Anton Chekhov

Anton Chekhov, great Russian dramatist and short story writer, was born on January 29, 1860, in Taganrog, Russia. In 1876 his father went bankrupt and, with the rest of his family, fled to Moscow, leaving Chekhov behind to live by his wits. Supporting himself by tutoring, Chekhov was able to graduate from school at nineteen and win a scholarship to study medicine in Moscow. In Moscow he became the family breadwinner by writing short comic sketches under a pseudonym. His first story appeared in March, 1880, in a St. Petersburg magazine, *Strekoza* (Dragonfly).

In 1884, he received his medical degree and by this time had already contracted tuberculosis, the disease that would finally cause his death. In 1890 Chekhov journeyed alone to Sakhalin, a penal colony on an island off Siberia, and wrote his only nonfiction work, *The Island of Sakhalin* (1893–94), which remains a classic in penology. Chekhov also began experimenting with drama and wrote several successful one-act farces. His prolific writing included over fifty great short stories.

His first produced play was *Ivanov* (1887). On October 17, 1896, *The Seagull* was performed in St. Petersburg. It was practically hissed off the stage, and Chekhov vowed to give up dramatic writing forever. In March, 1897, he had a violent lung hemorrhage, and his health worsened, but with the formation of the Moscow Art Theater, he again began to write for the stage. In 1898 at a rehearsal for a new production of *The Seagull* he met Olga Knipper, the actress whom he married in 1901. The Moscow Art Theater also produced *Uncle Vanya* (1899) and *The Three Sisters* (1901). But Chekhov's health deteriorated, and his work on *The Cherry Orchard* during the Moscow winter of 1903–04 led to his complete collapse. He died on July 15, 1904, at Badenweiler, a health resort in southern Germany.

C·A BANTAM CLASSIC·A BANTAM CLASSIC·A BANTAM CLASSIC·A BANTAM CLASSIC·A BANTAM CLASS

A DOCTOR'S VISIT
Short Stories
by Anton Chekhov

Edited and with an Introduction
by Tobias Wolff

BANTAM BOOKS
TORONTO • NEW YORK • LONDON • SYDNEY • AUCKLAND

A DOCTOR'S VISIT:
SHORT STORIES BY ANTON CHEKHOV
A Bantam Book

PRINTING HISTORY

"The Lady with the Pet Dog," "The Kiss," "Gusev," "In the Cart," "Heartache," "In the Ravine," "The Man in a Shell," "Gooseberries," and "About Love" from The Portable Chekhov, *edited and translated by Avrahm Yarmolinsky. Copyright 1947, © 1968 by The Viking Press, Inc. Copyright renewed © 1975 by Avrahm Yarmolinsky. Reprinted by Permission of Viking Penguin Inc.*

"Peasant Women," "The Student," and "Neighbours" from The Oxford Chekhov, *translated and edited by Ronald Hingley: vol 6 (1971) pp 99–117.*

"At Sea, and "In Exile" from Anton Chekhov: Selected Stories, *translated by Ann Dunnigan. Copyright © 1960 by Ann Dunnigan. Reprinted by arrangement with NAL Penguin Inc., New York, NY.*

"The Bishop" from Russian Silhouettes, *by Anton Chekhov, translated by Marian Fell is used with the permission of Charles Scribner's Sons, a div. of Macmillan, Inc. Copyright 1915 Charles Scribner's Sons; copyright renewed 1943 Olivia Fell Vans Agnew.*

"Dreams" from Stories of Russian Life *by Anton Chekhov, translated by Marian Fell is used with the permission of Charles Scribner's Sons, a div. of Macmillan, Inc. Copyright 1914 Charles Scribner's Sons; copyright renewed 1942 Olivia Fell Vans Agnew.*

"A Doctor's Visit" is reprinted with permission of Macmillan Publishing Company from The Lady with the Dog and Other Stories *by Anton Chekhov, translated from the Russian by Constance Garnett. Copyright 1917 by Macmillan Publishing Company, renewed 1945 by Constance Garnett.*

Bantam Classic edition / July 1988

*Cover painting "Evening Party"
by Vecherinka, from the Tretyakov
Gallery. Tass/Sovfoto.*

ISBN 0-553-21322-9

Published simultaneously in the United States and Canada

Bantam Books are published by Bantam Books, a division of Bantam Doubleday Dell Publishing Group, Inc. Its trademark, consisting of the words "Bantam Books" and the portrayal of a rooster, is Registered in U.S. Patent and Trademark Office and in other countries. Marca Registrada. Bantam Books, 666 Fifth Avenue, New York, New York 10103.

PRINTED IN THE UNITED STATES OF AMERICA

O 0 9 8 7 6 5 4 3 2 1

CONTENTS

Introduction by Tobias Wolff	vii
At Sea	1
Enemies	5
In the Cart	18
Neighbors	27
A Gentleman Friend	45
Peasant Women	49
The Bishop	63
Dreams	78
In Exile	87
A Doctor's Visit	96
Gusev	107
Heartache	120
The Kiss	126
The Lady With the Pet Dog	144
The Man in a Shell	161
Gooseberries	174
About Love	184
In the Ravine	193
The Student	232

INTRODUCTION

Anton Chekhov's life was the epic novel he never wrote. His paternal grandparents were serfs. When by prodigies of cunning and thrift they scraped together almost enough money to buy their freedom, their master, in a fit of generosity, threw in a daughter for free. One of their sons, Paul, hankering after riches and respectability, opened a grocery store in the muddy port town of Taganrog on the Sea of Azov. This Paul was a declaiming bully, a beater of children, a sanctimonious choirmaster who sold his customers tainted food, then cheated them on weight and change. This Paul was Chekhov's father.

When his children weren't minding the store he dragooned them into his choir and volunteered them for a numbing schedule of services, morning and night, day after day, piously basking in the admiration with which churchgoers regarded him and his model brood. It was a lesson in hypocrisy. Chekhov must have learned it well, because his fiction is bitter in its revelation of the selfish ends that religion can be made to serve, and canny in its recognition of the distance between the public presentation of a life and its private reality. As he writes of Gurov in *The Lady With the Pet Dog*: "Judging others by himself, he did not believe what he saw, and always fancied that every man led his real, most interesting life under cover of secrecy as under cover of night. The personal life of every individual is based on secrecy, and perhaps it was partly for that reason that civilized man is so nervously anxious that personal privacy should be respected."

Of course Chekhov had no way of knowing then that this would be the capital he'd someday live on, this hard education in human nature. At the time he was sickly, tired, and intimidated. "In my childhood," he wrote, "there was no childhood."

In 1876, when Chekhov was sixteen, his father went bankrupt and stole out of town under a carpet to save himself from prison. He settled in Moscow with his wife and five of his six children—all but Chekhov, who was left behind in Taganrog to make ends meet as best he could while finishing school. He kept himself afloat by tutoring other boys and accepting the hospitality of relatives and friends. For a time he stayed with a Cossack family whose passion for the hunt was so extreme that when no more challenging prey came to hand they hunted down their own chickens and cows. Chekhov's dependent condition rankled him; it encouraged, he later said, slavish tendencies that he had to dedicate his life to squeezing out—"drop by drop."

Chekhov did well enough in school to win a municipal scholarship for the purpose of studying medicine in Moscow. He joined his family there in 1879, and found them living in poverty; his father was no longer even living at home. Chekhov spent a good part of his stipend setting them up in decent lodgings, and before long he had effectively taken on the burden of support for the entire household. He seems to have done this without rancor. Those who knew the Chekhovs at that time later remarked on the raucous good humor of their life together.

This spirit owed much to Chekhov himself. He was a mimic, a prankster, a wag. He refused to be mastered by a moment's boredom. At a dull provincial wedding he amused himself by teaching one of the bridesmaids to exclaim "You are so naive!" at her suitors. He had a satirical eye that found rich fare on the streets of Moscow and led him, almost inevitably, to the writer's life. He began writing jokes and sketches to supplement his university stipend. The sketches grew into stories. By the time Chekhov finished his medical degree in 1884 he had become a regular contributor to the popular comic gazettes, and that same year he published his first collection of tales.

Chekhov was not inclined to take himself seriously as a writer.

He considered the work he'd done to be superficial and hesitated to take it farther, afraid to risk for the sake of art his reliable income from the comic papers. It was a matter of survival—his family needed the money. And now that he was a doctor he felt an obligation to begin treating people. "Medicine," he wrote, "is my lawful wife and Literature is my mistress. When I get fed up with one, I spend the night with the other." The joke by which he illustrates these competing claims on his talents and time does not obscure the moral predicament Chekhov felt himself to be in. He aspired to serve humanity and doubted that his writing had a legitimate place in this aspiration.

Chekhov needed to be roused to some more serious conception of his possibilities as a writer. This encouragement took the form of a letter from D. V. Grigorovitch, an older writer of particular renown and influence, one of the so-called Olympians. Grigorovitch wrote Chekhov in the spring of 1886. In his letter he pronounced Chekhov the most talented writer of his generation and scolded him for not doing justice to his gift. Chekhov replied immediately with an outpouring of gratitude, flattery, explanations, and the promise to "undertake something serious." His letter is a touching reminder that those whom we call great were once poor mortals distracted by debt, doubtful, worried, ignorant of future triumphs, dying for a kind word.

Chekhov kept his promise to undertake something serious. This something became the long story "The Steppe," a lyrical evocation of a young boy's journey across the Russian heartland. It won the Pushkin Prize in 1888, but Chekhov, always his own most demanding reader, was not entirely happy with it. He considered it too episodic, loose-knit. In this judgment he was probably right, though wrong in his opinion that whatever its faults, it was "the best work I can do." He had in fact written better stories during the period of his supposed frivolity: "Heartache," for example, and "A Gentleman Friend," and the dire, masterful story "Dreams." The most important change was not so much in Chekhov's work as in his attitude toward his work, and toward himself as a writer. Henceforth, though Chekhov continued intermittently to practice medicine, he did so more as a public service, even as a charity, than from any sense of vocation. It had become clear to him that his vocation was to write. He had a large and zealous audience. His work was moving in a direction that interested him, and he had won by now the goodwill of the Russian literary establishment: critics praised him; other writers treated him with respect; editors flooded him with letters of solicitation and advice, viciously slandering one another in hopes of maneuvering themselves into position for first crack at his manuscripts.

Chekhov settled in for the duration. He wrote steadily and seriously, volume upon volume of stories as well as *The Seagull, Three Sisters, Uncle Vanya, The Cherry Orchard*—plays that changed the theater and whose charge of life still show no sign of weakening. By 1899, five years before his death and with some of his best work still to be written, he estimated his output at "more than 10,000 pages of stories and tales in twenty years of literary activity." This reckoning did not include reviews, reportage, occasional pieces, serials, and a vast body of trivial pseudonymous work that he had no wish to bring to public attention. He was thirty-nine years old.

At the end of his account Chekhov added, "I also wrote plays."

Chekhov applied himself to his art as few other writers have done. But he never entirely overcame his feeling that literature wasn't enough, that even more was expected of him. At his country home near the village of Melikhovo he regularly treated ailing peasants, as many as a thousand a year. He did relief work during outbreaks of cholera and famine. He helped organize and finance the construction of schools. He gave help of every kind to young writers and built, in his home town of Taganrog, a library and a museum. His anger over the injustice of the Dreyfus trial reached such a pitch that he quarreled with A. S. Suvorin, the conservative editor who had been his close friend and mentor in the early days, and in the same spirit he resigned his membership in the Russian Academy when Gorky's membership was revoked for political reasons. But of all the deeds and gestures that came to characterize Chekhov's impatience with the meditative life, his need to *do something*, the most extravagant was his journey to the Siberian penal colony of Sakhalin Island.

"Sakhalin," Chekhov wrote, "is a place of unbearable sufferings, such as only human beings can endure." Yet beyond that fact outsiders knew almost nothing about the place, not even how many sufferers it held or in what particular ways they suffered. This ignorance seemed insupportable to Chekhov. "From the books I have been reading it is clear that we have let *millions* of people rot in prison, destroying them carelessly, thoughtlessly, barbarously; we drove people in chains through the cold across thousands of miles, infected them with syphilis, depraved them, multiplied criminals, and placed the blame for all this on red-nosed prison wardens . . . yet this is no concern of ours, we are not interested.''

In hope of arousing some interest while satisfying his own curiosity, Chekhov set out for Sakhalin in April of 1890. He had before him over five thousand miles of some of the most forbidding terrain on earth. He traveled for a short distance by rail, until the tracks gave out. Then he jolted along by coach when he could, or by cart, or sledge. This was not always possible. The roads were unpaved and boggy, often to the point of disappearing altogether, so that Chekhov was forced to make a significant part of the journey on foot. He passed through blizzards and torrential rains. The heat and dust, he wrote, were ''dreadful.'' The rivers were swollen, the ferrymen unreliable, the inns filthy, the food disgusting. But the tone of his letters is exultant rather than complaining; ''I am content and thank God for having given me the strength and opportunity to make this journey. I have seen and lived through a great deal, and everything is exceedingly interesting and new to me, not as a man of letters but simply as a human being. The river, the forest, the stations, untamed Nature, the wildlife, the physical agonies caused by the hardships of travel, the delights of resting—altogether everything is so wonderful that I can't even describe it.''

It took him almost three months to get to Sakhalin. He stayed on the island another three months, visiting the labor camps and prisons and small, hardscrabble holdings where some of the convicts were allowed to live with their families. He had set himself an impossible task—to take a personal, comprehensive census of every prisoner and settler on the island. That meant coming face to face with over 25,000 people. It was impossible but Chekhov did it, meeting along the way, often over dinner, some of the most notoriously blackhearted criminals in Russia. He kept a list of particulars on every convict, and later published an account of his findings: *The Island of Sakhalin: Travel Notes*. The book is a vision of almost complete darkness; only in the children of Sakhalin did he find any alternative to despair. Just before he left, he wrote his mother: ''I've seen nothing for three months but convicts and people who can talk only of hard labor, convicts, and the lash. What a dismal life!''

It has been suggested, logically enough, that the hardships of this expedition shortened Chekhov's life. By 1890 his lungs were causing him enough trouble to indicate that he had tuberculosis. But health is not a purely physical condition. It renews itself on spiritual resources as well, and in this respect Chekhov's journey to Sakhalin was cathartic and invigorating. It delivered him from a literary and personal life that seemed to him narrow, petty, incidental to the main drama. In taking on this great adventure, he was forced day by day to jettison his gloom and guilt—excess baggage in Siberia—while strengthening himself with faith and courage. A man like Chekhov suffers more from safety than from risk.

Chekhov sailed home by way of the Indian Ocean. After stopping in Ceylon—"the site of Paradise"—he wrote: "When I have children, I'll say to them, not without pride: 'You sons of bitches, in my time I had dalliance with a dark-eyed Hindu—and where? In a cocoanut grove, on a moonlit night!' "

Chekhov never had those children. In 1901 he married Olga Knipper, an actress with Konstantin Stanislavsky's Moscow Art Theater whom Chekhov had met when she played the lead in *The Seagull,* but his health had by then reached so fragile a state that he was forced to live in Yalta while his wife's career kept her in Moscow. Her one pregnancy ended in miscarriage.

By the spring of 1904 Chekhov was failing rapidly, which did not keep him from thoughts of entering the Russo-Japanese War as a doctor. Instead he let himself be persuaded to go to the German health resort of Badenweiler, near the Black Forest, for treatment. On the night of June 29 he described to his wife an idea he had for a story. A few hours later he was dead. His body was sent back to Moscow in a railroad car marked Fresh Oysters. It arrived on a rainy, dreary day, and part of the crowd that had turned out for his funeral mistakenly attached themselves to another procession. The rest of the mourners followed Chekhov to Novodevicy Convent, where he was buried beside his father.

Of this absurd business Maxim Gorky wrote, "Vulgarity triumphed over the coffin and the grave of her quiet but stubborn enemy, triumphed in every way." But Gorky's righteous gravity seems misplaced (as gravity so often does), perhaps because the whole episode has the distinctive character of a Chekhov invention—as if, for a kind of last meal, he had been granted the boon of choreographing his own departure.

* * *

Chekhov's life is so interesting not because it was exemplary, but because it was so emphatically *his*. It shows in every detail his authorship, his refusal to let others decide the shape it would take. His short stories bear the same mark. Chekhov's early work, slight as most of it is, betrays his impatience with received attitudes and forms. "At Sea," for example, draws a picture of the brutish life of sailors and then gives that picture an unexpected quality of innocence by juxtaposing it to a revelation of the greed, sensuality, and religious hypocrisy of the class that the sailors consider their betters. But Chekhov does not allow the story to proceed in the straight moral line implied by this contrast; he complicates its path by exposing the sailors' need to believe in the superiority of others, and in their own baseness, as a way of denying responsibility for themselves. The result is a story that resists appropriation by any class or party. Its atmosphere, drawn from details of ship life unobtrusively mingled with allusions to the Crucifixion, is close, ominous, relieved only by the callow humanity of the narrator's voice. The story ends almost in mid-breath, yet without any sense of incompleteness. All this is accomplished in the space of four pages.

In "At Sea" we feel Chekhov pushing at the limits imposed on him by the journals he wrote for, turning them into occasions for originality. If he could not write at length then he would write in depth, making every detail suggest others, capturing a moment of someone's life in such a way that we intuitively trace that life beyond the story, drawing the circle from the arc. This became Chekhov's signature method of constructing narrative. He had no real precedent for it in the short fiction of his time. Turgenev's *A Sportsman's Sketches,* published in 1852, offers models of characterization, evocative description—especially of nature—and trenchant social portraiture, but the individual pieces are not meant to stand alone. They qualify each other and depend on each other, compelling in themselves but not complete in themselves.

Tolstoy, whose work Chekhov also admired, even to the point of reverence, came to short fiction with the impulses of a novelist. His stories have discernible beginnings in which the characters are introduced and the situation set forth, middles in which the characters are tested by the developing situation, and endings that resolve these complications with rich, satisfying finality. This form lends itself to Tolstoy's edifying purposes. His conclusions are not intended to release the mind into avenues of possibility but to teach particular truths.

Chekhov held these two writers in particular regard, but neither of them worked in a form congenial to Chekhov's needs and temperament. He did not have room to develop his narratives at a Tolstoyan pace, nor was he inclined to. At the same time he wanted to move beyond incidental anecdotes, caricatures, and sketches toward a fiction of integrity and consequence. We see the results of this ambition even in early stories such as "At Sea" and "Oysters," brief narratives of such density that they expand in the reader's memory when the act of reading is done, taking on the weight of experience itself.

Chekhov has been accused of writing shapeless stories, "all middle like a tortoise" as John Galsworthy put it. It is true that Chekhov's stories do not have conventional beginnings and endings. Instead they tell us what we need to know by implication and indirection. They are not shapeless at all, but methodically shaped according to Chekhov's instinct for the essential and his impatience with the inessential. And he arrived at his method not by inadvertence but by the most unsparing, rigorous calculation. Whenever other writers called on him for advice he counseled brevity. "Cross out as many adjectives and adverbs as you can," he advised Gorky. Of beginnings, he said: "Fledgling authors frequently should do the following; bend the notebook in half and tear off the first half . . . you'll only have to change the beginning of the second half a little bit and the story will be utterly comprehensible. Everything that has no direct relation to the story must be ruthlessly thrown out." On description: "Eliminate commonplaces . . . choose small details . . . grouping them in such a way that if you close your eyes after reading it you can picture the whole thing. For example, you'll get a picture of a moonlit night if you write that on the dam of the mill a piece of broken bottle flashed like a bright star and the black shadow of a dog or a wolf rolled by like a ball."

This is an austere program. But its effect is not austere—not arid or cold. The opposite is true. By cutting away the gauze of convention, Chekhov is able to dissolve that safe distance between reader and story that convention maintains. The result is a sense of proximity and unpredictability. You never know what a Chekhov story will say to you, or demand of you.

Technical mastery, however hard and self-consciously he worked to achieve it, was not for Chekhov an end in itself. He writes of

Vassilyev in "A Nervous Breakdown" that "he had a talent for humanity." It was this same talent in himself that Chekhov meant to serve and to which he subordinated all his other talents. *Humanity*—the word has been so sentimentalized by politicians and hucksters that at the very sound of it one tenses, waiting for the pitch. It conjures up a mass of virtuous victims ready to be saved as soon as we send in our dollars and get behind the program. That is not the humanity Chekhov had a talent for. He wrote about particular people. If peasants were his subject, he did not haze them over with the condescension of romance as Tolstoy sometimes did, rejoicing in their hardships as food for their souls. "Peasant blood runs in my veins," Chekhov wrote, "and you can't astonish me with peasant virtues." He portrayed their sufferings with furious accuracy but did not pretend that their sufferings ennobled them. If they were bullied, they also bullied each other. Meanness begets meanness. When he wrote about a sick chorus girl suddenly overwhelmed with horror at the ugliness of her life, he did not show her knocking on the convent door the next day; he showed her back at the dance hall. Love, happiness, right behavior, kindness, peace of mind—all these enter Chekhov's stories as luminous possibilities bestowing a momentary dignity on those who long for them, until, unredeemed by action, they glimmer away.

Chekhov wrote with sympathy, but without the usual flourishes of fine feeling by which writers identify themselves as Caring Souls. His eyes were on the facts of human conduct. He did not pattern the events of his stories to conform to the wish list of any party or creed. He did not seek to reassure the reader by forcing his stories to uplifting conclusions, or by firing improbable insights and resolutions into the heads of his characters. He examined humanity, in short, with the same objectivity that a doctor must bring to the examination of a patient, counting it no favor to tell lies about his findings. "Man will become better," he wrote, "when you show him what he is like."

Not everyone appreciated this objectivity. Chekhov came under fire from ideologues of all kinds for failing to advance the Cause, whatever that might be. Simply to write the truth was not enough; the truth must serve the revolution. Not to take sides was a dereliction of responsibility. The radical critic N. K. Mikhaylovsky wrote of Chekhov: "I seemed to see a giant walking down a road, not knowing where he was going or why." This criticism bothered Chekhov, too, more than he cared

AT SEA
A Sailor's Story

Only the dimming lights of the receding harbor were visible in an ink-black sky. We could feel the heavy storm clouds overhead about to burst into rain, and it was suffocating, in spite of the wind and cold.

Crowded together in the crew's quarters we, the sailors, were casting lots. Loud, drunken laughter filled the air. One of our comrades was playfully crowing like a cock. A slight shiver ran through me from the back of my neck to my heels, as if cold small shot were pouring down my naked body from a hole in the back of my head. I was shivering both from the cold and certain other causes, which I wish to describe.

In my opinion man is, as a rule, foul; and the sailor can sometimes be the foulest of all the creatures of the earth—fouler than the lowest beast, which has at least the excuse of obeying his instincts. It is possible that I may be mistaken, since I do not know life, but it appears to me that a sailor has more occasion than anyone else to despise and curse himself. A man who at any moment may fall headlong from a mast to be forever hidden beneath a wave, a man who may drown, God alone knows when, has need of nothing, and no one on dry land feels pity for him. We sailors drink a lot of vodka and are dissolute because we do not know what one needs virtue for at sea. However, I shall continue.

We were casting lots. There were twenty-two of us who, having stood watch, were now at liberty. Out of this number only two were to have the luck of enjoying a rare spectacle. On this particular night the honeymoon cabin was occupied, but the wall of the cabin had only two holes at our disposal. One of them I myself had made with a fine saw, after boring through with a corkscrew; the other had been cut out with a knife by one of my comrades. We had worked at it for more than a week.

"You got one hole!"

"Who?"

They pointed to me. "Who got the other?"

"Your father."

My father, a humpbacked old sailor with a face like a baked apple, came up to me and clapped me on the back. "Today, my boy, we're lucky!" he said. "Do you hear, boy? Luck came to us both at the same time. That means something." Impatiently he asked the time; it was only eleven o'clock.

I went up on deck, lit my pipe, and gazed out to sea. It was dark, but it can be assumed that my eyes reflected what was taking place in my soul as I made out images on the black background of the night, visualizing what was so lacking in my own still young but already ruined life. . . .

At midnight I walked past the saloon and glanced in at the door. The bridegroom, a young pastor with a handsome blond head, sat at a table holding the Gospels in his hands. He was explaining something to a tall, gaunt Englishwoman. The bride, a very beautiful, shapely young woman, sat at her husband's side with her light blue eyes fixed on him. A tall, plump, elderly Englishman, a banker, with a repulsive red face, paced up and down the saloon. He was the husband of the middle-aged lady to whom the pastor was talking.

"Pastors have a habit of talking for hours," I thought. "He won't finish before morning." At one o'clock my father came to me, pulled me by the sleeve and said: "It's time. They've left the saloon."

In the twinkling of an eye I flew down the companionway and approached the familiar wall. Between this wall and the side of the ship there was a space where soot, water, and rats collected. I soon heard the heavy tread of the old man, my father. He cursed as he stumbled over a mat-sack and some kerosene cans. I felt for the hole in the wall and pulled out the square piece of wood I had so painstakingly sawed. I was looking at a thin, transparent muslin through which penetrated a soft, rosy light. Together with the light, my burning face was caressed by a delightful, sultry fragrance; this, no doubt, was the smell of an aristocratic bedroom. In order to see the room it was necessary to draw aside the muslin with two fingers, which I hastened to do. I saw bronze, velvet, lace, all bathed in a pink glow. About ten feet from my face stood the bed.

“Let me have your place,” said my father, impatiently pushing me aside. “I can see better here.” I did not answer him. “Your eyes are better than mine, boy, and it makes no difference to you if you look from far or near.”

“Be quiet,” I said, “they might hear us.”

The bride sat on the side of the bed, dangling her little feet in a foot muff. She was staring at the floor. Before her stood her husband, the young pastor. He was telling her something, what I do not know; the noise of the steamer made it impossible for me to hear. He spoke passionately, with gestures, his eyes flashing. She listened and shook her head in refusal.

“The devil!” my father muttered. “A rat bit me!”

I pressed my chest to the wall, as if fearing my heart would jump out. My head was burning.

The bride and groom talked at great length. At last he sank to his knees and held out his arms, imploring her. She shook her head in refusal. He leaped to his feet, crossed the cabin, and from the expression on his face and the movements of his arms I surmised that he was threatening her. The young wife rose and went slowly toward the wall where I was standing. She stopped near the opening and stood motionless in thought. I devoured her face with my eyes. It seemed to me that she was suffering, struggling with herself, not knowing what to do; but at the same time her features expressed anger. I did not understand it.

We continued to stand there face to face for about five minutes, then she moved slowly away and, pausing in the middle of the cabin, nodded to the pastor—a sign of consent, undoubtedly. He smiled happily, kissed her hand, and went out.

Within three minutes the door opened and the pastor reentered followed by the tall, plump Englishman whom I mentioned above. The Englishman went over to the bed and asked the beautiful woman a question. Pale, not looking at him, she nodded her head affirmatively. The banker then took out of his pocket a packet of some sort—evidently bank notes—and handed it to the pastor, who examined it, counted it, bowed, and went out. The elderly Englishman locked the door after him.

I sprang away from the wall as if I had been stung. I was frightened. It seemed to me the wind was tearing our ship to pieces, that we were going down. My father, that drunken, debauched old man, took me by the arm and said: ‘‘Let's go away from here! You shouldn't see that. You're still a boy.’’

He was hardly able to stand. I carried him up the steep winding stairs. Above, an autumn rain had begun to fall.

ENEMIES

About ten o'clock of a dark September evening the Zemstvo doctor Kirilov's only son, six-year-old Andrey, died of diphtheria. As the doctor's wife dropped onto her knees before the dead child's cot and the first paroxysm of despair took hold of her, the bell rang sharply in the hall.

When the diphtheria came all the servants were sent away from the house, that very morning. Kirilov himself went to the door, just as he was, in his shirtsleeves with his waistcoat unbuttoned, without wiping his wet face or hands, which had been burnt with carbolic acid. It was dark in the hall, and of the person who entered could be distinguished only his middle height, a white scarf, and a big, extraordinarily pale face, so pale that it seemed as though its appearance made the hall brighter. . . .

"Is the doctor in?" the visitor asked abruptly.

"I'm at home," answered Kirilov. "What do you want?"

"Oh, you're the doctor? I'm so glad!" The visitor was overjoyed and began to seek for the doctor's hand in the darkness. He found it and squeezed it hard in his own. "I'm very . . . very glad! We were introduced. . . . I am Aboguin . . . had the pleasure of meeting you this summer at Mr. Gnouchev's. I am very glad to have found you at home. . . . For God's sake, don't say you won't come with me immediately. . . . My wife has been taken dangerously ill. . . . I have the carriage with me. . . ."

From the visitor's voice and movements it was evident that he had been in a state of violent agitation. Exactly as though he had been frightened by a fire or a mad dog, he could hardly restrain his hurried breathing, and he spoke quickly in a trembling voice. In his speech there sounded a note of real sincerity, of childish fright. Like all men who are frightened and dazed, he spoke in short, abrupt phrases and uttered many superfluous, quite unnecessary words.

"I was afraid I shouldn't find you at home," he continued. "While I was coming to you I suffered terribly. . . . Dress yourself and let us go, for God's sake. . . . It happened like this, Papchinsky came to me—Alexander Siemionovich, you know him. . . . We were chatting. . . . Then we sat down to tea. Suddenly my wife cries out, presses her hands to her heart, and falls back in her chair. We carried her off to her bed and . . . and I rubbed her forehead with sal volatile, and splashed her with water. . . . She lies like a corpse. . . . I'm afraid that her heart's failed. . . . Let us go. . . . Her father, too, died of heart failure."

Kirilov listened in silence as though he did not understand the Russian language.

When Aboguin once more mentioned Papchinsky and his wife's father, and once more began to seek for the doctor's hand in the darkness, the doctor shook his head and said, drawling each word listlessly:

"Excuse me, but I can't go. . . . Five minutes ago my . . . son died."

"Is that true?" Aboguin whispered, stepping back. "My God, what an awful moment to come! It's a terribly fated day . . . terribly! What a coincidence . . . and it might have been on purpose!"

Aboguin took hold of the door handle and dropped his head in meditation. Evidently he was hesitating, not knowing whether to go away or to ask the doctor once more.

"Listen," he said eagerly, seizing Kirilov by the sleeve. "I fully understand your state! God knows I'm ashamed to try to hold your attention at such a moment, but what can I do? Think yourself—who can I go to? There isn't another doctor here besides you. For heaven's sake come. I'm not asking for myself. It's not I that's ill!"

Silence began, Kirilov turned his back to Aboguin, stood still for a while, and slowly went out of the hall into the drawing room. To judge by his uncertain, machine-like movement and by the attentiveness with which he arranged the hanging shade on the unlighted lamp in the drawing room and consulted a thick book which lay on the table—at such a moment he had neither purpose nor desire, nor did he think of anything, and probably had already forgotten that there was a stranger standing in his hall. The gloom and the quiet of the drawing room apparently increased his insanity. As he went from the drawing room to his study he raised his right foot higher than he need, felt with his hands for the doorposts, and then one felt a certain perplexity in his whole figure, as though he had entered a strange house by chance, or for the first time in his life had got drunk, and now was giving himself up in bewilderment to the new sensation. A wide line of light stretched across the bookshelves on one wall of the study; this light, together with the heavy stifling smell of carbolic acid and ether, came from the door ajar that led from the study into the bedroom. . . . The doctor sank into a chair before the table; for a while he looked drowsily at the shining books, then rose, and went into the bedroom.

Here, in the bedroom, dead quiet reigned. Everything, down to the last trifle, spoke eloquently of the tempest undergone, of weariness, and everything rested. The candle which stood among a close crowd of phials, boxes, and jars on the stool and the big lamp on the chest of drawers brightly lit the room. On the bed, by the window, the boy lay open-eyed, with a look of wonder on his face. He did not move, but it seemed that his open eyes became darker and darker every second and sank into his skull. Having laid her hands on his body and hid her face in the folds of the bedclothes, the mother now was on her knees before the bed. Like the boy she did not move, but how much living movement was felt in the coil of her body and in her hands! She was pressing close to the bed with her whole being, with eager vehemence, as though she were afraid to violate the quiet and comfortable pose which she had found at last for her weary body. Blankets, cloths, basins, splashes on the floor, brushes, and spoons scattered everywhere, a white bottle of limewater, the stifling heavy air itself—everything died away and, as it were, plunged into quietude.

The doctor stopped by his wife, thrust his hands into his trouser pockets, and, bending his head on one side, looked fixedly at his son. His face showed indifference; only the drops which glistened on his beard revealed that he had been lately weeping.

The repulsive terror of which we think when we speak of death was absent from the bedroom. In the pervading dumbness, in the mother's pose, in the indifference of the doctor's face was something attractive that touched the heart, the subtle and elusive beauty of human grief, which it will take men long to understand and describe, and only music, it seems, is able to express. Beauty too was felt in the stern stillness. Kirilov and his wife were silent and did not weep, as though they confessed all the poetry of their condition. As once the season of their youth passed away, so now in this boy their right to bear children had passed away, alas! for ever to eternity. The doctor is forty-four years old, already gray, and looks like an old man; his faded, sick wife is thirty-five. Andrey was not merely the only son but the last.

In contrast to his wife, the doctor's nature belonged to those which feel the necessity of movement when their soul is in pain. After standing by his wife for about five minutes, he passed from the bedroom, lifting his right foot too high, into a little room half filled with a big, broad divan. From there he went to the kitchen. After wandering about the fireplace and the cook's bed, he stooped through a little door and came into the hall.

Here he saw the white scarf and the pale face again.

"At last," sighed Aboguin, seizing the door handle. "Let us go, please."

The doctor shuddered, glanced at him, and remembered.

"Listen. I've told you already that I can't go," he said, livening. "What a strange idea!"

"Doctor, I'm made of flesh and blood too. I fully understand your condition. I sympathize with you," Aboguin said in an imploring voice, putting his hand to his scarf. "But I am not asking for myself. My wife is dying. If you had heard her cry, if you'd seen her face, you would understand my insistence! My God—and I thought that you'd gone to dress yourself. The time is precious, Doctor! Let us go, I beg of you."

"I can't come," Kirilov said after a pause, and stepped into his drawing room.

Aboguin followed him and seized him by the sleeve.

"You're in sorrow. I understand. But I'm not asking you to cure a toothache or to give expert evidence—but to save a human life." He went on imploring like a beggar. "This life is more than any personal grief. I ask you for courage, for a brave deed—in the name of humanity."

"Humanity cuts both ways," Kirilov said irritably. "In the name of the same humanity I ask you not to take me away. My God, what a strange idea! I can hardly stand on my feet and you frighten me with humanity. I'm not fit for anything now. I won't go for anything. With whom shall I leave my wife? No, no. . . ."

Kirilov flung out his open hands and drew back.

"And . . . and don't ask me," he continued, disturbed. "I'm sorry. . . . Under the Laws, Volume Thirteen, I'm obliged to go and you have the right to drag me by the neck. . . . Well, drag me, but . . . I'm not fit. . . . I'm not even able to speak. Excuse me."

"It's quite unfair to speak to me in that tone, Doctor," said Aboguin, again taking the doctor by the sleeve. "The thirteenth volume be damned! I have no right to do violence to your will. If you want to, come; if you don't, then God be with you; but it's not to your will that I apply, but to your feelings. A young woman is dying! You say your son died just now. Who could understand my terror better than you?"

Aboguin's voice trembled with agitation. His tremor and his tone were much more convincing than his words. Aboguin was sincere, but it is remarkable that every phrase he used came out stilted, soulless, inopportunely florid, and, as it were, insulted the atmosphere of the doctor's house and the woman who was dying. He felt it himself, and in his fear of being misunderstood he exerted himself to the utmost to make his voice soft and tender so as to convince by the sincerity of his tone, at least, if not by his words. As a rule, however deep and beautiful the words, they affect only the unconcerned. They cannot always satisfy those who are happy or distressed because the highest expression of happiness or distress is most often silence. Lovers understand each other best when they are silent, and a fervent passionate speech at the graveside affects only outsiders. To the widow and children it seems cold and trivial.

Kirilov stood still and was silent. When Aboguin uttered some more words on the higher vocation of a doctor, and self-sacrifice, the doctor sternly asked:

"Is it far?"

"Thirteen or fourteen versts. I've got good horses, Doctor. I give you my word of honor that I'll take you there and back in an hour. Only an hour."

The last words impressed the doctor more strongly than the

references to humanity or the doctor's vocation. He thought for a while and said with a sigh:

"Well, let us go!"

He went off quickly, with a step that was not sure, to his study, and soon after returned in a long coat. Aboguin, delighted, danced impatiently round him, helped him on with his overcoat, and accompanied him out of the house.

Outside it was dark, but brighter than in the hall. Now in the darkness the tall stooping figure of the doctor was clearly visible with the long, narrow beard and the aquiline nose. Besides his pale face Aboguin's big face could now be seen and a little student cap which hardly covered the crown of his head. The scarf showed white only in front, but behind it was hid under his long hair.

"Believe me, I'm able to appreciate your magnanimity," murmured Aboguin, as he helped the doctor to a seat in the carriage. "We'll whirl away. Luke, dear man, drive as fast as you can, do!"

The coachman drove quickly. First appeared a row of bare buildings, which stood along the hospital yard. It was dark everywhere, save that at the end of the yard a bright light from someone's window broke through the garden fence, and three windows in the upper story of the separate house seemed to be paler than the air. Then the carriage drove into dense obscurity where you could smell mushroom damp and hear the whisper of the trees. The noise of the wheels awoke the rooks, who began to stir in the leaves and raised a doleful, bewildered cry as if they knew that the doctor's son was dead and Aboguin's wife ill. Then began to appear separate trees, a shrub. Sternly gleamed the pond, where big black shadows slept. The carriage rolled along over an even plain. Now the cry of the rooks was but faintly heard far away behind. Soon it became completely still.

Almost all the way Kirilov and Aboguin were silent; save that once Aboguin sighed profoundly and murmured:

"It's terrible pain. One never loves his nearest so much as when there is the risk of losing them."

And when the carriage was quietly passing through the river, Kirilov gave a sudden start, as though the dashing of the water frightened him, and he began to move impatiently.

"Let me go," he said in anguish. "I'll come to you later. I only want to send the attendant to my wife. She is all alone."

Aboguin was silent. The carriage, swaying and rattling against the stones, drove over the sandy bank and went on. Kirilov began to toss about in anguish, and glanced around. Behind, the road was visible in the scant light of the stars and the willows that fringed the bank disappearing into the darkness. To the right the plain stretched smooth and boundless as heaven. On it in the distance here and there dim lights were burning, probably on the turf pits. To the left parallel with the road stretched a little hill, tufted with tiny shrubs, and on the hill a big half-moon stood motionless, red, slightly veiled with a mist, and surrounded with fine clouds which seemed to be gazing upon it from every side, and guarding it, lest it should disappear.

In all nature one felt something hopeless and sick. Like a fallen woman who sits alone in a dark room trying not to think of her past, the earth languished with reminiscence of spring and summer and waited in apathy for ineluctable winter. Wherever one's glance turned, nature showed everywhere like a dark, cold, bottomless pit, whence neither Kirilov nor Aboguin nor the red half-moon could escape. . . .

The nearer the carriage approached the destination the more impatient did Aboguin become. He moved about, jumped up, and stared over the driver's shoulder in front of him. And when at last the carriage drew up at the foot of the grand staircase, nicely covered with a striped linen awning, and he looked up at the lighted windows of the first floor, one could hear his breath trembling.

"If anything happens . . . I shan't survive it," he said, entering the hall with the doctor and slowly rubbing his hands in his agitation. "But I can't hear any noise. That means it's all right so far," he added, listening to the stillness.

No voices or steps were heard in the hall. For all the bright illumination, the whole house seemed asleep. Now the doctor and Aboguin, who had been in darkness up till now, could examine each other. The doctor was tall, with a stoop, slovenly dressed, and his face was plain. There was something unpleasantly sharp, ungracious, and severe in his thick Negro lips, his aquiline nose, and his faded, indifferent look. His tangled hair, his sunken temples, the early gray in his long thin beard that showed his shining chin, his pale gray complexion, and the slipshod awkwardness of his manners—the hardness of it all suggested to the mind bad times undergone, an unjust lot, and weariness of life and men. To look at the hard figure of the man, you could not believe that he had a wife and could weep over his child. Aboguin revealed something different. He was robust, solid, and fair haired, with a big head and large, yet soft, features, exquisitely dressed in the latest fashion. In his carriage, his tight-buttoned coat, and his mane of hair you felt something noble and leonine. He walked with his head straight and his chest prominent, he spoke in a pleasant baritone, and in his manner of removing his scarf or arranging his hair there appeared a subtle, almost feminine, elegance. Even his pallor and childish fear as he glanced upwards to the staircase while taking off his coat did not disturb his carriage or take from the satisfaction, the health and aplomb, which his figure breathed.

"There's no one about, nothing I can hear," he said, walking upstairs. "No commotion. May God be good!"

He accompanied the doctor through the hall to a large salon, where a big piano showed dark and a luster hung in a white cover. Thence they both passed into a small and beautiful drawing room, very cosy, filled with a pleasant, rosy half darkness.

"Please sit here a moment, Doctor," said Aboguin, "I . . . I won't be a second. I'll just have a look and tell them."

Kirilov was left alone. The luxury of the drawing room, the pleasant half darkness, even his presence in a stranger's unfamiliar house evidently did not move him. He sat in a chair looking at his hands burnt with carbolic acid. He had no more than a glimpse of the bright red lampshade, the cello case, and when he looked sideways across the room to where the clock was ticking he noticed a stuffed wolf, as solid and satisfied as Aboguin himself.

It was still. . . . Somewhere far away in the other rooms someone uttered a loud "Ah!" A glass door, probably a cupboard door, rang, and again everything was still. After five minutes had passed, Kirilov did not look at his hands any more. He raised his eyes to the door through which Aboguin had disappeared.

Aboguin was standing on the threshold, but not the same man as went out. The expression of satisfaction and subtle elegance had disappeared from him. His face and hands, the attitude of his body were distorted with a disgusting expression either of horror or of tormenting physical pain. His nose, lips, mustache, all his features were moving and, as it were, trying to tear themselves away from his face, but the eyes were as though laughing from pain.

Aboguin took a long, heavy step into the middle of the room, stooped, moaned, and shook his fists.

"Deceived!" he cried, emphasizing the syllable *cei*. "She deceived me! She's gone! She fell ill and sent me for the doctor only to run away with this fool Papchinsky. My God!"

Aboguin stepped heavily toward the doctor, thrust his white soft fists before his face, and went on wailing, shaking his fists the while.

"She's gone off! She's deceived me! But why this lie? My God, my God! Why this dirty, foul trick, this devilish, serpent's game? What have I done to her? She's gone off."

Tears gushed from his eyes. He turned on his heel and began to pace the drawing room. Now in his short jacket and his fashionable narrow trousers in which his legs seemed too thin for his body, he was extraordinarily like a lion. Curiosity kindled in the doctor's impassive face. He rose and eyed Aboguin.

"Well, where's the patient?"

"The patient, the patient," cried Aboguin, laughing, weeping, and still shaking his fists. "She's not ill, but accursed. Vile—dastardly. The devil himself couldn't have planned a fouler trick. She sent me so that she could run away with a fool, an utter clown, an Alphonse! My God, far better she should have died. I'll not bear it. I shall not bear it."

The doctor stood up straight. His eyes began to blink, filled with tears; his thin beard began to move with his jaw right and left.

"What's this?" he asked, looking curiously about. "My child's dead. My wife in anguish, alone in all the house. . . . I can hardly stand on my feet, I haven't slept for three nights . . . and I'm made to play in a vulgar comedy, to play the part of a stage property! I don't . . . I don't understand it!"

Aboguin opened one fist, flung a crumpled note on the floor, and trod on it, as upon an insect he wished to crush.

"And I didn't see . . . didn't understand," he said through his set teeth, brandishing one fist round his head, with an expression as though someone had trod on a corn. "I didn't notice how he came to see us every day. I didn't notice that he came in a carriage today! What was the carriage for? And I didn't see! Innocent!"

"I don't . . . I don't understand," the doctor murmured. "What's it all mean? It's jeering at a man, laughing at a man's suffering! That's impossible. . . . I've never seen it in my life before!"

With the dull bewilderment of a man who has just begun to understand that someone has bitterly offended him, the doctor shrugged his shoulders, waved his hands, and, not knowing what to say or do, dropped exhausted into a chair.

"Well, she didn't love me anymore. She loved another man. Very well. But why the deceit, why this foul treachery?" Aboguin spoke with tears in his voice. "Why, why? What have I done to you? Listen, Doctor," he said passionately, approaching Kirilov. "You were the unwilling witness of my misfortune, and I am not going to hide the truth from you. I swear I loved this woman. I loved her with devotion, like a slave. I sacrificed everything for her. I broke with my family, I gave up the service and my music. I forgave her things I could not have forgiven my mother and sister . . . I never once gave her an angry look . . . I never gave her any cause. Why this lie, then? I do not demand love, but why this abominable deceit? If you don't love anymore then speak out honestly, above all when you know what I feel about this matter. . . ."

With tears in his eyes and trembling in all his bones, Aboguin was pouring out his soul to the doctor. He spoke passionately, pressing both hands to his heart. He revealed all the family secrets without hesitation, as though he were glad that these secrets were being torn from his heart. Had he spoken thus for an hour or two and poured out all his soul, he would surely have been easier.

Who can say whether, had the doctor listened and given him friendly sympathy, he would not, as so often happens, have been reconciled to his grief unprotesting, without turning to unprofitable follies? But it happened otherwise. While Aboguin was speaking, the offended doctor changed countenance visibly. The indifference and amazement in his face gradually gave way to an expression of bitter outrage, indignation, and anger. His features became still sharper, harder, and more forbidding. When Aboguin put before his eyes the photograph of his young wife, with a pretty but dry, inexpressive face like a nun's, and asked if it were possible to look at that face and grant that it could express a lie, the doctor suddenly started away, with flashing eyes, and said, coarsely forging out each several word:

"Why do you tell me all this? I do not want to hear! I don't want to," he cried and banged his fist upon the table. "I don't want your trivial vulgar secrets—to hell with them. You dare not tell me such trivialities. Or do you think I have not yet been insulted enough! That I'm a lackey to whom you can give the last insult? Yes?''

Aboguin drew back from Kirilov and stared at him in surprise.

''Why did you bring me here?'' the doctor went on, shaking his beard. ''You marry out of high spirits, get angry out of high spirits, and make a melodrama—but where do I come in? What have I got to do with your romances? Leave me alone! Get on with your noble grabbing, parade your humane ideas, play'' —the doctor gave a side-glance at the cello case—''the double bass and the trombone, stuff yourselves like capons, but don't dare to jeer at a real man! If you can't respect him, then you can at least spare him your attentions.''

''What does all this mean?'' Aboguin asked, blushing.

''It means that it's vile and foul to play with a man! I'm a doctor. You consider doctors and all men who work and don't reek of scent and harlotry your footmen, your *mauvais tons*. Very well, but no one gave you the right to turn a man who suffers into a property.''

''How dare you say that?'' Aboguin asked quietly. Again his face began to twist about, this time in visible anger.

''How dare *you* bring me here to listen to trivial rubbish, when you know that I'm in sorrow?'' the doctor cried and banged his fists on the table once more. ''Who gave you the right to jeer at another's grief?''

''You're mad,'' cried Aboguin. ''You're ungenerous. I, too, am deeply unhappy and . . . and . . .''

''Unhappy''—the doctor gave a sneering laugh—''don't touch the word, it's got nothing to do with you. Wasters who can't get money on a bill call themselves unhappy too. A capon's unhappy, oppressed with all its superfluous fat. You worthless lot!''

''Sir, you're forgetting yourself,'' Aboguin gave a piercing scream. ''For words like those, people are beaten. Do you understand?''

Aboguin thrust his hand into his side pocket, took out a pocketbook, found two notes, and flung them on the table.

''There's your fee,'' he said, and his nostrils trembled. ''You're paid.''

''You dare not offer me money,'' said the doctor, and brushed the notes from the table to the floor. "You don't settle an insult with money."

Aboguin and the doctor stood face to face, heaping each other with undeserved insults. Never in their lives, even in a frenzy, had they said so much that was unjust and cruel and absurd. In both the selfishness of the unhappy is violently manifest. Unhappy men are selfish, wicked, unjust, and less able to understand each other than fools. Unhappiness does not unite people, but separates them; and just where one would imagine that people should be united by the community of grief, there is more injustice and cruelty done than among the comparatively contented.

"Send me home, please," the doctor cried, out of breath.

Aboguin rang the bell violently. Nobody came. He rang once more, then flung the bell angrily to the floor. It struck dully on the carpet and gave out a mournful sound like a death moan. The footman appeared.

"Where have you been hiding, damn you?" The master sprang upon him with clenched fists. "Where have you been just now? Go away and tell them to send the carriage round for this gentleman, and get the brougham ready for me. Wait," he called out as the footman turned to go. "Not a single traitor remains tomorrow. Pack off all of you! I will engage new ones. . . . Rabble!"

While they waited, Aboguin and the doctor were silent. Already the expression of satisfaction and the subtle elegance had returned to the former. He paced the drawing room, shook his head elegantly, and evidently was planning something. His anger was not yet cool, but he tried to make as if he did not notice his enemy. . . . The doctor stood with one hand on the edge of the table, looking at Aboguin with that deep, rather cynical, ugly contempt with which only grief and an unjust lot can look, when they see satiety and elegance before them.

A little later, when the doctor took his seat in the carriage and drove away, his eyes still glanced contemptuously. It was dark, much darker than an hour ago. The red half-moon had now disappeared behind the little hill, and the clouds which watched it lay in dark spots round the stars. The brougham with the red lamps began to rattle on the road and passed the doctor. It was Aboguin on his way to protest, to commit all manner of folly.

All the way the doctor thought not of his wife or Andrey, but only of Aboguin and those who lived in the house he just left. His thoughts were unjust, inhuman, and cruel. He passed sentence on Aboguin, his wife, Papchinsky, and all those who live in rosy semidarkness and smell of scent. All the way he hated them, and his heart ached with his contempt for them. The conviction he formed about them would last his life long.

Time will pass and Kirilov's sorrow, but this conviction, unjust and unworthy of the human heart, will not pass, but will remain in the doctor's mind until the grave.

IN THE CART

They drove out of the town at half past eight in the morning.

The paved road was dry, a splendid April sun was shedding warmth, but there was still snow in the ditches and in the woods. Winter, evil, dark, long, had ended so recently; spring had arrived suddenly, but neither the warmth nor the languid, transparent woods, warmed by the breath of spring, nor the black flocks flying in the fields over huge puddles that were like lakes, nor this marvelous, immeasurably deep sky, into which it seemed that one would plunge with such joy, offered anything new and interesting to Marya Vasilyevna, who was sitting in the cart. She had been teaching school for thirteen years, and in the course of all those years she had gone to the town for her salary countless times; and whether it was spring, as now, or a rainy autumn evening, or winter, it was all the same to her, and what she always, invariably longed for was to reach her destination as soon as possible.

She felt as though she had been living in these parts for a long, long time, for a hundred years, and it seemed to her that she knew every stone, every tree on the road from the town to her school. Here was her past and her present, and she could imagine no other future than the school, the road to the town and back, and again the school and again the road.

She had lost the habit of thinking of the time before she became a schoolmistress and had almost forgotten all about it. She had once had a father and mother; they had lived in Moscow in a big apartment near the Red Gate, but all that remained in her memory of that part of her life was something vague and formless like a dream. Her father had died when she was ten years old, and her mother had died soon after. She had a brother, an officer; at first they used to write to each other, then her brother had stopped answering her letters, he had lost the habit. Of her former belongings, all that remained was a photograph of her mother, but the dampness in the school had faded it, and now nothing could be seen on it but the hair and the eyebrows.

When they had gone a couple of miles, old Semyon, who was driving, turned round and said:

"They have nabbed an official in the town. They have sent him away. They say that he and some Germans killed Alexeyev, the mayor, in Moscow."

"Who told you that?"

"They read it in the papers, in Ivan Ionov's teahouse."

And again there was a long silence. Marya Vasilyevna thought of her school, of the examinations that were coming soon, and of the girl and the four boys whom she was sending up for them. And just as she was thinking about the examinations she was overtaken by a landowner named Hanov in a carriage with four horses, the very man who had acted as examiner in her school the previous year. As he drew alongside he recognized her and bowed.

"Good morning," he said. "Are you driving home, madam?"

This Hanov, a man of about forty with a worn face and a lifeless expression, was beginning to age noticeably, but was still handsome and attractive to women. He lived alone on his large estate, was not in the service, and it was said of him that he did nothing at home but pace from one end of the room to the other whistling, or play chess with his old footman. It was said, too, that he drank heavily. And indeed, at the examination the previous year the very papers he had brought with him smelt of scent and wine. On that occasion everything he wore was brand-new, and Marya Vasilyevna had found him very attractive and, sitting next to him, had felt embarrassed. She was used to seeing cold, hardheaded examiners at the school, but this one did not remember a single prayer, did not know what questions to ask, was exceedingly polite and considerate, and gave only the highest marks.

"I am on my way to visit Bakvist," he continued, addressing Marya Vasilyevna, "but I wonder if he is at home."

They turned off the highway onto a dirt road, Hanov leading the way and Semyon following. The team of four horses kept to the road, slowly pulling the heavy carriage through the mud. Semyon changed his course continually, leaving the road now to drive over a hillock, now to skirt a meadow, often jumping down from the cart and helping the horse. Marya Vasilyevna kept thinking about the school, and wondering whether the arithmetic problem at the examination would be hard or easy. And she was annoyed with the Zemstvo office, where she had found no one the previous day. What negligence! For the past two years she had been asking them to discharge the janitor, who did nothing, was rude to her, and cuffed the boys, but no one paid any attention to her. It was hard to find the chairman at the office and when you did find him, he would say with tears in his eyes that he had no time; the inspector visited the school once in three years and had no understanding of anything connected with it, since he had formerly been employed in the finance department and had obtained the post of school inspector through pull; the school board met very rarely and no one knew where; the trustee was a half-literate peasant, the owner of a tannery, stupid, coarse, and a bosom friend of the janitor's—and heaven knows to whom she could turn with complaints and inquiries.

"He is really handsome," she thought, glancing at Hanov.

Meanwhile the road was growing worse and worse. They drove into the woods. Here there was no turning off the road, the ruts were deep, and water flowed and gurgled in them. Twigs struck them stingingly in the face.

"How's the road?" asked Hanov, and laughed.

The schoolmistress looked at him and could not understand why this odd fellow lived here. What could his money, his interesting appearance, his refinement get him in this godforsaken place, with its mud, its boredom? Life granted him no privileges, and here, like Semyon, he was jogging slowly along over an abominable road and suffering the same discomforts. Why live here, when one had a chance to live in Petersburg or abroad? And it seemed as though it would be a simple matter for a rich man like him to turn this bad road into a good one so as to avoid having to endure this misery and seeing the despair written on the faces of his coachman and Semyon. But he merely laughed, and apparently it was all the same to him, and he asked nothing better of life. He was kind, gentle, naive; he had no grasp of this coarse life, he did not know it, any more than he had known the prayers at the examination. He presented nothing to the schools but globes, and sincerely regarded himself as a useful person and a prominent worker in the field of popular education. And who had need of his globes here?

"Hold on, Vasilyevna!" said Semyon.

The cart lurched violently and was about to turn over; something heavy fell on Marya Vasilyevna's feet—it was her purchases. There was a steep climb uphill over a clayey road; noisy rivulets were flowing in winding ditches; the water had gullied the road; and how could one drive here! The horses breathed heavily. Hanov got out of the carriage and walked at the edge of the road in his long coat. He was hot.

"How's the road?" he repeated, and laughed. "This is the way to smash your carriage."

"But who tells you to go driving in such weather?" asked Semyon in a surly voice. "You ought to stay home."

"I'm bored at home, grandfather. I don't like staying home."

Next to old Semyon he seemed well built and vigorous, but there was something barely perceptible in his gait which betrayed him as a weak creature, already blighted, approaching its end. And suddenly it seemed as though there were a whiff of liquor in the woods. Marya Vasilyevna felt frightened and was filled with pity for this man who was going to pieces without rhyme or reason, and it occurred to her that if she were his wife or his sister she would devote her whole life to his rescue. His wife! Life was so ordered that here he was living in his great house alone, while she was living in a godforsaken village alone, and yet for some reason the mere thought that he and she might meet on an equal footing and become intimate seemed impossible, absurd. Fundamentally, life was so arranged and human relations were complicated so utterly beyond all understanding that when you thought about it you were terrified and your heart sank.

"And you can't understand," she thought, "why God gives good looks, friendliness, charming, melancholy eyes to weak, unhappy, useless people—why they are so attractive."

"Here we must turn off to the right," said Hanov, getting into his carriage. "Good-bye! All good wishes!"

And again she thought of her pupils, of the examination, of

the janitor, of the school board; and when the wind brought her the sound of the receding carriage these thoughts mingled with others. She wanted to think of beautiful eyes, of love, of the happiness that would never be. . . .

His wife? It is cold in the morning, there is no one to light the stove, the janitor has gone off somewhere; the children come in as soon as it is light, bringing in snow and mud and making a noise; it is all so uncomfortable, so unpleasant. Her quarters consist of one little room and a kitchen close by. Every day when school is over she has a headache and after dinner she has heartburn. She has to collect money from the children for firewood and to pay the janitor, and to turn it over to the trustee, and then to implore him—that overfed, insolent peasant—for God's sake to send her firewood. And at night she dreams of examinations, peasants, snowdrifts. And this life has aged and coarsened her, making her homely, angular, and clumsy, as though they had poured lead into her. She is afraid of everything, and in the presence of a member of the Zemstvo board or of the trustee, she gets up and does not dare sit down again. And she uses obsequious expressions when she mentions any one of them. And no one likes her, and life is passing drearily, without warmth, without friendly sympathy, without interesting acquaintances. In her position how terrible it would be if she were to fall in love!

"Hold on, Vasilyevna!"

Another steep climb.

She had begun to teach school from necessity, without feeling called to it; and she had never thought of a call, of the need for enlightenment; and it always seemed to her that what was most important in her work was not the children, not enlightenment, but the examinations. And when did she have time to think of a call, of enlightenment? Teachers, impecunious physicians, doctors' assistants, for all their terribly hard work, do not even have the comfort of thinking that they are serving an ideal or the people, because their heads are always filled with thoughts of their daily bread, of firewood, of bad roads, of sickness. It is a hard, humdrum existence, and only stolid cart horses like Marya Vasilyevna can bear it a long time; lively, alert, impressionable people who talk about their calling and about serving the ideal are soon weary of it and give up the work.

Semyon kept on picking out the driest and shortest way, traveling now across a meadow, now behind the cottages, but in one place the peasants would not let them pass and in another the land belonged to the priest and so they could not cross it, in yet another Ivan Ionov had bought a plot from the landowner and had dug a ditch round it. They kept turning back.

They reached Nizhneye Gorodishche. Near the teahouse, on the dung-strewn, snowy ground, there stood wagons loaded with great bottles of oil of vitriol. There were a great many people in the teahouse, all drivers, and it smelled of vodka, tobacco, and sheepskins. The place was noisy with loud talk and the banging of the door, which was provided with a pulley. In the shop next door someone was playing an accordion steadily. Marya Vasilyevna was sitting down, having tea, while at the next table some peasants were drinking vodka and beer, sweaty with the tea they had had and the bad air.

"Hey, Kuzma!" people kept shouting confusedly. "What's doing?" "The Lord bless us!" "Ivan Dementyich, that I can do for you!" "See here, friend!"

A little pockmarked peasant with a black beard, who was quite drunk, was suddenly taken aback by something and began using foul language.

"What are you cursing about, you there?" Semyon, who was sitting some way off, remarked angrily. "Don't you see the young lady?"

"The young lady!" someone jeered in another corner.

"The swine!"

"I didn't mean nothing—" The little peasant was embarrassed. "Excuse me. I pays my money and the young lady pays hers. How-de-do, ma'am?"

"How do you do?" answered the schoolmistress.

"And I thank you kindly."

Marya Vasilyevna drank her tea with pleasure, and she, too, began turning red like the peasants, and again she fell to thinking about firewood, about the janitor. . . .

"Wait, brother," came from the next table. "It's the schoolma'am from Vyazovye. I know; she's a good sort."

"She's all right!"

The door was banging continually, some coming in, others going out. Marya Vasilyevna went on sitting there, thinking of the same things all the time, while the accordion went on playing and playing behind the wall. There had been patches of sunlight on the floor, they shifted to the counter, then to the wall, and finally disappeared altogether; this meant that it was past midday. The peasants at the next table were getting ready to leave. The little peasant went up to Marya Vasilyevna somewhat unsteadily and shook hands with her; following his example, the others shook hands with her at parting and filed out singly, and the door squeaked and slammed nine times.

"Vasilyevna, get ready," Semyon called to her.

They drove off. And again they went at a walking pace.

"A little while back they were building a school here at this Nizhneye Gorodishche," said Semyon, turning round. "There were wicked doings then!"

"Why, what?"

"They say the chairman pocketed a cool thousand, and the trustee another thousand, and the teacher five hundred."

"The whole school only cost a thousand. It's wrong to slander people, grandfather. That's all nonsense."

"I don't know. I only repeat what folks say."

But it was clear that Semyon did not believe the schoolmistress. The peasants did not believe her. They always thought she received too large a salary, twenty-one rubles a month (five would have been enough), and that she kept for herself the greater part of the money that she received for firewood and for the janitor's wages. The trustee thought as the peasants did, and he himself made something on the firewood and received a salary from the peasants for acting as trustee—without the knowledge of the authorities.

The woods, thank God, were behind them, and now it would be clear, level ground all the way to Vyazovye, and they had not far to go now. All they had to do was to cross the river and then the railway line, and then they would be at Vyazovye.

"Where are you going?" Marya Vasilyevna asked Semyon. "Take the road to the right across the bridge."

"Why, we can go this way just as well, it's not so deep."

"Mind you don't drown the horse."

"What?"

"Look, Hanov is driving to the bridge too," said Marya Vasilyevna, seeing the four-horse team far away to the right. "I think it's he."

"It's him all right. So he didn't find Bakvist in. What a blockhead he is. Lord have mercy on us! He's driving over there, and what for? It's all of two miles nearer this way."

They reached the river. In summer it was a shallow stream, easily forded and usually dried up by August, but now, after the spring floods, it was a river forty feet wide, rapid, muddy, and cold; on the bank, and right up to the water, there were fresh wheel tracks, so it had been crossed there.

"Giddap!" shouted Semyon angrily and anxiously, tugging violently at the reins and flapping his elbows as a bird does its wings. "Giddap!"

The horse went into the water up to its belly and stopped, but at once went on again, straining its muscles, and Marya Vasilyevna felt a sharp chill in her feet.

"Giddap!" she shouted, too, standing up. "Giddap!"

They got to the bank.

"Nice mess, Lord have mercy on us!" muttered Semyon, setting the harness straight. "It's an affliction, this Zemstvo."

Her shoes and rubbers were full of water, the lower edge of her dress and of her coat and one sleeve were wet and dripping; the sugar and flour had got wet, and that was the worst of it, and Marya Vasilyevna only struck her hands together in despair and said:

"Oh, Semyon, Semyon! What a fellow you are, really!"

The barrier was down at the railway crossing. An express was coming from the station. Marya Vasilyevna stood at the crossing waiting for the train to pass, and shivering all over with cold. Vyazovye was in sight now, and the school with the green roof and the church with its blazing crosses that reflected the setting sun; and the station windows were aflame, too, and a pink smoke rose from the engine. . . . And it seemed to her that everything was shivering with cold.

Here was the train; the windows, like the crosses on the church, reflected the blazing light; it hurt her eyes to look at them. On the platform of one of the first-class carriages a lady was standing, and Marya Vasilyevna glanced at her as she flashed by. Her mother! What a resemblance! Her mother had had just such luxuriant hair, just such a forehead, and that way of holding her head. And with amazing distinctness, for the first time in those thirteen years, she imagined vividly her mother, her father, her brother, their apartment in Moscow, the aquarium with the little fishes, everything down to the smallest detail; she suddenly heard the piano playing, her father's voice; she felt as then, young, good-looking, well dressed, in a bright warm room among her own people. A feeling of joy and happiness suddenly overwhelmed her, she pressed her hands to her temples in ecstasy and called softly, imploringly:

"Mama!"

And she began to cry, she did not know why. Just at that moment Hanov drove up with his team of four horses, and seeing him she imagined such happiness as had never been, and smiled and nodded to him as an equal and an intimate, and it seemed to her that the sky, the windows, the trees, were glowing with her happiness, her triumph. No, her father and mother had never died, she had never been a schoolmistress, that had been a long, strange, oppressive dream, and now she had awakened. . . .

"Vasilyevna, get in!"

And suddenly it all vanished. The barrier was slowly rising. Marya Vasilyevna, shivering and numb with cold, got into the cart. The carriage with the four horses crossed the railway track, Semyon followed. The guard at the crossing took off his cap.

"And this is Vyazovye. Here we are."

NEIGHBORS

Peter Ivashin was in very bad humor. His unmarried sister had gone to live with Vlasich, a married man. Somehow hoping to shake off the irksome, depressed mood which obsessed him indoors and out of doors, he would summon up his sense of fair play and all his high-minded, worthy principles. (Hadn't he always stood out for free love?) But it was no use and he could never help reaching the same conclusion as stupid Nanny: his sister had behaved badly, Vlasich had stolen his sister. It was all most distressing.

His mother stayed closeted in her room all day, Nanny spoke in whispers and kept sighing, his aunt was on the point of leaving every day, so they kept bringing her suitcases into the hall and then taking them back to her room. In house, courtyard, and garden it was as quiet as if they had a corpse laid out. Aunt, servants, even the peasants . . . all seemed to give Ivashin enigmatic, baffled looks as if to say that his sister had been seduced and what was he going to do about it? And he blamed himself for doing nothing, though what he should actually *be* doing he had no idea.

Thus six days passed. On the afternoon of the seventh, a Sunday, a messenger rode over with a letter. The address was in a familiar feminine hand: "Her Excell. Mrs. Anna Ivashin."

Ivashin rather felt that there was something provocative, defiant and liberal about the envelope, the handwriting, and that unfinished word "Excell." And female liberalism is intolerant, pitiless, and harsh.

"She'd rather die than give in to her unhappy mother and ask forgiveness," thought Ivashin, taking the letter to his mother.

Mother was lying on her bed fully clothed. Seeing her son, she abruptly sat up and patted the gray hairs which had strayed from under her cap.

"What is it, what is it?" she asked impatiently.

"This came," said her son, handing over the letter.

The name Zina, even the word "she," were not spoken in that house. They talked of Zina impersonally: "this was sent," "a departure took place." The mother recognized her daughter's writing, her face grew ugly and disagreeable, and the gray hairs once more escaped from her cap.

"Never!" she said, gesticulating as if the letter had scorched her fingers. "No, no, never! Nothing would induce me."

The mother sobbed hysterically in her grief and shame. She obviously wanted to read the letter, but pride would not permit her. Ivashin realized that he ought to open it himself and read it out, but he suddenly felt angrier than he had ever felt in his life and he rushed out into the yard.

"Say there will be no answer!" he shouted to the messenger. "No answer, I say! Tell her that, you swine!"

He tore up the letter. Then tears came into his eyes and he went out into the fields, feeling cruel, guilty, and wretched.

He was only twenty-seven years old, but he was already fat, he dressed like an old man in loose, roomy clothes and was short of breath. He had all the qualities of an old bachelor landowner. He never fell in love, never thought of marriage, and the only people he was fond of were his mother, his sister, Nanny, and Vasilyich the gardener. He liked a good meal, his afternoon nap, and conversation about politics or lofty abstractions. He had taken a university degree in his time, but had come to think of that as a sort of conscription incumbent on young men between eighteen and twenty-five years of age. Anyway, the thoughts which now daily haunted his mind . . . they had nothing to do with the university and his course of studies.

In the fields it was hot and still, as if rain was in the offing. The wood was steaming, and there was an oppressive, fragrant smell of pines and rotting leaves. Ivashin kept stopping to wipe his wet brow. He inspected his winter corn and his spring corn, went round his clover field, and twice chased off a partridge and her chicks at the edge of the wood. And all the time he was conscious that this insufferable situation could not go on forever, that he must end it one way or the other. He might end it stupidly and brutally somehow, but end it he must.

How, though? What could he do, he wondered, casting supplicatory glances at sky and trees as if begging their help.

But sky and trees were mute, nor were high-minded principles of any avail. Common sense suggested that the agonizing problem admitted only a stupid solution and that today's scene with the messenger was not the last of its kind. He was afraid to think what might happen next.

The sun was setting as he made his way home, now feeling the problem to be utterly insoluble. To accept what had happened was impossible, but it was equally impossible not to accept it and there was no middle way. Removing his hat, he fanned himself with his handkerchief and was walking down the road with over a mile to go when he heard a ringing behind him. It was an ingenious, highly successful combination of bells and chimes which sounded like tinkling glass. Only one person went abroad with this tintinnabulation: Inspector Medovsky of the police, a former hussar officer who had wasted his substance and had a pretty rough time, an invalid and a distant relative of Ivashin's. He was an old friend of the family and had a fatherly affection for Zina, whom he much admired.

"I was just coming to see you," he said as he caught Ivashin up. "Get in and I'll give you a lift."

He was smiling and looked cheerful, clearly not yet aware that Zina had gone to live with Vlasich. He might have been informed, but if so he hadn't believed it. Ivashin found himself in an awkward situation.

"You're most welcome," he muttered, blushing until tears came into his eyes and uncertain what lie to tell or how to tell it. "Delighted," he went on, trying to smile, "but, er, Zina's away and Mother's ill."

"What a pity," said the inspector, looking at Ivashin thoughtfully. "And I was hoping to spend an evening with you. Where has Zina gone?"

"To the Sinitskys', and then she wanted to go on to a convent, I think. I don't know definitely."

The inspector talked a little longer, then turned back, and

Ivashin walked home, horrified to think what the other would feel when he learnt the truth. Ivashin imagined his feelings and savored them as he entered the house.

"Lord help us," he thought.

Only his aunt was taking afternoon tea in the dining room. Her face held its usual expression suggestive of a weak, defenseless woman, but one who would not permit herself to be insulted. Ivashin sat at the far end of the table (he disliked his aunt) and began drinking his tea in silence.

"Your mother missed lunch again today," said his aunt. "You might bear it in mind, Peter. Starving herself to death won't cure her troubles."

Ivashin found it absurd for his aunt to meddle in other people's business and make her own departure depend on Zina's having left home. He felt like saying something rude but restrained himself—realizing even as he did so that the time had come for action and that he could let things slide no longer. It was a matter of either doing something straight away or of falling down, screaming and banging his head on the floor. He pictured Vlasich and Zina, both freethinking, both well pleased with themselves, kissing under some maple tree, and then his seven days' accumulated depression and anger all seemed to topple over on Vlasich.

"One man seduces and abducts my sister," he thought. "A second will come and cut my mother's throat, a third will set fire to the house or burgle us: and all this under the mask of friendship, lofty principles, and sufferings.

"I won't have it!" Ivashin suddenly shouted, thumping the table.

He jumped up and ran out of the dining room. His estate manager's horse was saddled up in the stables, so he mounted it and galloped off to see Vlasich.

Stormy emotions raged within him. He felt the urge to do something striking and impetuous even if it meant regretting it for the rest of his life. Should he call Vlasich a blackguard, slap his face, challenge him to a duel? But Vlasich wasn't the sort who fights duels. As for calling him a blackguard and slapping his face, that would only increase his wretchedness and make him retreat further inside himself. These miserable, meek specimens are the limit, they are more trouble than anyone. They get away with murder. When a miserable man counters a well-deserved reproach with his look of profound guilt and sickly smile, when he submissively bows his head before you . . . then, it seems, Justice herself has not the heart to strike.

"Never mind," decided Ivashin. "I'll horsewhip him in Zina's presence and I'll give him a piece of my mind."

He rode through his woodland and scrub, and imagined Zina trying to justify what she had done by talking of women's rights, of the freedom of the individual, and by saying that there is no difference between being married in church and being a common-law wife. Just like a woman, she would argue about things she didn't understand, and she would probably end up by asking what this had to do with him and what right he had to interfere.

"True, I haven't any right," muttered Ivashin. "But so much the better. The ruder, the more in the wrong I am the better."

The air was sultry, clouds of gnats hung low above the ground, and peewits wept piteously in the scrub. There was every sign of rain, yet not a cloud in the sky. Crossing the boundary of his estate, Ivashin galloped over a level, smooth field—he often took this way, and he knew every bush and hollow. That object looming far ahead of him in the twilight like a dark cliff . . . it was a red church. He could picture it all in the smallest detail, even the plaster on the gate and the calves which were always browsing on the hedge. Nearly a mile from the church, on the right, was the dark copse belonging to Count Koltovich and beyond that copse Vlasich's land began.

From behind church and Count's copse a huge black cloud advanced with white lightnings flashing on it.

"Well, here we are, Lord help us," thought Ivashin.

The horse soon tired of the pace and Ivashin tired too. The thunderhead glared at him, apparently advising him to turn back, and he felt a little scared.

"I'll prove they're in the wrong," he tried to reassure himself. "They'll talk of free love and freedom of the individual, yet freedom means self-control, surely, not giving way to passions. It's sheer licentiousness, their freedom is."

Here was the count's large pond, dark blue and glowering under the cloud, breathing damp and slime. Near the log path two willows—one old, one young—were leaning tenderly into each other. Ivashin and Vlasich had walked past this very spot a fortnight ago, softly singing the students' song about it being love that makes the world go round.

Wretched song!

Thunder rumbled as Ivashin rode through the wood, and the

trees roared and bent in the wind. He must hurry. From the copse to Vlasich's estate he had less than a mile of meadow to cover along a path flanked on both sides by old birch trees. Like Vlasich they were a wretched, dismal sight, being every bit as spindly and lanky as their owner. Heavy rain rustled in birches and grass. The wind suddenly dropped, there was a whiff of wet earth and poplars. Then Vlasich's yellow acacia hedge, also lanky and spindly, came into view. At the point where some latticework had collapsed his neglected orchard appeared.

No longer thinking about slapping Vlasich's face or horse-whipping him, Ivashin did not know what he was going to do at the man's house. He felt nervous. He was afraid on his own behalf and on his sister's—scared at the thought of seeing her any moment. How would she behave toward her brother? What would the two of them talk about? And should he not turn back while there was yet time? Thus brooding, he galloped down the avenue of lime trees to the house, rounded the broad lilac bushes—and suddenly saw Vlasich.

Bareheaded, in cotton shirt and top boots, stooping under the rain, Vlasich was going from a corner of the house toward the front door followed by a workman with a hammer and a box of nails. They must have been mending a shutter which had been banging in the wind. Vlasich saw Ivashin and stopped.

"Is it you Peter?" he smiled. "What a very nice surprise."

"Yes, it's me, as you see," said Ivashin quietly, brushing off rain drops with both hands.

"Well, what a good idea. Delighted," said Vlasich, but did not hold out his hand, obviously hesitating and waiting for the other to make the first move.

"Good for the oats, this," he said with a glance at the sky.

"Quite so."

They went silently into the house. A door on the right led from the hall into another hall and then into a reception room, and there was a door on the left into the small room occupied by Vlasich's manager in winter. Ivashin and Vlasich went into that room.

"Where did the rain catch you?" Vlasich asked.

"Not far from here, quite close to the house."

Ivashin sat on the bed, glad of the rain's noise, glad that the room was dark. It was better that way—not so unnerving, and he need not look his companion in the eye. His rage had passed, but he felt afraid and vexed with himself. He had got off to a bad start, he felt, and his trip boded ill.

For some time neither man spoke and they pretended to be listening to the rain.

"Thanks, Peter," began Vlasich, clearing his throat. "Most obliged to you for coming. It's generous of you, very decent. I appreciate it, I value it greatly, believe you me."

He looked out of the window and continued, standing in the middle of the room.

"Somehow everything happened secretly as if we were keeping you in the dark. Knowing that we might have hurt you, made you angry . . . it has cast a cloud over our happiness all this time. But let me defend myself. It was not that we didn't trust you, that wasn't why we were so secretive. In the first place, it all happened on the spur of the moment and there was no time to discuss things. Secondly, this is such an intimate, sensitive business and it was awkward to bring in a third party, even one as close to us as you. But the real point is, we were banking heavily on your generosity all along. You're the most generous of men, you're such a frightfully decent chap. I'm infinitely obliged to you. If you should ever need my life, then come and take it."

Vlasich spoke in a low, hollow, deep voice, all on one note like a fog horn. He was obviously upset. Ivashin felt that it was his turn to speak now, and that for him to listen in silence really would be to pose as the most generous and frightfully decent of nitwits—which was not what he had come for.

He got quickly to his feet.

"Look here, Gregory," he panted in a low voice, "you know I liked you—couldn't want a better husband for my sister. But what's happened is frightful, it doesn't bear thinking of."

"What's so horrible, though?" asked Vlasich in quaking tones. "It would be horrible if we had done wrong, but we haven't, have we?"

"Look here, Gregory, you know I'm not the least bit stuffy, but—well, I'm sorry to be so blunt, but you have both been very selfish, to my way of thinking. I shan't say anything to Zina about this, of course, it would only upset her, but you ought to know that Mother's sufferings are practically indescribable."

"Yes, very lamentable," sighed Vlasich. "We foresaw that, Peter, but what on earth could we do about it? Just because your actions upset someone it doesn't mean they're wrong. It can't be helped. Any serious step you take . . . it's bound to upset somebody. If you went to fight for freedom that would hurt your mother, too, it can't be helped. If you make your family's peace of mind your main priority it means good-bye to any idealism in life."

Lightning flared beyond the window and the flash seemed to switch Vlasich's thoughts into a different channel. He sat down by Ivashin's side and started saying things which would have been far better left unsaid.

"I worship your sister, Peter," he said. "Visiting your place, I always felt I was on pilgrimage. I absolutely idolized Zina and now I worship her more each day. She is more than a wife to me! More sacred, I tell you!"

Vlasich waved his arms.

"I adore her. Since she has been living here I have entered my house as if it were a shrine. She is a rare, an outstanding, a most frightfully decent woman."

What a ghastly rigmarole, thought Ivashin, irked by the word "woman."

"Why don't you get married properly?" he asked. "How much does your wife want for a divorce?"

"Seventy-five thousand."

"That's a bit much, but why not beat her down?"

"She won't give an inch. She's an awful woman, old man."

Vlasich sighed. "I never told you about her before, it has been such a hideous memory, but as the subject has come up I'll go on. I married her on a decent, chivalrous impulse. In our regiment, if you want the details, a certain battalion commander took up with her as a girl of eighteen—simply seduced her, in other words, lived with her a couple of months and then dropped her.

"She was in a most ghastly plight, old man. She was ashamed to go home to her parents, who wouldn't have her anyway, and her lover had deserted her. What could she do—set up as barrack-room whore? My fellow officers were horrified. Not that they were little plaster saints themselves, but this was such a rotten show, even they found it a bit thick! Besides, no one in the regiment could stand that colonel. All the second lieutenants and ensigns were furious and they decided to do him in the eye by getting up a subscription for the wretched girl, see? So we junior officers met in conclave and each started putting down his five or ten rubles, when I had a rush of blood to the head. The situation seemed to cry out for some heroic gesture, so I dashed off to the girl and said how sorry I was—I spoke with tremendous feeling. On my way to see her, and then as I was speaking, I loved her passionately as a woman insulted and injured. Yes, quite so.

"Well—the upshot was, I proposed a week later. My superiors and comrades found my marriage unbecoming to an officer's dignity. That only added fuel to the flames, though. So I wrote a great epistle, see? I argued that what I had done should be inscribed in regimental history in letters of gold, and all that. I sent the letter to my colonel with copies to my brother officers. Now, I was a bit upset, of course, and I did rather overstep the mark. I was asked to leave the regiment. I have a rough copy hidden somewhere, I'll let you read it some time. It's written with real feeling—I enjoyed some sublime moments of sheer decency, as you'll see. I resigned my commission and came here with my wife. My father had left a debt or two and I had no money, but my wife embarked on a social whirl from the start, dressing up and playing cards, so I had to mortgage my estate. She was no better than she should be, if you see what I mean, and you are the only one of my neighbors who hasn't been her lover. About two years later I gave her some money—all I had at the time—to go away, and away she went to town. Yes, quite so.

"Now I'm paying the ghastly creature twelve hundred a year. There is a certain fly, old man, that puts its larva on a spider's back and the spider can't get rid of it. The grub attaches itself and drinks the spider's heart's blood. That's just how this woman fixed on me. She's a regular vampire. She loaths and scorns me for my folly: for marrying someone like her, that is. She despises my chivalry. A wise man dropped her, says she, and a fool picked her up. Only a wretched half-wit could do what I did, she reckons. It really is a bit hard to take, old man. And by the way, old man, I've had a pretty raw deal, one way and another, it really has got me down."

Ivashin became quite mystified as he listened to Vlasich. What ever could Zina see in the man? He was not young (he was forty-one), he was lean, lanky, narrow-chested, long-nosed and his beard was turning gray. He spoke like a fog horn, he had a sickly smile and an ungainly trick of flapping his arms about when he was talking. Instead of health, handsome, manly bearing, urbanity and good humor, he was just vaguely dim so far as looks went. He dressed so badly, everything about him was so dismal, he rejected poetry and painting as "irrelevant to modern needs"— didn't appreciate them, in other words. Music left him cold. He was a poor farmer. His estate was in utter chaos, and was mortgaged too. He was paying twelve percent on a second mortgage and on top of that he owed another ten thousand in personal loans. When his interest or alimony fell due he went round cadging money with the air of a man whose house is on fire. At these times he'd say oh, to hell with it, and he would sell up his whole winter store of firewood for five rubles or a straw rick for three, and then have his garden fence or some old seedbed frames used to heat his stores. Pigs had ruined his pastures, the villagers' cattle trampled his saplings, and each winter there were fewer and fewer of his old trees left. Beehives and rusty pails bestrewed his vegetable plot and garden. He lacked all talents and gifts, even the humble knack of leading an average life. In practical matters he was an innocent, a weakling easily cheated and done down. No wonder the peasants said he was "a bit touched."

He was a liberal and was thought quite a firebrand in the county, but in this, too, he wore a humdrum air. There was no panache or verve about his freethinking. Whether indignant, irate, or enthusiastic, he was all on one note, so to speak—it all lacked flair, it fell so very flat. Even at times of extreme agitation he never raised his head or stood up straight. But the main snag was his trick of trotting out even his finest and loftiest ideas in a way that made them seem hackneyed and dated. Whenever he embarked on a sluggish, portentous-sounding exegesis, all about impulses of sublime integrity and the best years of his life, whenever he raved about young folk always being, and always having been, in the van of social progress, whenever he condemned Russians for donning their dressing gowns at thirty and forgetting their *alma mater*'s traditions, it all sounded like something you had read in a book long, long ago. When you stayed in his house he would put a Pisarev or Darwin on your bedside table, and if you said you had already read them he'd go and fetch a Dobrolyubov!

In the county this rated as freethinking, and many thought it an innocent, harmless quirk. Yet it made him profoundly unhappy. For him it was that maggot to which he had just alluded and which had fastened on him to batten on his life's blood. There was his past with that weird marriage *à la* Dostoyevsky, those long letters and the copies written in a poor, illegible hand but with great emotion, there were the interminable misunderstandings, explanations, disillusionments. Then there were his debts, his second mortgage, his wife's alimony, and his monthly loans, none of which was any good to anybody, either him or anyone else. Now, in the present, he was still as restless as he always had been, he still sought some great mission in life and he still couldn't mind his own business. There were still these long letters and copies of them in season and out of season, there were still those exhausting, hackneyed tirades about the village community, reviving local handicrafts, starting up cheese dairies—each speech exactly like the one before as if they were machine made rather than hatched by a live brain. Finally, there was this scandal over Zina which might end heaven knew how.

And the thing was, Zina was so young, she was only twenty-two. She was pretty, elegant, high-spirited, she liked laughing, chattering, arguing, she was crazy about music. She was good with clothes and books, she knew how to create a civilized environment: at home she would never have put up with a room like this with its smell of boots and cheap vodka. She was a liberal, too, but her freethinking seemed to brim over with energy, with the pride of a young girl, vigorous, bold, eagerly yearning to excel and show more originality than others.

How *could* she love a Vlasich?

"The man's so quixotic, so pigheaded, so fanatical, so lunatic," thought Ivashin. "But she's as wishy-washy, characterless and pliable as me. She and I both give in quickly, we don't stand up for ourselves. She fell in love with him—but then I like him, too, don't I, in spite of everything?"

Ivashin thought Vlasich a good, decent man, but narrow and one-sided. In Vlasich's emotions and sufferings, in his whole life, Ivashin saw no lofty aims, either near or distant, he saw only boredom and lack of *savoir-vivre*. Vlasich's self-martyrdom, what he called his achievements and decent impulses . . . they struck Ivashin as so much wasted effort like firing off purposeless blank shots and using up a lot of powder. As for Vlasich's obsession with the outstanding integrity and rectitude of his own mental processes, that struck Ivashin as naive—morbid, even. Then there was the man's lifelong knack of confusing the trivial and the sublime, his making a stupid marriage and regarding that as a stupendous feat—and then having affairs with women and calling them the triumph of ideals or something. None of it made any kind of sense.

Still, Ivashin did like him and felt that there was a certain power about him. He somehow never had the heart to contradict the man.

Vlasich sat down very near Ivashin in the dark, wanting to talk to the sound of the rain. He had already cleared his throat to tell some other long story like the history of his marriage, but Ivashin couldn't bear to hear it, tormented as he was by the thought of seeing his sister any moment.

"Yes, you have had a raw deal," he said gently. "But I'm sorry, we're digressing, you and I. This is beside the point."

"Yes, yes, quite," said Vlasich, rising to his feet. "So let's get back to the subject. Our conscience is clear, Peter, I can tell you. We aren't married, but that we're man and wife in every real sense is neither for me to argue nor for you to hear. You're as free from prejudice as I am, so there can be no disagreement between us on that score, thank God. As for our future, you have no cause for apprehension. I shall work my fingers to the bone, I'll work day and night—I'll do all in my power to make Zina happy, in other words. Her life will be a beautiful thing. Shall I pull it off, you ask? I shall, old boy. When a man's obsessed with one idea every minute of the day it isn't hard for him to get his way. But let's go and see Zina, we must give her a nice surprise."

Ivashin's heart pounded. He stood up and followed Vlasich into the hall, and then into the drawing room. The huge, grim room contained only an upright piano and a long row of antique bronzed chairs on which no one ever sat. A single candle burnt on the piano. From the drawing room they went silently into the dining room. This, too, was spacious and uncomfortable. In the center of the room was a round, two-leaved table with six legs. There was only one candle. A clock in a large red case like an icon holder showed half past two.

Vlasich opened the door into the next room.

"Peter's here, Zina," he said.

At once rapid footsteps were heard and Zina came into the dining room—a tall, buxom, very pale girl, looking exactly as Ivashin had last seen her at home in her black skirt and red blouse with a large buckle on the belt. She put one arm round her brother and kissed him on the temple.

"What a storm!" she said. "Gregory went off somewhere and I was left alone in the house."

She betrayed no embarrassment, and she looked at her brother as frankly and openly as at home. Looking at her, Ivashin, too, ceased to feel embarrassed.

"But you aren't afraid of thunder, are you?" he said, sitting down at the table.

"No, but the rooms are so vast here. It's an old house, and the thunder makes it all rattle like a cupboardful of crockery.

"Altogether it's a nice little house," she went on, sitting opposite her brother. "Every room has some delightful association—Gregory's grandfather shot himself in my room, believe it or not."

"We'll have some money in August and I'll do up the cottage in the garden," said Vlasich.

"Somehow one always thinks of that grandfather when it thunders," Zina went on. "And in this dining room a man was flogged to death."

"It's a fact," Vlasich confirmed, gazing wide-eyed at Ivashin. "Some time in the forties this place was leased to a certain Olivier, a Frenchman. His daughter's portrait is lying about in our attic now: a very pretty girl. This Olivier, my father told me, despised Russians as dunces and mocked them cruelly. For instance, he insisted that when the priest walked past the manor he should remove his cap a quarter of a mile away, and whenever the Olivier family drove through the village the church bells had to be rung. Serfs and small fry got even shorter shrift, of course. Now, one day one of the cheeriest members of the Russian tramping fraternity chanced to roll along—the lad had a bit of Gogol's theological student Khoma Brut about him. He asked for a night's lodging, the managers liked him, and they let him stay in the office.

"There are a lot of versions of the story. Some say the boy incited the peasants, while others have it that Olivier's daughter fell in love with the boy. What really happened I don't know, except that Olivier called him in here one fine evening, cross-examined him, and then gave orders to flog him. The master sits at this table drinking claret, see, while the grooms are beating the student. Olivier must have been trying to wring something out of him. By morning the lad was dead of torture and they hid the body somewhere. They are said to have thrown it in Koltovich's pond. An official inquiry was started, but the Frenchman paid several thousand in the right quarter and went off to Alsace. His lease ran out just then and that was the end of the matter."

"What scoundrels," shuddered Zina.

"My father remembered Olivier and his daughter well. He said she was a remarkably beautiful girl, and eccentric to boot. Myself, I think the young fellow did both: incited the peasants *and* took the daughter's fancy. Perhaps, even, he wasn't a theological student at all, but someone traveling incognito."

Zina grew pensive. The story of the student and the beautiful French girl had obviously run away with her imagination. Her appearance hadn't changed at all in the last week, Ivashin thought, she had only grown a little paler. She looked calm and normal as if she and her brother were now visiting Vlasich together. But some change had taken place in himself, Ivashin felt. The fact was that he had been able to discuss absolutely anything with her when she was still living at home, but now he couldn't even bring himself to ask her quite simply how she was getting on. The question seemed clumsy, superfluous. And a similar change must have affected her, for she was in no hurry to mention their mother, their home, her affair with Vlasich. She didn't try to justify herself, nor did she say that free unions are better than being married in church, but she remained calm, quietly pondering the story of Olivier.

Why, though, had they suddenly spoken about Olivier?

"You both got your shoulders wet in the rain," Zina said with a happy smile, touched by this small resemblance between her brother and Vlasich.

Ivashin felt the full bitterness and horror of his situation. He remembered his deserted home, the closed piano, and Zina's bright little room where no one went anymore. He remembered that her small footprints had vanished from their garden paths and that now no one went bathing with a noisy laugh before afternoon tea. The things that had increasingly claimed his affections since earliest childhood, that he used to like contemplating sometimes when sitting in a stuffy classroom or lecture hall—serenity, integrity, joy, everything that filled a home with life and light . . . those things had gone without trace, they had vanished and merged with the crude, clumsy story of some battalion commander, chivalrous subaltern, loose woman, and grandfather who had shot himself.

To start talking about his mother, to think that there could be any return to the past . . . that would mean misunderstanding what was perfectly clear.

Ivashin's eyes brimmed with tears and his hand trembled

where it lay on the table. Zina guessed what he was thinking about, and her eyes also reddened and glistened.

"Come here, Gregory," she said to Vlasich.

Both went over to the window and started whispering. From Vlasich's way of bending down toward her and from her way of looking at him Ivashin again realized that the matter was settled, that it couldn't be mended, and that there was nothing more to be said. Zina went out.

"Well, old boy," said Vlasich after a short pause, rubbing his hands and smiling. "Just now I said we were happy, but that was a bit of poetic license, so to speak. We haven't yet experienced happiness, in fact. Zina has been thinking of you and her mother all the time and she has been suffering, while I've suffered, too, watching her. Hers is a free, undaunted nature, but it's hard to go against the grain, you know—besides which she's young. The servants call her Miss. It seems a trifle, but it upsets her. That's the way of it, old man."

Zina brought in a dish of strawberries. She was followed by a little maidservant, seemingly meek and downtrodden, who put a jug of milk on the table and gave a very low bow. She had something in common with the antique furniture which was comparably torpid and dreary.

The sound of rain had ceased. Ivashin ate strawberries while Vlasich and Zina looked at him in silence. The time had come for a conversation pointless but unavoidable, and all three were depressed by the prospect. Ivashin's eyes again brimmed with tears. He pushed the bowl away, saying that it was time to go home, or else he would be late and it might rain again. The moment had arrived when it behooved Zina to speak of her family and her new life.

"How are things at home?" she asked rapidly, her pale face trembling. "How's Mother?"

"Well, you know Mother—" answered Ivashin, not looking at her.

"You have thought a lot about what's happened, Peter," she said, taking her brother by the sleeve, and he realized how hard it was for her to speak. "You have given it a lot of thought, so tell me: is there any chance Mother will ever accept Gregory . . . and the situation in general?"

She stood close to her brother, facing him, and he marveled at her beauty, and at his own apparent failure to notice it before. His sister, this sensitive, elegant girl who looked so much like their mother, now lived with Vlasich and shared Vlasich's home with a torpid maid and six-legged table in a house where a man had been flogged to death. And now she wouldn't be going home with her brother, but would stay the night here. All of this struck Ivashin as incredibly absurd.

"You know Mother," he said, not answering her question. "In my view you should conform with . . . you should, er, do something, sort of ask her forgiveness or—"

"But asking forgiveness would mean pretending we had done wrong. I don't mind telling lies to comfort Mother, but it won't work, will it? I know Mother.

"Well, we shall just have to see," said Zina, cheering up now that the most unpleasant bit was over. "We shall just have to put up with it for five or ten years and see what happens then."

She took her brother's arm and pressed against his shoulder as they went through the dark hall.

They went on to the steps. Ivashin said good-bye, mounted his horse, and started off at a walk. Zina and Vlasich walked a little way with him. It was quiet and warm, there was a delicious smell of hay. Between the clouds stars blazed vividly in the sky. Vlasich's old garden, witness of so many distressing episodes in its time, slumbered in the enveloping darkness, and riding through it was saddening, somehow.

"This afternoon Zina and I experienced a number of truly sublime moments," said Vlasich. "I read her a first-rate article on the agricultural resettlement problem. You really must read it, old man, it has outstanding integrity. I couldn't resist writing to the author, care of the editor. I wrote only a single line: 'I thank you and firmly shake your honest hand.' "

Ivashin wanted to tell him not to meddle in other people's business for heaven's sake, but remained silent.

Vlasich walked by his right stirrup, Zina by the left. Both seemed to have forgotten that they had to go back home, that it was damp, that they had nearly reached Koltovich's copse. They were expecting something from him, Ivashin felt, but what it was they expected they didn't know themselves and he felt desperately sorry for them. Now, as they walked by his horse so meekly and pensively, he felt absolutely convinced that they were unhappy—that they never could be happy—and their love seemed a deplorable and irrevocable mistake. Pitying them and aware that he could do nothing to help them, he fell prey to weakmindedness which made him ready for any sacrifice, could he but rid himself of this onerous feeling of compassion.

"I'll come and stay the night with you sometimes," he said.

But that looked like giving in to them and didn't satisfy him. When they stopped to say good-bye near Koltovich's copse he leant toward Zina and touched her shoulder.

"You're quite right, Zina," he said. "You have done the right thing."

To stop himself saying more and bursting into tears, he lashed his horse and galloped into the wood. Riding into darkness, he looked back and saw Vlasich and Zina walking home along the path—he with long strides, she at his side with quick, jerky steps. They were conducting an animated conversation.

"I'm like a silly old woman," thought Ivashin. "I went there to solve a problem, but only complicated it. Ah well, never mind."

He felt depressed. When the wood ended he rode at a walk, then stopped his horse near the pond. He wanted to sit and think. On the far side of the pond the rising moon was reflected as a red streak and there were hollow rumbles of thunder somewhere. Ivashin gazed steadily at the water, picturing his sister's despair, her anguished pallor and the dry eyes with which she would hide her degradation from the world. He imagined her pregnancy, their mother's death and funeral, Zina's horror. Nothing but death could break that proud, superstitious old woman. Appalling visions of the future appeared before him on the dark, smooth water, and amid pale feminine figures he saw himself—cowardly, weak, hunted-looking.

On the pond's right bank about a hundred yards away stood some dark, unmoving object—was it a man or a tall tree-stump? Ivashin remembered the murdered student who had been thrown into this pond.

"Olivier behaved cruelly," he thought, gazing at the dark, ghostly figure. "But at least he did solve his problem one way or the other, while I have solved nothing, I've only made a worse mess. He did and said what he thought, whereas I do and say what I don't think. Besides, I don't really know what I do think—"

He rode up to the dark figure. It was an old, rotting post, the relic of some building.

From Koltovich's copse and garden came a strong whiff of lily of the valley and honey-laden herbs. Ivashin rode along the edge of the pond, gazed mournfully at the water, and remembered his past life. So far he had not done or said what he thought, he concluded, and others had repaid him in like coin, which was why all life now seemed as dark as this pond with its reflections of the night sky and its tangled waterweed. There was no mending matters either, he thought.

A GENTLEMAN FRIEND

When she came out of the hospital the charming Vanda, or, according to her passport, "the honorable lady-citizen Nastasya Kanavkina," found herself in a position in which she had never been before: without a roof and without a sou. What was to be done?

First of all, she went to a pawnshop to pledge her turquoise ring, her only jewelry. They gave her a ruble for the ring . . . but what can you buy for a ruble? For that you can't get a short jacket *à la mode,* or an elaborate hat, or a pair of brown shoes; yet without these things she felt naked. She felt as though not only the people, but even the horses and dogs were staring at her and laughing at the plainness of her clothes. And her only thought was for her clothes; she did not care at all what she ate or where she slept.

"If only I were to meet a gentleman friend . . ." she thought. "I could get some money. . . . Nobody would say 'No,' because . . ."

But she came across no gentleman friends. It's easy to find them of nights in the *Renaissance,* but they wouldn't let her go into the *Renaissance* in that plain dress and without a hat. What's to be done? After a long time of anguish, vexed and weary with walking, sitting, and thinking, Vanda made up her mind to play her last card: to go straight to the rooms of some gentleman friend and ask him for money.

"But who shall I go to?" she pondered. "I can't possibly go to Misha. . . . He's got a family. . . . The ginger-headed old man is at his office . . ."

Vanda recollected Finkel, the dentist, the converted Jew, who gave her a bracelet three months ago. Once she poured a glass of beer on his head at the German club. She was awfully glad that she had thought of Finkel.

"He'll be certain to give me some, if only I find him in . . ." she thought on her way to him. "And if he won't, then I'll break every single thing there."

She had her plan already prepared. She approached the dentist's door. She would run up the stairs with a laugh, fly into his private room, and ask for twenty-five rubles. . . . But when she took hold of the bellpull, the plan went clean out of her head. Vanda suddenly began to be afraid and agitated, a thing which had never happened to her before. She was never anything but bold and independent in drunken company; but now, dressed in common clothes, and just like any ordinary person begging a favor, she felt timid and humble.

"Perhaps he has forgotten me. . . ." she thought, not daring to pull the bell. "And how can I go up to him in a dress like this? As if I were a pauper, or a dowdy respectable . . ."

She rang the bell irresolutely.

There were steps behind the door. It was the porter.

"Is the doctor at home?" she asked.

She would have been very pleased now if the porter had said no, but instead of answering, he showed her into the hall and took her jacket. The stairs seemed to her luxurious and magnificent, but what she noticed first of all in all the luxury was a large mirror in which she saw a ragged creature without an elaborate hat, without a modish jacket, and without a pair of brown shoes. And Vanda found it strange that, now that she was poorly dressed and looking more like a seamstress or a washerwoman, for the first time she felt ashamed, and had no more assurance or boldness left. In her thoughts she began to call herself Nastya Kanavkina, instead of Vanda as she used.

"This way, please!" said the maidservant, leading her to the private room. "The doctor will be here immediately. . . . Please, take a seat."

Vanda dropped into an easy chair.

"I'll say: 'Lend me . . .' " she thought. "That's the right thing, because we are acquainted. But the maid must go out of the room. . . . It's awkward in front of the maid. . . . What is she standing there for?"

In five minutes the door opened and Finkel entered—a tall, swarthy, convert Jew, with fat cheeks and goggle eyes. His cheeks, eyes, belly, fleshy hips—were all so full, repulsive, and coarse! At the *Renaissance* and the German club he used always to be a little drunk, to spend a lot of money on women, patiently put up with all their tricks—for instance, when Vanda poured the beer on his head, he only smiled and shook his finger at her—but now he looked dull and sleepy; he had the pompous, chilly expression of a superior, and he was chewing something.

"What is the matter?" he asked, without looking at Vanda. Vanda glanced at the maid's serious face, at the blown out figure of Finkel, who obviously did not recognize her, and she blushed.

"What's the matter?" the dentist repeated, irritated.

"To-oth ache . . ." whispered Vanda.

"Ah . . . which tooth . . . where?"

Vanda remembered she had a tooth with a hole.

"At the bottom . . . to the right," she said.

"H'm . . . open your mouth."

Finkel frowned, held his breath, and began to work the aching tooth loose.

"Do you feel any pain?" he asked, picking at her tooth with some instrument.

"Yes, I do . . ." Vanda lied. "Shall I remind him?" she thought. "He'll be sure to remember. . . . But . . . the maid . . . what is she standing there for?"

Finkel suddenly snorted like a steam engine, straight into her mouth, and said:

"I don't advise you to have a stopping. . . . Anyhow the tooth is quite useless."

Again he picked at the tooth for a little and soiled Vanda's lips and gums with his tobacco-stained fingers. Again he held his breath and dived into her mouth with something cold. . . .

Vanda suddenly felt a terrible pain, shrieked, and seized Finkel's hand. . . .

"Never mind. . . ." he murmured. "Don't be frightened. . . . This tooth isn't any use."

And his tobacco-stained fingers, covered with blood, held up the extracted tooth before her eyes. The maid came forward and put a bowl to her lips.

"Rinse your mouth with cold water at home," said Finkel. "That will make the blood stop."

He stood before her in the attitude of a man impatient to be left alone at last.

"Good-bye . . ." she said, turning to the door.

"H'm! And who's to pay me for the work?" Finkel asked laughingly.

"Ah . . . yes!" Vanda recollected, blushed, and gave the dentist the ruble she had got for the turquoise ring.

When she came into the street she felt still more ashamed than before, but she was not ashamed of her poverty anymore. Nor did she notice anymore that she hadn't an elaborate hat or a modish jacket. She walked along the street spitting blood and each red spittle told her about her life, a bad, hard life; about the insults she had suffered and had still to suffer—tomorrow, a week, a year hence—her whole life, till death . . .

"Oh, how terrible it is!" she whispered. "My God, how terrible!"

But the next day she was at the *Renaissance* and she danced there. She wore a new, immense red hat, a new jacket *à la mode* and a pair of brown shoes. She was treated to supper by a young merchant from Kazan.

PEASANT WOMEN

Just opposite the church in the village of Raybuzh stands an iron-roofed, two-story house with a stone foundation. The owner, Philip Kashin, also known as Dyudya, lives on the ground floor with his family, while on the upper story—extremely hot in summer, extremely cold in winter—are lodgings for passing officials, merchants, and country gentlemen. Dyudya rents plots of land, keeps a tavern on the highway, deals in tar, honey, cattle, and bonnets, and has saved about eight thousand rubles which he keeps in the town bank.

His elder son Theodore is foreman mechanic in a factory—having gone up in the world, as the locals say, and left the rest of them standing. Theodore's wife Sophia, a plain woman in poor health, makes her home with her father-in-law, is always crying, and drives over to hospital for treatment every Sunday. Dyudya's second son, hunchbacked Alyoshka, lives at home with his father and was recently married to a girl from a poor family called Barbara—a pretty young thing who enjoys the best of health and likes to dress smartly. When officials and merchants put up at the house, they always insist on Barbara serving the samovar and making their beds.

One June evening—the sun was setting and a scent of hay, warm dung, and fresh milk filled the air—a plain cart with three occupants drove into Dyudya's yard. There was a man of about thirty in a sailcloth suit sitting beside a boy of seven or eight in a long, black coat with big bone buttons, and there was a red-shirted youth as driver.

The youth unhitched the horses and walked them up and down the street, while the man washed, faced the church to say a prayer, spread out a rug by the cart, and sat down with the boy to have supper.

He ate with leisurely dignity. Having seen plenty of travelers in his day, Dyudya recognized his bearing as that of a business-like, serious man who knows his own worth.

Dyudya sat in his porch in his waistcoat, without a cap, waiting for the traveler to speak—he was used to visitors telling various bedtime stories of an evening and liked listening to them. His wife, old Afanasyevna, and his daughter-in-law, Sophia, were milking in the cowshed, while Barbara—the other daughter-in-law—sat upstairs by an open window eating sunflower seeds.

"Would the little boy be your son, then?" Dyudya asked the traveler.

"No, he's adopted—an orphan. I took him in for my soul's salvation."

They fell into conversation, and the visitor turned out a talkative man with quite a turn of phrase. From what he said, Dyudya learnt that he was a local townsman of the lower sort and a householder, that he went by the name of Matthew Savvich, that he was now on his way to look at some allotments which he had rented from some German settlers, and that the boy was called Kuzka. It was a hot, stifling evening, and no one felt like sleep. When it was dark, and pale stars twinkled here and there in the sky, Matthew Savvich began telling the story of how Kuzka had come into his care. Afanasyevna and Sophia stood a little way off listening, and Kuzka went to the gate.

"It's a complicated story in the extreme, old man," Matthew began. "To tell you all of it would take all night and more. Ten years ago there lived in our street, in the cottage next to mine—where the chandlery and dairy now are—an old widow called Martha Kapluntsev, who had two sons. One was a railway guard. The other, Vasya, was about my age, and lived at home with his mother. Old Kapluntsev had kept horses, about five pair, and had a carting business in town. The widow carried on her husband's business, and was as good at managing her carriers as the old man, so that the carting cleared about five rubles' profit some days. The lad made a bit of money, too, breeding pedigree pigeons and selling them to fanciers. He was forever standing on the roof, throwing up a broom and whistling, while his tumblers flew right up in the sky—but not high enough for him, he wanted them higher still. He caught goldfinches and starlings, and made them cages.

"It seemed a waste of time, but his time wasting was soon bringing in ten rubles a month. Well now, in course of time the old lady loses the use of her legs and takes to her bed, for which reason the house has no woman to run it, and that's about as good as a man having no eyes! So the old lady bestirs herself and decides to get Vasya married. They call in the matchmaker at once, one thing leads to another, there's lots of women's talk, and Vasya goes to inspect the local girls. He picks on Mashenka, Widow Samokhvalikha's daughter. They're betrothed without much ado, and it's all fixed up in one week. She's a young girl of about seventeen, a small, short little thing, but fair-complexioned and attractive, with all the makings of a high-class young lady, and her dowry isn't bad—about five hundred rubles in cash, a cow, and a bed. But the old lady knew what was coming, and two days after the wedding she departs for that heavenly Jerusalem where there's neither illness nor sighing. The young couple bury her and settle down. For six months everything's fine, but then disaster suddenly strikes again—it never rains but it pours. Vasya's summoned to an office for the conscription balloting, and they take him for a soldier, poor boy—won't even grant him any exemptions, but shave his head and pack him off to Poland. God's will it was, it couldn't be helped. He's all right as he says good-bye to the wife in his yard, but when he takes his last look at his pigeon loft he weeps buckets—a sorry sight he is. At first Mashenka gets her mother to live with her to keep her company, and the mother stays on till the confinement, when this boy Kuzka is born. But then she goes to another married daughter in Oboyan, leaving Mashenka alone with her baby. There are the five carters—a drunken, rowdy crew. She has the horses and drays on her hands, besides which there's her fence falling down, or her chimney catching fire, see? It's not woman's work, so she turns to me for every little thing, since we're neighbors. I go and fix things up, give her a few tips.

"Well, of course, all this means going indoors, having tea and a chat. I'm a young chap—a bit brainy, like, fond of talking about this and that—and she's a cultured, polite girl too. She dresses nicely and carries a parasol in summer. I'll start talking religion or politics, which flatters her, and she'll give me tea and jam.

"In fact, old man, to cut a long story short, within a twelvemonth the devil, the adversary of mankind, has me in a proper muddle, I can tell you. I notice that if I don't go and see her, I never feel right that day—I'm bored. And I keep thinking of excuses to call.

" 'It's time to put in your window frames for winter,' I say. And I hang around all day with her—putting in her frames, but taking care to leave a couple over for next day.

" 'I'd better count Vasya's pigeons,' I say, 'and see that none of them gets lost'—and so on.

"I keep talking to her over the fence, and end by making a little gate in it as a short cut. There's a lot of evil and nastiness in this world from the female sex—even saints have been led astray, let alone us sinners. Mashenka doesn't keep me at arm's length, and instead of thinking of her husband and keeping herself for him, she falls in love with me. I begin noticing that she misses me, too, and is always walking near the fence and looking into my yard through the cracks. My mind reels at the thought of her. Early one morning, at dawn on a Thursday in Easter Week, I'm going past her gate on my way to market when up pops the Evil One. I look through the trellis thing at the top of her gate, and there she is—already awake and feeding her ducks in the middle of the yard. I can't resist calling her. She comes and looks at me through the trellis, her little face all pale, her eyes soft and sleepy looking.

"I find her very attractive and begin complimenting her, like as if we were at a party instead of standing by that gate, while she blushes, laughs and looks me straight in the eye without blinking. I lose all sense and begin declaring my amorous feelings.

"She opens the gate to let me in, and we live together as man and wife from that morning on."

Hunchbacked Alyoshka came into the yard from the street and ran gasping into the house without looking at anyone. A minute later he ran out of doors again with his accordion and vanished through the gate, jingling copper coins in his pocket and cracking sunflower seeds on his way.

"Who's that?" asked Matthew Savvich.

"It's my son Alyoshka," answered Dyudya. "The rascal's off

on a spree. He's a hunchback, God having afflicted him that way, so we don't ask much of him."

"He's always with the lads, always having his bit of fun," sighed Afanasyevna. "We married him off just before Shrovetide, and thought he'd improve—but he's even worse, I do declare."

"It didn't work out," Dyudya said. "We only made a strange girl's fortune when we didn't need to."

Beyond the church someone began singing a magnificent, sad song. The words were inaudible, and only the voices could be heard—two tenors and a bass. While everyone listened, the yard grew as quiet as can be.

Two of the singers suddenly broke off with a peal of laughter, but the third—a tenor—went on singing, taking so high a note that all felt impelled to gaze upwards as if the voice had reached the very height of heaven. Barbara came out of doors and looked at the church, shading her eyes with her hand as if blinded by sunlight.

"It's the priest's sons and the schoolmaster," she said.

The three voices once more sang in unison. Matthew Savvich sighed.

"Well, that's the way of it, old man," he went on. "Two years later we get a letter from Vasya in Warsaw. He's being invalided out of the army, he writes—he isn't well. By this time I've banished all that nonsense from my head, and arrangements are under way to marry me to a decent young woman, but what I don't know is how to be rid of this wretched love affair. I make up my mind to speak to Mashenka every day, but I don't know how I can do it without a lot of female squawking. The letter frees my hands. Mashenka and I read it together, and she turns white as a sheet.

" 'Thank God,'' says I. 'This means you can be an honest woman again.'

" 'I won't live with him,' she tells me.

" 'He's your husband, ain't he?' says I.

" 'It ain't so simple. I never loved him—I married him against my will because Mother made me.'

" 'Now don't try and wriggle out of it, you little fool,' I say. 'Just tell me this—were you married in church or weren't you?'

" 'Yes I was,' says she. 'But it's you I love, and I'll live with you till my dying day. People may laugh at me, but I don't care.'

" 'You're a God-fearing woman,' say I. 'You've read what the Scripture says, haven't you?' "

"If she's married, she should cleave to her husband," said Dyudya.

"Yes, husband and wife are one flesh.

" 'You and I have sinned,' I tell her, 'and we must stop. We must repent and fear God. Let's beg Vasya's pardon,' say I. 'He's a quiet, mild fellow—he won't kill us. And it's better,' I say, 'to suffer agonies from a lawful husband in this world than gnash your teeth on the Day of Judgment.'

"The woman won't listen, she's set on having her own way, and takes no notice.

" 'I love you,' says she, and that was that.

"Vasya arrives home on the Saturday before Trinity Sunday, early in the morning—I can see everything through the fence. He runs into the house and comes out a minute later with Kuzka in his arms, laughing and crying. He kisses Kuzka and looks at his pigeon loft—he wants to go to his pigeons, but hasn't the heart to put Kuzka down. A soft, sentimental sort of fellow, he was. The day passes off all right, quietly and uneventfully. The bells are rung for evening service.

" 'Tomorrow's Trinity Sunday,' I think. 'So why don't they decorate their gate and fence with green boughs? Something's wrong,' thinks I.

"So I go over. I look, and there he is sitting on the floor in the middle of the room, rolling his eyes as if he was drunk, with tears streaming down his cheeks and his hands trembling. He takes some cracknels, necklaces, gingerbread, and various sweets out of his bundle, and throws them all over the floor. Kuzka, about three years old at the time, crawls around munching gingerbread, while Mashenka stands by the stove, pale and shuddering.

" 'I'm no wife to you, I don't want to live with you,' she mutters, and all sorts of silly rubbish.

"I bow low to Vasya.

" 'We have done you wrong, Vasya,' I say. 'Forgive us, for Christ's sake!'

"Then I get up and speak to Mashenka.

" 'You, Mashenka, must now wash Vasya's feet and drink the dirty water. Be his obedient wife, and pray God for me that He may forgive my transgressions in His mercy.'

"As if inspired by an angel in heaven, I read her a lecture and speak with such feeling that I actually break down and cry. Well, two days later Vasya comes to see me.

" 'I'll forgive you, Matthew, and forgive my wife too,'' he says. 'God help you both. She's a soldier's wife, it's a common way of behaving for a young female, it's hard to keep yourself to yourself. She ain't the first and she won't be the last. The only thing is,' says he, 'I ask you to act as if there had never been anything between you—don't let on. And I,' says he, 'will try to please her every way I can, so she'll love me again.'

"He shakes hands with me, has some tea, and goes away looking happy. Well, thinks I, thank God for that, and I'm glad it's all turned out so well. But no sooner is Vasya out of my yard than in comes Mashenka—something terrible, it was. She hangs on my neck, crying.

" 'Don't leave me, for Christ's sake,' she begs. 'I can't live without you.' "

"The shameless hussy!" sighed Dyudya.

"I shout at her, I stamp my feet, I drag her out in the lobby, and I put the door on the latch.

" 'Go to your husband,' I shout. 'Don't shame me in public. Have some fear of God in your heart.'

"So it goes on every day. One morning I'm standing in my yard by the stable, mending a bridle, and suddenly I see her run in through the gate, barefoot, just as she was in her petticoat, coming straight toward me. She picks up the bridle and gets tar all over her, trembling and crying.

" 'I can't live with that hateful creature, I can't bear it. If you don't love me, kill me.'

"I get angry and hit her twice with the bridle, and meanwhile Vasya runs in through the gate.

" 'Don't hit her, don't hit her!' he shouts, quite frantic.

"But he runs up himself and lashes out like a maniac, punching her with all his might, then throws her on the ground and starts kicking her. I try to protect her, but he picks up the reins and goes for her with those. And all the time he's thrashing her, he's squealing and whinnying like a foal."

"I'd give you reins if I had my way!" muttered Barbara, moving off. "Torturing us women, you rotten swine!"

"Shut up, bitch!" shouted Dyudya.

"Squealing away he was," Matthew Savvich went on. "One of the carters runs out of his yard, I call my own workman, and the three of us take Mashenka away from him and lead her home by the arms. Disgraceful it was! That evening I go along to see how she is, and she's lying in bed all wrapped up with fomentations on her. Only her eyes and nose can be seen, and she's looking at the ceiling.

" 'Hello, Mashenka,' I say. No answer.

"Vasya's sitting in the next room clutching his head.

" 'I'm a wicked man, I've ruined my life!' he weeps. 'Let me die, O Lord!'

"I sit with Mashenka for half an hour and read her a lecture—put the fear of God into her.

" 'The righteous will go to heaven in the next world,' say I. 'But you'll go into the fiery Gehenna along with all the other whores. Don't disobey your husband—down on your knees to him!'

"But not a word does she answer, she doesn't even wink an eye—I might have been talking to a stone. Next day Vasya sickens with something like cholera, and by evening I hear he's dead. They bury him.

"Not wanting to show people her shameless face and bruises, Mashenka doesn't go to the cemetery. And soon the rumor spreads among the townsfolk that Vasya's death wasn't natural, and that Mashenka did him in. The story reaches the authorities, who dig up Vasya, slit his guts and find arsenic in his belly—an open and shut case, it was. The police come and take Mashenka away together with that little innocent Kuzka, and put them in prison. That's where her flighty ways got her, it was punishment from God.

"They tried her eight months later. I remember her sitting in the dock wearing a white kerchief and gray prison coat. She was thin, pale, sharp-eyed—a pathetic sight. Behind her was a soldier with a gun. She wouldn't plead not guilty. There were some in court who said she'd poisoned her husband, while others argued that her husband had taken the poison himself in his grief. I was one witness. When they cross-examined me, I told the whole truth.

" 'She done it, the sinful creature,' said I. 'She didn't love her husband, you can't get away from it—and she was used to having her own way.'

"They began the trial in the morning, and that night they sentenced her to thirteen years' hard labor in Siberia. After the sentence, Mashenka was in the local prison for three months, and I used to go and see her—take her tea and sugar out of common humanity. But when she sees me she trembles all over and throws her arms about.

" 'Go away,' she mutters. 'Go away!'

"And she clasps Kuzka to her as if afraid I might take him off her.

" 'Now,' I say, 'see what you've sunk to! Oh Mashenka, Mashenka, you lost soul! You wouldn't listen when I tried to talk sense into you, and now you must pay for it. It's your fault,' say I, 'you've only yourself to blame.'

"I read her a lecture, and she keeps telling me to go away, go away, huddling against the wall with Kuzka and shivering. When they're taking her to our county town, I go to see her off at the railway station and slip a ruble in her bundle to save my soul. But she never got to Siberia—she fell sick of a fever in the county town and died in gaol."

"Serve the bitch right!" said Dyudya.

"They brought Kuzka back home. I thought it over, and decided to adopt him. And why not? Gaol-bird's spawn he may be—still he's a living soul, a Christian. I felt sorry for him. I'll make him a clerk, and if I don't have children of my own I'll make him a merchant. Nowadays I take him with me wherever I go, so he can learn something."

All the time while Matthew Savvich was telling his story, Kuzka sat on a stone near the gate, his head cupped in his hands, and looking at the sky. In the darkness he looked like a tree stump from a distance.

"Go to bed, Kuzka," Matthew Savvich yelled.

"Yes, it's time," said Dyudya, getting up and yawning noisily. "They all try to be too clever," he added. "They won't listen, and then they end up getting what they asked for."

The moon was already sailing in the sky above the yard. It was moving swiftly to one side, while the clouds below it sped the other way. The clouds drifted off, but the moon was still clearly seen above the yard. Matthew Savvich turned toward the church and prayed, then wished them good night and lay down on the ground near the cart. Kuzka also said his prayers, then lay in the cart, covering himself with his coat. To make himself comfortable, he burrowed in the hay, curling up with his elbows touching his knees. From the yard Dyudya could be seen lighting a candle in a downstairs room, putting on his spectacles, and standing in the corner with a book. For a long time he read, bowing before the icon.

The visitors fell asleep. Afanasyevna and Sophia went up to the cart and looked at Kuzka.

"He's asleep, poor little orphan," the old woman said. "He's thin and pale, nothing but skin and bones. He has no mother, and no one to feed him properly."

"My Grishutka's two years older, I reckon," Sophia said. "He's no better than a slave, living in that factory without his mother. The master beats him, I'll warrant. When I looked at this little boy just now, I remembered Grishutka, and it made my blood turn cold."

A minute passed in silence.

"He won't remember his mother, I reckon," said the old woman.

"How could he?"

Huge tears flowed from Sophia's eyes.

"He's curled up like a kitten," she said, sobbing and laughing with tender pity. "Poor little orphan."

Kuzka started, and opened his eyes. He saw an ugly, wrinkled, tear-stained face before him, and next to it another, an old woman's—toothless, sharp-chinned, hook-nosed. Above was the fathomless sky with its racing clouds and moon. He screamed in terror, and Sophia screamed too. Echo answered both of them, and their alarm flashed through the stifling air. A neighboring watchman started banging, and a dog barked. Matthew Savvich muttered in his sleep, and turned over.

Late at night, when Dyudya, the old woman, and the watchman next door were all asleep, Sophia went out through the gate and sat on a bench. The heat was stifling, and her head ached from crying. Broad and long—with two verst-posts visible on the right, and another two on the left—the street seemed to go on forever. The moon had abandoned the yard to stand behind the church, and one side of the street was bathed in moonlight, while the other was black with shadows. The long shadows of poplars and starling cotes spanned the entire street, and the church's shadow, black and menacing, lay in a broad band, clasping Dyudya's gate and half his house. There was no one about and it was quiet. From time to time faint strains of music were wafted from the end of the street—Alyoshka playing his accordion, no doubt.

In the shadow near the church fence someone was walking. Was it man or cow—or no more than a large bird rustling in the trees? One could not tell. Then a figure emerged from the shadows, paused, said something in a man's voice, and vanished down the church lane. A little later another figure appeared about five yards from the gate. This person was moving straight to the gate from the church, and stopped still on seeing Sophia on the bench.

"Is that you, Barbara?" Sophia asked.

"What if it is?"

Barbara it was. She stood still for a minute, then came and sat on the bench.

"Where have you been?" asked Sophia.

Barbara made no answer.

"You mind you don't get into trouble," Sophia said. "Playing around like this, and you only just married. Did you hear how they kicked Mashenka and whipped her with the reins? You mind that don't happen to you."

"I don't care."

Barbara laughed into her handkerchief.

"I've been having a bit of fun with the priest's son," she whispered.

"You don't mean it!"

"It's God's truth."

"That's a sin," Sophia whispered.

"Who cares? Why bother? Sin or no sin, I'd rather be struck by lightning than live this way. I'm young and healthy, and I have a hunchbacked husband that I can't abide—he's that pig-headed, he's worse than that blasted Dyudya. I never had enough to eat as a girl, and I went barefoot. To escape such misery I took the bait of Alyoshka's money, and became a slave. I was caught like a rat in a trap, and now I'd rather sleep with a viper than with that rotten Alyoshka. And your life too—it don't bear thinking of! Your Theodore threw you out of the factory—sent you to his father's—and took up with another woman. They took your boy off you and made a slave out of him. You work like a horse, and never hear a kind word. Better pine away as an old maid all your life, better take your half-rubles from the priest's sons, better go begging, better throw yourself head first down a well—"

"That's a sin," Sophia whispered again.

"Who cares?"

Somewhere beyond the church the same three voices—the two tenors and the bass—started another sad song. Once again the words were inaudible.

"They're making quite a night of it," Barbara laughed.

She began whispering about the fun she was having with the priest's son of a night—what he said, what his friends were like, and about how she also carried on with officials and merchants who stayed at the house. The sad song bore a whiff of freedom, and Sophia began laughing. It was all very sinful and frightening and sweet to the ear. She envied Barbara, sorry that she hadn't sinned herself when she was young and beautiful.

Midnight struck in the old church by the cemetery.

"We'd better go to bed, or else Dyudya may miss us," said Sophia, getting up.

Both went quietly into the yard.

"I went away and missed the end of his story about Mashenka," said Barbara, making her bed under the window.

"She died in gaol, he said. She'd poisoned her husband."

Barbara lay down by Sophia and thought for a moment.

"I could kill Alyoshka," she said. "I'd think nothing of it."

"You don't mean that, God help you."

As Sophia was dropping off, Barbara huddled up to her.

"Let's do away with Dyudya and Alyoshka," she whispered in her ear.

Sophia shuddered and said nothing, then opened her eyes and stared at the sky for a long time without winking.

"They'd find out," she said.

"No, they wouldn't. Dyudya's an old man, he's not long for this world. And they'll say Alyoshka died of drink."

"I'm afraid— God would strike us dead."

"Who cares?"

Both lay awake, silently thinking.

"It's cold," said Sophia, shivering all over. "It'll soon be morning, I reckon. Are you asleep?"

"No. Don't take any notice of me, dear," whispered Barbara. "I'm so angry with them swine, I don't know what I'm saying. Go to sleep, it's nearly daylight. Sleep."

Both were silent. They calmed down and soon fell asleep.

The old woman was the first to wake up. She woke Sophia, and they both went to the shed to milk the cows. Hunchbacked Alyoshka walked in, dead drunk, without his accordion, his chest and knees covered with dust and straw—so he must have fallen down on the way. He staggered into the shed, flopped on to a sledge without undressing, and started snoring at once. When the crosses on the church, and then the windows, were blazing in the bright flame of the rising sun, and the shadows from trees and well sweep spanned the dewy grass of the yard, Matthew Savvich jumped up and bestirred himself.

"Get up, Kuzka!" he shouted. "Time to harness up! Look slippy there!"

The morning's bustle began. A young Jewish woman in a flounced brown dress led a horse into the yard to water it. The pulley of the well creaked piteously, the pail rattled.

Sleepy, listless, covered with dew, Kuzka sat in the cart, lazily putting on his coat, listening to water splashing out of the pail in the well, and shivering with cold.

"Give my lad a nudge, missus, so he'll go and harness up," shouted Matthew Savvich to Sophia.

Then Dyudya yelled from a window. "Sophia, charge that woman a kopeck for watering her horse. They're always doing that, the Jewish scum."

In the street, sheep were running to and fro, bleating. Women shouted at the shepherd, who played his pipe, cracked his whip, or answered them in a heavy, rough, deep voice. Three sheep ran into the yard, couldn't find the gate, butted the fence—and the noise woke Barbara, who seized her bedding in both arms and made for the house.

"You might have driven the sheep out," the old woman shouted at her. "You're too high and mighty, I suppose!"

"There she goes again—why should I work for such monsters?" muttered Barbara as she went indoors.

The cart was greased, the horses harnessed. Dyudya came out of the house carrying an abacus, and sat in the porch working out what to charge the visitor for his night's lodging, oats, and water.

"That's a lot for oats, old man," said Matthew Savvich.

"Then don't take them. No one's forcing you, Mister Merchant."

Just as the travelers were going to get in the cart and leave, something held them up for a moment—Kuzka had lost his cap.

"Where did you put it, you little swine?" Matthew Savvich roared angrily. "Where is it?"

Kuzka's face was contorted with terror as he rushed this way and that near the cart. Not finding it there, he ran to the gate, then to the cow shed. The old woman and Sophia helped him look.

"I'll tear your ears off!" shouted Matthew Savvich. "Little bleeder!"

The cap was found at the bottom of the cart. Brushing off the hay with his sleeves, Kuzka put it on and mounted the cart—nervously, still looking terrified, as if fearing to be struck from behind. Matthew Savvich crossed himself, the lad tugged the reins. The cart moved off and rolled out of the yard.

THE BISHOP

It was on the eve of Palm Sunday; vespers were being sung in the Staro-Petrovski Convent. The hour was nearly ten when the palm leaves were distributed, and the little icon-lamps were growing dim; their wicks had burnt low, and a soft haze hung in the chapel. As the worshippers surged forward in the twilight like the waves of the sea, it seemed to His Reverence Pyotr, who had been feeling ill for three days, that the people who came to him for palm leaves all looked alike, and, men or women, old or young, all had the same expression in their eyes. He could not see the doors through the haze; the endless procession rolled toward him, and seemed as if it must go on rolling forever. A choir of women's voices was singing and a nun was reading the canon.

How hot and close the air was, and how long the prayers! His Reverence was tired. His dry, parching breath was coming quickly and painfully, his shoulders were aching, and his legs were trembling. The occasional cries of an idiot in the gallery annoyed him. And now, as a climax, His Reverence saw, as in a delirium, his own mother whom he had not seen for nine years coming toward him in the crowd. She, or an old woman exactly like her, took a palm leaf from his hands, and moved away looking at him all the while with a glad, sweet smile, until she was lost in the crowd. And for some reason the tears began to course down his cheeks. His heart was happy and peaceful, but his eyes were fixed on a distant part of the chapel where the prayers were being read, and where no human being could be distinguished among the shadows. The tears glistened on his cheeks and beard. Then someone who was standing near him began to weep, too, and then another, and then another, until little by little the chapel was filled with a low sound of weeping. Then the convent choir began to sing, the weeping stopped, and everything went on as before.

Soon afterward the service ended. The fine, jubilant notes of the heavy chapel-bells were throbbing through the moonlit garden as the bishop stepped into his coach and drove away. The white walls, the crosses on the graves, the silvery birches, and the faraway moon hanging directly over the monastery all seemed to be living a life of their own, incomprehensible, but very near to mankind. It was early in April, and a chilly night had succeeded a warm spring day. A light frost was falling, but the breath of spring could be felt in the soft, cool air. The road from the monastery was sandy, the horses were obliged to proceed at a walk, and, bathed in the bright, tranquil moonlight, a stream of pilgrims was crawling along on either side of the coach. All were thoughtful, no one spoke. Everything around them, the trees, the sky, and even the moon, looked so young and intimate and friendly that they were reluctant to break the spell which they hoped might last forever.

Finally the coach entered the city and rolled down the main street. All the stores were closed but that of Erakin, the millionaire merchant. He was trying his electric lights for the first time, and they were flashing so violently that a crowd had collected in front of the store. Then came wide, dark streets in endless succession, and then the highway, and fields, and the smell of pines. Suddenly a white crenelated wall loomed before him, and beyond it rose a tall belfry flanked by five flashing golden cupolas, all bathed in moonlight. This was the Pankratievski Monastery, where His Reverence Pyotr lived. Here, too, the calm, brooding moon was floating directly above the monastery. The coach drove through the gate, its wheels crunching on the sand. Here and there the dark forms of monks started out into the moonlight and footsteps rang along the flagstone paths.

"Your mother has been here while you were away, Your

Reverence,'' a lay brother told the bishop as he entered his room.

''My mother? When did she come?''

''Before vespers. She first found out where you were, and then drove to the convent.''

''Then it was she whom I saw just now in the chapel! Oh, Father in heaven!''

And His Reverence laughed for joy.

''She told me to tell you, Your Reverence,'' the lay brother continued, ''that she would come back tomorrow. She had a little girl with her, a grandchild, I think. She is stopping at Ovsianikov's inn.''

''What time is it now?''

''It is after eleven.''

''What a nuisance!''

His Reverence sat down irresolutely in his sitting room, unwilling to believe that it was already so late. His arms and legs were racked with pain, the back of his neck was aching, and he felt uncomfortable and hot. When he had rested a few moments he went into his bedroom and there, too, he sat down and dreamed of his mother. He heard the lay brother walking away and Father Sisoi, the priest, coughing in the next room. The monastery clock struck the quarter.

His Reverence undressed and began his prayers. He spoke the old, familiar words with scrupulous attention, and at the same time he thought of his mother. She had nine children, and about forty grandchildren. She had lived from the age of seventeen to the age of sixty with her husband, the deacon, in a little village. His Reverence remembered her from the days of his earliest childhood, and, ah, how he had loved her! Oh, that dear, precious, unforgettable childhood of his! Why did those years that had vanished forever seem so much brighter and richer and gayer than they really had been? How tender and kind his mother had been when he was ill in his childhood and youth! His prayers mingled with the memories that burned ever brighter and brighter in his heart like a flame, but they did not hinder his thoughts of his mother.

When he had prayed he lay down, and as soon as he found himself in the dark there rose before his eyes the vision of his dead father, his mother, and Lyesopolye, his native village. The creaking of wagon wheels, the bleating of sheep, the sound of church bells on a clear summer morning, ah, how pleasant it was to think of these things! He remembered Father Semyon, the old priest at Lyesopolye, a kind, gentle, good-natured old man. He himself had been small, and the priest's son had been a huge strapping novice with a terrible bass voice. He remembered how this young priest had scolded the cook once, and had shouted: "Ah, you she-ass of Jehovah!" And Father Semyon had said nothing, and had only been mortified because he could not for the life of him remember reading of an ass of that name in the Bible!

Father Semyon had been succeeded by Father Demyan, a hard drinker who sometimes even went so far as to see green snakes. He had actually borne the nickname of "Demian the Snake-Seer" in the village. Matvey Nikolaich had been the schoolmaster, a kind, intelligent man, but a hard drinker, too. He never thrashed his scholars, but for some reason he kept a little bundle of birch twigs hanging on his wall, under which was a tablet bearing the absolutely unintelligible inscription: *Betula Kinderbalsamica Secuta.*[1] He had had a woolly black dog whom he called Syntax.

The bishop laughed. Eight miles from Lyesopolye lay the village of Obnino, possessing a miraculous icon. A procession started from Obnino every summer bearing the wonder-working icon and making the rounds of all the neighboring villages. The church bells would ring all day long first in one village, then in another, and to little Pavel (His Reverence was called little Pavel then) the air itself seemed tremulous with rapture. Barefoot, hatless, and infinitely happy, he followed the icon with a naive smile on his lips and naive faith in his heart.

Until the age of fifteen little Pavel had been so slow at his lessons that his parents had even thought of taking him out of the ecclesiastical school and putting him to work in the village store.

The bishop turned over so as to break the train of his thoughts, and tried to go to sleep.

"My mother has come!" he remembered, and laughed.

The moon was shining in through the window, and the floor was lit by its rays while he lay in shadow. A cricket was chirping. Father Sisoi was snoring in the next room, and there was a forlorn, friendless, even a vagrant note in the old man's cadences.

Sisoi had once been the steward of a diocesan bishop and was

---

[1]Fractured Latin and German: "Twigs children-healing flogger."

known as Father Former Steward. He was seventy years old, and lived sometimes in a monastery sixteen miles away, sometimes in the city, sometimes wherever he happened to be. Three days ago he had turned up at the Pankratievski Monastery, and the bishop had kept him here in order to discuss with him at his leisure the affairs of the monastery.

The bell for matins rang at half past one. Father Sisoi coughed, growled something, and got up.

"Father Sisoi!" called the bishop.

Sisoi came in dressed in a white cassock, carrying a candle in his hand.

"I can't go to sleep," His Reverence said. "I must be ill. I don't know what the matter is; I have fever."

"You have caught cold, your Lordship. I must rub you with tallow."

Father Sisoi stood looking at him for a while and yawned: "Ah-h—the Lord have mercy on us!

"Erakin has electricity in his store now—I hate it!" he continued.

Father Sisoi was aged and round shouldered and gaunt. He was always displeased with something or other, and his eyes, which protruded like those of a crab, always wore an angry expression.

"I don't like it at all," he repeated—"I hate it."

II

Next day, on Palm Sunday, His Reverence officiated at the cathedral in the city. Then he went to the diocesan bishop's, then to see a general's wife who was very ill, and at last he drove home. At two o'clock two beloved guests were having dinner with him, his aged mother, and his little niece Katya, a child of eight. The spring sun was peeping cheerily in through the windows as they sat at their meal, and was shining merrily on the white tablecloth and on Katya's red hair. Through the double panes they heard the rooks cawing and the magpies chattering in the garden.

"It is nine years since I saw you last," said the old mother, "and yet when I caught sight of you in the convent chapel yesterday I thought to myself: 'God bless me, he has not changed a bit!' Only perhaps you are a little thinner than you were, and your beard has grown longer. Oh, holy Mother, Queen of heaven! Everybody was crying yesterday. As soon as I saw you, I began to cry myself, I don't know why. His holy will be done!"

In spite of the tenderness with which she said this, it was clear that she was not at her ease. It was as if she did not know whether to address the bishop by the familiar "thee" or the formal "you," and whether she ought to laugh or not. She seemed to feel herself more of a poor deacon's wife than a mother in his presence. Meanwhile Katya was sitting with her eyes glued to the face of her uncle the bishop as if she were trying to make out what manner of man this was. Her hair had escaped from her comb and her bow of velvet ribbon, and was standing straight up around her head like a halo. Her eyes were foxy and bright. She had broken a glass before sitting down, and now, as she talked, her grandmother kept moving first a glass, and then a wineglass, out of her reach. As the bishop sat listening to his mother, he remembered how, many, many years ago, she had sometimes taken him and his brothers and sisters to visit relatives whom they considered rich. She had been busy with her own children in those days, and now she was busy with her grandchildren, and had come to visit him with Katya here.

"Your sister Varenka has four children"—she was telling him—"Katya is the oldest. God knows why, her father fell ill and died three days before Assumption. So my Varenka has been thrown out into the cold world."

"And how is my brother Nikanor?" the bishop asked.

"He is well, thank the Lord. He is pretty well, praise be to God. But his son Nikolasha wouldn't go into the church, and is at college instead learning to be a doctor. He thinks it is best, but who knows? However, God's will be done!"

"Nikolasha cuts up dead people!" said Katya, spilling some water into her lap.

"Sit still, child!" her grandmother said, quietly taking the glass out of her hands.

"How long it is since we have seen one another!" exclaimed His Reverence, tenderly stroking his mother's shoulder and hand. "I missed you when I was abroad, I missed you dreadfully."

"Thank you very much!"

"I used to sit by my window in the evening listening to the band playing, and feeling lonely and forlorn. Sometimes I would suddenly grow so homesick that I used to think I would gladly give everything I had in the world for a glimpse of you and home."

His mother smiled and beamed, and then immediately drew a long face and said stiffly:

"Thank you very much!"

The bishop's mood changed. He looked at his mother and could not understand where she had acquired that deferential, humble expression of face and voice, and what the meaning of it might be. He hardly recognized her and felt sorrowful and vexed. Besides, his head was still aching, and his legs were racked with pain. The fish he was eating tasted insipid and he was very thirsty.

After dinner two wealthy lady landowners visited him and sat for an hour and a half with faces a mile long, never uttering a word. Then an archimandrite, a gloomy, taciturn man, came on business. Then the bells rang for vespers, the sun set behind the woods, and the day was done. As soon as he got back from church the bishop said his prayers and went to bed, drawing the covers up closely about his ears. The moonlight troubled him, and soon the sound of voices came to his ears. Father Sisoi was talking politics with his mother in the next room.

"There is a war in Japan now," he was saying. "The Japanese belong to the same race as the Montenegrins. They fell under the Turkish yoke at the same time."

And then the bishop heard his mother's voice say:

"And so, you see, when we had said our prayers, and had our tea, we went to Father Yegor—"

She kept saying over and over again that they "had tea," as if all she knew of life was tea drinking.

The memory of his seminary and college life slowly and mistily took shape in the bishop's mind. He had been a teacher of Greek for three years, until he could no longer read without glasses, and then he had taken the vows, and had been made an inspector. When he was thirty-two he had been made the rector of a seminary, and then an archimandrite. At that time his life had been so easy and pleasant, and had seemed to stretch so far, far into the future that he could see absolutely no end to it. But his health had failed, and he had nearly lost his eyesight. His doctors had advised him to give up his work and go abroad.

"And what did you do next?" asked Father Sisoi in the adjoining room.

"And then we had tea," answered his mother.

"Why, Father, your beard is green!" exclaimed Katya suddenly. And she burst out laughing.

The bishop remembered that the color of Father Sisoi's beard really did verge on green, and he, too, laughed.

"My goodness! What a plague that child is!" cried Father Sisoi in a loud voice, for he was growing angry. "You're a spoiled baby, you are! Sit still!"

The bishop recalled the new white church in which he had officiated when he was abroad, and the sound of a warm sea. Eight years had slipped by while he was there; then he had been recalled to Russia, and now he was already a bishop, and the past had faded away into mist as if it had been but a dream.

Father Sisoi came into his room with a candle in his hand.

"Well, well!" he exclaimed, surprised. "Asleep already, Your Reverence?"

"Why not?"

"It's early yet, only ten o'clock! I bought a candle this evening and wanted to rub you with tallow."

"I have a fever," the bishop said, sitting up. "I suppose something ought to be done. My head feels so queer."

Sisoi began to rub the bishop's chest and back with tallow.

"There—there—" he said. "Oh, Lord God Almighty! There! I went to town today, and saw that—what do you call him?—that archpresbyter Sidonski. I had tea with him. I hate him! Oh, Lord God Almighty! There! I hate him!"

III

The diocesan bishop was very old and very fat, and had been ill in bed with gout for a month. So His Reverence Pyotr had been visiting him almost every day and had received his suppliants for him. And now that he was ill he was appalled to think of the futilities and trifles they asked for and wept over. He felt annoyed at their ignorance and cowardice. The very number of all those useless trivialities oppressed him, and he felt as if he could understand the diocesan bishop who had written "Lessons in Free Will" when he was young, and now seemed so absorbed in details that the memory of everything else, even of God, had forsaken him. Pyotr must have grown out of touch with Russian life while he was abroad, for it was hard for him to grow used to it now. The people seemed rough, the women stupid and tiresome, the novices and their teachers uneducated and often disorderly. And then the documents that passed through his hands by the hundreds of thousands! The provosts gave all the priests in the diocese, young and old, and their wives and children[1] marks for good behavior, and he was obliged to talk about all this, and read about it, and write serious articles on it. His Reverence never had a moment which he could call his own; all day his nerves were on edge, and he grew calm only when he found himself in church.

He could not grow accustomed to the terror which he involuntarily inspired in every breast in spite of his quiet and modest ways. Everyone in the district seemed to shrivel and quake and apologize as soon as he looked at them. Everyone trembled in his presence; even the old archpresbyters fell down at his feet, and not long ago one suppliant, the old wife of a village priest, had been prevented by terror from uttering a word, and had gone away without asking for anything. And he, who had never been able to say a harsh word in his sermons, and who never blamed people because he pitied them so, would grow exasperated with these suppliants, and hurl their petitions to the ground. Not a soul had spoken sincerely and naturally to him since he had been here; even his old mother had changed, yes, she had changed very much! Why did she talk so freely to Sisoi when all the while she was so serious and ill at ease with him, her own son? It was not like her at all! The only person who behaved naturally in his presence, and who said whatever came into his head, was old man Sisoi, who had lived with bishops all his life, and had outlasted eleven of them. And therefore His Reverence felt at ease with Sisoi, even though he was, without a doubt, a rough and quarrelsome person.

After morning prayers on Tuesday the bishop received his suppliants and lost his temper with them. He felt ill, as usual, and longed to go to bed, but he had hardly entered his room before he was told that the young merchant Erakin, a benefactor of the monastery, had called on very important business. The bishop was obliged to receive him. Erakin stayed about an hour talking in a very loud voice, and it was hard to understand what he was trying to say.

After he had gone there came an abbess from a distant con-

---

[1]Lower Russian Orthodox clergy are permitted to marry.

vent, and by the time she had gone the bells were tolling for vespers; it was time for the bishop to go to church.

The monks sang melodiously and rapturously that evening; a young, black-bearded priest officiated. His Reverence listened as they sang of the Bridegroom and of the chamber swept and garnished, and felt neither repentance nor sorrow, but only a deep peace of mind. He sat by the altar where the shadows were deepest, and was swept in imagination back into the days of his childhood and youth, when he had first heard these words sung. The tears trickled down his cheeks, and he meditated on how he had attained everything in life that it was possible for a man in his position to attain; his faith was unsullied, and yet all was not clear to him; something was lacking, and he did not want to die. It still seemed to him that he was leaving unfound the most important thing of all. Something of which he had dimly dreamed in the past, hopes that had thrilled his heart as a child, a schoolboy, and a traveler in foreign lands, troubled him still.

"How beautifully they are singing today!" he thought. "Oh, how beautifully!"

IV

On Thursday he held a service in the cathedral. It was the festival of the Washing of Feet. When the service was over, and the people had gone to their several homes, the sun was shining brightly and cheerily, and the air was warm. The gutters were streaming with bubbling water, and the tender songs of larks came floating in from the fields beyond the city, bringing peace to his heart. The trees were already awake, and over them brooded the blue, unfathomable sky.

His Reverence went to bed as soon as he reached home, and told the lay brother to close his shutters. The room grew dark. Oh, how tired he was!

As on the day before, the sound of voices and the tinkling of glasses came to him from the next room. His mother was gaily recounting some tale to Father Sisoi, with many a quaint word and saying, and the old man was listening gloomily and answering in a gruff voice:

"Well, I never! Did they, indeed? What do you think of that!"

And once more the bishop felt annoyed and then hurt that the old lady should be so natural and simple with strangers, and so silent and awkward with her own son. It even seemed to him that she always tried to find some pretext for standing in his presence, as if she felt uneasy sitting down. And his father? If he had been alive, he would probably not have been able to utter a word when the bishop was there.

Something in the next room fell to the floor with a crash. Katya had evidently broken a cup or a saucer, for Father Sisoi suddenly snorted, and cried angrily:

"What a terrible plague this child is! Merciful heavens! No one could keep her supplied with china!"

Then silence fell. When he opened his eyes again, the bishop saw Katya standing by his bedside staring at him, her red hair standing up around her head like a halo, as usual.

"Is that you, Katya?" he asked. "Who is that opening and shutting doors down there?"

"I don't hear anything."

He stroked her head.

"So your cousin Nikolasha cuts up dead people, does he?" he asked, after a pause.

"Yes, he is learning to."

"Is he nice?"

"Yes, very, only he drinks a lot."

"What did your father die of?"

"Papa grew weaker and weaker, and thinner and thinner, and then came his sore throat. And I was ill, too, and so was my brother Fedia. We all had sore throats. Papa died, Uncle, but we got well."

Her chin quivered, her eyes filled with tears.

"Oh, Your Reverence!" she cried in a shrill voice, beginning to weep bitterly. "Dear Uncle, Mother and all of us are so unhappy! Do give us a little money! Help us, Uncle darling!"

He also shed tears, and for a moment could not speak for emotion. He stroked her hair, and touched her shoulder, and said:

"All right, all right, little child. Wait until Easter comes, then we will talk about it. I'll help you."

His mother came quietly and timidly into the room, and said a prayer before the icon. When she saw that he was awake, she asked:

"Would you like a little soup?"

"No, thanks," he answered. "I'm not hungry."

"I don't believe you are well—I can see that you are not well. You really mustn't fall ill! You have to be on your feet all day long. My goodness, it makes one tired to see you! Never mind, Easter is no longer over the hills and far away. When Easter comes you will rest. God will give us time for a little talk then, but now I'm not going to worry you any more with my silly chatter. Come, Katya, let His Lordship have another forty winks—"

And the bishop remembered that, when he was a boy, she had used exactly the same half-playful, half-respectful tone to all high dignitaries of the church. Only by her strangely tender eyes and by the anxious look which she gave him as she left the room could anyone have guessed that she was his mother. He shut his eyes and seemed to be asleep, but he heard the clock strike twice, and Father Sisoi coughing next door. His mother came in again and looked shyly at him. Suddenly there came a bang, and a door slammed; a vehicle of some kind drove up to the front steps. The lay brother came into the bishop's room, and called:

"Your Reverence!"

"What is it?"

"Here is the coach! It is time to go to our Lord's Passion— "

"What time is it?"

"Quarter to eight."

The bishop dressed and drove to the cathedral. He had to stand motionless in the center of the church while the twelve Gospels were being read, and the first and longest and most beautiful of them all he read himself. A strong, valiant mood took hold of him. He knew this Gospel, beginning "The Son of Man is risen today—," by heart, and as he repeated it, he raised his eyes and saw a sea of little lights about him. He heard the sputtering of candles, but the people had disappeared. He felt surrounded by those whom he had known in his youth; he felt that they would always be here until—God knows when!

His father had been a deacon, his grandfather had been a priest, and his great-grandfather a deacon. He sprang from a race that had belonged to the church since Christianity first came to Russia, and his love for the ritual of the church, the clergy, and the sound of church bells was inborn in him, deeply, irradicably implanted in his heart. When he was in church, especially when he was taking part in the service himself, he felt active and valorous and happy. And so it was with him now. Only, after the eighth Gospel had been read, he felt that his voice was becoming so feeble that even his cough was inaudible; his head was aching, and he began to fear that he might collapse. His legs were growing numb; in a little while he ceased to have any sensation in them at all, and could not imagine what he was standing on and why he did not fall down.

It was quarter to twelve when the service ended. The bishop went to bed as soon as he reached home, without even saying his prayers. As he pulled his blanket up over him, he suddenly wished that he were abroad; he passionately wished it. He would give his life, he thought, to cease from seeing these cheap, wooden walls and that low ceiling, to cease from smelling the stale scent of the monastery.

If there were only someone with whom he could talk, someone to whom he could unburden his heart!

He heard steps in the adjoining room, and tried to recall who it might be. At last the door opened, and Father Sisoi came in with a candle in one hand and a teacup in the other.

"In bed already, Your Reverence?" he asked. "I have come to rub your chest with vinegar and vodka. It is a fine thing, if rubbed in good and hard. Oh, Lord God Almighty! There—there—I have just come from our monastery. I hate it. I am going away from here tomorrow, my Lord. Oh, Lord, God Almighty—there—"

Sisoi never could stay long in one place, and he now felt as if he had been in this monastery for a year. It was hard to tell from what he said where his home was, whether there was anyone or anything in the world that he loved, and whether he believed in God or not. He himself never could make out why he had become a monk, but then, he never gave it any thought, and the time when he had taken the vows had long since faded from his memory. He thought he must have been born a monk.

"Yes, I am going away tomorrow. Bother this place!"

"I want to have a talk with you—I never seem to have the time—" whispered the bishop, making a great effort to speak. "You see, I don't know anyone—or anything—here—"

"Very well then, I shall stay until Sunday, but no longer! Bother this place!"

"What sort of a bishop am I?" His Reverence went on, in a faint voice. "I ought to have been a village priest, or a deacon, or a plain monk. All this is choking me—it is choking me—"

"What's that? Oh, Lord God Almighty! There—go to sleep

now, Your Reverence. What do you mean? What's all this you are saying? Good night!''

All night long the bishop lay awake, and in the morning he grew very ill. The lay brother took fright and ran first to the archimandrite and then for the monastery doctor who lived in the city. The doctor, a stout, elderly man with a long, gray beard, looked intently at His Reverence, shook his head, knit his brows, and finally said:

''I'll tell you what, Your Reverence; you have typhoid.''

The bishop grew very thin and pale in the next hour, his eyes grew larger, his face became covered with wrinkles, and he looked quite small and old. He felt as if he were the thinnest, weakest, puniest man in the whole world, and as if everything that had occurred before this had been left far, far behind, and would never happen again.

''How glad I am of that!'' he thought. ''Oh, how glad!''

His aged mother came into the room. When she saw his wrinkled face and his great eyes, she was seized with fear, and, falling down on her knees by his bedside, she began kissing his face, his shoulders, and his hands. He seemed to her to be the thinnest, weakest, puniest man in the world, and she forgot that he was a bishop and kissed him as if he had been a little child whom she dearly, dearly loved.

''Little Pavel, my dearie!'' she cried. ''My little son, why do you look like this? Little Pavel, oh, answer me!''

Katya, pale and severe, stood near them, and could not understand what was the matter with her uncle, and why Granny wore such a look of suffering on her face and spoke such heart-rending words. And he, he was speechless, and knew nothing of what was going on around him. He was dreaming that he was an ordinary man once more, striding swiftly and merrily through the open country, a staff in his hand, bathed in sunshine, with the wide sky above him, as free as a bird to go wherever his fancy led him.

''My little son! My little Pavel! Answer me!'' begged his mother.

''Don't bother His Lordship,'' said Sisoi angrily, crossing the room. ''Let him sleep. Nothing to do there . . . what for! . . .''

Three doctors came, consulting together, and drove away. The day seemed long, incredibly long, and then came the long, long night. Just before dawn on Saturday morning the lay brother went to the old mother, who was lying on a sofa in the sitting room, and asked her to come into the bedroom; His Reverence had gone to eternal peace.

Next day was Easter. There were forty-two churches in the city and two monasteries, and the deep, joyous notes of their bells pealed out over the town from morning until night. The birds were caroling, the bright sun was shining. The big market-place was full of noise; barrel organs were droning, concertinas were squealing, and drunken voices were ringing through the air. Trotting races were held in the main street that afternoon; in a word, all was merry and gay, as had been the year before and as, doubtless, it would be the year to come.

A month later a new bishop was appointed, and everyone forgot His Reverence Pyotr. Only the dead man's mother, who is living now in a little country town with her son the deacon, when she goes out at sunset to meet her cow and joins the other women on the way, tells them about her children and grandchildren, and her boy who became a bishop.

And when she mentions him she looks at them shyly, for she is afraid they will not believe her.

And, as a matter of fact, not all of them do.

DREAMS

Two soldiers are escorting to the county seat a vagrant who refuses to give his name. One of them is black bearded and thickset, with legs so uncommonly short that, seen from behind, they seem to begin much lower down than those of other men; the other is long, lank, spare, and straight as a stick, with a thin beard of a dark-reddish hue. The first waddles along, looking from side to side and sucking now a straw and now the sleeve of his coat. He slaps his thigh and hums to himself, and looks, on the whole, lighthearted and carefree. The other, with his lean face and narrow shoulders, is staid and important looking; in build and in the expression of his whole person he resembles a priest of the Old Believers[1] or one of those warriors depicted on antique icons. "For his wisdom God has enlarged his brow," that is to say, he is bald, which still more enhances the resemblance. The first soldier is called Andrey Ptakha, the second Nikander Sapozhnikov.

The man they are escorting is not in the least like what everyone imagines a tramp should be. He is small and sickly and feeble, with little, colorless, absolutely undefined features. His eyebrows are thin, his glance is humble and mild, and his

---

[1]A religious sect that refused to accept the church reforms of 1682 and practiced its own rites.

whiskers have barely made their appearance though he is already past thirty. He steps timidly along, stooping, with his hands thrust into his sleeves. The collar of his threadbare, unpeasantlike little coat is turned right up to the brim of his cap, so that all that can venture to peep out at the world is his little red nose. When he speaks, it is in a high, obsequious little voice, and then he immediately coughs. It is hard, very hard to recognize in him a vagabond who is hiding his name. He looks more like some impoverished, godforsaken son of a priest, or a clerk discharged for intemperance, or a merchant's son who has essayed his puny strength on the stage and is now returning to his home to play out the last act of the parable of the prodigal son. Perhaps, judging from the dull patience with which he battles with the clinging autumn mud, he is a fanatic; some youth trained for a monk who is wandering from one monastery to another all over Russia, doggedly seeking "a life of peace and freedom from sin," which he cannot find.

The wayfarers have been walking a long time, but for all their efforts they cannot get away from the same spot of ground. Before them lie ten yards of dark brown, muddy road, behind them lies as much; beyond that, wherever they turn, rises a dense wall of white fog. They walk and walk, but the ground they walk on is always the same; the wall comes no nearer; the spot remains a spot. Now and then they catch glimpses of white, irregular cobblestones, a dip in the road, or an armful of hay dropped by some passing wagon; a large pool of muddy water gleams for a moment, or a shadow, vaguely outlined, suddenly and unexpectedly appears before them. The nearer they come to this, the smaller and darker it grows; they come nearer still, and before them rises a crooked mile-post with its numbers effaced, or a woebegone birch tree, naked and wet, like a wayside beggar. The birch tree is whispering something with the remains of its yellow foliage; one leaf breaks off and flutters sluggishly to the ground, and then again there come fog and mud and the brown grass by the roadside. Dim, evil tears hang on these blades—not the tears of quiet joy that the earth weeps when she meets and accompanies the summer sun, and with which at dawn she quenches the thirst of quail and rails and graceful, long-billed snipe! The feet of the travelers are caught by the thick, sticky mud; every step costs them an effort.

Andrey Ptakha is a trifle provoked. He is scrutinizing the

vagrant and trying to understand how a live, sober man could forget his name.

"You belong to the Orthodox Church, don't you?" he asks.

"I do," answers the tramp briefly.

"H'm—have you been christened?"

"Of course I have; I'm not a Turk! I go to church and observe the fasts and don't eat meat when it's forbidden to do so—"

"Well, then, what name shall I call you by?"

"Call me what you please, lad."

Ptakha shrugs his shoulders and slaps his thigh in extreme perplexity. The other soldier, Nikander, preserves a sedate silence. He is not so simple as Ptakha, and evidently knows very well reasons which might induce a member of the Orthodox Church to conceal his identity. His expressive face is stern and cold. He walks apart and disdains idle gossip with his companions. He seems to be endeavoring to show to everyone and everything, even to the mist, how grave and sensible he is.

"The Lord only knows what to think about you!" pursues Ptakha. "Are you a peasant or not? Are you a gentleman or not? Or are you something between the two? I was rinsing out a sieve in a pond one day and caught a little monster as long as my finger here, with gills and a tail. Thinks I—it's a fish! Then I take another look at it—and I'll be blessed if it didn't have feet! It wasn't a fish and it wasn't a reptile—the devil only knows what it was! That's just what you are. What class do you belong to?"

"I am a peasant by birth," sighs the tramp. "My mother was a house serf. In looks I'm not a peasant, and that is because fate has willed it so, good man. My mother was a nurse in a gentleman's house and had every pleasure the heart could desire, and I, as her flesh and blood, belonged, in her lifetime, to the household. They petted me and spoiled me and beat me till they beat me from common to well-bred. I slept in a bed, had a real dinner every day, and wore trousers and low shoes like any little noble. Whatever my mother had to eat, I had. They gave her dresses and dressed me too. Oh, we lived well! The candy and cake I ate in my childhood would buy a good horse now if I could sell them! My mother taught me to read and write, and from the time I was a baby, instilled the fear of God into me and trained me so well that to this day I couldn't use an impolite, peasant word. I don't drink vodka, lad, and I dress cleanly and can make a respectable appearance in good society. God give her health if she is still alive; if she is dead, take her soul, O Lord, to rest in Thy heavenly kingdom where the blessed find peace!''

The tramp uncovers his head, with its sparse bristles, casts his eyes upward, and makes the sign of the cross twice.

''Give her peace, O Lord, in green places!'' he says in a drawling voice, more like an old woman's than a man's. ''Keep thy slave Ksenya in all thy ways, O Lord! If it had not been for my good mother I should have been a simple peasant now, not knowing a thing. As it is, lad, ask me what you please; I know everything: the Holy Scriptures, all godly things, all the prayers, and the Catechisms. I live according to the Scriptures; I do wrong to no one; I keep my body pure; I observe the fasts and eat as it is ordered. Some men find pleasure only in vodka and brawling, but when I have time I sit in a corner and read a book, and as I read I cry and cry—''

''Why do you cry?''

''Because the things they tell of are so pitiful. Sometimes you pay only five kopecks for a book and weep and wail over it to despair—''

''Is your father dead?'' asks Ptakha.

''I don't know, lad. It's no use hiding a sin; I don't know who my father was. What I think is that I was an illegitimate son of my mother's. My mother lived all her life with the gentry and never would marry a common peasant.''

''So she flew higher, up to his master!'' laughs Ptakha.

''That is so. My mother was pious and godly, and of course it is a sin, a great sin, to say so, but, nevertheless, maybe I have noble blood in my veins. Maybe I am a peasant in station only and am really a high-born gentleman.''

The ''high-born gentleman'' utters all this in a soft, sickly sweet voice, wrinkling his narrow brows and emitting squeaky noises from his cold, red, little nose.

Ptakha listens to him, eyes him with astonishment, and still shrugs his shoulders.

After going four miles the soldiers and the tramp sit down on a little knoll to rest.

''Even a dog can remember his name,'' mutters Ptakha. ''I am called Andrey and he is called Nikander; every man has his God-given name and no one could possibly forget it—not possibly!''

''Whose business is it of anyone's to know who I am?'' sighs the tramp, leaning his cheek on his hand. ''And what good would it do me if they knew? If I were allowed to go wherever I liked I should be worse off than I am now. I know the law, my Christian friends—now I am a vagrant who does not remember his name, and the worst they could do to me would be to send me to eastern Siberia with thirty or forty lashes, but if I should tell them my real name and station I should be sent to hard labor again—I know!"

"You mean to say you have been a convict?"

"I have, my good friend. My head was shaved and I wore chains for four years."

"What for?"

"For murder, good man. When I was still a boy, about eighteen years old, my mother put arsenic into our master's glass by mistake instead of soda. There were a great many different little boxes in the store room and it was not hard to mistake them."

The tramp sighs, shakes his head, and continues:

"She was a godly woman, but who can say? The soul of another is a dark forest. Maybe she did it by mistake. Maybe it was because her master had attached another servant to himself and her heart could not forgive the insult. Perhaps she did put it in on purpose—God only knows! I was young then and couldn't understand everything. I remember now that our master did, in fact, take another mistress at that time and that my mother was deeply hurt. Our trial went on for two years after that. My mother was condemned to twenty years' penal servitude and I to seven on account of my youth."

"And what charge were you convicted on?"

"For being an accomplice. I handed our master the glass. It was always that way: my mother would prepare the soda and I would hand him the glass. But I am confessing all this before you, brothers, as before God. You won't tell anyone—"

"No one will ever ask us," says Ptakha. "So that means you ran away from prison, does it?"

"Yes, I ran away, good friend. Fourteen of us escaped. God be with them! They ran away and took me along too. Now judge for yourself, lad, and tell me honestly whether I have any reason for telling my name? I should be condemned to penal servitude again; and what sort of a convict am I? I am delicate and sickly; I like cleanliness in my food and in the places where I sleep. When I pray to God I like to have a little shrine-lamp or a candle burning, and I don't like to have noises going on round me when

I'm praying. When I prostrate myself I don't like to have the floor all filthy and spat over, and I prostrate myself forty times morning and night for my mother's salvation."

The tramp takes off his cap and crosses himself.

"But let them send me to eastern Siberia if they want to!" he cries. "I'm not afraid of that."

"What? Is that better?"

"It is an entirely different affair. At hard labor you are no better off than a crab in a basket. You are crowded and pushed and hustled; there's not a quiet corner to take breath; it's a hell on earth—the Mother of God forbid it! A ruffian you are, and a ruffian's treatment you receive—worse than any dog's. You get nothing to eat; there is nowhere to sleep and nowhere to say your prayers. In exile it's different. You first enroll yourself in the company, as everyone else does. The government is compelled by law to give you your share of land. Yes, indeed! Land, they say, is cheap there, as cheap as snow. You can take all you want! They would give me land for farming, lad, and land for a garden, and land for a house. Then I would plow and sow, as other men do, raise cattle and bees and sheep and dogs—I'd get myself a Siberian cat to keep the rats and mice from eating my property, I'd build me a house, brothers, and buy icons; and, God willing, I'd marry and have children—"

The tramp is murmuring to himself now and has ceased looking at his listeners; he is gazing off somewhere to one side. Artless as his reveries are, he speaks with such sincerity and such heartfelt earnestness that it is hard not to believe what he says. The little mouth of the vagrant is twisted by a smile, and his whole face, his eyes, and his nose are numbed and paralyzed by the foretaste of far-off happiness. The soldiers listen and regard him earnestly, not without compassion. They also believe what he says.

"I am not afraid of Siberia," the tramp murmurs on. "Siberia and Russia are the same thing. They have the same God there as here, and the same Tsar, and they speak the language of Orthodox Christians, as I am speaking with you; only there is greater plenty, and the people are richer. Everything is better there. Take, for example, the rivers. They are a thousand times finer than ours. And fish! The fishing in them is simply beyond words! Fishing, brothers, is the greatest joy of my life. I don't ask for bread; only let me sit and hold a fishing line! Indeed, that is true! I catch fish on a hook and line and in pots and with bow nets, and when the ice comes I use cast nets. I am not strong enough to fish with a cast net myself; so I have to hire a peasant for five kopecks to do that for me. Heavens, what fun it is! It's like seeing your own brother again to catch an eel or a mudfish! And you have to treat every fish differently, I can tell you. You use a minnow for one, and a worm for another, and a frog or a grasshopper for a third; you've got to know all that. Take, for example, the eel. The eel isn't a dainty fish; it will take even a newt. Pikes like earthworms—garfish, butterflies. There is no greater joy on earth than fishing for chubs in swift water. You bait your hook with a butterfly or a beetle, so that it will float on the surface; and you let your line run out some twenty or thirty yards without a sinker; then you stand in the water without your trousers and let the bait float down with the current till—tug! and there's a chub on the hook! Then you have to watch ever so closely for just the right moment to hook it or the confounded thing will go off with your bait. The moment it twitches the line you've got to pull; there isn't a second to lose! The number of fish I have caught in my life is a caution! When we were escaping and the other convicts were asleep in the forest, I couldn't sleep and would go off in search of a river. The rivers there are so wide and swift and steep-banked—it's a caution. And all along their shores lie dense forests. The trees are so high that it makes your head swim to look up to the top of them. According to prices here every one of those pine trees is worth ten rubles—"

Under the confused stress of his imagination, the dream pictures of the past, and the sweet foretaste of happiness, the piteous little man stops speaking and only moves his lips as if whispering to himself. The feeble, beatific smile does not leave his face. The soldiers say nothing. Their heads have sunk forward onto their breasts, and they are lost in meditation. In the autumn silence, when a chill, harsh fog from the earth settles on the soul and rises like a prison wall before one to testify to the narrow limits of man's freedom, ah! then it is sweet to dream of wide, swift rivers with bold, fertile banks, of dense forests, of boundless plains! Idly, peacefully, the fancy pictures to itself a man, a tiny speck, appearing on the steep, uninhabited bank of a river in the early morning, before the flush of dawn has faded from the sky. The summits of the everlasting pines rise piled high in terraces on either side of the stream and, muttering darkly, look sternly at that free man. Roots, great rocks, and thorny bushes obstruct his path, but he is strong of body and valiant of heart and fears neither the pines nor the rocks nor the solitude nor the rolling echoes that reiterate every footfall.

The imagination of the soldiers is painting for them pictures of a free life which they have never lived. Is it that they darkly recall images of things heard long ago? Or have these visions of a life of liberty come down to them with their flesh and blood as an inheritance from their remote, wild ancestors? God only knows!

The first to break the silence is Nikander, who until now has not let fall a word. Perhaps he is jealous of the vagrant's visionary happiness; perhaps he feels in his heart that dreams of bliss are incongruous amidst surroundings of gray mist and brown-black mud—at any rate, he looks sternly at the tramp and says:

"That is all very well, brother; that is all very fine, but you'll never reach that land of plenty! How could you? You would go thirty miles and then give up the ghost—a little half-dead creature like you! You've only walked four miles today, and yet look at you! You can't seem to get rested at all!"

The tramp turns slowly to Nikander and the blissful smile fades from his face. He looks with dismay at the grave countenance of the soldier as if he had been caught doing wrong and seems to have recollected something, for he nods his head. Silence falls once more. All three are busy with their own thoughts. The soldiers are trying to force their minds to grasp what perhaps God alone can conceive of: the terrible expanse that lies between them and that land of freedom. Images more clear, precise, and terrifying are crowding into the vagrant's head—courts of justice, dungeons for exiles and for convicts, prison barracks, weary halts along the road, the cold of winter, illness, the death of his companions—all rise vividly before him.

The tramp blinks, and little drops stand out upon his brow. He wipes his forehead with his sleeve, draws a deep breath as if he had just jumped out of a hot oven, wipes his forehead with the other sleeve, and glances fearfully behind him.

"It is quite true that you could never get there," Ptakha assents. "You're not a walker! Look at yourself—all skin and bone! It would kill you, brother."

"Of course it would kill him; he couldn't possibly do it," declares Nikander. "He'll be sent straight to the hospital, anyway, as it is. That's a fact!"

The nameless wanderer looks with terror at the stern, impassive faces of his evil-boding fellow travelers; then, lowering his eyes, he rapidly crosses himself without taking off his cap. He is trembling all over, his head is shaking, and he is beginning to writhe like a caterpillar that someone has stepped on.

"Come on! Time to go!" cries Nikander, rising. "We have rested long enough!"

Another minute and the travelers are plodding along the muddy road. The tramp is stooping more than before and has thrust his hands still deeper into the sleeves of his coat. Ptakha is silent.

IN EXILE

Old Semyon, whose nickname was Preacher, and a young Tartar, whose name no one knew, were sitting by a campfire on the bank of the river; the other three ferrymen were inside the hut. Semyon, a gaunt, toothless old man of sixty, broad shouldered and still healthy looking, was drunk; he would have gone to bed long ago, but he had a bottle in his pocket and was afraid his comrades in the hut would ask him for a drink of vodka. The Tartar was worn out and ill, and, wrapping himself in his rags, he talked about how good it was in the province of Simbirsk, and what a beautiful and clever wife he had left at home. He was not more than twenty-five, and in the firelight his pale, sickly face and woebegone expression made him seem like a boy.

"Well, this is no paradise, of course," said Preacher. "You can see for yourself: water, bare banks, nothing but clay wherever you look. . . . It's long past Easter and there's still ice on the river . . . and this morning there was snow."

"Bad! Bad!" said the Tartar, surveying the landscape with dismay.

A few yards away the dark, cold river flowed, growling and sluicing against the pitted clay banks as it sped on to the distant sea. At the edge of the bank loomed a capacious barge, which ferrymen call a *karbas*. Far away on the opposite bank, crawling snakes of fire were dying down then reappearing—last year's grass being burned. Beyond the snakes there was darkness again. Little blocks of ice could be heard knocking against the barge. It was cold and damp. . . .

The Tartar glanced at the sky. There were as many stars as there were at home, the same blackness, but something was lacking. At home in the province of Simbirsk, the stars and the sky seemed altogether different.

"Bad! Bad!" he repeated.

"You'll get used to it!" said Preacher with a laugh. "You're still young and foolish—the milk's hardly dry on your lips—and in your foolishness you think there's no one more unfortunate than you, but the time will come when you'll say to yourself: 'May God give everyone such a life.' Just look at me. In a week's time the floods will be over and we'll launch the ferry; you'll all go gadding about Siberia, while I stay here, going back and forth, from one bank to the other. For twenty-two years now that's what I've been doing. Day and night. The pike and the salmon under the water and me on it. That's all I want. God give everyone such a life."

The Tartar threw some brushwood onto the fire, lay down closer to it, and said, "My father is sick man. When he dies, my mother, my wife, will come here. Have promised."

"And what do you want a mother and a wife for?" asked Preacher. "Just foolishness, brother. It's the devil stirring you up, blast his soul! Don't listen to him, the Evil One! Don't give in to him. When he goes on about women, spite him: I don't want them! When he talks to you about freedom, you stand up to him: I don't want it! I want nothing! No father, no mother, no wife, no freedom, no house nor home! I want nothing, damn their souls!"

Preacher took a swig at the bottle and went on, "I'm no simple peasant, brother; I don't come from the servile class; I'm a deacon's son, and when I was free I lived in Kursk, and used to go around in a frock coat; but now I've brought myself to such a point that I can sleep naked on the ground and eat grass. And God give everyone such a life. I don't want anything, I'm not afraid of anyone, and the way I see it, there's no man richer or freer than I am. When they sent me here from Russia, from the very first day I jibbed: I want nothing! The devil was at me about my wife, about my kin, about freedom, but I told him: I want nothing! And I stuck to it; and here, you see, I live well, I don't complain. But if anyone humors the devil and listens to him even once, he's lost, no salvation for him. He'll be stuck fast in the bog, up to his ears, and he'll never get out.

"It's not only the likes of you, foolish peasants, that are lost, but even the wellborn and educated. Fifteen years ago they sent a gentleman here from Russia. He forged a will or something—wouldn't share with his brothers. It was said he was a prince or a baron, but maybe he was only an official, who knows? Well, the gentleman came here, and the first thing, he bought himself a house and land in Mukhortinskoe. 'I want to live by my own labor,' says he, 'in the sweat of my brow, because I'm no longer a gentleman, but an exile.' . . . 'Well,' says I, 'may God help you, that's the right thing.' He was a young man then, a hustler, always on the move; he used to do the mowing himself, catch fish, ride sixty versts on horseback. But here was the trouble: from the very first year he began riding to Gyrino to the post office. He used to stand on my ferry and sigh, 'Ah, Semyon, for a long time now they haven't sent me any money from home.' . . . 'You don't need money, Vasily Sergeich. What good is it? Throw off the past, forget it as if it had never happened, as if it was only a dream, and start life afresh. Don't listen to the devil,' I tell him, 'he'll bring you to no good; he'll tighten the noose. Now you want money,' says I, 'and in a little while, before you know it, you'll want something else, and then more and more. But,' says I, 'if you want to be happy, the very first thing is not to want anything.' Yes. . . . 'And if fate has cruelly wronged you and me,' says I, 'it's no good going down on your knees to her and asking her favor; you have to spurn her and laugh at her, otherwise she'll laugh at you.' That's what I said to him. . . .

"Two years later I ferried him over to this side, and he was rubbing his hands together and laughing. 'I'm going to Gyrino,' says he, 'to meet my wife. She has taken pity on me and come here. She's so kind and good!' He was panting with joy. Next day he comes with his wife. A young, beautiful lady in a hat, carrying a baby girl in her arms. And plenty of baggage of all sorts. My Vasily Sergeich was spinning around her; couldn't take his eyes off her; couldn't praise her enough. 'Yes, brother Semyon, even in Siberia people can live!' . . . 'Well,' thinks I, 'just you wait; better not rejoice too soon.' . . . And from that time on, almost every week he went to Gyrino to find out if money had been sent from Russia. As for money—it took plenty! 'It's for my sake that her youth and beauty are going to ruin here in Siberia,' he says, 'sharing with me my bitter fate, and for this,' he says, 'I ought to provide her with every diversion.' To make it more cheerful for his lady he took up with the officials and with all sorts of riffraff. And there had to be food and drink for this crowd, of course, and they must have a piano, and a fuzzy little lap dog on the sofa—may it croak! . . . Luxury, in short, indulgence. The lady did not stay with him long. How could she? Clay, water, cold, no vegetables for you, no fruit; uneducated and drunken people all around, no manners at all, and she a pampered lady from the capital. . . . Naturally, she grew tired of it. Besides, her husband, say what you like, was no longer a gentleman, but an exile—not exactly an honor.

"Three years later, I remember, on the eve of the Assumption, someone shouted from the other side. I went over in the ferry, and what do I see but the lady—all muffled up, and with her a young gentleman, an official. There was a troika. . . . And after I ferried them across, they got in it and vanished into thin air! That was the last that was seen of them. Toward morning Vasily Sergeich galloped up to the ferry. 'Didn't my wife pass this way, Semyon, with a gentleman in spectacles?' . . . 'She did,' says I. 'Seek the wind in the fields!' He galloped off in pursuit of them, and didn't stop for five days and five nights. Afterwards, when I took him over to the other side, he threw himself down on the ferry, beat his head against the planks, and howled. 'So that's how it is,' says I. . . . I laughed and recalled to him: 'Even in Siberia people can live!' And he beat his head all the more.

"After that he began to long for freedom. His wife had slipped away to Russia, so, naturally, he was drawn there, both to see her and to rescue her from her lover. And, my friend, he took to galloping off every day, either to the post office or the authorities; he kept sending in petitions, and presenting them personally, asking to be pardoned so he could go back home; and he used to tell how he had spent some two hundred rubles on telegrams alone. He sold his land, and mortgaged his house to the Jews. He grew gray, stooped, and yellow in the face, as if he was consumptive. He'd talk to you and go: khe-khe-khe . . . and there would be tears in his eyes. He struggled with those petitions for eight years, but now he has recovered his spirits and is more cheerful: he's thought up a new indulgence. His daughter, you see, has grown up. He keeps an eye on her, dotes on her. And, to tell the truth, she's all right, a pretty little thing, black browed, and with a lively disposition. Every Sunday he goes to church with her in Gyrino. Side by side they stand on the ferry, she laughing and he not taking his eyes off her. 'Yes, Semyon,' says he, 'even in Siberia people can live. Even in Siberia there is happiness. Look,' says he, 'see what a daughter I've got! I suppose you wouldn't find another like her if you went a thousand versts.' . . . 'Your daughter,' says I, 'is a fine young lady, that's true, certainly. . . .' But I think to myself: 'Wait a while. . . . The girl is young, her blood is dancing, she wants to live, and what life is there here?' And, my friend, she did begin to fret. . . . She withered and withered, wasted away, fell ill; and now she's completely worn out. Consumption.

"That's your Siberian happiness for you, the pestilence take it! That's how people can live in Siberia! . . . He's taken to running after doctors and taking them home with him. As soon as he hears that there's a doctor or quack two or three hundred versts away, he goes to fetch him. A terrible lot of money has been spent on doctors; to my way of thinking, it would have been better to spend it on drink. . . . She'll die anyway. She's certain to die, and then he'll be completely lost. He'll hang himself from grief, or run away to Russia—that's sure. He'll run away, they'll catch him, there'll be a trial, and then hard labor; they'll give him a taste of the lash. . . ."

"Good, good," muttered the Tartar, shivering with cold.

"What's good?" asked Preacher.

"Wife and daughter. . . . Let hard labor, let suffer; he saw his wife and daughter. . . . You say: want nothing. But nothing is bad! Wife was with him three years—God gave him that. Nothing is bad; three years is good. How you not understand?"

Shivering and stuttering, straining to pick out the Russian words, of which he knew so few, the Tartar said God forbid one should fall sick and die in a strange land, and be buried in the cold, sodden earth; that if his wife came to him even for one day, even for one hour, he would be willing to accept any torture whatsoever, and thank God for it. Better one day of happiness than nothing.

After that he again described the beautiful and clever wife he had left at home; then, clutching his head with both hands, he began crying and assuring Semyon that he was innocent and had been falsely accused. His two brothers and his uncle stole some horses from a peasant, and beat the old man till he was half dead, and the commune had not judged fairly, but had contrived a sentence by which all three brothers were sent to Siberia, while the uncle, a rich man, remained at home.

"You'll get u-u-used to it!" said Semyon.

The Tartar relapsed into silence and fixed his tearful eyes on the fire; his face expressed bewilderment and fright, as though he still did not understand why he was here in the dark, in the damp, among strangers, instead of in the province of Simbirsk. Preacher lay down near the fire, chuckled at something, and began singing in an undertone.

"What joy has she with her father?" he said a little later. "He loves her, she's a consolation to him, it's true; but you have to mind your p's and q's with him, brother: he's a strict old man, a severe old man. And strictness is not what young girls want. . . . They want petting and ha-ha-ha and ho-ho-ho, scents and pomades! Yes. . . . Ekh, life, life!" sighed Semyon, getting up with difficulty. "The vodka's all gone, so it's time to sleep. Eh? I'm going, my boy."

Left alone, the Tartar put more brushwood onto the fire, lay down, and, looking into the blaze, began thinking of his native village, and of his wife: if she would come only for a month, even for a day, then, if she liked, she might go back again. Better a month or even a day than nothing. But if she kept her promise and came, how could he provide for her? Where could she live?

"If not something to eat, how you live?" the Tartar asked aloud.

He was paid only ten kopecks for working at the oars a day and a night; the passengers gave him tips, it was true, but the ferrymen shared everything among themselves, giving nothing to the Tartar, but only making fun of him. And he was hungry, cold, and frightened from want. . . . Now, when his whole body was shivering and aching, he ought to go into the hut and lie down to sleep, but he had nothing there to cover himself with, and it was colder there than on the river bank; here, too, he had nothing to put over him, but at least he could make a fire. . . .

In another week, when the floods had subsided and the ferry could sail, none of the ferrymen except Semyon would be needed, and the Tartar would begin going from village to village looking for work and begging alms. His wife was only seventeen years old; beautiful, pampered, shy—could she possibly go from village to village, her face unveiled, begging? No, even to think of it was dreadful. . . .

It was already growing light; the barge, the bushes of rose willow, and the ripples on the water were clearly distinguishable, and looking back there was the steep clay precipice, below it the little hut thatched with brown straw, and above clung the huts of the villagers. The cocks were already crowing in the village.

The red clay precipice, the barge, the river, the strange, unkind people, hunger, cold, illness—perhaps all this did not exist in reality. Probably it was all a dream, thought the Tartar. He felt that he was asleep, and hearing his own snoring. . . . Of course, he was at home in the province of Simbirsk, and he had only to call his wife by name for her to answer, and in the next room his mother. . . . However, what awful dreams there are! Why? The Tartar smiled and opened his eyes. What river was this? The Volga?

"Bo-o-at!" someone shouted from the other side. "Karba-a-s!"

The Tartar woke up and went to wake his comrades, to row over to the other side. Putting on their torn sheepskins as they came, the ferrymen appeared on the bank, swearing in hoarse, sleepy voices, and shivering from the cold. After their sleep, the river, from which there came a piercing gust of cold air, evidently struck them as revolting and sinister. They were not quick to jump into the barge. The Tartar and the three ferrymen took up the long, broad-bladed oars, which looked like crabs' claws in the darkness. Semyon leaned his belly against the long tiller. The shouting from the other side continued, and two shots were fired from a revolver; the man probably thought that the ferrymen were asleep or had gone off to the village tavern.

"All right, plenty of time!" said Preacher in the tone of a man who is convinced that there is no need to hurry in this world—that it makes no difference, really, and nothing will come of it.

The heavy, clumsy barge drew away from the bank and floated between the rose willows; and only because the willows slowly receded was it possible to see that the barge was not standing still but moving. The ferrymen plied the oars evenly, in unison; Preacher hung over the tiller on his belly, and, describing an arc in the air, flew from one side of the boat to the other. In the darkness it looked as if the men were sitting on some antediluvian animal with long paws, and sailing to a cold, bleak land, the very one of which we sometimes dream in nightmares.

They passed beyond the willows and floated out into the open. The rhythmic thump and splash of the oars were now audible on the further shore, and someone shouted, "Hurry! Hurry!" Another ten minutes passed and the barge bumped heavily against the landing stage.

"And it keeps coming down, and coming down!" muttered Semyon, wiping the snow from his face. "Where it comes from, God only knows!"

On the other side stood a thin old man of medium height wearing a jacket lined with fox fur and a white lambskin cap. He was standing at a little distance from his horses and not moving; he had a concentrated, morose expression, as if, trying to remember something, he had grown angry with his unyielding memory. When Semyon went up to him with a smile and took off his cap, he said, "I'm hastening to Anastasyevka. My daughter is worse again, and they say there's a new doctor at Anastasyevka."

They dragged the tarantass onto the barge and rowed back. The man, whom Semyon called Vasily Sergeich, stood motionless all the way back, his thick lips tightly compressed, his eyes fixed on one spot; when the coachman asked permission to smoke in his presence, he made no reply, as if he had not heard. And Semyon, hanging over the tiller on his belly, glanced mockingly at him and said, "Even in Siberia people can live. Li-i-ve!"

There was a triumphant expression on Preacher's face, as if he had proved something and was rejoicing that it had turned out exactly as he had surmised. The helpless, unhappy look of the man in the fox-lined jacket evidently afforded him great satisfaction.

"It's muddy driving now, Vasily Sergeich," he said when the horses were harnessed on the bank. "You'd better have waited a week or two till it gets drier. . . . Or else not have gone at all. . . . If there were any sense in going, but, as you yourself know, people have been driving about for ever and ever, by day and by night, and there's never any sense in it. That's the truth!"

Vasily Sergeich tipped him without a word, got into the tarantass, and drove off.

"See there, he's gone galloping off for a doctor!" said Semyon, shrinking with cold. "Yes, looking for a real doctor is like chasing the wind in the fields, or catching the devil by the tail, damn your soul! What freaks! Lord forgive me, a sinner!"

The Tartar went up to Preacher and, looking at him with hatred and abhorrence, trembling, mixing Tartar words with his broken Russian, said, "He is good—good. You bad! You bad! Gentleman is good soul, excellent, and you beast, you bad! Gentleman alive and you dead. . . . God created man to be live, be joyful, be sad and sorrow, but you want nothing. . . . You not live, you stone, clay! Stone want nothing and you want nothing. . . . You stone—and God not love you, love gentleman!"

Everyone laughed; the Tartar frowned scornfully and, with a gesture of despair, wrapped himself in his rags and went to the fire. Semyon and the ferrymen trailed off to the hut.

"It's cold," said one of the ferrymen hoarsely, as he stretched out on the straw that covered the damp floor.

"Well, it's not warm!" one of the others agreed. "It's a hard life!"

They all lay down. The door was blown open by the wind, and snow drifted into the hut. No one felt like getting up and closing the door; it was cold and they were lazy.

"I'm all right!" said Semyon, falling asleep. "God give everyone such a life."

"You're a hard case, we know that. Even the devils won't take you!"

From outside there came sounds like the howling of a dog.

"What's that? Who's there?"

"It's the Tartar crying."

"He'll get u-u-used to it!" said Semyon, and instantly fell asleep.

Soon the others fell asleep too. And the door remained unclosed.

A DOCTOR'S VISIT

The professor received a telegram from the Lyalikovs' factory; he was asked to come as quickly as possible. The daughter of some Madame Lyalikov, apparently the owner of the factory, was ill, and that was all that one could make out of the long, incoherent telegram. And the professor did not go himself, but sent instead his assistant, Korolyov.

It was two stations from Moscow, and there was a drive of three miles from the station. A carriage with three horses had been sent to the station to meet Korolyov; the coachman wore a hat with a peacock's feather on it, and answered every question in a loud voice like a soldier: "No, sir!" "Certainly, sir!"

It was Saturday evening; the sun was setting, the workpeople were coming in crowds from the factory to the station, and they bowed to the carriage in which Korolyov was driving. And he was charmed with the evening, the farmhouses and villas on the road, and the birch trees, and the quiet atmosphere all around, when the fields and woods and the sun seemed preparing, like the workpeople now on the eve of the holiday, to rest, and perhaps to pray. . . .

He was born and had grown up in Moscow; he did not know the country, and he had never taken any interest in factories, or been inside one, but he had happened to read about factories, and had been in the houses of manufacturers and had talked to them; and whenever he saw a factory far or near, he always thought how quiet and peaceable it was outside, but within there was always sure to be impenetrable ignorance and dull egoism on the side of the owners, wearisome, unhealthy toil on the side of the workpeople, squabbling, vermin, vodka. And now when the workpeople timidly and respectfully made way for the carriage, in their faces, their caps, their walk, he read physical impurity, drunkenness, nervous exhaustion, bewilderment.

They drove in at the factory gates. On each side he caught glimpses of the little houses of workpeople, of the faces of women, of quilts and linen on the railings. "Look out!" shouted the coachman, not pulling up the horses. It was a wide courtyard without grass, with five immense blocks of buildings with tall chimneys a little distance one from another, warehouses and barracks, and over everything a sort of gray powder as though from dust. Here and there, like oases in the desert, there were pitiful gardens, and the green and red roofs of the houses in which the managers and clerks lived. The coachman suddenly pulled up the horses, and the carriage stopped at the house, which had been newly painted gray; here was a flower garden, with a lilac bush covered with dust, and on the yellow steps at the front door there was a strong smell of paint.

"Please come in, Doctor," said women's voices in the passage and the entry, and at the same time he heard sighs and whisperings. "Pray walk in. . . . We've been expecting you so long . . . we're in real trouble. Here, this way."

Madame Lyalikov—a stout elderly lady wearing a black silk dress with fashionable sleeves, but, judging from her face, a simple uneducated woman—looked at the doctor in a flutter, and could not bring herself to hold out her hand to him; she did not dare. Beside her stood a personage with short hair and a pince-nez; she was wearing a blouse of many colors, and was very thin and no longer young. The servants called her Christina Dmitryevna, and Korolyov guessed that this was the governess. Probably, as the person of most education in the house, she had been charged to meet and receive the doctor, for she began immediately, in great haste, stating the causes of the illness, giving trivial and tiresome details, but without saying who was ill or what was the matter.

The doctor and the governess were sitting talking while the lady of the house stood motionless at the door, waiting. From the conversation Korolyov learned that the patient was Madame Lyalikov's only daughter and heiress, a girl of twenty, called Liza; she had been ill for a long time and had consulted various doctors, and the previous night she had suffered till morning from such violent palpitations of the heart that no one in the house had slept, and they had been afraid she might die.

"She has been, one may say, ailing from a child," said Christina Dmitryevna in a singsong voice, continually wiping her lips with her hand. "The doctors say it is nerves; when she was a little girl she was scrofulous, and the doctors drove it inwards, so I think it may be due to that."

They went to see the invalid. Fully grown up, big and tall, but ugly like her mother, with the same little eyes and disproportionate breadth of the lower part of her face, lying with her hair in disorder, muffled up to the chin, she made upon Korolyov at the first minute the impression of a poor, destitute creature, sheltered and cared for here out of charity, and he could hardly believe this was the heiress of the five huge buildings.

"I am the doctor come to see you," said Korolyov. "Good evening."

He mentioned his name and pressed her hand, a large, cold, ugly hand; she sat up, and, evidently accustomed to doctors, let herself be sounded, without showing the least concern that her shoulders and chest were uncovered.

"I have palpitations of the heart," she said. "It was so awful all night. . . . I almost died of fright! Do give me something."

"I will, I will; don't worry yourself."

Korolyov examined her and shrugged his shoulders.

"The heart is all right," he said; "it's all going on satisfactorily; everything is in good order. Your nerves must have been playing pranks a little, but that's so common. The attack is over by now, one must suppose; lie down and go to sleep."

At that moment a lamp was brought into the bedroom. The patient screwed up her eyes at the light, then suddenly put her hands to her head and broke into sobs. And the impression of a destitute, ugly creature vanished, and Korolyov no longer noticed the little eyes or the heavy development of the lower part of the face. He saw a soft, suffering expression which was intelligent and touching: she seemed to him altogether graceful, feminine, and simple; and he longed to soothe her, not with drugs, not with advice, but with simple, kindly words. Her mother put her arms round her head and hugged her. What despair, what grief was in the old woman's face! She, her mother, had reared her and brought her up, spared nothing, and devoted her whole life to having her daughter taught French, dancing, music: had engaged a dozen teachers for her; had consulted the best doctors, kept a governess. And now she could not make out the reason of these tears, why there was all this misery, she could not understand, and was bewildered; and she had a guilty, agitated, despairing expression, as though she had omitted something very important, had left something undone, had neglected to call in somebody—and whom, she did not know.

"Lizanka, you are crying again . . . again," she said, hugging her daughter to her. "My own, my darling, my child, tell me what it is! Have pity on me! Tell me."

Both wept bitterly. Korolyov sat down on the side of the bed and took Liza's hand.

"Come, give over; it's no use crying," he said kindly. "Why, there is nothing in the world that is worth those tears. Come, we won't cry; that's no good. . . ."

And inwardly he thought:

"It's high time she was married. . . ."

"Our doctor at the factory gave her kalibromati," said the governess, "but I notice it only makes her worse. I should have thought that if she is given anything for the heart it ought to be drops. . . . I forget the name. . . . Convallaria, isn't it?"

And there followed all sorts of details. She interrupted the doctor, preventing his speaking, and there was a look of effort on her face, as though she supposed that, as the woman of most education in the house, she was duty bound to keep up a conversation with the doctor, and on no other subject but medicine.

Korolyov felt bored.

"I find nothing special the matter," he said, addressing the mother as he went out of the bedroom. "If your daughter is being attended by the factory doctor, let him go on attending her. The treatment so far has been perfectly correct, and I see no reason for changing your doctor. Why change? It's such an ordinary trouble; there's nothing seriously wrong."

He spoke deliberately as he put on his gloves, while Madame Lyalikov stood without moving, and looked at him with her tearful eyes.

"I have half an hour to catch the ten o'clock train," he said. "I hope I am not too late."

"And can't you stay?" she asked, and tears trickled down her cheeks again. "I am ashamed to trouble you, but if you would be so good. . . . For God's sake," she went on in an undertone, glancing toward the door, "do stay tonight with us! She is all I have . . . my only daughter. . . . She frightened me last night; I can't get over it. . . . Don't go away, for goodness' sake! . . ."

He wanted to tell her that he had a great deal of work in Moscow, that his family were expecting him home; it was disagreeable to him to spend the evening and the whole night in a strange house quite needlessly; but he looked at her face, heaved a sigh, and began taking off his gloves without a word.

All the lamps and candles were lighted in his honor in the drawing room and the dining room. He sat down at the piano and began turning over the music. Then he looked at the pictures on the walls, at the portraits. The pictures, oil paintings in gold frames, were views of the Crimea—a stormy sea with a ship, a Catholic monk with a wineglass; they were all dull, smooth daubs, with no trace of talent in them. There was not a single good-looking face among the portraits, nothing but broad cheekbones and astonished-looking eyes. Lyalikov, Liza's father, had a low forehead and a self-satisfied expression; his uniform sat like a sack on his bulky plebeian figure; on his breast was a medal and a Red Cross Badge. There was little sign of culture, and the luxury was senseless and haphazard, and was as ill fitting as that uniform. The floors irritated him with their brilliant polish, the lusters on the chandelier irritated him, and he was reminded for some reason of the story of the merchant who used to go to the baths with a medal on his neck. . . .

He heard a whispering in the entry; someone was softly snoring. And suddenly from outside came harsh, abrupt, metallic sounds, such as Korolyov had never heard before, and which he did not understand now; they roused strange, unpleasant echoes in his soul.

"I believe nothing would induce me to remain here to live . . ." he thought, and went back to the music books again.

"Doctor, please come to supper!" the governess called him in a low voice.

He went into supper. The table was large and laid with a vast number of dishes and wines, but there were only two to supper: himself and Christina Dmitryevna. She drank Madeira, ate rapidly, and talked, looking at him through her pince-nez:

"Our workpeople are very contented. We have performances at the factory every winter; the workpeople act themselves. They have lectures with a magic lantern, a splendid tearoom, and everything they want. They are very much attached to us, and when they heard that Lizanka was worse they had a service sung for her. Though they have no education, they have their feelings too."

"It looks as though you have no man in the house at all," said Korolyov.

"Not one. Pyotr Nikanoritch died a year and a half ago, and left us alone. And so there are the three of us. In the summer we live here, and in winter we live in Moscow, in Polianka. I have been living with them for eleven years—as one of the family."

At supper they served sterlet, chicken rissoles, and stewed fruit; the wines were expensive French wines.

"Please don't stand on ceremony, Doctor," said Christina Dmitryevna, eating and wiping her mouth with her fist, and it was evident she found her life here exceedingly pleasant. "Please have some more."

After supper the doctor was shown to his room, where a bed had been made up for him, but he did not feel sleepy. The room was stuffy and it smelt of paint; he put on his coat and went out.

It was cool in the open air; there was already a glimmer of dawn, and all the five blocks of buildings, with their tall chimneys, barracks, and warehouses, were distinctly outlined against the damp air. As it was a holiday, they were not working and the windows were dark, and in only one of the buildings was there a furnace burning; two windows were crimson, and fire mixed with smoke came from time to time from the chimney. Far away beyond the yard the frogs were croaking and the nightingales singing.

Looking at the factory buildings and the barracks, where the workpeople were asleep, he thought again what he always thought when he saw a factory. They may have performances for the workpeople, magic lanterns, factory doctors, and improvements of all sorts, but, all the same, the workpeople he had met that day on his way from the station did not look in any way different from those he had known long ago in his childhood, before there were factory performances and improvements. As a doctor accustomed to judging correctly of chronic complaints, the radical cause of which was incomprehensible and incurable, he looked upon factories as something baffling, the cause of which also was obscure and not removable, and all the improvements in the life of the factory hands he looked upon not as superfluous, but as comparable with the treatment of incurable illnesses.

"There is something baffling in it, of course . . ." he thought, looking at the crimson windows. "Fifteen hundred or two thousand workpeople are working without rest in unhealthy surroundings, making bad cotton goods, living on the verge of starvation, and only waking from this nightmare at rare intervals in the tavern; a hundred people act as overseers, and the whole life of that hundred is spent in imposing fines, in abuse, in injustice, and only two or three so-called owners enjoy the profits, though they don't work at all, and despise the wretched cotton. But what are the profits, and how do they enjoy them? Madame Lyalikov and her daughter are unhappy—it makes one wretched to look at them; the only one who enjoys her life is Christina Dmitryevna, a stupid, middle-aged maiden lady in pince-nez. And so it appears that all these five blocks of buildings are at work, and inferior cotton is sold in the Eastern markets, simply that Christina Dmitryevna may eat sterlet and drink Madeira."

Suddenly there came a strange noise, the same sound Korolyov had heard before supper. Someone was striking on a sheet of metal near one of the buildings; he struck a note, and then at once checked the vibrations, so that short, abrupt, discordant sounds were produced, rather like "Dair . . . dair . . . dair. . . ." Then there was half a minute of stillness, and from another building there came sounds equally abrupt and unpleasant, lower bass notes: "Drin . . . drin . . . drin. . . ." Eleven times. Evidently it was the watchman striking the hour.

Near the third building he heard: "Zhuk . . . zhuk . . . zhuk. . . ." And so near all the buildings, and then behind the barracks and beyond the gates. And in the stillness of the night it seemed as though these sounds were uttered by a monster with crimson eyes—the devil himself, who controlled the owners and the workpeople alike, and was deceiving both.

Korolyov went out of the yard into the open country.

"Who goes there?" someone called to him at the gates in an abrupt voice.

"It's just like being in prison," he thought, and made no answer.

Here the nightingales and the frogs could be heard more distinctly, and one could feel it was a night in May. From the station came the noise of a train; somewhere in the distance drowsy cocks were crowing; but, all the same, the night was still, the world was sleeping tranquilly. In a field not far from the factory there could be seen the framework of a house and heaps of building material: Korolyov sat down on the planks and went on thinking.

"The only person who feels happy here is the governess, and the factory hands are working for her gratification. But that's only apparent: she is only the figurehead. The real person, for whom everything is being done, is the devil."

And he thought about the devil, in whom he did not believe, and he looked round at the two windows where the fires were gleaming. It seemed to him that out of those crimson eyes the devil himself was looking at him—that unknown force that had created the mutual relation of the strong and the weak, that coarse blunder which one could never correct. The strong must hinder the weak from living—such was the law of nature; but only in a newspaper article or in a schoolbook was that intelligible and easily accepted. In the hotchpotch which was everyday life, in the tangle of trivialities out of which human relations were woven, it was no longer a law, but a logical absurdity, when the strong and the weak were both equally victims of their mutual relations, unwillingly submitting to some directing force, unknown, standing outside life, apart from man.

So thought Korolyov, sitting on the planks, and little by little he was possessed by a feeling that this unknown and mysterious force was really close by and looking at him. Meanwhile the east was growing paler, time passed rapidly; when there was not a soul anywhere near, as though everything were dead, the five buildings and their chimneys against the gray background of the dawn had a peculiar look—not the same as by day; one forgot altogether that inside there were steam motors, electricity, telephones, and kept thinking of lake dwellings, of the Stone Age, feeling the presence of a crude, unconscious force. . . .

And again there came the sound: "Dair . . . dair . . . dair . . . dair . . ." twelve times. Then there was stillness, stillness for half a minute, and at the other end of the yard there rang out:

"Drin . . . drin . . . drin. . . ."

"Horribly disagreeable," thought Korolyov.

"Zhuk . . . zhuk . . ." there resounded from a third place, abruptly, sharply, as though with annoyance—"Zhuk . . . zhuk. . . ."

And it took four minutes to strike twelve. Then there was a hush; and again it seemed as though everything were dead.

Korolyov sat a little longer, then went to the house, but sat up for a good while longer. In the adjoining rooms there was whispering, there was a sound of shuffling slippers and bare feet.

"Is she having another attack?" thought Korolyov.

He went out to have a look at the patient. By now it was quite light in the rooms, and a faint glimmer of sunlight, piercing through the morning mist, quivered on the floor and on the wall of the drawing room. The door of Liza's room was open, and she was sitting in a low chair beside her bed, with her hair down, wearing a dressing gown and wrapped in a shawl. The blinds were down on the windows.

"How do you feel?" asked Korolyov.

"Thank you."

He touched her pulse, then straightened her hair that had fallen over her forehead.

"You are not asleep," he said. "It's beautiful weather outside. It's spring. The nightingales are singing, and you sit in the dark and think of something."

She listened and looked into his face; her eyes were sorrowful and intelligent, and it was evident she wanted to say something to him.

"Does this happen to you often?" he said.

She moved her lips, and answered:

"Often, I feel wretched almost every night."

At that moment the watchman in the yard began striking two o'clock. They heard: "Dair . . . dair . . ." and she shuddered.

"Do those knockings worry you?" he asked.

"I don't know. Everything here worries me," she answered, and pondered. "Everything worries me. I hear sympathy in your voice; it seemed to me as soon as I saw you that I could tell you all about it."

"Tell me, I beg you."

"I want to tell you of my opinion. It seems to me that I have no illness, but that I am weary and frightened, because it is bound to be so and cannot be otherwise. Even the healthiest person can't help being uneasy if, for instance, a robber is moving about under his window. I am constantly being doctored," she went on, looking at her knees, and she gave a shy smile. "I am very grateful, of course, and I do not deny that the treatment is a benefit; but I should like to talk, not with a doctor, but with some intimate friend who would understand me and would convince me that I was right or wrong."

"Have you no friends?" asked Korolyov.

"I am lonely. I have a mother; I love her, but, all the same, I am lonely. That's how it happens to be. . . . Lonely people read a great deal, but say little and hear little. Life for them is mysterious; they are mystics and often see the devil where he is not. Lermontov's Tamara was lonely and she saw the devil."

"Do you read a great deal?"

"Yes. You see, my whole time is free from morning till night. I read by day, and by night my head is empty; instead of thoughts there are shadows in it."

"Do you see anything at night?" asked Korolyov.

"No, but I feel. . . ."

She smiled again, raised her eyes to the doctor, and looked at him so sorrowfully, so intelligently; and it seemed to him that she trusted him, and that she wanted to speak frankly to him, and that she thought the same as he did. But she was silent, perhaps waiting for him to speak.

And he knew what to say to her. It was clear to him that she needed as quickly as possible to give up the five buildings and the million if she had it—to leave that devil that looked out at night; it was clear to him, too, that she thought so herself, and was only waiting for someone she trusted to confirm her.

But he did not know how to say it. How? One is shy of asking men under sentence what they have been sentenced for; and in the same way it is awkward to ask very rich people what they want so much money for, why they make such a poor use of their wealth, why they don't give it up, even when they see in it their unhappiness; and if they begin a conversation about it themselves, it is usually embarrassing, awkward, and long.

"How is one to say it?" Korolyov wondered. "And is it necessary to speak?"

And he said what he meant in a roundabout way:

"You in the position of a factory owner and a wealthy heiress are dissatisfied; you don't believe in your right to it; and here now you can't sleep. That, of course, is better than if you were satisfied, slept soundly, and thought everything was satisfactory. Your sleeplessness does you credit; in any case, it is a good sign. In reality, such a conversation as this between us now would have been unthinkable for our parents. At night they did not talk, but slept sound; we, our generation, sleep badly, are restless, but talk a great deal, and are always trying to settle whether we are right or not. For our children or grandchildren that question—

whether they are right or not—will have been settled. Things will be clearer for them than for us. Life will be good in fifty years' time; it's only a pity we shall not last out till then. It would be interesting to have a peep at it."

"What will our children and grandchildren do?" asked Liza.

"I don't know. . . . I suppose they will throw it all up and go away."

"Go where?"

"Where? . . . Why, where they like," said Korolyov; and he laughed. "There are lots of places a good, intelligent person can go to."

He glanced at his watch.

"The sun has risen, though," he said. "It is time you were asleep. Undress and sleep soundly. Very glad to have made your acquaintance," he went on, pressing her hand. "You are a good, interesting woman. Good night!"

He went to his room and went to bed.

In the morning they all came out on to the steps to see him off. Liza, pale and exhausted, was in a white dress as though for a holiday, with a flower in her hair; she looked at him, as yesterday, sorrowfully and intelligently, smiled and talked, and all with an expression as though she wanted to tell him something special, important—him alone. They could hear the larks trilling and the church bells pealing. The windows in the factory buildings were sparkling gaily, and, driving across the yard and afterwards along the road to the station, Korolyov thought neither of the workpeople nor of lake dwellings, nor of the devil, but thought of the time, perhaps close at hand, when life would be as bright and joyous as that still Sunday morning; and he thought how pleasant it was on such a morning in the spring to drive with three horses in a good carriage, and to bask in the sunshine.

GUSEV

It is already dark, it will soon be night.

Gusev, a discharged private, half rises in his bunk and says in a low voice:

"Do you hear me, Pavel Ivanych? A soldier in Suchan was telling me: while they were sailing, their ship bumped into a big fish and smashed a hole in its bottom."

The individual of uncertain social status whom he is addressing, and whom everyone in the ship infirmary calls Pavel Ivanych, is silent as though he hasn't heard.

And again all is still. The wind is flirting with the rigging, the screw is throbbing, the waves are lashing, the bunks creak, but the ear has long since become used to these sounds, and everything around seems to slumber in silence. It is dull. The three invalids—two soldiers and a sailor—who were playing cards all day are dozing and talking deliriously.

The ship is apparently beginning to roll. The bunk slowly rises and falls under Gusev as though it were breathing, and this occurs once, twice, three times . . . Something hits the floor with a clang: a jug must have dropped.

"The wind has broken loose from its chain," says Gusev, straining his ears.

This time Pavel Ivanych coughs and says irritably:

"One minute a vessel bumps into a fish, the next the wind breaks loose from its chain. . . . Is the wind a beast that it breaks loose from its chain?"

"That's what Christian folks say."

"They are as ignorant as you. . . . They say all sorts of things. One must have one's head on one's shoulders and reason it out. You have no sense."

Pavel Ivanych is subject to seasickness. When the sea is rough he is usually out of sorts, and the merest trifle irritates him. In Gusev's opinion there is absolutely nothing to be irritated about. What is there that is strange or out of the way about that fish, for instance, or about the wind breaking loose from its chain? Suppose the fish were as big as the mountain and its back as hard as a sturgeon's, and supposing, too, that over yonder at the end of the world stood great stone walls and the fierce winds were chained up to the walls. If they haven't broken loose, why then do they rush all over the sea like madmen and strain like hounds tugging at their leash? If they are not chained up what becomes of them when it is calm?

Gusev ponders for a long time about fishes as big as a mountain and about stout, rusty chains. Then he begins to feel bored and falls to thinking about his home, to which he is returning after five years' service in the Far East. He pictures an immense pond covered with drifts. On one side of the pond is the brick-colored building of the pottery with a tall chimney and clouds of black smoke; on the other side is a village. His brother Alexey drives out of the fifth yard from the end in a sleigh; behind him sits his little son Vanka in big felt boots, and his little girl Akulka also wearing felt boots. Alexey has had a drop. Vanka is laughing, Akulka's face cannot be seen, she is muffled up.

"If he doesn't look out, he will have the children frostbitten," Gusev reflects. "Lord send them sense that they may honor their parents and not be any wiser than their father and mother."

"They need new soles," a delirious sailor says in a bass voice. "Yes, yes!"

Gusev's thoughts abruptly break off and suddenly without rhyme or reason the pond is replaced by a huge bull's head without eyes, and the horse and sleigh are no longer going straight ahead but are whirling round and round, wrapped in black smoke. But still he is glad he has had a glimpse of his people. In fact, he is breathless with joy, and his whole body, down to his fingertips, tingles with it. "Thanks be to God we have seen each other again," he mutters deliriously, but at once opens his eyes and looks for water in the dark.

He drinks and lies down, and again the sleigh is gliding along, then again there is the bull's head without eyes, smoke, clouds . . . And so it goes till daybreak.

II

A blue circle is the first thing to become visible in the darkness—it is the porthole; then, little by little, Gusev makes out the man in the next bunk, Pavel Ivanych. The man sleeps sitting up, as he cannot breathe lying down. His face is gray, his nose long and sharp, his eyes look huge because he is terribly emaciated, his temples are sunken, his beard skimpy, his hair long. His face does not reveal his social status: you cannot tell whether he is a gentleman, a merchant, or a peasant. Judging from his expression and his long hair, he may be an assiduous churchgoer or a lay brother, but his manner of speaking does not seem to be that of a monk. He is utterly worn out by his cough, by the stifling heat, his illness, and he breathes with difficulty, moving his parched lips. Noticing that Gusev is looking at him he turns his face toward him and says:

"I begin to guess . . . Yes, I understand it all perfectly now."

"What do you understand, Pavel Ivanych?"

"Here's how it is. . . . It has always seemed strange to me that terribly ill as you fellows are, you should be on a steamer where the stifling air, the heavy seas, in fact everything, threatens you with death; but now it is all clear to me. . . . Yes. . . . The doctors put you on the steamer to get rid of you. They got tired of bothering with you, cattle. . . . You don't pay them any money, you are a nuisance, and you spoil their statistics with your deaths. . . . So, of course, you are just cattle. And it's not hard to get rid of you. . . . All that's necessary is, in the first place, to have no conscience or humanity, and, secondly, to deceive the ship authorities. The first requirement need hardly be given a thought—in that respect we are virtuosos, and as for the second condition, it can always be fulfilled with a little practice. In a crowd of four hundred healthy soldiers and sailors, five sick ones are not conspicuous; well, they got you all onto the steamer, mixed you with the healthy ones, hurriedly counted you over and in the confusion nothing untoward was noticed, and when the steamer was on the way, people discovered that there were paralytics and consumptives on their last legs lying about the deck . . ."

Gusev does not understand Pavel Ivanych; thinking that he is being reprimanded, he says in self-justification:

"I lay on the deck because I was so sick; when we were being unloaded from the barge onto the steamer, I caught a bad chill."

"It's revolting," Pavel Ivanych continues. "The main thing is, they know perfectly well that you can't stand the long journey and yet they put you here. Suppose you last as far as the Indian Ocean, and then what? It's horrible to think of. . . . And that's the gratitude for your faithful, irreproachable service!"

Pavel Ivanych's eyes flash with anger. He frowns fastidiously and says, gasping for breath, "Those are the people who ought to be given a drubbing in the newspapers till the feathers fly in all directions."

The two sick soldiers and the sailor have waked up and are already playing cards. The sailor is half reclining in his bunk, the soldiers are sitting nearby on the floor in most uncomfortable positions. One of the soldiers has his right arm bandaged and his wrist is heavily swathed in wrappings that look like a cap, so that he holds his cards under his right arm or in the crook of his elbow while he plays with his left. The ship is rolling heavily. It is impossible to stand up, or have tea, or take medicine.

"Were you an orderly?" Pavel Ivanych asks Gusev.

"Yes, sir, an orderly."

"My God, my God!" says Pavel Ivanych and shakes his head sadly. "To tear a man from his home, drag him a distance of ten thousand miles, then wear him out till he gets consumption and . . . and what is it all for, one asks? To turn him into an orderly for some Captain Kopeykin or Midshipman Dyrka! How reasonable!"

"It's not hard work, Pavel Ivanych. You get up in the morning and polish the boots, start the samovars going, tidy the rooms, and then you have nothing more to do. The lieutenant drafts plans all day, and if you like, you can say your prayers or read a book or go out on the street. God grant everyone such a life."

"Yes, very good! The lieutenant drafts plans all day long, and you sit in the kitchen and long for home. . . . Plans, indeed!

. . . It's not plans that matter but human life. You have only one life to live and it mustn't be wronged."

"Of course, Pavel Ivanych, a bad man gets no break anywhere, either at home or in the service, but if you live as you ought and obey orders, who will want to wrong you? The officers are educated gentlemen, they understand. . . . In five years I have never once been in the guard house, and I was struck, if I remember right, only once."

"What for?"

"For fighting. I have a heavy hand, Pavel Ivanych. Four Chinks came into our yard; they were bringing firewood or something, I forget. Well, I was bored and I knocked them about a bit, the nose of one of them, damn him, began bleeding. . . . The lieutenant saw it all through the window, got angry, and boxed me on the ear."

"You are a poor, foolish fellow. . . ." whispers Pavel Ivanych. "You don't understand anything."

He is utterly exhausted by the rolling of the ship and shuts his eyes; now his head drops back, now it sinks forward on his chest. Several times he tries to lie down but nothing comes of it: he finds it difficult to breathe.

"And what did you beat up the four Chinks for?" he asks after a while.

"Oh, just like that. They came into the yard and I hit them."

There is silence. . . . The card players play for two hours, eagerly, swearing sometimes, but the rolling and pitching of the ship overcomes them too; they throw aside the cards and lie down. Again Gusev has a vision: the big pond, the pottery, the village . . . Once more the sleigh is gliding along, once more Vanka is laughing and Akulka, the silly thing, throws open her fur coat and thrusts out her feet, as much as to say: "Look, good people, my felt boots are not like Vanka's, they're new ones."

"Going on six, and she has no sense yet," Gusev mutters in his delirium. "Instead of showing off your boots you had better come and get your soldier uncle a drink. I'll give you a present."

And here is Andron with a flintlock on his shoulder, carrying a hare he has killed, and behind him is the decrepit old Jew Isaychik, who offers him a piece of soap in exchange for the hare; and here is the black calf in the entry, and Domna sewing a shirt and crying about something, and then again the bull's head without eyes, black smoke . . .

Someone shouts overhead, several sailors run by; it seems that something bulky is being dragged over the deck, something falls with a crash. Again some people run by. . . . Has there been an accident? Gusev raises his head, listens, and sees that the two soldiers and the sailor are playing cards again; Pavel Ivanych is sitting up and moving his lips. It is stifling, you haven't the strength to breathe, you are thirsty, the water is warm, disgusting. The ship is still rolling and pitching.

Suddenly something strange happens to one of the soldiers playing cards. He calls hearts diamonds, gets muddled over his score, and drops his cards, then with a frightened, foolish smile looks round at all of them.

"I shan't be a minute, fellows . . ." he says, and lies down on the floor.

Everybody is nonplussed. They call to him, he does not answer.

"Stepan, maybe you are feeling bad, eh?" the soldier with the bandaged arm asks him. "Perhaps we had better call the priest, eh?"

"Have a drink of water, Stepan . . ." says the sailor. "Here, brother, drink."

"Why are you knocking the jug against his teeth?" says Gusev angrily. "Don't you see, you cabbage head?"

"What?"

"What?" Gusev mimicks him. "There is no breath in him, he's dead! That's what! Such stupid people, Lord God!"

III

The ship has stopped rolling and Pavel Ivanych is cheerful. He is no longer cross. His face wears a boastful, challenging, mocking expression. It is as though he wants to say: "Yes, right away I'll tell you something that will make you burst with laughter." The round porthole is open and a soft breeze is blowing on Pavel Ivanych. There is a sound of voices, the splash of oars in the water . . . Just under the porthole someone is droning in a thin, disgusting voice; must be a Chinaman singing.

"Here we are in the harbor," says Pavel Ivanych with a mocking smile. "Only another month or so and we shall be in Russia. M'yes, messieurs of the armed forces! I'll arrive in Odessa and from there go straight to Kharkov. In Kharkov I have a friend, a man of letters. I'll go to him and say, 'Come, brother, put aside your vile subjects, women's amours and the beauties of nature, and show up the two-legged vermin. . . . There's a subject for you.' "

For a while he reflects, then says:

"Gusev, do you know how I tricked them?"

"Tricked who, Pavel Ivanych?"

"Why, these people. . . . You understand, on this steamer there is only a first class and a third class, and they only allow peasants, that is, the common herd, to go in the third. If you have got a jacket on and even at a distance look like a gentleman or a bourgeois, you have to go first class, if you please. You must fork out five hundred rubles if it kills you. 'Why do you have such a regulation?' I ask them. 'Do you mean to raise the prestige of the Russian intelligentsia thereby?' 'Not a bit of it. We don't let you simply because a decent person can't go third class; it is too horrible and disgusting there.' 'Yes, sir? Thank you for being so solicitous about decent people's welfare. But in any case, whether it's nasty there or nice, I haven't got five hundred rubles. I didn't loot the treasury, I didn't exploit the natives, I didn't traffic in contraband, I flogged nobody to death, so judge for yourselves if I have the right to occupy a first class cabin and even to reckon myself among the Russian intelligentsia.' But logic means nothing to them. So I had to resort to fraud. I put on a peasant coat and high boots, I pulled a face so that I looked like a common drunk, and went to the agents: 'Give us a little ticket, your Excellency,' said I—"

"You're not of the gentry, are you?" asked the sailor.

"I come of a clerical family. My father was a priest, and an honest one; he always told the high and mighty the truth to their faces and, as a result, he suffered a great deal."

Pavel Ivanych is exhausted from talking and gasps for breath, but still continues:

"Yes, I always tell people the truth to their faces. I'm not afraid of anyone or anything. In this respect, there is a great difference between me and all of you, men. You are dark people, blind, crushed; you see nothing and what you do see, you don't understand. . . . You are told that the wind breaks loose from its chain, that you are beasts, savages, and you believe it; someone gives it to you in the neck—you kiss his hand; some animal in a racoon coat robs you and then tosses you a fifteen-kopeck tip and you say: 'Let me kiss your hand, sir.' You are outcasts, pitiful wretches. I am different, my mind is clear. I see it all plainly like a hawk or an eagle when it hovers over the earth, and I understand everything. I am protest personified. I see tyranny—I protest. I see a hypocrite—I protest, I see a triumphant swine—I protest. And I cannot be put down, no Spanish Inquisition can silence me. No. Cut out my tongue and I will protest with gestures. Wall me up in a cellar—I will shout so that you will hear me half a mile away, or will starve myself to death, so that they may have another weight on their black consciences. Kill me and I will haunt them. All my acquaintances say to me: 'You are a most insufferable person, Pavel Ivanych.' I am proud of such a reputation. I served three years in the Far East and I shall be remembered there a hundred years. I had rows there with everybody. My friends wrote to me from Russia: 'Don't come back,' but here I am going back to spite them. . . . Yes. . . . That's life as I understand it. That's what one can call life."

Gusev is not listening; he is looking at the porthole. A junk, flooded with dazzling hot sunshine, is swaying on the transparent turquoise water. In it stand naked Chinamen, holding up cages with canaries in them and calling out: "It sings, it sings!"

Another boat knocks against it; a steam cutter glides past. Then there is another boat: a fat Chinaman sits in it, eating rice with chopsticks. The water sways lazily, white sea gulls languidly hover over it.

"Would be fine to give that fat fellow one in the neck," reflects Gusev, looking at the stout Chinaman and yawning.

He dozes off and it seems to him that all nature is dozing too. Time flies swiftly by. Imperceptibly the day passes. Imperceptibly darkness descends. . . . The steamer is no longer standing still but is on the move again.

IV

Two days pass. Pavel Ivanych no longer sits up but is lying down. His eyes are closed, his nose seems to have grown sharper.

"Pavel Ivanych," Gusev calls to him. "Hey, Pavel Ivanych."

Pavel Ivanych opens his eyes and moves his lips.

"Are you feeling bad?"

"No. . . . It's nothing. . . ." answers Pavel Ivanych gasping for breath. "Nothing, on the contrary . . . I am better. . . . You see, I can lie down now. . . . I have improved . . ."

"Well, thank God for that, Pavel Ivanych."

"When I compare myself to you, I am sorry for you, poor fellows. My lungs are healthy, mine is a stomach cough. . . . I can stand hell, let alone the Red Sea. Besides, I take a critical attitude toward my illness and the medicines. While you— Your minds are dark. . . . It's hard on you, very, very hard!"

The ship is not rolling, it is quiet, but as hot and stifling as a Turkish bath; it is hard, not only to speak, but even to listen. Gusev hugs his knees, lays his head on them and thinks of his home. God, in this stifling heat, what a relief it is to think of snow and cold! You're driving in a sleigh; all of a sudden, the horses take fright at something and bolt. Careless of the road, the ditches, the gullies, they tear like mad things right through the village, across the pond, past the pottery, across the open fields. "Hold them!" the pottery hands and the peasants they meet shout at the top of their voices. "Hold them!" But why hold them? Let the keen cold wind beat in your face and bite your hands; let the lumps of snow, kicked up by the horses, slide down your collar, your neck, your chest; let the runners sing, and the traces and the whippletrees break, the devil take them. And what delight when the sleigh upsets and you go flying full tilt into a drift, face right in the snow, and then you get up, white all over with icicles on your mustache, no cap, no gloves, your belt undone. . . . People laugh, dogs bark . . .

Pavel Ivanych half opens one eye, fixes Gusev with it and asks softly:

"Gusev, did your commanding officer steal?"

"Who can tell, Pavel Ivanych? We can't say, we didn't hear about it."

And after that, a long time passes in silence. Gusev broods, his mind wanders, and he keeps drinking water: it is hard for him to talk and hard for him to listen, and he is afraid of being talked to. An hour passes, a second, a third; evening comes, then night, but he doesn't notice it; he sits up and keeps dreaming of the frost.

There is a sound as though someone were coming into the infirmary, voices are heard, but five minutes pass and all is quiet again.

"The kingdom of heaven be his and eternal peace," says the soldier with a bandaged arm. "He was an uneasy chap."

"What?" asks Gusev. "Who?"

"He died, they have just carried him up."

"Oh, well," mutters Gusev, yawning, "the kingdom of heaven be his."

"What do you think, Gusev?" the soldier with the bandaged arm says after a while. "Will he be in the kingdom of heaven or not?"

"Who do you mean?"

"Pavel Ivanych."

"He will. . . . He suffered so long. Then again, he belonged to the clergy and priests have a lot of relatives. Their prayers will get him there."

The soldier with the bandage sits down on Gusev's bunk and says in an undertone:

"You too, Gusev, aren't long for this world. You will never get to Russia."

"Did the doctor or the nurse say so?" asks Gusev.

"It isn't that they said so, but one can see it. It's plain when a man will die soon. You don't eat, you don't drink, you've got so thin it's dreadful to look at you. It's consumption, in a word. I say it not to worry you, but because maybe you would like to receive the sacrament and extreme unction. And if you have any money, you had better turn it over to the senior officer."

"I haven't written home," Gusev sighs. "I shall die and they won't know."

"They will," the sick sailor says in a bass voice. "When you die, they will put it down in the ship's log, in Odessa they will send a copy of the entry to the army authorities, and they will notify your district board or somebody like that."

Such a conversation makes Gusev uneasy and a vague craving begins to torment him. He takes a drink—it isn't that; he drags himself to the porthole and breathes the hot, moist air—it isn't that; he tries to think of home, of the frost—it isn't that. . . . At last it seems to him that if he stays in the infirmary another minute, he will certainly choke to death.

"It's stifling, brother," he says. "I'll go on deck. Take me there, for Christ's sake."

"All right," the soldier with the bandage agrees. "You can't walk, I'll carry you. Hold on to my neck."

Gusev puts his arm around the soldier's neck, the latter places his uninjured arm round him and carries him up. On the deck, discharged soldiers and sailors are lying asleep side by side; there are so many of them it is difficult to pass.

"Get down on the floor," the soldier with the bandage says softly. "Follow me quietly, hold on to my shirt."

It is dark, there are no lights on deck or on the masts or anywhere on the sea around. On the prow the seaman on watch stands perfectly still like a statue, and it looks as though he, too, were asleep. The steamer seems to be left to its own devices and to be going where it pleases.

"Now they'll throw Pavel Ivanych into the sea," says the soldier with the bandage, "in a sack and then into the water."

"Yes, that's the regulation."

"At home, it's better to lie in the earth. Anyway, your mother will come to the grave and shed a tear."

"Sure."

There is a smell of dung and hay. With drooping heads, steers stand at the ship's rail. One, two, three—eight of them! And there's a pony. Gusev puts out his hand to stroke it, but it shakes its head, shows its teeth, and tries to bite his sleeve.

"Damn brute!" says Gusev crossly.

The two of them thread their way to the prow, then stand at the rail, peering. Overhead there is deep sky, bright stars, peace and quiet, exactly as at home in the village. But below there is darkness and disorder. Tall waves are making an uproar for no reason. Each one of them as you look at it is trying to rise higher than all the rest and to chase and crush its neighbor; it is thunderously attacked by a third wave that has a gleaming white mane and is just as ferocious and ugly.

The sea has neither sense nor pity. If the steamer had been smaller, not made of thick iron plates, the waves would have crushed it without the slightest remorse, and would have devoured all the people in it without distinguishing between saints and sinners. The steamer's expression was equally senseless and cruel. This beaked monster presses forward, cutting millions of waves in its path; it fears neither darkness nor the wind, nor space, nor solitude—it's all child's play for it, and if the ocean had its population, this monster would crush it, too, without distinguishing between saints and sinners.

"Where are we now?" asks Gusev.

"I don't know. Must be the ocean."

"You can't see land. . . ."

"No chance of it! They say we'll see it only in seven days."

The two men stare silently at the white phosphorescent foam, and brood. Gusev is first to break the silence.

"There is nothing frightening here," he says. "Only you feel queer as if you were in a dark forest; but if, let's say, they lowered the boat this minute and an officer ordered me to go fifty miles across the sea to catch fish, I'll go. Or, let's say, if a Christian were to fall into the water right now, I'd jump in after him. A German or a Chink I wouldn't try to save, but I'd go in after a Christian."

"And are you afraid to die?"

"I am. I am sorry about the farm. My brother at home, you know, isn't steady; he drinks, he beats his wife for no reason, he doesn't honor his father and mother. Without me everything will go to rack and ruin, and before long it's my fear that my father and old mother will be begging their bread. But my legs won't hold me up, brother, and it's stifling here. Let's go to sleep."

V

Gusev goes back to the infirmary and gets into his bunk. He is again tormented by a vague desire and he can't make out what it is that he wants. There is a weight on his chest, a throbbing in his head, his mouth is so dry that it is difficult for him to move his tongue. He dozes and talks in his sleep and, worn out with nightmares, with coughing and the stifling heat, toward morning he falls into a heavy sleep. He dreams that they have just taken the bread out of the oven in the barracks and that he has climbed into the oven and is having a steam bath there, lashing himself with a besom of birch twigs. He sleeps for two days and on the third at noon two sailors come down and carry him out of the infirmary. He is sewn up in sailcloth and to make him heavier, they put two gridirons in with him. Sewn up in sailcloth, he looks like a carrot or a radish: broad at the head and narrow at the feet. Before sunset, they carry him on deck and put him on a plank. One end of the plank lies on the ship's rail, the other on a box placed on a stool. Round him stand the discharged soldiers and the crew with heads bared.

"Blessed is our God," the priest begins, "now, and ever, and unto ages of ages."

"Amen," three sailors chant.

The discharged men and the crew cross themselves and look

off at the waves. It is strange that a man should be sewn up in sailcloth and should soon be flying into the sea. Is it possible that such a thing can happen to anyone?

The priest strews earth upon Gusev and makes obeisance to him. The men sing "Memory Eternal."

The seaman on watch duty raises the end of the plank, Gusev slides off it slowly and then flying, head foremost, turns over in the air and—plop! Foam covers him, and for a moment, he seems to be wrapped in lace, but the instant passes and he disappears in the waves.

He plunges rapidly downward. Will he reach the bottom? At this spot the ocean is said to be three miles deep. After sinking sixty or seventy feet, he begins to descend more and more slowly, swaying rhythmically as though in hesitation, and, carried along by the current, moves faster laterally than vertically.

And now he runs into a school of fish called pilot fish. Seeing the dark body, the little fish stop as though petrified and suddenly all turn round together and disappear. In less than a minute they rush back at Gusev, swift as arrows, and begin zigzagging round him in the water. Then another dark body appears. It is a shark. With dignity and reluctance, seeming not to notice Gusev, as it were, it swims under him; then while he, moving downward, sinks upon its back, the shark turns, belly upward, basks in the warm transparent water and languidly opens its jaws with two rows of teeth. The pilot fish are in ecstasy; they stop to see what will happen next. After playing a little with the body, the shark nonchalantly puts his jaws under it, cautiously touches it with his teeth and the sailcloth is ripped the full length of the body, from head to foot; one of the gridirons falls out, frightens the pilot fish and striking the shark on the flank, sinks rapidly to the bottom.

Meanwhile, up above, in that part of the sky where the sun is about to set, clouds are massing, one resembling a triumphal arch, another a lion, a third a pair of scissors. A broad shaft of green light issues from the clouds and reaches to the middle of the sky; a while later, a violet beam appears alongside of it and then a golden one and a pink one. . . . The heavens turn a soft lilac tint. Looking at this magnificent enchanting sky, the ocean frowns at first, but soon it, too, takes on tender, joyous, passionate colors for which it is hard to find a name in the language of man.

HEARTACHE

"To whom shall I tell my sorrow?"[1]

Evening twilight. Large flakes of wet snow are circling lazily about the street lamps which have just been lighted, settling in a thin soft layer on roofs, horses' backs, peoples' shoulders, caps. Iona Potapov, the cabby, is all white like a ghost. As hunched as a living body can be, he sits on the box without stirring. If a whole snowdrift were to fall on him, even then, perhaps, he would not find it necessary to shake it off. His nag, too, is white and motionless. Her immobility, the angularity of her shape, and the sticklike straightness of her legs make her look like a penny gingerbread horse. She is probably lost in thought. Anyone who has been torn away from the plow, from the familiar gray scenes, and cast into this whirlpool full of monstrous lights, of ceaseless uproar and hurrying people, cannot help thinking.

Iona and his nag have not budged for a long time. They had driven out of the yard before dinnertime and haven't had a single fare yet. But now evening dusk is descending upon the city. The pale light of the street lamps changes to a vivid color and the bustle of the street grows louder.

"Sleigh to the Vyborg District!" Iona hears. "Sleigh!"

---

[1]From an old Russian song comparable to a black Spiritual.

Iona starts, and through his snow-plastered eyelashes sees an officer in a military overcoat with a hood.

"To the Vyborg District!" repeats the officer. "Are you asleep, eh? To the Vyborg District!"

As a sign of assent Iona gives a tug at the reins, which sends layers of snow flying from the horse's back and from his own shoulders. The officer gets into the sleigh. The driver clucks to the horse, cranes his neck like a swan, rises in his seat and, more from habit than necessity, flourishes his whip. The nag, too, stretches her neck, crooks her sticklike legs, and irresolutely sets off.

"Where are you barging in, damn you?" Iona is promptly assailed by shouts from the massive dark wavering to and fro before him. "Where the devil are you going? Keep to the right!"

"Don't you know how to drive? Keep to the right," says the officer with vexation.

A coachman driving a private carriage swears at him; a pedestrian who was crossing the street and brushed against the nag's nose with his shoulder looks at him angrily and shakes the snow off his sleeve. Iona fidgets on the box as if sitting on needles and pins, thrusts out his elbows, and rolls his eyes like a madman, as though he did not know where he was or why he was there.

"What rascals they all are," the officer jokes. "They are doing their best to knock into you or be trampled by the horse. It's a conspiracy."

Iona looks at his fare and moves his lips. He wants to say something, but the only sound that comes out is a wheeze.

"What is it?" asks the officer.

Iona twists his mouth into a smile, strains his throat and croaks hoarsely: "My son, sir . . . er, my son died this week."

"H'm, what did he die of?"

Iona turns his whole body around to his fare and says, "Who can tell? It must have been a fever. He lay in the hospital only three days and then he died. . . . It is God's will."

"Get over, you devil!" comes out of the dark. "Have you gone blind, you old dog? Keep your eyes peeled!"

"Go on, go on," says the officer. "We shan't get there until tomorrow at this rate. Give her the whip!"

The driver cranes his neck again, rises in his seat, and with heavy grace swings his whip. Then he looks around at the officer several times, but the latter keeps his eyes closed and is apparently indisposed to listen. Letting his fare off in the Vyborg

District, Iona stops by a teahouse and again sits motionless and hunched on the box. Again the wet snow paints him and his nag white. One hour passes, another . . .

Three young men, two tall and lanky, one short and hunchbacked, come along swearing at each other and loudly pound the pavement with their galoshes.

"Cabby, to the Police Bridge!" the hunchback shouts in a cracked voice. "The three of us . . . twenty kopecks!"

Iona tugs at the reins and clucks to his horse. Twenty kopecks is not fair, but his mind is not on that. Whether it is a ruble or five kopecks, it is all one to him now, so long as he has a fare. . . . The three young men, jostling each other and using foul language, go up to the sleigh and all three try to sit down at once. They start arguing about which two are to sit and who shall be the one to stand. After a long ill-tempered and abusive altercation, they decide that the hunchback must stand up because he is the shortest.

"Well, get going," says the hunchback in his cracked voice, taking up his station and breathing down Iona's neck. "On your way! What a cap you've got, brother! You won't find a worse one in all Petersburg—"

"Hee, hee . . . hee, hee . . ." Iona giggles, "as you say— "

"Well, then, 'as you say,' drive on. Are you going to crawl like this all the way, eh? D'you want to get it in the neck?"

"My head is splitting," says one of the tall ones. "At the Dukmasov's yesterday, Vaska and I killed four bottles of cognac between us."

"I don't get it, why lie?" says the other tall one angrily. "He is lying like a trouper."

"Strike me dead, it's the truth!"

"It is about as true as that a louse sneezes."

"Hee, hee," giggles Iona. "The gentlemen are feeling good!"

"Faugh, the devil take you!" cries the hunchback indignantly. "Will you get a move on, you old pest, or won't you? Is that the way to drive? Give her a crack of the whip! Giddap, devil! Giddap! Let her feel it!"

Iona feels the hunchback's wriggling body and quivering voice behind his back. He hears abuse addressed to him, sees people, and the feeling of loneliness begins little by little to lift from his heart. The hunchback swears till he chokes on an elaborate three-decker oath and is overcome by cough. The tall youths begin discussing a certain Nadezhda Petrovna. Iona looks round at them. When at last there is a lull in the conversation for which he has been waiting, he turns around and says: "This week . . . er . . . my son died."

"We shall all die," says the hunchback, with a sigh, wiping his lips after his coughing fit. "Come, drive on, drive on. Gentlemen, I simply cannot stand this pace! When will he get us there?"

"Well, you give him a little encouragement. Biff him in the neck!"

"Do you hear, you old pest? I'll give it to you in the neck. If one stands on ceremony with fellows like you, one may as well walk. Do you hear, you old serpent? Or don't you give a damn what we say?"

And Iona hears rather than feels the thud of a blow on his neck.

"Hee, hee," he laughs. "The gentlemen are feeling good. God give you health!"

"Cabby, are you married?" asks one of the tall ones.

"Me? Hee, hee! The gentlemen are feeling good. The only wife for me now is the damp earth. . . . Hee, haw, haw! The grave, that is! . . . Here my son is dead and me alive. . . . It is a queer thing, death comes in at the wrong door. . . . It don't come for me, it comes for my son. . . ."

And Iona turns round to tell them how his son died, but at that point the hunchback gives a sigh of relief and announces that, thank God, they have arrived at last. Having received his twenty kopecks, for a long while Iona stares after the revelers, who disappear into a dark entrance. Again he is alone and once more silence envelops him. The grief which has been allayed for a brief space comes back again and wrenches his heart more cruelly than ever. There is a look of anxiety and torment in Iona's eyes as they wander restlessly over the crowds moving to and fro on both sides of the street. Isn't there someone among those thousands who will listen to him? But the crowds hurry past, heedless of him and his grief. His grief is immense, boundless. If his heart were to burst and his grief to pour out, it seems that it would flood the whole world, and yet no one sees it. It has found a place for itself in such an insignificant shell that no one can see it in broad daylight.

Iona notices a doorkeeper with a bag and makes up his mind to speak to him.

"What time will it be, friend?" he asks.

"Past nine. What have you stopped here for? On your way!"

Iona drives a few steps away, hunches up and surrenders himself to his grief. He feels it is useless to turn to people. But before five minutes are over, he draws himself up, shakes his head as though stabbed by a sharp pain, and tugs at the reins. . . . He can bear it no longer.

"Back to the yard!" he thinks. "To the yard!"

And his nag, as though she knew his thoughts, starts out at a trot. An hour and a half later, Iona is sitting beside a large, dirty stove. On the stove, on the floor, on benches are men snoring. The air is stuffy and foul. Iona looks at the sleeping figures, scratches himself, and regrets that he has come home so early.

"I haven't earned enough to pay for the oats," he reflects. "That's what's wrong with me. A man that knows his job . . . who has enough to eat and has enough for his horse don't need to fret."

In one of the corners a young driver gets up, hawks sleepily, and reaches for the water bucket.

"Thirsty?" Iona asks him.

"Guess so."

"H'm, may it do you good, but my son is dead, brother . . . did you hear? This week in the hospital. . . . What a business!"

Iona looks to see the effect of his words, but he notices none. The young man has drawn his cover over his head and is already asleep. The old man sighs and scratches himself. Just as the young man was thirsty for water so he thirsts for talk. It will soon be a week since his son died and he hasn't talked to anybody about him properly. He ought to be able to talk about it, taking his time, sensibly. He ought to tell how his son was taken ill, how he suffered, what he said before he died, how he died. . . . He ought to describe the funeral, and how he went to the hospital to fetch his son's clothes. His daughter Anisya is still in the country. . . . And he would like to talk about her too. Yes, he has plenty to talk about now. And his listener should gasp and moan and keen. . . . It would be even better to talk to women. Though they are foolish, two words will make them blubber.

"I must go out and have a look at the horse," Iona thinks. "There will be time enough for sleep. You will have enough sleep, no fear. . . ."

He gets dressed and goes into the stable where his horse is standing. He thinks about oats, hay, the weather. When he is alone, he dares not think of his son. It is possible to talk about him with someone, but to think of him when one is alone, to evoke his image is unbearably painful.

"You chewing?" Iona asks his mare seeing her shining eyes. "There, chew away, chew away. . . . If we haven't earned enough for oats, we'll eat hay. . . . Yes. . . . I've grown too old to drive. My son had ought to be driving, not me. . . . He was a real cabby. . . . He had ought to have lived. . . ."

Iona is silent for a space and then goes on: "That's how it is, old girl. . . . Kuzma Ionych is gone. . . . Departed this life. . . . He went and died to no purpose. . . . Now let's say you had a little colt, and you were that little colt's own mother. And suddenly, let's say, that same little colt departed this life. . . . You'd be sorry, wouldn't you?"

The nag chews, listens, and breathes on her master's hands. Iona is carried away and tells her everything.

THE KISS

At eight o'clock on the evening of the twentieth of May all the six batteries of the N—— Reserve Artillery Brigade halted for the night in the village of Mestechki on their way to camp. At the height of the general commotion, while some officers were busily occupied around the guns, and others, gathered together in the square near the church enclosure, were receiving the reports of the quartermasters, a man in civilian dress, riding a queer horse, came into sight round the church. The little dun-colored horse with a fine neck and a short tail came, moving not straight forward, but, as it were, sideways, with a sort of dance step, as though it were being lashed about the legs. When he reached the officers the man on the horse took off his hat and said:

"His Excellency Lieutenant General von Rabbeck, a local landowner, invites the officers to have tea with him this minute. . . ."

The horse bowed, danced, and retired sideways; the rider raised his hat once more and in an instant disappeared with his strange horse behind the church.

"What the devil does it mean?" grumbled some of the officers, dispersing to their quarters. "One is sleepy, and here this von Rabbeck with his tea! We know what tea means."

The officers of all the six batteries remembered vividly an

incident of the previous year, when during maneuvers they, together with the officers of a Cossack regiment, were in the same way invited to tea by a count who had an estate in the neighborhood and was a retired army officer; the hospitable and genial count made much of them, dined and wined them, refused to let them go to their quarters in the village, and made them stay the night. All that, of course, was very nice—nothing better could be desired, but the worst of it was, the old army officer was so carried away by the pleasure of the young men's company that till sunrise he was telling the officers anecdotes of his glorious past, taking them over the house, showing them expensive pictures, old engravings, rare guns, reading them autograph letters from great people, while the weary and exhausted officers looked and listened, longing for their beds and yawning in their sleeves; when at last their host let them go, it was too late for sleep.

Might not this von Rabbeck be just such another? Whether he were or not, there was no help for it. The officers changed their uniforms, brushed themselves, and went all together in search of the gentleman's house. In the square by the church they were told they could get to his Excellency's by the lower road—going down behind the church to the river, walking along the bank to the garden, and there the alleys would take them to the house; or by the upper way—straight from the church by the road which, half a mile from the village, led right up to his Excellency's barns. The officers decided to go by the upper road.

"Which von Rabbeck is it?" they wondered on the way. "Surely not the one who was in command of the N—— cavalry division at Plevna?"

"No, that was not von Rabbeck, but simply Rabbe and no 'von.' "

"What lovely weather!"

At the first of the barns the road divided in two: one branch went straight on and vanished in the evening darkness, the other led to the owner's house on the right. The officers turned to the right and began to speak more softly. . . . On both sides of the road stretched stone barns with red roofs, heavy and sullen looking, very much like barracks in a district town. Ahead of them gleamed the windows of the manor house.

"A good omen, gentlemen," said one of the officers. "Our setter leads the way; no doubt he scents game ahead of us! . . ."

Lieutenant Lobytko, who was walking in front, a tall and

stalwart fellow, though entirely without mustache (he was over twenty-five, yet for some reason there was no sign of hair on his round, well-fed face), renowned in the brigade for his peculiar ability to divine the presence of women at a distance, turned round and said:

"Yes, there must be women here; I feel that by instinct."

On the threshold the officers were met by von Rabbeck himself, a comely looking man of sixty in civilian dress. Shaking hands with his guests, he said that he was very glad and happy to see them, but begged them earnestly for God's sake to excuse him for not asking them to stay the night; two sisters with their children, his brothers, and some neighbors, had come on a visit to him, so that he had not one spare room left.

The General shook hands with everyone, made his apologies, and smiled, but it was evident by his face that he was by no means so delighted as last year's count, and that he had invited the officers simply because, in his opinion, it was a social obligation. And the officers themselves, as they walked up the softly carpeted stairs, as they listened to him, felt that they had been invited to this house simply because it would have been awkward not to invite them; and at the sight of the footmen, who hastened to light the lamps at the entrance below and in the anteroom above, they began to feel as though they had brought uneasiness and discomfort into the house with them. In a house in which two sisters and their children, brothers, and neighbors were gathered together, probably on account of some family festivity or event, how could the presence of nineteen unknown officers possibly be welcome?

Upstairs at the entrance to the drawing room the officers were met by a tall, graceful old lady with black eyebrows and a long face, very much like the Empress Eugénie. Smiling graciously and majestically, she said she was glad and happy to see her guests, and apologized that her husband and she were on this occasion unable to invite *messieurs les officiers* to stay the night. From her beautiful majestic smile, which instantly vanished from her face every time she turned away from her guests, it was evident that she had seen numbers of officers in her day, that she was in no humor for them now, and if she invited them to her house and apologized for not doing more, it was only because her breeding and position in society required it of her.

When the officers went into the big dining room, there were about a dozen people, men and ladies, young and old, sitting at tea at the end of a long table. A group of men wrapped in a haze of cigar smoke was dimly visible behind their chairs; in the midst of them stood a lanky young man with red whiskers, talking loudly in English, with a burr. Through a door beyond the group could be seen a light room with pale blue furniture.

"Gentlemen, there are so many of you that it is impossible to introduce you all!" said the General in a loud voice, trying to sound very gay. "Make each other's acquaintance, gentlemen, without any ceremony!"

The officers—some with very serious and even stern faces, others with forced smiles, and all feeling extremely awkward—somehow made their bows and sat down to tea.

The most ill at ease of them all was Ryabovich—a short, somewhat stooped officer in spectacles, with whiskers like a lynx's. While some of his comrades assumed a serious expression, while others wore forced smiles, his face, his lynxlike whiskers, and spectacles seemed to say, "I am the shyest, most modest, and most undistinguished officer in the whole brigade!" At first, on going into the room and later, sitting down at table, he could not fix his attention on any one face or object. The faces, the dresses, the cut-glass decanters of brandy, the steam from the glasses, the molded cornices—all blended in one general impression that inspired in Ryabovich alarm and a desire to hide his head. Like a lecturer making his first appearance before the public, he saw everything that was before his eyes, but apparently only had a dim understanding of it (among physiologists this condition, when the subject sees but does not understand, is called "mental blindness"). After a little while, growing accustomed to his surroundings, Ryabovich regained his sight and began to observe. As a shy man, unused to society, what struck him first was that in which he had always been deficient—namely, the extraordinary boldness of his new acquaintances. Von Rabbeck, his wife, two elderly ladies, a young lady in a lilac dress, and the young man with the red whiskers, who was, it appeared, a younger son of von Rabbeck, very cleverly, as though they had rehearsed it beforehand, took seats among the officers, and at once got up a heated discussion in which the visitors could not help taking part. The lilac young lady hotly asserted that the artillery had a much better time than the cavalry and the infantry, while von Rabbeck and the elderly ladies maintained the opposite. A brisk interchange followed. Ryabovich looked at the lilac young lady who argued so hotly about what was unfamiliar and utterly uninteresting to her, and watched artificial smiles come and go on her face.

Von Rabbeck and his family skillfully drew the officers into the discussion, and meanwhile kept a sharp eye on their glasses and mouths to see whether all of them were drinking, whether all had enough sugar, why someone was not eating cakes or not drinking brandy. And the longer Ryabovich watched and listened, the more he was attracted by this insincere but splendidly disciplined family.

After tea the officers went into the drawing room. Lieutenant Lobytko's instinct had not deceived him. There were a great many girls and young married ladies. The "setter" lieutenant was soon standing by a very young blond in a black dress, and, bending over her jauntily, as though leaning on an unseen sword, smiled and twitched his shoulders coquettishly. He probably talked very interesting nonsense, for the blond looked at his well-fed face condescendingly and asked indifferently, "Really?" And from that indifferent "Really?" the "setter," had he been intelligent, might have concluded that she would never call him to heel.

The piano struck up; the melancholy strains of a waltz floated out of the wide open windows, and everyone, for some reason, remembered that it was spring, a May evening. Everyone was conscious of the fragrance of roses, of lilac, and of the young leaves of the poplar. Ryabovich, who felt the brandy he had drunk, under the influence of the music stole a glance toward the window, smiled, and began watching the movements of the women, and it seemed to him that the smell of roses, of poplars, and lilac came not from the garden, but from the ladies' faces and dresses.

Von Rabbeck's son invited a scraggy-looking young lady to dance, and waltzed round the room twice with her. Lobytko, gliding over the parquet floor, flew up to the lilac young lady and whirled her away. Dancing began. . . . Ryabovich stood near the door among those who were not dancing and looked on. He had never once danced in his whole life, and he had never once in his life put his arm round the waist of a respectable woman. He was highly delighted that a man should in the sight of all take a girl he did not know round the waist and offer her his shoulder to put her hand on, but he could not imagine himself in the position of such a man. There were times when he envied the boldness and swagger of his companions and was inwardly wretched; the knowledge that he was timid, round-shouldered, and uninteresting, that he had a long waist and lynxlike whiskers deeply mortified him, but with years he had grown used to this feeling, and now, looking at his comrades dancing or loudly talking, he no longer envied them, but only felt touched and mournful.

When the quadrille began, young von Rabbeck came up to those who were not dancing and invited two officers to have a game at billiards. The officers accepted and went with him out of the drawing room. Ryabovich, having nothing to do and wishing to take at least some part in the general movement, slouched after them. From the big drawing room they went into the little drawing room, then into a narrow corridor with a glass roof, and thence into a room in which on their entrance three sleepy-looking footmen jumped up quickly from couches. At last, after passing through a long succession of rooms, young von Rabbeck and the officers came into a small room where there was a billiard table. They began to play.

Ryabovich, who had never played any game but cards, stood near the billiard table and looked indifferently at the players, while they in unbuttoned coats, with cues in their hands, stepped about, made puns, and kept shouting out unintelligible words.

The players took no notice of him, and only now and then one of them, shoving him with his elbow or accidentally touching him with his cue, would turn round and say, "*Pardon!*" Before the first game was over he was weary of it, and began to feel that he was not wanted and in the way. . . . He felt disposed to return to the drawing room and he went out.

On his way back he met with a little adventure. When he had gone halfway he noticed that he had taken a wrong turning. He distinctly remembered that he ought to meet three sleepy footmen on his way, but he had passed five or six rooms, and those sleepy figures seemed to have been swallowed up by the earth. Noticing his mistake, he walked back a little way and turned to the right; he found himself in a little room which was in semi-darkness and which he had not seen on his way to the billiard room. After standing there a little while, he resolutely opened the first door that met his eyes and walked into an absolutely dark room. Straight ahead could be seen the crack in the doorway through which came a gleam of vivid light; from the other side of the door came the muffled sound of a melancholy mazurka.

Here, too, as in the drawing room, the windows were wide open and there was a smell of poplars, lilac, and roses. . . .

Ryabovich stood still in hesitation. . . . At that moment, to his surprise, he heard hurried footsteps and the rustling of a dress, a breathless feminine voice whispered, "At last!" and two soft, fragrant, unmistakably feminine arms were clasped about his neck; a warm cheek was pressed against his, and simultaneously there was the sound of a kiss. But at once the bestower of the kiss uttered a faint shriek and sprang away from him, as it seemed to Ryabovich, with disgust. He, too, almost shrieked and rushed toward the gleam of light at the door. . . .

When he returned to the drawing room his heart was palpitating and his hands were trembling so noticeably that he made haste to hide them behind his back. At first he was tormented by shame and dread that the whole drawing room knew that he had just been kissed and embraced by a woman. He shrank into himself and looked uneasily about him, but as he became convinced that people were dancing and talking as calmly as ever, he gave himself up entirely to the new sensation which he had never experienced before in his life. Something strange was happening to him. . . . His neck, round which soft, fragrant arms had so lately been clasped, seemed to him to be anointed with oil; on his left cheek near his mustache where the unknown had kissed him, there was a faint chilly tingling sensation as from peppermint drops, and the more he rubbed the place the more distinct was the chilly sensation; all of him, from head to foot, was full of a strange new feeling which grew stronger and stronger. . . . He wanted to dance, to talk, to run into the garden, to laugh aloud. . . . He quite forgot that he was round-shouldered and uninteresting, that he had lynxlike whiskers and an "undistinguished appearance" (that was how his appearance had been described by some ladies whose conversation he had accidentally overheard). When von Rabbeck's wife happened to pass by him, he gave her such a broad and friendly smile that she stood still and looked at him inquiringly.

"I like your house immensely!" he said, setting his spectacles straight.

The general's wife smiled and said that the house had belonged to her father; then she asked whether his parents were living, whether he had long been in the army, why he was so thin, and so on. . . . After receiving answers to her questions, she went on, and after his conversation with her his smiles were more friendly than ever, and he thought he was surrounded by splendid people. . . .

At supper Ryabovich ate mechanically everything offered him, drank, and without listening to anything, tried to understand what had just happened to him. . . . The adventure was of a mysterious and romantic character, but it was not difficult to explain it. No doubt some girl or young married lady had arranged a tryst with some man in the dark room, had waited a long time, and being nervous and excited, had taken Ryabovich for her hero; this was the more probable as Ryabovich had stood still hesitating in the dark room, so that he, too, had looked like a person waiting for something. . . . This was how Ryabovich explained to himself the kiss he had received.

"And who is she?" he wondered, looking round at the women's faces. "She must be young, for elderly ladies don't arrange rendezvous. That she was a lady, one could tell by the rustle of her dress, her perfume, her voice. . . ."

His eyes rested on the lilac young lady, and he thought her very attractive; she had beautiful shoulders and arms, a clever face, and a delightful voice. Ryabovich, looking at her, hoped that she and no one else was his unknown. . . . But she laughed somehow artificially and wrinkled her long nose, which seemed to him to make her look old. Then he turned his eyes upon the blond in a black dress. She was younger, simpler, and more genuine, had a charming brow, and drank very daintily out of her wineglass. Ryabovich now hoped that it was she. But soon he began to think her face flat, and fixed his eyes upon the one next her.

"It's difficult to guess," he thought, musing. "If one were to take only the shoulders and arms of the lilac girl, add the brow of the blond and the eyes of the one on the left of Lobytko, then. . ."

He made a combination of these things in his mind and so formed the image of the girl who had kissed him, the image that he desired but could not find at the table. . . .

After supper, replete and exhilarated, the officers began to take leave and say thank you. Von Rabbeck and his wife began again apologizing that they could not ask them to stay the night.

"Very, very glad to have met you, gentlemen," said von Rabbeck, and this time sincerely (probably because people are far more sincere and good humored at speeding their parting guests than on meeting them). "Delighted. Come again on your way back! Don't stand on ceremony! Where are you going? Do you want to go by the upper way? No, go across the garden; it's nearer by the lower road."

The officers went out into the garden. After the bright light and the noise the garden seemed very dark and quiet. They walked in silence all the way to the gate. They were a little drunk, in good spirits, and contented, but the darkness and silence made them thoughtful for a minute. Probably the same idea occurred to each one of them as to Ryabovich: would there ever come a time for them when, like von Rabbeck, they would have a large house, a family, a garden—when they, too, would be able to welcome people, even though insincerely, feed them, make them drunk and contented?

Going out of the garden gate, they all began talking at once and laughing loudly about nothing. They were walking now along the little path that led down to the river and then ran along the water's edge, winding round the bushes on the bank, the gulleys, and the willows that overhung the water. The bank and the path were scarcely visible, and the other bank was entirely plunged in darkness. Stars were reflected here and there in the dark water; they quivered and were broken up—and from that alone it could be seen that the river was flowing rapidly. It was still. Drowsy sandpipers cried plaintively on the farther bank, and in one of the bushes on the hither side a nightingale was trilling loudly, taking no notice of the crowd of officers. The officers stood round the bush, touched it, but the nightingale went on singing.

"What a fellow!" they exclaimed approvingly. "We stand beside him and he takes not a bit of notice! What a rascal!"

At the end of the way the path went uphill, and, skirting the church enclosure, led into the road. Here the officers, tired with walking uphill, sat down and lighted their cigarettes. On the farther bank of the river a murky red fire came into sight, and having nothing better to do, they spent a long time in discussing whether it was a camp fire or a light in a window, or something else. . . . Ryabovich, too, looked at the light, and he fancied that the light looked and winked at him, as though it knew about the kiss.

On reaching his quarters, Ryabovich undressed as quickly as possible and got into bed. Lobytko and Lieutenant Merzlyakov—a peaceable, silent fellow, who was considered in his own circle a highly educated officer, and was always, whenever it was possible, reading *The Messenger of Europe,* which he carried about with him everywhere—were quartered in the same cottage with Ryabovich. Lobytko undressed, walked up and down the room for a long while with the air of a man who has not been satisfied, and sent his orderly for beer. Merzlyakov got into bed, put a candle by his pillow and plunged into *The Messenger of Europe*.

"Who was she?" Ryabovich wondered, looking at the sooty ceiling.

His neck still felt as though he had been anointed with oil, and there was still the chilly sensation near his mouth as though from peppermint drops. The shoulders and arms of the young lady in lilac, the brow and the candid eyes of the blond in black, waists, dresses, and brooches, floated through his imagination. He tried to fix his attention on these images, but they danced about, broke up and flickered. When these images vanished altogether from the broad dark background which everyone sees when he closes his eyes, he began to hear hurried footsteps, the rustle of skirts, the sound of a kiss—and an intense baseless joy took possession of him. . . . Abandoning himself to this joy, he heard the orderly return and announce that there was no beer. Lobytko was terribly indignant, and began pacing up and down the room again.

"Well, isn't he an idiot?" he kept saying, stopping first before Ryabovich and then before Merzlyakov. "What a fool and a blockhead a man must be not to get hold of any beer! Eh? Isn't he a blackguard?"

"Of course you can't get beer here," said Merzlyakov, not removing his eyes from *The Messenger of Europe*.

"Oh! Is that your opinion?" Lobytko persisted. "Lord have mercy upon us, if you dropped me on the moon I'd find you beer and women directly! I'll go and find some at once. . . . You may call me a rascal if I don't!"

He spent a long time in dressing and pulling on his high boots, then finished smoking his cigarette in silence and went out.

"Rabbeck, Grabbeck, Labbeck," he muttered, stopping in the outer room. "I don't care to go alone, damn it all! Ryabovich, wouldn't you like to go for a walk? Eh?"

Receiving no answer, he returned, slowly undressed, and got into bed. Merzlyakov sighed, put *The Messenger of Europe* away, and extinguished the light.

"H'm! . . ." muttered Lobytko, lighting a cigarette in the dark.

Ryabovich pulled the bedclothes over his head, curled himself up in bed, and tried to gather together the flashing images in his mind and to combine them into a whole. But nothing came of it. He soon fell asleep, and his last thought was that someone had caressed him and made him happy—that something extraordinary, foolish, but joyful and delightful, had come into his life. The thought did not leave him even in his sleep.

When he woke up the sensations of oil on his neck and the chill of peppermint about his lips had gone, but joy flooded his heart just as the day before. He looked enthusiastically at the window frames, gilded by the light of the rising sun, and listened to the movement of the passersby in the street. People were talking loudly close to the window. Lebedetzky, the commander of Ryabovich's battery, who had only just overtaken the brigade, was talking to his sergeant at the top of his voice, having lost the habit of speaking in ordinary tones.

"What else?" shouted the commander.

"When they were shoeing the horses yesterday, your Honor, they injured Pigeon's hoof with a nail. The vet put on clay and vinegar; they are leading him apart now. Also, your Honor, Artemyev got drunk yesterday, and the lieutenant ordered him to be put in the limber of a spare gun-carriage."

The sergeant reported that Karpov had forgotten the new cords for the trumpets and the pegs for the tents, and that their Honors the officers had spent the previous evening visiting General von Rabbeck. In the middle of this conversation the red-bearded face of Lebedetzky appeared in the window. He screwed up his short-sighted eyes, looking at the sleepy faces of the officers, and greeted them.

"Is everything all right?" he asked.

"One of the horses has a sore neck from the new collar," answered Lobytko, yawning.

The commander sighed, thought a moment, and said in a loud voice:

"I am thinking of going to see Alexandra Yevgrafovna. I must call on her. Well, good-bye. I shall catch up with you in the evening."

A quarter of an hour later the brigade set off on its way. When it was moving along the road past the barns, Ryabovich looked at the house on the right. The blinds were down in all the windows. Evidently the household was still asleep. The one who had kissed Ryabovich the day before was asleep too. He tried to imagine her asleep. The wide-open window of the bedroom, the green branches peeping in, the morning freshness, the scent of the poplars, lilac, and roses, the bed, a chair, and on it the skirts that had rustled the day before, the little slippers, the little watch on the table—all this he pictured to himself clearly and distinctly, but the features of the face, the sweet sleepy smile, just what was characteristic and important, slipped through his imagination like quicksilver through the fingers. When he had ridden a third of a mile, he looked back: the yellow church, the house, and the river were all bathed in light; the river with its bright green banks, with the blue sky reflected in it and glints of silver in the sunshine here and there, was very beautiful. Ryabovich gazed for the last time at Mestechki, and he felt as sad as though he were parting with something very near and dear to him.

And before him on the road were none but long-familiar, uninteresting scenes. . . . To right and to left, fields of young rye and buckwheat with rooks hopping about in them; if one looked ahead, one saw dust and the backs of men's heads; if one looked back, one saw the same dust and faces. . . . Foremost of all marched four men with sabers—this was the vanguard. Next came the singers, and behind them the trumpeters on horseback. The vanguard and the singers, like torchbearers in a funeral procession, often forgot to keep the regulation distance and pushed a long way ahead. . . . Ryabovich was with the first cannon of the fifth battery. He could see all the four batteries moving in front of him. To a civilian the long tedious procession which is a brigade on the move seems an intricate and unintelligible muddle; one cannot understand why there are so many people round one cannon, and why it is drawn by so many horses in such a strange network of harness, as though it really were so terrible and heavy. To Ryabovich it was all perfectly comprehensible and therefore uninteresting. He had known for ever so long why at the head of each battery beside the office there rode a stalwart noncom, called bombardier; immediately behind him could be seen the horsemen of the first and then of the middle units. Ryabovich knew that of the horses on which they rode, those on the left were called one name, while those on the right were called another—it was all extremely uninteresting. Behind the horsemen came two shaft horses. On one of them sat a rider still covered with the dust of yesterday and with a clumsy and funny-looking wooden guard on his right leg. Ryabovich knew the object of this guard, and did not think it funny. All the riders waved their whips mechanically and shouted from time to time. The cannon itself was not presentable. On the limber lay sacks of oats covered with a tarpaulin, and the cannon itself was hung all over with kettles, soldiers' knapsacks, bags, and looked like some small harmless animal surrounded for some unknown reason by men and horses. To the leeward of it marched six men, the gunners, swinging their arms. After the cannon there came again more bombardiers, riders, shaft horses, and behind them another cannon, as unpresentable and unimpressive as the first. After the second came a third, a fourth; near the fourth there was an officer, and so on. There were six batteries in all in the brigade, and four cannon in each battery. The procession covered a third of a mile; it ended in a string of wagons near which an extremely appealing creature—the ass, Magar, brought by a battery commander from Turkey—paced pensively, his long-eared head drooping.

Ryabovich looked indifferently ahead and behind him, at the backs of heads and at faces; at any other time he would have been half asleep, but now he was entirely absorbed in his new agreeable thoughts. At first when the brigade was setting off on the march he tried to persuade himself that the incident of the kiss could only be interesting as a mysterious little adventure, that it was in reality trivial, and to think of it seriously, to say the least, was stupid; but now he bade farewell to logic and gave himself up to dreams. . . . At one moment he imagined himself in von Rabbeck's drawing room beside a girl who was like the young lady in lilac and the blond in black; then he would close his eyes and see himself with another, entirely unknown girl, whose features were very vague. In his imagination he talked, caressed her, leaned over her shoulder, pictured war, separation, then meeting again, supper with his wife, children. . . .

"Brakes on!" The word of command rang out every time they went downhill.

He, too, shouted, "Brakes on!" and was afraid this shout would disturb his reverie and bring him back to reality. . . .

As they passed by some landowner's estate Ryabovich looked over the fence into the garden. A long avenue, straight as a ruler, strewn with yellow sand and bordered with young birch trees, met his eyes. . . . With the eagerness of a man who indulges in daydreaming, he pictured to himself little feminine feet tripping along yellow sand, and quite unexpectedly had a clear vision in his imagination of her who had kissed him and whom he had succeeded in picturing to himself the evening before at supper. This image remained in his brain and did not desert him again.

At midday there was a shout in the rear near the string of wagons:

"Attention! Eyes to the left! Officers!"

The general of the brigade drove by in a carriage drawn by a pair of white horses. He stopped near the second battery and shouted something which no one understood. Several officers, among them Ryabovich, galloped up to him.

"Well? How goes it?" asked the general, blinking his red eyes. "Are there any sick?"

Receiving an answer, the general, a little skinny man, chewed, thought for a moment and said, addressing one of the officers:

"One of your drivers of the third cannon has taken off his leg guard and hung it on the fore part of the cannon, the rascal. Reprimand him."

He raised his eyes to Ryabovich and went on:

"It seems to me your breeching is too long."

Making a few other tedious remarks, the general looked at Lobytko and grinned.

"You look very melancholy today, Lieutenant Lobytko," he said. "Are you pining for Madame Lopuhova? Eh? Gentlemen, he is pining for Madame Lopuhova."

Madame Lopuhova was a very stout and very tall lady long past forty. The general, who had a predilection for large women, whatever their ages, suspected a similar taste in his officers. The officers smiled respectfully. The general, delighted at having said something very amusing and biting, laughed loudly, touched his coachman's back, and saluted. The carriage rolled on. . . .

"All I am dreaming about now which seems to me so impossible and unearthly is really quite an ordinary thing," thought Ryabovich, looking at the clouds of dust racing after the general's carriage. "It's all very ordinary, and everyone goes through it. . . . That general, for instance, was in love at one time; now he is married and has children. Captain Wachter, too, is married and loved, though the nape of his neck is very red and ugly and he has no waist. . . . Salmanov is coarse and too much of a Tartar, but he had a love affair that has ended in marriage. . . . I am the same as everyone else, and I, too, shall have the same experience as everyone else, sooner or later. . . ."

And the thought that he was an ordinary person and that his

life was ordinary delighted him and gave him courage. He pictured *her* and his happiness boldly, just as he liked. . . .

When the brigade reached their halting-place in the evening, and the officers were resting in their tents, Ryabovich, Merzlyakov, and Lobytko were sitting round a chest having supper. Merzlyakov ate without haste and, as he munched deliberately, read *The Messenger of Europe,* which he held on his knees. Lobytko talked incessantly and kept filling up his glass with beer, and Ryabovich, whose head was confused from dreaming all day long, drank and said nothing. After three glasses he got a little drunk, felt weak, and had an irresistible desire to relate his new sensations to his comrades.

"A strange thing happened to me at those von Rabbecks'," he began, trying to impart an indifferent and ironical tone to his voice. "You know I went into the billiard room. . . ."

He began describing very minutely the incident of the kiss, and a moment later relapsed into silence. . . . In the course of that moment he had told everything, and it surprised him dreadfully to find how short a time it took him to tell it. He had imagined that he could have been telling the story of the kiss till next morning. Listening to him, Lobytko, who was a great liar and consequently believed no one, looked at him skeptically and laughed. Merzlyakov twitched his eyebrows and, without removing his eyes from *The Messenger of Europe,* said:

"That's an odd thing! How strange! . . . throws herself on a man's neck, without addressing him by name. . . . She must have been some sort of lunatic."

"Yes, she must," Ryabovich agreed.

"A similar thing once happened to me," said Lobytko, assuming a scared expression. "I was going last year to Kovno. . . . I took a second-class ticket. The train was crammed, and it was impossible to sleep. I gave the guard half a ruble; he took my luggage and led me to another compartment. . . . I lay down and covered myself with a blanket. . . . It was dark, you understand. Suddenly I felt someone touch me on the shoulder and breathe in my face. I made a movement with my hand and felt somebody's elbow. . . . I opened my eyes and only imagine—a woman. Black eyes, lips red as a prime salmon, nostrils breathing passionately—a bosom like a buffer. . . ."

"Excuse me," Merzlyakov interrupted calmly. "I understand about the bosom, but how could you see the lips if it was dark?"

Lobytko began trying to put himself right and laughing at

Merzlyakov's being so dull witted. It made Ryabovich wince. He walked away from the chest, got into bed, and vowed never to confide again.

Camp life began. . . . The days flowed by, one very much like another. All those days Ryabovich felt, thought, and behaved as though he were in love. Every morning when his orderly handed him what he needed for washing, and he sluiced his head with cold water, he recalled that there was something warm and delightful in his life.

In the evenings when his comrades began talking of love and women, he would listen and draw up closer; and he wore the expression of a soldier listening to the description of a battle in which he has taken part. And on the evenings when the officers, out on a spree with the setter Lobytko at their head, made Don-Juanesque raids on the neighboring "suburb," and Ryabovich took part in such excursions, he always was sad, felt profoundly guilty, and inwardly begged *her* forgiveness. . . . In hours of leisure or on sleepless nights when he felt moved to recall his childhood, his father and mother—everything near and dear, in fact—he invariably thought of Mestechki, the queer horse, von Rabbeck, his wife who resembled Empress Eugénie, the dark room, the light in the crack of the door. . . .

On the thirty-first of August he was returning from the camp, not with the whole brigade, but with only two batteries. He was dreamy and excited all the way, as though he were going home. He had an intense longing to see again the queer horse, the church, the insincere family of the von Rabbecks, the dark room. The "inner voice," which so often deceives lovers, whispered to him for some reason that he would surely see her. . . . And he was tortured by the questions: How would he meet her? What would he talk to her about? Had she forgotten the kiss? If the worst came to the worst, he thought, even if he did not meet her, it would be a pleasure to him merely to go through the dark room and recall the past. . . .

Toward evening there appeared on the horizon the familiar church and white barns. Ryabovich's heart raced. . . . He did not hear the officer who was riding beside him and saying something to him, he forgot everything and looked eagerly at the river shining in the distance, at the roof of the house, at the dovecote round which the pigeons were circling in the light of the setting sun.

When they reached the church and were listening to the quartermaster, he expected every second that a man on horseback would come round the church enclosure and invite the officers to tea, but . . . the quartermaster ended his report, the officers dismounted and strolled off to the village, and the man on horseback did not appear.

"Von Rabbeck will hear at once from the peasants that we have come and will send for us," thought Ryabovich as he went into the peasant cottage, unable to understand why a comrade was lighting a candle and why the orderlies were hastening to get the samovars going.

A crushing uneasiness took possession of him. He lay down, then got up and looked out of the window to see whether the messenger were coming. But there was no sign of him.

He lay down again, but half an hour later he got up and, unable to restrain his uneasiness, went into the street and strode toward the church. It was dark and deserted in the square near the church enclosure. Three soldiers were standing silent in a row where the road began to go downhill. Seeing Ryabovich, they roused themselves and saluted. He returned the salute and began to go down the familiar path.

On the farther bank of the river the whole sky was flooded with crimson: the moon was rising; two peasant women, talking loudly, were pulling cabbage leaves in the kitchen garden; beyond the kitchen garden there were some cottages that formed a dark mass. . . . Everything on the near side of the river was just as it had been in May: the path, the bushes, the willows overhanging the water . . . but there was no sound of the brave nightingale and no scent of poplar and young grass.

Reaching the garden, Ryabovich looked in at the gate. The garden was dark and still. . . . He could see nothing but the white stems of the nearest birch trees and a little bit of the avenue; all the rest melted together into a dark mass. Ryabovich looked and listened eagerly, but after waiting for a quarter of an hour without hearing a sound or catching a glimpse of a light, he trudged back. . . .

He went down to the river. The general's bathing cabin and the bath sheets on the rail of the little bridge showed white before him. . . . He walked up on the bridge, stood a little, and quite unnecessarily touched a sheet. It felt rough and cold. He looked down at the water. . . . The river ran rapidly and with a faintly audible gurgle round the piles of the bathing cabin. The red moon was reflected near the left bank; little ripples ran over the reflection, stretching it out, breaking it into bits, and seemed trying to carry it away. . . .

"How stupid, how stupid!" thought Ryabovich, looking at the running water. "How unintelligent it all is!"

Now that he expected nothing, the incident of the kiss, his impatience, his vague hopes and disappointment presented themselves to him in a clear light. It no longer seemed to him strange that the general's messenger never came and that he would never see the girl who had accidentally kissed him instead of someone else; on the contrary, it would have been strange if he had seen her. . . .

The water was running, he knew not where or why, just as it did in May. At that time it had flowed into a great river, from the great river into the sea; then it had risen in vapor, turned into rain, and perhaps the very same water was running now before Ryabovich's eyes again. . . . What for? Why?

And the whole world, the whole of life, seemed to Ryabovich an unintelligible, aimless jest. . . . And turning his eyes from the water and looking at the sky, he remembered again how Fate in the person of an unknown woman had by chance caressed him, he recalled his summer dreams and fancies, and his life struck him as extraordinarily meager, poverty-stricken, and drab. . . .

When he had returned to the cottage he did not find a single comrade. The orderly informed him that they had all gone to "General Fontryabkin, who had sent a messenger on horseback to invite them. . . ."

For an instant there was a flash of joy in Ryabovich's heart, but he quenched it at once, got into bed, and in his wrath with his fate, as though to spite it, did not go to the general's.

THE LADY WITH THE PET DOG

A new person, it was said, had appeared on the esplanade: a lady with a pet dog. Dmitry Dmitrich Gurov, who had spent a fortnight at Yalta and had got used to the place, had also begun to take an interest in new arrivals. As he sat in Vernet's confectionery shop he saw, walking on the esplanade, a fair-haired young woman of medium height, wearing a beret; a white Pomeranian was trotting behind her.

And afterwards he met her in the public garden and in the square several times a day. She walked alone, always wearing the same beret and always with the white dog; no one knew who she was and everyone called her simply "the lady with the pet dog."

"If she is here alone without a husband or friends," Gurov reflected, "it wouldn't be a bad thing to make her acquaintance."

He was under forty, but he already had a daughter twelve years old, and two sons at school. They had found a wife for him when he was very young, a student in his second year, and by now she seemed half as old again as he. She was a tall, erect woman with dark eyebrows, stately and dignified and, as she said of herself, intellectual. She read a great deal, used simplified spelling in her letters, called her husband, not Dmitry, but Dimitry, while he privately considered her of limited intelligence, narrow-minded, dowdy, was afraid of her, and did not like to be at home. He had begun being unfaithful to her long ago—had been unfaithful to her often and, probably for that reason, almost always spoke ill of women, and when they were talked of in his presence used to call them "the inferior race."

It seemed to him that he had been sufficiently tutored by bitter experience to call them what he pleased, and yet he could not have lived without "the inferior race" for two days together. In the company of men he was bored and ill at ease, he was chilly and uncommunicative with them; but when he was among women he felt free, and knew what to speak to them about and how to comport himself; and even to be silent with them was no strain on him. In his appearance, in his character, in his whole makeup there was something attractive and elusive that disposed women in his favor and allured them. He knew that, and some force seemed to draw him to them too.

Oft-repeated and really bitter experience had taught him long ago that with decent people—particularly Moscow people—who are irresolute and slow to move, every affair which at first seems a light and charming adventure inevitably grows into a whole problem of extreme complexity, and in the end a painful situation is created. But at every new meeting with an interesting woman this lesson of experience seemed to slip from his memory, and he was eager for life, and everything seemed so simple and diverting.

One evening while he was dining in the public garden the lady in the beret walked up without haste to take the next table. Her expression, her gait, her dress, and the way she did her hair told him that she belonged to the upper class, that she was married, that she was in Yalta for the first time and alone, and that she was bored there. The stories told of the immorality in Yalta are to a great extent untrue; he despised them, and knew that such stories were made up for the most part by persons who would have been glad to sin themselves if they had had the chance; but when the lady sat down at the next table three paces from him, he recalled these stories of easy conquests, of trips to the mountains, and the tempting thought of a swift, fleeting liaison, a romance with an unknown woman of whose very name he was ignorant suddenly took hold of him.

He beckoned invitingly to the Pomeranian, and when the dog approached him, shook his finger at it. The Pomeranian growled; Gurov threatened it again.

The lady glanced at him and at once dropped her eyes.

"He doesn't bite," she said and blushed.

"May I give him a bone?" he asked; and when she nodded he inquired affably, "Have you been in Yalta long?"

"About five days."

"And I am dragging out the second week here."

There was a short silence.

"Time passes quickly, and yet it is so dull here!" she said, not looking at him.

"It's only the fashion to say it's dull here. A provincial will live in Belyov or Zhizdra and not be bored, but when he comes here it's 'Oh, the dullness! Oh, the dust!' One would think he came from Granada."

She laughed. Then both continued eating in silence, like strangers, but after dinner they walked together and there sprang up between them the light banter of people who are free and contented, to whom it does not matter where they go or what they talk about. They walked and talked of the strange light on the sea: the water was a soft, warm, lilac color, and there was a golden band of moonlight upon it. They talked of how sultry it was after a hot day. Gurov told her that he was a native of Moscow, that he had studied languages and literature at the university, but had a post in a bank; that at one time he had trained to become an opera singer but had given it up, that he owned two houses in Moscow. And he learned from her that she had grown up in Petersburg, but had lived in S—— since her marriage two years previously, that she was going to stay in Yalta for about another month, and that her husband, who needed a rest, too, might perhaps come to fetch her. She was not certain whether her husband was a member of a government board or served on a Zemstvo council, and this amused her. And Gurov learned, too, that her name was Anna Sergeyevna.

Afterwards in his room at the hotel he thought about her—and was certain that he would meet her the next day. It was bound to happen. Getting into bed he recalled that she had been a schoolgirl only recently, doing lessons like his own daughter; he thought how much timidity and angularity there was still in her laugh and her manner of talking with a stranger. It must have been the first time in her life that she was alone in a setting in which she was followed, looked at, and spoken to for one secret purpose alone, which she could hardly fail to guess. He thought of her slim, delicate throat, her lovely gray eyes.

"There's something pathetic about her, though," he thought, and dropped off.

II

A week had passed since they had struck up an acquaintance. It was a holiday. It was close indoors, while in the street the wind whirled the dust about and blew people's hats off. One was thirsty all day, and Gurov often went into the restaurant and offered Anna Sergeyevna a soft drink or ice cream. One did not know what to do with oneself.

In the evening when the wind had abated they went out on the pier to watch the steamer come in. There were a great many people walking about the dock; they had come to welcome someone and they were carrying bunches of flowers. And two peculiarities of a festive Yalta crowd stood out: the elderly ladies were dressed like young ones and there were many generals.

Owing to the choppy sea, the steamer arrived late, after sunset, and it was a long time tacking about before it put in at the pier. Anna Sergeyevna peered at the steamer and the passengers through her lorgnette as though looking for acquaintances, and whenever she turned to Gurov her eyes were shining. She talked a great deal and asked questions jerkily, forgetting the next moment what she had asked; then she lost her lorgnette in the crush.

The festive crowd began to disperse; it was now too dark to see people's faces; there was no wind anymore, but Gurov and Anna Sergeyevna still stood as though waiting to see someone else come off the steamer. Anna Sergeyevna was silent now, and sniffed her flowers without looking at Gurov.

"The weather has improved this evening," he said. "Where shall we go now? Shall we drive somewhere?"

She did not reply.

Then he looked at her intently, and suddenly embraced her and kissed her on the lips, and the moist fragrance of her flowers enveloped him; and at once he looked round him anxiously, wondering if anyone had seen them.

"Let us go to your place," he said softly. And they walked off together rapidly.

The air in her room was close and there was the smell of the perfume she had bought at the Japanese shop. Looking at her,

Gurov thought: "What encounters life offers!" From the past he preserved the memory of carefree, good-natured women whom love made gay and who were grateful to him for the happiness he gave them, however brief it might be; and of women like his wife who loved without sincerity, with too many words, affectedly, hysterically, with an expression that it was not love or passion that engaged them but something more significant; and of two or three others, very beautiful, frigid women, across whose faces would suddenly flit a rapacious expression—an obstinate desire to take from life more than it could give, and these were women no longer young, capricious, unreflecting, domineering, unintelligent, and when Gurov grew cold to them their beauty aroused his hatred, and the lace on their lingerie seemed to him to resemble scales.

But here there was the timidity, the angularity of inexperienced youth, a feeling of awkwardness; and there was a sense of embarrassment, as though someone had suddenly knocked at the door. Anna Sergeyevna, "the lady with the pet dog," treated what had happened in a peculiar way, very seriously, as though it were her fall—so it seemed, and this was odd and inappropriate. Her features drooped and faded, and her long hair hung down sadly on either side of her face; she grew pensive and her dejected pose was that of a Magdalene in a picture by an old master.

"It's not right," she said. "You don't respect me now, you first of all."

why There was a watermelon on the table. Gurov cut himself a slice and began eating it without haste. They were silent for at least half an hour.

There was something touching about Anna Sergeyevna; she had the purity of a well-bred, naive woman who has seen little of life. The single candle burning on the table barely illumined her face, yet it was clear that she was unhappy.

"Why should I stop respecting you, darling?" asked Gurov. "You don't know what you're saying."

"God forgive me," she said, and her eyes filled with tears. "It's terrible."

"It's as though you were trying to exonerate yourself."

"How can I exonerate myself? No. I am a bad, low woman; I despise myself and I have no thought of exonerating myself. It's not my husband but myself I have deceived. And not only just now; I have been deceiving myself for a long time. My husband may be a good, honest man, but he is a flunky! I don't know what he does, what his work is, but I know he is a flunky! I was twenty when I married him. I was tormented by curiosity; I wanted something better. 'There must be a different sort of life,' I said to myself. I wanted to live! To live, to live! Curiosity kept eating at me—you don't understand it, but I swear to God I could no longer control myself; something was going on in me: I could not be held back. I told my husband I was ill, and came here. And here I have been walking about as though in a daze, as though I were mad; and now I have become a vulgar, vile woman whom anyone may despise."

Gurov was already bored with her; he was irritated by her naive tone, by her repentance, so unexpected and so out of place; but for the tears in her eyes he might have thought she was joking or playacting.

"I don't understand, my dear," he said softly. "What do you want?"

She hid her face on his breast and pressed close to him.

"Believe me, believe me, I beg you," she said, "I love honesty and purity, and sin is loathsome to me; I don't know what I'm doing. Simple people say, 'The Evil One has led me astray.' And I may say of myself now that the Evil One has led me astray."

"Quiet, quiet," he murmured.

He looked into her fixed, frightened eyes, kissed her, spoke to her softly and affectionately, and by degrees she calmed down, and her gaiety returned; both began laughing.

Afterwards when they went out there was not a soul on the esplanade. The town with its cypresses looked quite dead, but the sea was still sounding as it broke upon the beach; a single launch was rocking on the waves and on it a lantern was blinking sleepily.

They found a cab and drove to Oreanda.

"I found out your surname in the hall just now: it was written on the board—von Dideritz," said Gurov. "Is your husband German?"

"No; I believe his grandfather was German, but he is Greek Orthodox himself."

At Oreanda they sat on a bench not far from the church, looked down at the sea, and were silent. Yalta was barely visible through the morning mist; white clouds rested motionlessly on the mountaintops. The leaves did not stir on the trees, cicadas twanged, and the monotonous muffled sound of the sea that rose from below spoke of the peace, the eternal sleep awaiting us. So it rumbled below when there was no Yalta, no Oreanda here; so it rumbles now, and it will rumble as indifferently and as hollowly when we are no more. And in this constancy, in this complete indifference to the life and death of each of us, there lies, perhaps, a pledge of our eternal salvation, of the unceasing advance of life upon earth, of unceasing movement toward perfection. Sitting beside a young woman who in the dawn seemed so lovely, Gurov, soothed and spellbound by these magical surroundings—the sea, the mountains, the clouds, the wide sky—thought how everything is really beautiful in this world when one reflects: everything except what we think or do ourselves when we forget the higher aims of life and our own human dignity.

A man strolled up to them—probably a guard—looked at them and walked away. And this detail, too, seemed so mysterious and beautiful. They saw a steamer arrive from Feodosia, its lights extinguished in the glow of dawn.

"There is dew on the grass," said Anna Sergeyevna, after a silence.

"Yes, it's time to go home."

They returned to the city.

Then they met every day at twelve o'clock on the esplanade, lunched and dined together, took walks, admired the sea. She complained that she slept badly, that she had palpitations, asked the same questions, troubled now by jealousy and now by the fear that he did not respect her sufficiently. And often in the square or the public garden, when there was no one near them, he suddenly drew her to him and kissed her passionately. Complete idleness, these kisses in broad daylight exchanged furtively in dread of someone's seeing them, the heat, the smell of the sea, and the continual flitting before his eyes of idle, well-dressed, well-fed people, worked a complete change in him; he kept telling Anna Sergeyevna how beautiful she was, how seductive, was urgently passionate; he would not move a step away from her, while she was often pensive and continually pressed him to confess that he did not respect her, did not love her in the least, and saw in her nothing but a common woman. Almost every evening rather late they drove somewhere out of town, to Oreanda or to the waterfall; and the excursion was always a success, the scenery invariably impressed them as beautiful and magnificent.

They were expecting her husband, but a letter came from him saying that he had eye trouble, and begging his wife to return home as soon as possible. Anna Sergeyevna made haste to go.

"It's a good thing I am leaving," she said to Gurov. "It's the hand of Fate!"

She took a carriage to the railway station, and he went with her. They were driving the whole day. When she had taken her place in the express, and when the second bell had rung, she said, "Let me look at you once more—let me look at you again. Like this."

She was not crying but was so sad that she seemed ill, and her face was quivering.

"I shall be thinking of you—remembering you," she said. "God bless you; be happy. Don't remember evil against me. We are parting forever—it has to be, for we ought never to have met. Well, God bless you."

The train moved off rapidly, its lights soon vanished, and a minute later there was no sound of it, as though everything had conspired to end as quickly as possible that sweet trance, that madness. Left alone on the platform, and gazing into the dark distance, Gurov listened to the twang of the grasshoppers and the hum of the telegraph wires, feeling as though he had just waked up. And he reflected, musing, that there had now been another episode or adventure in his life, and it, too, was at an end, and nothing was left of it but a memory. He was moved, sad, and slightly remorseful: this young woman whom he would never meet again had not been happy with him; he had been warm and affectionate with her, but yet in his manner, his tone, and his caresses there had been a shade of light irony, the slightly coarse arrogance of a happy male who was, besides, almost twice her age. She had constantly called him kind, exceptional, high-minded; obviously he had seemed to her different from what he really was, so he had involuntarily deceived her.

Here at the station there was already a scent of autumn in the air; it was a chilly evening.

"It is time for me to go north too," thought Gurov as he left the platform. "High time!"

III

At home in Moscow the winter routine was already established: the stoves were heated, and in the morning it was still dark when the children were having breakfast and getting ready for school, and the nurse would light the lamp for a short time. There were frosts already. When the first snow falls, on the first day the sleighs are out, it is pleasant to see the white earth, the white roofs; one draws easy, delicious breaths, and the season brings back the days of one's youth. The old limes and birches, white with hoarfrost, have a good-natured look; they are closer to one's heart than cypresses and palms, and near them one no longer wants to think of mountains and the sea.

Gurov, a native of Moscow, arrived there on a fine frosty day, and when he put on his fur coat and warm gloves and took a walk along Petrovka, and when on Saturday night he heard the bells ringing, his recent trip and the places he had visited lost all charm for him. Little by little he became immersed in Moscow life, greedily read three newspapers a day, and declared that he did not read the Moscow papers on principle. He already felt a longing for restaurants, clubs, formal dinners, anniversary celebrations, and it flattered him to entertain distinguished lawyers and actors, and to play cards with a professor at the physicians' club. He could eat a whole portion of meat stewed with pickled cabbage and served in a pan, Moscow style.

A month or so would pass and the image of Anna Sergeyevna, it seemed to him, would become misty in his memory, and only from time to time he would dream of her with her touching smile as he dreamed of others. But more than a month went by, winter came into its own, and everything was still clear in his memory as though he had parted from Anna Sergeyevna only yesterday. And his memories glowed more and more vividly. When in the evening stillness the voices of his children preparing their lessons reached his study, or when he listened to a song or to an organ playing in a restaurant, or when the storm howled in the chimney, suddenly everything would rise up in his memory: what had happened on the pier and the early morning with the mist on the mountains, and the steamer coming from Feodosia, and the kisses. He would pace about his room a long time, remembering and smiling; then his memories passed into reveries, and in his imagination the past would mingle with what was to come. He did not dream of Anna Sergeyevna, but she followed him about everywhere and watched him. When he shut his eyes he saw her before him as though she were there in the flesh, and she seemed to him lovelier, younger, tenderer than she had been, and he imagined himself a finer man than he had been in Yalta. Of evenings she peered out at him from the bookcase, from the fireplace, from the corner—he heard her breathing, the caressing rustle of her clothes. In the street he followed the women with his eyes, looking for someone who resembled her.

Already he was tormented by a strong desire to share his memories with someone. But in his home it was impossible to talk of his love, and he had no one to talk to outside; certainly he could not confide in his tenants or in anyone at the bank. And what was there to talk about? He hadn't loved her then, had he? Had there been anything beautiful, poetical, edifying, or simply interesting in his relations with Anna Sergeyevna? And he was forced to talk vaguely of love, of women, and no one guessed what he meant; only his wife would twitch her black eyebrows and say, "The part of a philanderer does not suit you at all, Dimitry."

One evening, coming out of the physicians' club with an official with whom he had been playing cards, he could not resist saying:

"If you only knew what a fascinating woman I became acquainted with at Yalta!"

The official got into his sledge and was driving away, but turned suddenly and shouted:

"Dmitry Dmitrich!"

"What is it?"

"You were right this evening: the sturgeon was a bit high."

These words, so commonplace, for some reason moved Gurov to indignation, and struck him as degrading and unclean. What savage manners, what mugs! What stupid nights, what dull, humdrum days! Frenzied gambling, gluttony, drunkenness, continual talk always about the same things! Futile pursuits and conversations always about the same topics take up the better part of one's time, the better part of one's strength, and in the end there is left a life clipped and wingless, an absurd mess, and there is no escaping or getting away from it—just as though one were in a madhouse or a prison.

Gurov, boiling with indignation, did not sleep all night. And he had a headache all the next day. And the following nights too he slept badly; he sat up in bed, thinking, or paced up and down his room. He was fed up with his children, fed up with the bank; he had no desire to go anywhere or to talk of anything.

In December during the holidays he prepared to take a trip and told his wife he was going to Petersburg to do what he could for a young friend—and he set off for S——. What for? He did not know, himself. He wanted to see Anna Sergeyevna and talk with her, to arrange a rendezvous if possible.

He arrived at S—— in the morning, and at the hotel took the best room, in which the floor was covered with gray army cloth, and on the table there was an inkstand, gray with dust and topped by a figure on horseback, its hat in its raised hand and its head broken off. The porter gave him the necessary information: von Dideritz lived in a house of his own on Staro-Goncharnaya Street, not far from the hotel: he was rich and lived well and kept his own horses; everyone in the town knew him. The porter pronounced the name "Dridiritz."

Without haste Gurov made his way to Staro-Goncharnaya Street and found the house. Directly opposite the house stretched a long gray fence studded with nails.

"A fence like that would make one run away," thought Gurov, looking now at the fence, now at the windows of the house.

He reflected: this was a holiday, and the husband was apt to be at home. And in any case, it would be tactless to go into the house and disturb her. If he were to send her a note it might fall into her husband's hands, and that might spoil everything. The best thing was to rely on chance. And he kept walking up and down the street and along the fence, waiting for the chance. He saw a beggar go in at the gate and heard the dogs attack him; then an hour later he heard a piano, and the sound came to him faintly and indistinctly. Probably it was Anna Sergeyevna playing. The front door opened suddenly, and an old woman came out, followed by the familiar white Pomeranian. Gurov was on the point of calling to the dog, but his heart began beating violently, and in his excitement he could not remember the Pomeranian's name.

He kept walking up and down, and hated the gray fence more and more, and by now he thought irritably that Anna Sergeyevna had forgotten him and was perhaps already diverting herself with another man, and that that was very natural in a young woman who from morning till night had to look at that damn fence. He went back to his hotel room and sat on the couch for a long while not knowing what to do, then he had dinner and a long nap.

"How stupid and annoying all this is!" he thought when he woke and looked at the dark windows: it was already evening.

"Here I've had a good sleep for some reason. What am I going to do at night?"

He sat on the bed, which was covered with a cheap gray blanket of the kind seen in hospitals, and he twitted himself in his vexation:

"So there's your lady with the pet dog. There's your adventure. A nice place to cool your heels in."

That morning at the station a playbill in large letters had caught his eye. *The Geisha* was to be given for the first time. He thought of this and drove to the theater.

"It's quite possible that she goes to first nights," he thought.

The theater was full. As in all provincial theaters, there was a haze above the chandelier, the gallery was noisy and restless; in the front row, before the beginning of the performance, the local dandies were standing with their hands clasped behind their backs; in the governor's box the governor's daughter, wearing a boa, occupied the front seat, while the governor himself hid modestly behind the portiere and only his hands were visible; the curtain swayed; the orchestra was a long time tuning up. While the audience were coming in and taking their seats, Gurov scanned the faces eagerly.

Anna Sergeyevna, too, came in. She sat down in the third row, and when Gurov looked at her his heart contracted, and he understood clearly that in the whole world there was no human being so near, so precious, and so important to him; she, this little, undistinguished woman, lost in a provincial crowd, with a vulgar lorgnette in her hand, filled his whole life now, was his sorrow and his joy, the only happiness that he now desired for himself, and to the sounds of the bad orchestra, of the miserable local violins, he thought how lovely she was. He thought and dreamed.

A young man with small side-whiskers, very tall and stooped, came in with Anna Sergeyevna and sat down beside her; he nodded his head at every step and seemed to be bowing continually. Probably this was the husband whom at Yalta, in an access of bitter feeling, she had called a flunky. And there really was in his lanky figure, his side-whiskers, his small bald patch, something of a flunky's retiring manner; his smile was mawkish, and in his buttonhole there was an academic badge like a waiter's number.

During the first intermission the husband went out to have a smoke; she remained in her seat. Gurov, who was also sitting in the orchestra, went up to her and said in a shaky voice, with a forced smile:

"Good evening!"

She glanced at him and turned pale, then looked at him again in horror, unable to believe her eyes, and gripped the fan and the lorgnette tightly together in her hands, evidently trying to keep herself from fainting. Both were silent. She was sitting, he was standing, frightened by her distress and not daring to take a seat beside her. The violins and the flute that were being tuned up sang out. He suddenly felt frightened: it seemed as if all the people in the boxes were looking at them. She got up and went hurriedly to the exit; he followed her, and both of them walked blindly along the corridors and up and down stairs, and figures in the uniforms prescribed for magistrates, teachers, and officials of the Department of Crown Lands, all wearing badges, flitted before their eyes, as did also ladies and fur coats on hangers; they were conscious of drafts and the smell of stale tobacco. And Gurov, whose heart was beating violently, thought:

"Oh, Lord! Why are these people here and this orchestra!"

And at that instant he suddenly recalled how when he had seen Anna Sergeyevna off at the station he had said to himself that all was over between them and that they would never meet again. But how distant the end still was!

On the narrow, gloomy staircase over which it said "To the Amphitheater," she stopped.

"How you frightened me!" she said, breathing hard, still pale and stunned. "Oh, how you frightened me! I am barely alive. Why did you come? Why?"

"But do understand, Anna, do understand—" he said hurriedly, under his breath. "I implore you, do understand—"

She looked at him with fear, with entreaty, with love; she looked at him intently, to keep his features more distinctly in her memory.

"I suffer so," she went on, not listening to him. "All this time I have been thinking of nothing but you; I live only by the thought of you. And I wanted to forget, to forget; but why, oh, why have you come?"

On the landing above them two highschool boys were looking down and smoking, but it was all the same to Gurov; he drew Anna Sergeyevna to him and began kissing her face and her hands.

"What are you doing, what are you doing!" she was saying in horror, pushing him away. "We have lost our senses. Go away today; go away at once— I conjure you by all that is sacred, I implore you— People are coming this way!"

Someone was walking up the stairs.

"You must leave," Anna Sergeyevna went on in a whisper. "Do you hear, Dmitry Dmitrich? I will come and see you in Moscow. I have never been happy; I am unhappy now, and I never, never shall be happy, never! So don't make me suffer still more! I swear I'll come to Moscow. But now let us part. My dear, good, precious one, let us part!"

She pressed his hand and walked rapidly downstairs, turning to look round at him, and from her eyes he could see that she really was unhappy. Gurov stood for a while, listening, then when all grew quiet, he found his coat and left the theater.

IV

And Anna Sergeyevna began coming to see him in Moscow. Once every two or three months she left S——, telling her husband that she was going to consult a doctor about a woman's ailment from which she was suffering—and her husband did and did not believe her. When she arrived in Moscow she would stop at the Slavyansky Bazaar Hotel, and at once send a man in a red cap to Gurov. Gurov came to see her, and no one in Moscow knew of it.

Once he was going to see her in this way on a winter morning (the messenger had come the evening before and not found him in). With him walked his daughter, whom he wanted to take to school: it was on the way. Snow was coming down in big wet flakes.

"It's three degrees above zero, and yet it's snowing," Gurov was saying to his daughter. "But this temperature prevails only on the surface of the earth; in the upper layers of the atmosphere there is quite a different temperature."

"And why doesn't it thunder in winter, Papa?"

He explained that too. He talked, thinking all the while that he was on his way to a rendezvous, and no living soul knew of it, and probably no one would ever know. He had two lives: an open one, seen and known by all who needed to know it, full of conventional truth and conventional falsehood, exactly like the lives of his friends and acquaintances; and another life that went on in secret. And through some strange, perhaps accidental, combination of circumstances, everything that was of interest and importance to him, everything that was essential to him, everything about which he felt sincerely and did not deceive himself, everything that constituted the core of his life was going on concealed from others; while all that was false, the shell in which he hid to cover the truth—his work at the bank, for instance, his discussions at the club, his references to the "inferior race," his appearances at anniversary celebrations with his wife—all that went on in the open. Judging others by himself, he did not believe what he saw, and always fancied that every man led his real, most interesting life under cover of secrecy as under cover of night. The personal life of every individual is based on secrecy, and perhaps it is partly for that reason that civilized man is so nervously anxious that personal privacy should be respected.

Having taken his daughter to school, Gurov went on to the Slavyansky Bazaar Hotel. He took off his fur coat in the lobby, went upstairs, and knocked gently at the door. Anna Sergeyevna, wearing his favorite gray dress, exhausted by the journey and by waiting, had been expecting him since the previous evening. She was pale and looked at him without a smile, and he had hardly entered when she flung herself on his breast. Their kiss was a long, lingering one, as though they had not seen one another for two years.

"Well, darling, how are you getting on there?" he asked. "What news?"

"Wait; I'll tell you in a moment— I can't speak."

She could not speak; she was crying. She turned away from him and pressed her handkerchief to her eyes.

"Let her have her cry; meanwhile I'll sit down," he thought, and he seated himself in an armchair.

Then he rang and ordered tea, and while he was having his tea she remained standing at the window with her back to him. She was crying out of sheer agitation, in the sorrowful consciousness that their life was so sad; that they could only see each other in secret and had to hide from people like thieves! Was it not a broken life?

"Come, stop now, dear!" he said.

It was plain to him that this love of theirs would not be over soon, that the end of it was not in sight. Anna Sergeyevna was growing more and more attached to him. She adored him, and it was unthinkable to tell her that their love was bound to come to an end some day; besides, she would not have believed it!

He went up to her and took her by the shoulders, to fondle her and say something diverting, and at that moment he caught sight of himself in the mirror.

His hair was already beginning to turn gray. And it seemed odd to him that he had grown so much older in the last few years, and lost his looks. The shoulders on which his hands rested were warm and heaving. He felt compassion for this life, still so warm and lovely, but probably already about to begin to fade and wither like his own. Why did she love him so much? He always seemed to women different from what he was, and they loved in him not himself, but the man whom their imagination created and whom they had been eagerly seeking all their lives; and afterwards, when they saw their mistake, they loved him nevertheless. And not one of them had been happy with him. In the past he had met women, come together with them, parted from them, but he had never once loved; it was anything you please, but not love. And only now when his head was gray he had fallen in love, really, truly—for the first time in his life.

Anna Sergeyevna and he loved each other as people do who are very close and intimate, like man and wife, like tender friends; it seemed to them that fate itself had meant them for one another, and they could not understand why he had a wife and she a husband; and it was as though they were a pair of migratory birds, male and female, caught and forced to live in different cages. They forgave each other what they were ashamed of in their past, they forgave everything in the present, and felt that this love of theirs had altered them both.

Formerly in moments of sadness he had soothed himself with whatever logical arguments came into his head, but now he no longer cared for logic; he felt profound compassion, he wanted to be sincere and tender.

"Give it up now, my darling," he said. "You've had your cry; that's enough. Let us have a talk now, we'll think up something."

Then they spent a long time taking counsel together, they talked of how to avoid the necessity for secrecy, for deception, for living in different cities, and not seeing one another for long stretches of time. How could they free themselves from these intolerable fetters?

"How? How?" he asked, clutching his head. "How?"

THE MAN IN A SHELL

On the outskirts of the village of Mironositzkoe two belated huntsmen had settled for the night in the barn belonging to the elder, Prokofy. They were the veterinary, Ivan Ivanych, and the high-school teacher, Burkin. Ivan Ivanych had a rather queer double surname—Chimsha-Himalaisky—which did not suit him at all, and he was known as Ivan Ivanych all over the province. He lived on a stud farm near the town and had gone out shooting to breathe some fresh air. As for Burkin, the high-school teacher, he spent every summer at Count P——'s, and had long been thoroughly at home in the district.

They did not sleep. Ivan Ivanych, a tall, spare old man with long mustaches, was sitting outside the door, smoking a pipe in the moonlight. Burkin was lying inside on the hay, and could not be seen for the darkness.

They were telling each other stories. Among other things, they spoke of the elder's wife, Mavra, a healthy and by no means stupid woman, observing that she had never been beyond her native village, had never seen a city or a railway in her life, and had spent the last ten years hugging the stove and only going out into the street at night.

"There's nothing remarkable about that!" said Burkin. "There are not a few people in the world, temperamentally unsociable, who try to withdraw into a shell like a hermit crab or a snail. Perhaps it is a manifestation of atavism, a return to the time when man's ancestor was not yet a gregarious animal and lived alone in his lair, or perhaps it is only one of the varieties of human character—who knows? I am no naturalist, and it is not my business to settle such questions; I only mean to say that people like Mavra are by no means rare. Why, not to go far afield, there was Belikov, a colleague of mine, a teacher of Greek, who died in our town two months ago. You have heard of him, no doubt. The curious thing about him was that he wore rubbers and a warm coat with an interlining, and carried an umbrella even in the finest weather. And he kept his umbrella in its cover and his watch in a gray chamois case, and when he took out his penknife to sharpen his pencil, his penknife, too, was in a little case; and his face seemed to be in a case, too, because it was always hidden in his turned-up collar. He wore dark spectacles and a sweater, stuffed his ears with cotton wool, and when he got into a cab always told the driver to put up the hood. In short, the man showed a constant and irrepressible inclination to keep a covering about himself, to create for himself a membrane, as it were, which would isolate him and protect him from outside influences. Actuality irritated him, frightened him, kept him in a state of continual agitation, and, perhaps to justify his timidity, his aversion for the present, he would always laud the past and things that had never existed, and the dead languages that he taught were in effect for him the same rubbers and umbrella in which he sought concealment from real life.

" 'Oh, how sonorous, how beautiful the Greek language is!' he would say, with a saccharine expression; and as though to prove his point, he would screw up his eyes and, raising one finger, utter: 'Anthropos!'

"His thoughts, too, Belikov tried to tuck away in a sheath. The only things that were clear to him were government regulations and newspapers notices in which something was forbidden. When some ruling prohibited high-school students from appearing on the streets after nine o'clock at night, or some article censured carnal love, this he found clear and definite: it was forbidden, and that was that. But there was always a doubtful element for him, something vague and not fully expressed in any sanction or permission. When a dramatic club or a reading room or a teahouse was licensed in the town, he would shake his head and say in a low voice:

" 'Of course, it's all very well, but you can't tell what may come of it.'

"Any infringement of the rules, any deviation or departure from them, plunged him into gloom, though one would have thought it was no concern of his. If one of his colleagues was late for the thanksgiving service, or if rumors reached him of some prank of the high-school boys, or if one of the female members of the staff had been seen late in the evening in the company of an officer, he would become very much agitated and keep saying that one couldn't tell what might come of it. At faculty meetings he simply crushed us with his cautiousness, his suspiciousness, and his typical remarks to the effect that the young people in the girls' as well as in the boys' high school were unruly, that there was much noise in the classrooms, that it might reach the ears of the authorities, that one couldn't tell what might come of it, and that it would be a good thing if Petrov were expelled from the second form and Yegorov from the fourth. And what do you think, with his sighs, his moping, the dark spectacles on his pale little face, a little face like a pole-cat's, you know, he weighed us all down, and we submitted, reduced Petrov's and Yegorov's marks for conduct, detained them, and in the end expelled them both.

"He had a peculiar habit of visiting our lodgings. He would call on some teacher, would sit down, and remain silently staring, as though he were trying to detect something. He would sit like this in silence for an hour or two and then leave. This he called 'maintaining good relations with his colleagues'; and it was obvious that making these calls and sitting there like that was painful to him, and that he went to see us simply because he considered it his duty to his colleagues. We teachers were afraid of him. And even the principal was afraid of him. Would you believe it, our teachers were all thoughtful, decent people, brought up on Turgenev and Shchedrin, yet this little man, who always wore rubbers and carried an umbrella, had the whole high school under his thumb for fully fifteen years! The high school? The whole town! Our ladies did not get up private theatricals on Saturdays for fear he should find it out, and the clergy dared not eat meat in Lent or play cards in his presence. Under the influence of people like Belikov the whole town spent ten to fifteen frightened years. We were afraid to speak out loud, to write letters, to make acquaintances, to read books, to help the poor, to teach people how to read and write. . . ."

Ivan Ivanych coughed, as a preliminary to making some remark, but first lighted his pipe, gazed at the moon, and then said, between pauses:

"Yes, thoughtful, decent people, readers of Shchedrin and Turgenev, of Buckle and all the rest of them, yet they knuckled under and put up with it—that's just how it is."

"Belikov and I lived in the same house," Burkin went on, "on the same floor, his door facing mine; we often saw each other, and I was acquainted with his domestic arrangements. It was the same story: dressing gown, nightcap, blinds, bolts, prohibitions and restrictions of all sorts, and, 'Oh, you can't tell what may come of it!' Lenten fare didn't agree with him, yet he could not eat meat, as people might say that Belikov did not keep the fasts, and he ate perch fried in butter—not a Lenten dish, yet one could not call it meat. He did not keep a female servant for fear people might think evil of him, but instead employed an old man of sixty, called Afanasy, half-witted and given to drinking, who had once been an orderly and could cook after a fashion. This Afanasy was usually standing at the door with folded arms; he would sigh deeply and always mutter the same thing:

" 'The likes of *them* is thick as hops hereabouts!'

"Belikov's bedroom was tiny and boxlike; his bed was curtained. When he went to bed he drew the bedclothes over his head; it was hot and stuffy; the wind rattled the closed doors; a humming noise came from the stove and the sound of sighs from the kitchen, ominous sighs— And he lay under the quilt, terrified. He was afraid that something might happen, that Afanasy would murder him, that thieves would break in, and he had bad dreams all night long, and in the morning when we went to school together, he was downcast and pale, and it was plain that the place, swarming with people, toward which he was going, filled his whole being with dread and aversion, and that walking beside me was disagreeable to a man of his unsociable temperament.

" 'How noisy the classrooms are,' he used to say, as though trying to find an explanation for his distress. 'It's an outrage.'

"And imagine, this teacher of Greek—this man in a shell—came near to getting married."

Ivan Ivanych glanced rapidly into the barn and said, "You are joking!"

"Yes, strange as it seems, he nearly got married. A new teacher of geography and history, a certain Mihail Savvich

Kovalenko, a Ukrainian, was assigned to our school. He did not come alone, but with his sister, Varenka. He was a tall, dark young man with huge hands, and one could see from his face that he spoke in a deep voice, and, in fact, his voice seemed to come out of a barrel: 'Boom, boom, boom!' She was not so young, about thirty, but she, too, was tall, well built, with black eyebrows and red cheeks—in a word, she was not a girl but a peach, and so lively, so noisy; she was always singing Little Russian songs and laughing. At the least provocation, she would go off into ringing laughter: 'Ha-ha-ha!' We first got well acquainted with the Kovalenkos, I remember, at the principal's name-day party. Among the morose, emphatically dull pedagogues who attend even a name-day party as a duty, we suddenly saw a new Aphrodite risen from the foam; she walked with her arms akimbo, laughed, sang, danced. She sang with feeling 'The Winds Are Blowing' and then another Ukrainian song and another, and she fascinated us all, all, even Belikov. He sat down beside her and said with a saccharine smile:

" 'The Little Russian tongue reminds one of ancient Greek in its softness and agreeable sonority.'

"That flattered her, and she began telling him with feeling and persuasiveness that they had a farm in the Gadyach district, and that her Mummy lived there, and that they had such pears, such melons, such *kabaki*! The Little Russians call a pumpkin *kabak*,[1] while their taverns they call *shinki*, and they make a *borshch* with tomatoes and eggplant in it, 'which is so delicious—ever so delicious!'

"We listened, and listened, and suddenly the same idea occurred to all of us:

" 'It would be a good thing to marry them off,' the principal's wife whispered to me.

"For some reason we all recalled that our friend Belikov was unmarried, and it seemed strange to us now that we had failed to notice it before, and in fact had completely lost sight of so important a detail in his life. What was his attitude toward women? How had he settled for himself this vital problem? Until then we had had no interest in the matter; perhaps we had not even admitted the idea that a man who wore rubbers in all weathers and slept behind curtains was capable of love.

---

[1] Russian for tavern.

" 'He is way past forty and she is thirty,' the principal's wife clarified her idea. 'I believe she would marry him.'

"What isn't done in the provinces out of boredom, how many useless and foolish things! And that is because what is necessary isn't done at all. What need was there, for instance, for us to make a match for this Belikov, whom one could not even imagine as a married man? The principal's wife, the inspector's wife, and all our high-school ladies, grew livelier and even better looking, as though they had suddenly found an object in life. The principal's wife would take a box at the theater, and lo and behold! Varenka would be sitting in it, fanning herself, beaming and happy, and beside her would be Belikov, a twisted little man, looking as though he had been pulled out of his lodging by pincers. I would give an evening party and the ladies would insist on my inviting Belikov and Varenka. In short, the machine was set in motion. It turned out that Varenka was not averse to matrimony. Her life with her brother was not very cheerful: they did nothing but argue and quarrel with one another for days on end. Here is a typical scene: Kovalenko strides down the street, a tall, husky fellow, in an embroidered shirt, a lock of hair falling over his forehead from under his cap, in one hand a bundle of books, in the other a thick, knotted stick; he is followed by his sister, also carrying books.

" 'But you haven't read it, Mihailik!' she is arguing loudly. 'I tell you, I swear you haven't read it at all!'

" 'And I tell you I have read it,' bellows Kovalenko, banging his stick on the sidewalk.

" 'Oh, my goodness, Mihailik, why are you so cross? We are only discussing principles.'

" 'I tell you that I have read it!' Kovalenko shouts, more loudly than ever.

"And at home, if there was an outsider present, there was sure to be a fusillade. She must have been fed up with such a life and longed for a home of her own. Besides, there was her age; there was no time left to pick and choose; she was apt to marry anybody, even a teacher of Greek. Come to think of it, most of our young ladies don't care whom they marry so long as they do marry. Be that as it may, Varenka began to show an unmistakable inclination for Belikov.

"And Belikov? He used to call on Kovalenko just as he did on the rest of us. He would arrive, sit down, and go on sitting there in silence. He would sit quietly, and Varenka would sing to him

'The Winds Are Blowing' or would stare at him pensively with her dark eyes, or would suddenly go off into a peal of laughter—'Ha-ha-ha!'

"In amorous affairs and in marrying, suggestion plays a great part. Everybody—both his colleagues and the ladies—began assuring Belikov that he ought to get married, that there was nothing left for him in life but to get married; we all felicitated him, and with solemn faces delivered ourselves of various platitudes, such as 'Marriage is a serious step.' Besides, Varenka was good-looking and attractive; she was the daughter of a civil councilor, and she owned a farm; above all, she was the first woman who had treated him cordially and affectionately. His head was turned, and he decided that he really ought to get married."

"Well, at that point," said Ivan Ivanych, "you should have taken away his rubbers and umbrella."

"Just fancy, that proved to be impossible. He put Varenka's portrait on his table, kept calling on me and talking about Varenka and about family life, saying that marriage was a serious step. He went frequently to the Kovalenkos's, but he did not alter his habits in the least. On the contrary, his decision to get married seemed to have a deleterious effect on him. He grew thinner and paler and seemed to retreat further into his shell.

" 'I like Varvara Savvishna,' he would say to me, with a faint and crooked smile, 'and I know that everyone ought to get married, but—you know, all this has happened so suddenly—One must think it over a little.'

" 'What is there to think over?' I would say to him. 'Get married—that's all.'

" 'No; marriage is a serious step; one must first weigh the impending duties and responsibilities—so that nothing untoward may come of it. It worries me so much that I don't sleep nights. And I must confess I am afraid: she and her brother have such a peculiar way of thinking; they reason so strangely, you know, and she has a very impetuous disposition. You get married, and then, there is no telling, you may get into trouble.'

"And he did not propose; he kept putting it off, to the great vexation of the principal's wife and all our ladies; he kept weighing his future duties and responsibilities, and meanwhile he went for a walk with Varenka almost every day—possibly he thought that this was the proper thing under the circumstances—and came to see me to talk about family life. And in all probability he would have ended by proposing to her, and would have made one of those needless, stupid marriages thousands of which are made among us out of sheer boredom and idleness, if it had not been for a *kolossalischer Skandal*.

"I must tell you that Varenka's brother conceived a hatred of Belikov from the first day of their acquaintance and couldn't endure him.

" 'I don't understand,' he used to say to us, shrugging his shoulders, 'I don't understand how you can put up with that informer, that nasty mug. Ugh! how can you live here? The atmosphere you breathe is vile, stifling! Are you pedagogues, teachers? No, you are piddling functionaries; yours is not a temple of learning but a police station, and it has the same sour smell. No, brothers, I will stay with you for a while, and then I will go to my farm and catch crayfish there and teach Ukrainian brats. I will go, and you can stay here with your Judas—blast him!'

"Or he would laugh till tears came to his eyes, his laughter now deep, now shrill, and ask me, throwing up his hands, 'What does he come here for? What does he want? He sits and stares.'

"He even gave Belikov a nickname, 'the Spider.' Of course, we avoided talking to him about his sister's planning to marry the Spider. And when, on one occasion, the principal's wife hinted to him what a good thing it would be if his sister settled down with such a substantial, universally respected man as Belikov, he frowned and grumbled:

" 'It's none of my business; let her marry a viper if she likes. I don't care to meddle in other people's affairs.'

"Now listen to what happened next. Some wag drew a caricature of Belikov walking along under his umbrella, wearing his rubbers, his trousers tucked up, with Varenka on his arm; below there was the legend 'Anthropos in love.' The artist got the expression admirably, you know. He must have worked more than one night, for the teachers of both the boys' and the girls' high schools, the teachers of the theological seminary, and the government officials all received copies. Belikov received one too. The caricature made a very painful impression on him.

"We left the house together; it was the first of May, a Sunday, and all of us, the boys and the teachers, had agreed to meet at the high school and then to walk to a grove on the outskirts of the town. We set off, and he was green in the face and gloomier than a thundercloud.

" 'What wicked, malicious people there are!' he said, and his lips quivered.

"I couldn't help feeling sorry for him. We were walking along, and all of a sudden—imagine!—Kovalenko came rolling along on a bicycle, and after him, also on a bicycle, Varenka, flushed and exhausted, but gay and high-spirited.

" 'We are going on ahead,' she shouted. 'What lovely weather! Just too lovely!'

"And they both vanished. Belikov turned from green to white, and seemed petrified. He stopped short and stared at me.

" 'Good heavens, what is this?' he asked. 'Can my eyes be deceiving me? Is it proper for high-school teachers and ladies to ride bicycles?'

" 'What's improper about it?' I asked. 'Let them ride and may it do them good.'

" 'But you can't mean it,' he cried, amazed at my calm. 'What are you saying?'

"And he was so shocked that he refused to go farther, and returned home.

"Next day he was continually twitching and rubbing his hands nervously, and it was obvious from the expression of his face that he was far from well. And he left before the school day was over, for the first time in his life. And he ate no dinner. Toward evening he wrapped himself up warmly, though it was practically summer weather, and made his way to the Kovalenkos'. Varenka was out; he found only her brother at home.

" 'Please sit down,' Kovalenko said coldly, frowning. He had a sleepy look; he had just taken an after-dinner nap and was in a very bad humor.

"Belikov sat in silence for about ten minutes, and then began, 'I have come to you to relieve my mind. I am very, very much troubled. Some malicious fellow has drawn a caricature of me and of another person who is close to both of us. I regard it as my duty to assure you that I had nothing to do with it. I have given no grounds for such an attack—on the contrary, I have always behaved as a respectable person would.'

"Kovalenko sat there sulking without a word. Belikov waited awhile, and then went on in a low, mournful voice; 'And I have something else to say to you. I have been in the service for years, while you have entered it only lately, and I consider it my duty as an older colleague to give you a warning. You ride a bicycle, and that pastime is utterly improper for an educator of youth.'

" 'Why so?' asked Kovalenko in his deep voice.

" 'Surely that needs no explanation, Mihail Savvich—surely it is self-evident! If the teacher rides a bicycle, what can one expect of the pupils? The only thing left them is to walk on their heads! And so long as it is not explicitly permitted, it should not be done. I was horrified yesterday! When I saw your sister, everything went black before my eyes. A lady or a young girl on a bicycle—it's terrible!'

" 'What is it you wish exactly?'

" 'All I wish to do is to warn you, Mihail Savvich. You are a young man, you have a future before you, you must be very, very careful of your behavior, and you are so neglectful, oh, so neglectful! You go about in an embroidered shirt, are constantly seen in the street carrying books, and now the bicycle too. The principal will learn that you and your sister ride bicycles, and then it will reach the trustee's ears. No good can come of that.'

" 'It's nobody's business if my sister and I do bicycle,' said Kovalenko, and he turned crimson. 'And whoever meddles in my private affairs can go to the devil!'

"Belikov turned pale and got up.

" 'If you speak to me in that tone, I cannot continue,' he said. 'And I beg you never to express yourself in that manner about our superiors in my presence; you should be respectful to the authorities.'

" 'Have I said anything offensive about the authorities?' asked Kovalenko, looking at him angrily. 'Please leave me in peace. I am an honorable man, and do not care to talk to gentlemen of your stripe. I hate informers!'

"Belikov fidgeted nervously and hurriedly began putting on his coat, with an expression of horror on his face. It was the first time in his life he had been spoken to so rudely.

" 'You can say what you please,' he declared, as he stepped out of the entry onto the staircase landing. 'Only I must warn you: someone may have overheard us, and lest our conversation be misinterpreted and harm come of it, I shall have to inform the principal of the contents of our conversation—in a general way. I am obliged to do so.'

" 'Inform him? Go, make your report and be damned to you!'

"Kovalenko seized him from behind by the collar and gave him a shove, and Belikov rolled noisily downstairs, rubbers and all. The staircase was high and steep, but he arrived at the bottom safely, got up, and felt his nose to see whether his spectacles were intact. But just as he was rolling down the stairs, Varenka came in, accompanied by two ladies; they stood below, staring, and this was more dreadful to Belikov than anything else. I believe he would rather have broken his neck or both legs than have been an object of ridicule. Why, now the whole town would hear of it; it would come to the principal's ears, it would reach the trustee. Oh, there was no telling what might come of it! There would be another caricature, and it would all end in his being ordered to retire from his post.

"When he got up, Varenka recognized him and, looking at his ludicrous face, his crumpled overcoat, and his rubbers, not grasping the situation and supposing that he had fallen by accident, could not restrain herself and burst into laughter that resounded throughout the house:

" 'Ha-ha-ha!'

"And this reverberant, ringing 'Ha-ha-ha!' put an end to everything: to the expected match and to Belikov's earthly existence. He did not hear what Varenka was saying; he saw nothing. On reaching home, the first thing he did was to remove Varenka's portrait from the table; then he went to bed, and he never got up again.

"Two or three days later Afanasy came to me and asked whether the doctor should not be sent for, as there was something wrong with his master. I went in to see Belikov. He lay silent behind the curtains, covered with a quilt; when you questioned him, he answered 'yes' and 'no' and nothing more. He lay there while Afanasy, gloomy and scowling, hovered about him, sighing heavily and reeking of vodka like a tavern.

"A month later Belikov died. We all went to his funeral—that is, all connected with both high schools and with the theological seminary. Now when he was lying in his coffin his expression was mild, pleasant, even cheerful, as though he were glad that he had at last been put into a case that he would never leave again. Yes, he had attained his ideal! And as though in his honor, it was cloudy, rainy weather on the day of his funeral, and we all wore rubbers and carried umbrellas. Varenka, too, was at the funeral, and when the coffin was lowered into the grave, she dropped a tear. I have noticed that Ukrainian women always laugh or cry—there is no intermediate state for them.

"I confess, it is a great pleasure to bury people like Belikov.

As we were returning from the cemetery we wore discreet Lenten faces; no one wanted to display this feeling of pleasure—a feeling like that we had experienced long, long ago as children when the grown-ups had gone out and we ran about the garden for an hour or two, enjoying complete freedom. Ah, freedom, freedom! A mere hint, the faintest hope of its possibility, gives wings to the soul, isn't that true?

"We returned from the cemetery in good humor. But not more than a week had passed before life dropped into its old rut, and was as gloomy, tiresome, and stupid as before, the sort of life that is not explicitly forbidden, but on the other hand is not fully permitted; things were no better. And, indeed, though we had buried Belikov, how many such men in shells were left, how many more of them there will be!"

"That's the way it is," said Ivan Ivanych, and lit his pipe.

"How many more of them there will be!" repeated Burkin.

The high-school teacher came out of the barn. He was a short, stout man, completely bald, with a black beard that nearly reached his waist; two dogs came out with him.

"What a moon!" he said, looking up.

It was already midnight. On the right could be seen the whole village, a long street stretching far away for some three miles. Everything was sunk in deep, silent slumber; not a movement, not a sound; one could hardly believe that nature could be so still. When on a moonlit night you see a wide village street, with its cottages, its haystacks, and its willows that have dropped off to sleep, a feeling of serenity comes over the soul; as it rests thus, hidden from toil, care, and sorrow by the nocturnal shadows, the street is gentle, sad, beautiful, and it seems as though the stars look down upon it kindly and tenderly, and as if there were no more evil on earth, and all were well. On the left, where the village ended, the open country began; the fields could be seen stretching far away to the horizon, and there was no movement, no sound in that whole expanse drenched with moonlight.

"Yes, that's the way it is," repeated Ivan Ivanych; "and isn't our living in the airless, crowded town, our writing useless papers, our playing vint—isn't all that a sort of shell for us? And this spending our lives among pettifogging, idle men and silly, unoccupied women, our talking and our listening to all sorts of poppycock—isn't that a shell too? If you like, I will tell you a very instructive story."

"No; it's time to turn in," said Burkin. "Tomorrow's another day."

They went into the barn and lay down on the hay. And they were both covered up and had dozed off when suddenly there was the sound of light footsteps—tap, tap. Someone was walking near the barn, walking a little and stopping, and a minute later, tap, tap again. The dogs began to growl.

"That's Mavra," said Burkin.

The footsteps died away.

"To see and hear them lie," said Ivan Ivanych, turning over on the other side, "and to be called a fool for putting up with their lies; to endure insult and humiliation, and not dare say openly that you are on the side of the honest and the free, and to lie and smile yourself, and all for the sake of a crust of bread, for the sake of a warm nook, for the sake of a mean, worthless rank in the service—no, one cannot go on living like that!"

"Come, now, that's a horse of another color, Ivan Ivanych," said the teacher. "Let's go to sleep."

And ten minutes later Burkin was asleep. But Ivan Ivanych kept sighing and turning from one side to the other; then he got up, went outside again, and sitting himself near the door, lighted his pipe.

GOOSEBERRIES

The sky had been overcast since early morning; it was a still day, not hot, but tedious, as it usually is when the weather is gray and dull, when clouds have been hanging over the fields for a long time, and you wait for the rain that does not come. Ivan Ivanych, a veterinary, and Burkin, a high-school teacher, were already tired with walking, and the plain seemed endless to them. Far ahead were the scarcely visible windmills of the village of Mironositzkoe; to the right lay a range of hills that disappeared in the distance beyond the village, and both of them knew that over there were the river, and fields, green willows, homesteads, and if you stood on one of the hills, you could see from there another vast plain, telegraph poles, and a train that from afar looked like a caterpillar crawling, and in clear weather you could even see the town. Now, when it was still and when nature seemed mild and pensive, Ivan Ivanych and Burkin were filled with love for this plain, and both of them thought what a beautiful land it was.

"Last time when we were in Elder Prokofy's barn," said Burkin, "you were going to tell me a story."

"Yes; I wanted to tell you about my brother."

Ivan Ivanych heaved a slow sigh and lit his pipe before beginning his story, but just then it began to rain. And five minutes later there was a downpour, and it was hard to tell when it would be over. The two men halted, at a loss; the dogs, already wet, stood with their tails between their legs and looked at them feelingly.

"We must find shelter somewhere," said Burkin. "Let's go to Alyohin's; it's quite near."

"Let's."

They turned aside and walked across a mown meadow, now going straight ahead, now bearing to the right, until they reached the road. Soon poplars came into view, a garden, then the red roofs of barns; the river gleamed, and the view opened on a broad expanse of water with a mill and a white bathing cabin. That was Sofyino, Alyohin's place.

The mill was going, drowning out the sound of the rain; the dam was shaking. Wet horses stood near the carts, their heads drooping, and men were walking about, their heads covered with sacks. It was damp, muddy, dreary; and the water looked cold and unkind. Ivan Ivanych and Burkin felt cold and messy and uncomfortable through and through; their feet were heavy with mud and when, having crossed the dam, they climbed up to the barns, they were silent as though they were cross with each other.

The noise of a winnowing-machine came from one of the barns, the door was open, and clouds of dust were pouring from within. On the threshold stood Alyohin himself, a man of forty, tall and rotund, with long hair, looking more like a professor or an artist than a gentleman farmer. He was wearing a white blouse, badly in need of washing, that was belted with a rope, and drawers, and his high boots were plastered with mud and straw. His eyes and nose were black with dust. He recognized Ivan Ivanych and Burkin and was apparently very glad to see them.

"Please go up to the house, gentlemen," he said, smiling; "I'll be there directly, in a moment."

It was a large structure of two stories. Alyohin lived downstairs in what was formerly the stewards' quarters: two rooms that had arched ceilings and small windows; the furniture was plain, and the place smelled of rye bread, cheap vodka, and harness. He went into the showy rooms upstairs only rarely, when he had guests. Once in the house, the two visitors were met by a chambermaid, a young woman so beautiful that both of them stood still at the same moment and glanced at each other.

"You can't imagine how glad I am to see you, gentlemen," said Alyohin, joining them in the hall. "What a surprise! Pelageya," he said, turning to the chambermaid, "give the guests a change of clothes. And, come to think of it, I will change too. But I must go and bathe first, I don't think I've had a wash since spring. Don't you want to go into the bathing cabin? In the meanwhile things will be got ready here."

The beautiful Pelageya, with her soft, delicate air, brought them bath towels and soap, and Alyohin went to the bathing cabin with his guests.

"Yes, it's a long time since I've bathed," he said, as he undressed. "I've an excellent bathing cabin, as you see—it was put up by my father—but somehow I never find time to use it." He sat down on the steps and lathered his long hair and neck, and the water around him turned brown.

"I say—" observed Ivan Ivanych significantly, looking at his head.

"I haven't had a good wash for a long time," repeated Alyohin, embarrassed, and soaped himself once more; the water about him turned dark blue, the color of ink.

Ivan Ivanych came out of the cabin, plunged into the water with a splash, and swam in the rain, thrusting his arms out wide; he raised waves on which white lilies swayed. He swam out to the middle of the river and dived and a minute later came up in another spot and swam on and kept diving, trying to touch bottom. "By God!" he kept repeating delightedly, "by God!" He swam to the mill, spoke to the peasants there, and turned back and in the middle of the river lay floating, exposing his face to the rain. Burkin and Alyohin were already dressed and ready to leave, but he kept on swimming and diving. "By God!" he kept exclaiming. "Lord, have mercy on me."

"You've had enough!" Burkin shouted to him.

They returned to the house. And only when the lamp was lit in the big drawing room upstairs, and the two guests, in silk dressing gowns and warm slippers, were lounging in armchairs, and Alyohin himself, washed and combed, wearing a new jacket, was walking about the room evidently savoring the warmth, the cleanliness, the dry clothes and light footwear, and when pretty Pelageya, stepping noiselessly across the carpet and smiling softly, brought in a tray with tea and jam, only then did Ivan Ivanych begin his story, and it was as though not only Burkin and Alyohin were listening, but also the ladies, old and young, and the military men who looked down upon them, calmly and severely, from their gold frames.

"We are two brothers," he began, "I, Ivan Ivanych, and my brother, Nikolay Ivanych, who is two years my junior. I went in for a learned profession and became a veterinary; Nikolay at nineteen began to clerk in a provincial branch of the treasury. Our father was a *kantonist*,[1] but he rose to be an officer and so a nobleman, a rank that he bequeathed to us together with a small estate. After his death there was a lawsuit and we lost the estate to creditors, but be that as it may, we spent our childhood in the country. Just like peasant children we passed days and nights in the fields and the woods, herded horses, stripped bast from the trees, fished, and so on. And, you know, whoever even once in his life has caught a perch or seen thrushes migrate in the autumn, when on clear, cool days they sweep in flocks over the village, will never really be a townsman and to the day of his death will have a longing for the open. My brother was unhappy in the government office. Years passed, but he went on warming the same seat, scratching away at the same papers, and thinking of one and the same thing: how to get away to the country. And little by little his vague longing turned into a definite desire, into a dream of buying a little property somewhere on the banks of a river or a lake.

"He was a kind and gentle soul and I loved him, but I never sympathized with his desire to shut himself up for the rest of his life on a little property of his own. It is a common saying that a man needs only six feet of earth. But six feet is what a corpse needs, not a man. It is also asserted that if our educated class is drawn to the land and seeks to settle on farms, that's a good thing. But these farms amount to the same six feet of earth. To retire from the city, from the struggle, from the hubbub, to go off and hide on one's own farm—that's not life, it is selfishness, sloth, it is a kind of monasticism, but monasticism without works. Man needs not six feet of earth, not a farm, but the whole globe, all of nature, where unhindered he can display all the capacities and peculiarities of his free spirit.

"My brother Nikolay, sitting in his office, dreamed of eating his own *shchi*, which would fill the whole farmyard with a delicious aroma, of picnicking on the green grass, of sleeping in the sun, of sitting for hours on the seat by the gate gazing at field

[1] The son of a private, registered at birth in the army and trained in a military school.

and forest. Books on agriculture and the farming items in almanacs were his joy, the delight of his soul. He liked newspapers, too, but the only things he read in them were advertisements of land for sale, so many acres of tillable land and pasture, with house, garden, river, mill, and millpond. And he pictured to himself garden paths, flowers, fruit, birdhouses with starlings in them, crucians in the pond, and all that sort of thing, you know. These imaginary pictures varied with the advertisements he came upon, but somehow gooseberry bushes figured in every one of them. He could not picture to himself a single country house, a single rustic nook, without gooseberries.

" 'Country life has its advantages,' he used to say. 'You sit on the veranda having tea, and your ducks swim in the pond, and everything smells delicious and—the gooseberries are ripening.'

"He would draw a plan of his estate and invariably it would contain the following features: a) the master's house; b) servants' quarters; c) kitchen-garden; d) a gooseberry patch. He lived meagerly: he deprived himself of food and drink; he dressed God knows how, like a beggar, but he kept on saving and salting money away in the bank. He was terribly stingy. It was painful for me to see it, and I used to give him small sums and send him something on holidays, but he would put that away too. Once a man is possessed by an idea, there is no doing anything with him.

"Years passed. He was transferred to another province, he was already past forty, yet he was still reading newspaper advertisements and saving up money. Then I heard that he was married. Still for the sake of buying a property with a gooseberry patch he married an elderly, homely widow, without a trace of affection for her, but simply because she had money. After marrying her, he went on living parsimoniously, keeping her half starved, and he put her money in the bank in his own name. She had previously been the wife of a postmaster, who had got her used to pies and cordials. This second husband did not even give her enough black bread. She began to sicken, and some three years later gave up the ghost. And, of course, it never for a moment occurred to my brother that he was to blame for her death. Money, like vodka, can do queer things to a man. Once in our town a merchant lay on his deathbed; before he died, he ordered a plateful of honey and he ate up all his money and lottery tickets with the honey, so that no one should get it. One day when I was inspecting a drove of cattle at a railway station, a cattle dealer fell under a locomotive and it sliced off his leg. We carried him in to the infirmary, the blood was gushing from the wound—a terrible business, but he kept begging us to find his leg and was very anxious about it: he had twenty rubles in the boot that was on that leg, and he was afraid they would be lost.''

''That's a tune from another opera,'' said Burkin.

Ivan Ivanych paused a moment and then continued:

''After his wife's death, my brother began to look around for a property. Of course, you may scout about for five years and in the end make a mistake, and buy something quite different from what you have been dreaming of. Through an agent my brother bought a mortgaged estate of three hundred acres with a house, servants' quarters, a park, but with no orchard, no gooseberry patch, no duck pond. There was a stream, but the water in it was the color of coffee, for on one of its banks there was a brickyard and on the other a glue factory. But my brother was not at all disconcerted: he ordered a score of gooseberry bushes, planted them, and settled down to the life of a country gentleman.

''Last year I paid him a visit. I thought I would go and see how things were with him. In his letter to me my brother called his estate 'Chumbaroklov Waste, or Himalaiskoe' (our surname was Chimsha-Himalaisky). I reached the place in the afternoon. It was hot. Everywhere there were ditches, fences, hedges, rows of fir trees, and I was at a loss as to how to get to the yard and where to leave my horse. I made my way to the house and was met by a fat dog with reddish hair that looked like a pig. It wanted to bark, but was too lazy. The cook, a fat, barelegged woman, who also looked like a pig, came out of the kitchen and said that the master was resting after dinner. I went in to see my brother, and found him sitting up in bed, with a quilt over his knees. He had grown older, stouter, flabby; his cheeks, his nose, his lips jutted out: it looked as though he might grunt into the quilt at any moment.

''We embraced and dropped tears of joy and also of sadness at the thought that the two of us had once been young, but were now gray and nearing death. He got dressed and took me out to show me his estate.

'' 'Well, how are you getting on here?' I asked.

'' 'Oh, all right, thank God. I am doing very well.'

''He was no longer the poor, timid clerk he used to be but a real landowner, a gentleman. He had already grown used to his new manner of living and developed a taste for it. He ate a great deal, steamed himself in the bathhouse, was growing stout, was already having a lawsuit with the village commune and the two factories, and was very much offended when the peasants failed to address him as 'Your Honor.' And he concerned himself with his soul's welfare, too, in a substantial, upper-class manner, and performed good deeds not simply, but pompously. And what good works! He dosed the peasants with bicarbonate and castor oil for all their ailments and on his name day he had a thanksgiving service celebrated in the center of the village, and then treated the villagers to a gallon of vodka, which he thought was the thing to do. Oh, those horrible gallons of vodka! One day a fat landowner hauls the peasants up before the rural police officer for trespassing, and the next, to mark a feast day, treats them to a gallon of vodka, and they drink and shout 'Hurrah' and when they are drunk bow down at his feet. A higher standard of living, overeating, and idleness develop the most insolent self-conceit in a Russian. Nikolay Ivanych, who when he was a petty official was afraid to have opinions of his own even if he kept them to himself, now uttered nothing but incontrovertible truths and did so in the tone of a minister of state: 'Education is necessary, but the masses are not ready for it; corporal punishment is generally harmful, but in some cases it is useful and nothing else will serve.'

" 'I know the common people, and I know how to deal with them,' he would say. 'They love me. I only have to raise my little finger, and they will do anything I want.'

"And all this, mark you, would be said with a smile that bespoke kindness and intelligence. Twenty times over he repeated: 'We, of the gentry,' 'I, as a member of the gentry.' Apparently he no longer remembered that our grandfather had been a peasant and our father just a private. Even our surname, Chimsha-Himalaisky, which in reality is grotesque, seemed to him sonorous, distinguished, and delightful.

"But I am concerned now not with him, but with me. I want to tell you about the change that took place in me during the few hours that I spent on his estate. In the evening when we were having tea, the cook served a plateful of gooseberries. They were not bought, they were his own gooseberries, the first ones picked since the bushes were planted. My brother gave a laugh and for a minute looked at the gooseberries in silence, with tears in his eyes—he could not speak for excitement. Then he put one berry in his mouth, glanced at me with the triumph of a child who has at last been given a toy he was longing for, and said: 'How tasty!' And he ate the gooseberries greedily, and kept repeating: 'Ah, how delicious! Do taste them!'

"They were hard and sour, but as Pushkin has it,

> The falsehood that exalts we cherish more
> Than meaner truths that are a thousand strong.

I saw a happy man, one whose cherished dream had so obviously come true, who had attained his goal in life, who had got what he wanted, who was satisfied with his lot and with himself. For some reason an element of sadness had always mingled with my thoughts of human happiness, and now at the sight of a happy man I was assailed by an oppressive feeling bordering on despair. It weighed on me particularly at night. A bed was made up for me in a room next to my brother's bedroom, and I could hear that he was wakeful, and that he would get up again and again, go to the plate of gooseberries and eat one after another. I said to myself: 'How many contented, happy people there really are! What an overwhelming force they are! Look at life: the insolence and idleness of the strong, the ignorance and brutishness of the weak, horrible poverty everywhere, overcrowding, degeneration, drunkenness, hypocrisy, lying— Yet in all the houses and on all the streets there is peace and quiet; of the fifty thousand people who live in our town there is not one who would cry out, who would vent his indignation aloud. We see the people who go to market, eat by day, sleep by night, who babble nonsense, marry, grow old, good-naturedly drag their dead to the cemetery, but we do not see or hear those who suffer, and what is terrible in life goes on somewhere behind the scenes. Everything is peaceful and quiet and only mute statistics protest: so many people gone out of their minds, so many gallons of vodka drunk, so many children dead from malnutrition— And such a state of things is evidently necessary; obviously the happy man is at ease only because the unhappy ones bear their burdens in silence, and if there were not this silence, happiness would be impossible. It is a general hypnosis. Behind the door of every contented, happy man there ought to be someone standing with a little hammer and continually reminding him with a knock that there are unhappy people, that however happy he may be, life will sooner or later show him its claws, and trouble will come to him—illness, poverty, losses, and then no one will see or hear him, just as now he neither sees nor hears others. But there is no man with a hammer. The happy man lives at his ease, faintly fluttered by small daily cares, like an aspen in the wind—and all is well.'

"That night I came to understand that I, too, had been contented and happy," Ivan Ivanych continued, getting up. "I, too, over the dinner table or out hunting would hold forth on how to live, what to believe, the right way to govern the people. I, too, would say that learning was the enemy of darkness, that education was necessary but that for the common people the three R's were sufficient for the time being. Freedom is a boon, I used to say, it is as essential as air, but we must wait awhile. Yes, that's what I used to say, and now I ask: Why must we wait?" said Ivan Ivanych, looking wrathfully at Burkin. "Why must we wait, I ask you? For what reason? I am told that nothing can be done all at once, that every idea is realized gradually, in its own time. But who is it that says so? Where is the proof that it is just? You cite the natural order of things, the law governing all phenomena, but is there law, is there order in the fact that I, a living, thinking man, stand beside a ditch and wait for it to close up of itself or fill up with silt, when I could jump over it or throw a bridge across it? And again, why must we wait? Wait, until we have no strength to live, and yet we have to live and are eager to live!

"I left my brother's place early in the morning, and ever since then it has become intolerable for me to stay in town. I am oppressed by the peace and the quiet, I am afraid to look at the windows, for there is nothing that pains me more than the spectacle of a happy family sitting at table having tea. I am an old man now and unfit for combat, I am not even capable of hating. I can only grieve inwardly, get irritated, worked up, and at night my head is ablaze with the rush of ideas and I cannot sleep. Oh, if I were young!"

Ivan Ivanych paced up and down the room excitedly and repeated, "If I were young!"

He suddenly walked up to Alyohin and began to press now one of his hands, now the other.

"Pavel Konstantinovich," he said imploringly, "don't quiet down, don't let yourself be lulled to sleep! As long as you are young, strong, alert, do not cease to do good! There is no happiness and there should be none, and if life has a meaning and a purpose, that meaning and purpose is not our happiness but something greater and more rational. Do good!''

All this Ivan Ivanych said with a pitiful, imploring smile, as though he were asking a personal favor.

Afterwards all three of them sat in armchairs in different corners of the drawing room and were silent. Ivan Ivanych's story satisfied neither Burkin nor Alyohin. With the ladies and generals looking down from the golden frames, seeming alive in the dim light, it was tedious to listen to the story of the poor devil of a clerk who ate gooseberries. One felt like talking about elegant people, about women. And the fact that they were sitting in a drawing room where everything—the chandelier under its cover, the armchairs, the carpets underfoot—testified that the very people who were now looking down from the frames had once moved about here, sat and had tea, and the fact that lovely Pelageya was noiselessly moving about—that was better than any story.

Alyohin was very sleepy; he had gotten up early, before three o'clock in the morning, to get some work done, and now he could hardly keep his eyes open, but he was afraid his visitors might tell an interesting story in his absence, and he would not leave. He did not trouble to ask himself if what Ivan Ivanych had just said was intelligent or right. The guests were not talking about groats, or hay, or tar, but about something that had no direct bearing on his life, and he was glad of it and wanted them to go on.

''However, it's bedtime,'' said Burkin, rising. ''Allow me to wish you good night.''

Alyohin took leave of his guests and went downstairs to his own quarters, while they remained upstairs. They were installed for the night in a big room in which stood two old wooden beds decorated with carvings, and in the corner was an ivory crucifix. The wide cool beds which had been made by the lovely Pelageya gave off a pleasant smell of clean linen.

Ivan Ivanych undressed silently and got into bed.

''Lord forgive us sinners!'' he murmured, and drew the bedclothes over his head.

His pipe, which lay on the table, smelled strongly of burnt tobacco, and Burkin, who could not sleep for a long time, kept wondering where the unpleasant odor came from.

The rain beat against the window panes all night.

ABOUT LOVE

For breakfast next day delicious little patties, crayfish and mutton croquettes, were served, and while we were eating, Nikanor the cook came up to ask what the guests would like for dinner. He was a man of medium height, with a puffy face and small eyes; he was clean shaven, and it looked as though his mustache had not been shaven off but plucked out.

According to Alyohin, the beautiful Pelageya was in love with this cook. As he drank and had a violent temper, she did not want to marry him, but was willing to live with him just so. But he was very devout, and his religious convictions did not allow him to live "just so"; he insisted that she marry him, and didn't want it otherwise, and when he was drunk he used to swear at her and even beat her. Whenever he was drunk she would hide upstairs and sob, and on such occasions Alyohin and the servants stayed in the house to defend her if necessary.

The conversation turned to love.

"How love is born," said Alyohin, "why Pelageya hasn't fallen in love with somebody more like herself both inwardly and outwardly, and why she fell in love with Nikanor, that mug—we all call him 'the Mug'—to what extent personal happiness counts in love—all that is uncertain; and one can argue about it as one pleases. So far only one incontestable truth has been stated about love: 'This is a great mystery'; everything else that has been written or said about love is not a solution, but only a statement of questions that have remained unanswered. The explanation that would fit one case does not apply to a dozen others, and the very best thing, to my mind, would be to explain every case separately without attempting to generalize. Each case should be individualized, as the doctors say."

"Perfectly true," Burkin assented.

"We Russians who are cultivated have a weakness for these questions that remain unanswered. Love is usually poeticized, embellished with roses, nightingales; but we Russians embellish our loves with these fatal questions, and choose the least interesting of them, at that. In Moscow, when I was a student, there was a girl with whom I lived, a charming creature, and every time I held her in my arms she was thinking about what I would allow her a month for housekeeping and about the price of beef. Similarly, when we are in love, we never stop asking ourselves whether it is honorable or dishonorable, sensible or stupid, what this love will lead to, and so on. If that is a good thing or not I don't know, but that it is a hindrance and a source of dissatisfaction and irritation, of that I am certain."

It looked as though he wanted to tell a story. People who lead a lonely existence always have something on their minds that they are eager to talk about. In town bachelors visit baths and restaurants in order to have a chance to talk, and sometimes tell very interesting stories to bath attendants and waiters; in the country they usually unbosom themselves to their guests. At the moment we could see a gray sky from the windows and trees drenched with rain; in such weather we could go nowhere and there was nothing for us to do but to tell and listen to stories.

"I have been living at Sofyino and been farming for a long time," Alyohin began, "ever since I graduated from the university. My education did not fit me for rough work and temperamentally I am a bookish fellow, but when I came here the estate was heavily mortgaged, and as my father had gone into debt partly because he had spent a great deal on my education, I decided not to leave the place but to work till I had paid off the debt. I made up my mind to this and set to work, not, I must confess, without some repugnance. The land here does not yield much, and if you are not to farm at a loss you must employ serf labor or hired help, which comes to almost the same thing, or work it like a peasant—that is, you must work in the fields yourself with your family. There is no middle way. But in those days I did not go into such niceties. I did not leave an inch of earth unturned; I got together all the peasants, men and women, from the neighboring villages; the work hummed. I myself plowed and sowed and reaped, and found it awfully tedious, and frowned with disgust, like a village cat driven by hunger to eat cucumbers in the kitchen garden. My body ached, and I slept on my feet.

"At first it seemed to me that I could easily reconcile this life of toil with civilized living; to achieve that, I thought, all that was necessary was to secure a certain external order. I established myself upstairs here in the best rooms, and had them serve me coffee and liqueurs after lunch and dinner, and every night I read *The Messenger of Europe* in bed. But one day our priest, Father Ivan, came and drank up all my liqueurs at one sitting, and *The Messenger of Europe* went to the priest's daughters, because in summer, especially at haymaking time, I couldn't drag myself to bed at all, but fell asleep on a sledge in the shed or somewhere in a shack in the woods, and how could I think of reading? Little by little I moved downstairs, began to eat in the servants' kitchen, and nothing is left of my former luxury but the people who were in Father's service and whom it would be painful to discharge.

"Before I had been here many years I was elected honorary justice of the peace. Now and then I had to go to town and take part in the assizes of the peace and the sessions of the circuit court, and this diverted me. When you live here for two or three months without seeing a soul, especially in winter, you begin at last to pine for a black coat. And at the circuit court there were black coats and uniforms and frock coats, too, all worn by lawyers, educated men; there were always people to talk to. After sleeping on the sledge and dining in the kitchen, to sit in an armchair wearing clean linen, in light boots, with the chain of office around one's neck—that was such luxury!

"I would be warmly received in the town. I made friends readily. And of all my friendships the most intimate and, to tell the truth, the most agreeable to me was my acquaintance with Luganovich, the assistant president of the circuit court. You both know him: an extremely charming man. This was just after the celebrated arson case; the preliminary investigation had lasted two days and we were worn out. Luganovich looked at me and said:

" 'You know what? Come and dine with me.'

"This was unexpected, as I knew Luganovich very slightly, only officially, and I had never been to his house. I went to my hotel room for a minute to change and then went off to dinner. And here came my opportunity to meet Anna Alexeyevna, Luganovich's wife. She was then still a very young woman, not more than twenty-two, and her first baby had been born just six months before. It is all a thing of the past; and now I should find it hard to determine what was so exceptional about her, what it was about her that I liked so much; but at the time, at dinner, it was all perfectly clear to me. I saw a young woman, beautiful, kind, intelligent, fascinating, such a woman as I had never met before; and at once I sensed in her a being near to me and already familiar, as though I had seen that face, those friendly, intelligent eyes long ago, in my childhood, in the album which lay on my mother's chest of drawers.

"In the arson case the defendants were four Jews who were charged with collusion, and in my opinion they were quite innocent. At dinner I was very much agitated and out of sorts, and I don't recall what I said, but Anna Alexeyevna kept shaking her head, and saying to her husband,

" 'Dmitry, how can this be?'

"Luganovich is one of those good-natured, simpleminded people who firmly adhere to the belief that once a man is indicted in court he is guilty, and that one should not express doubt as to the correctness of a verdict except with all legal formalities on paper, but never at dinner and in private conversation.

" 'You and I didn't commit arson,' he said gently, 'and you see we are not on trial and not in prison.'

"Both husband and wife tried to make me eat and drink as much as possible. From some details, from the way they made the coffee together, for instance, and the way they understood each other without completing their phrases, I gathered that they lived in peace and harmony, and that they were glad of a guest. After dinner they played a duet on the piano; then it got dark, and I drove home.

"That was at the beginning of spring. I spent the whole summer at Sofyino without a break, and I had no time even to think of the town, but the memory of the willowy, fair-haired woman remained in my mind all those months; I did not think of her, but it was as though her shadow were lying lightly on my soul.

"In the late autumn a benefit performance was given in the

town. I entered the governor's box (I had been invited there in the intermission); and there I saw Anna Alexeyevna sitting beside the governor's wife; and again there was the same irresistible, striking impression of beauty and lovely, caressing eyes, and again the same feeling of nearness. We sat side by side, then went out into the foyer.

" 'You've grown thinner,' she said; 'have you been ill?'

" 'Yes, I had rheumatism in my shoulder, and in rainy weather I sleep badly.'

" 'You look listless. In spring, when you came to dinner, you seemed younger, livelier. You were animated, and talked a great deal then; you were very interesting, and I must confess I was a little carried away. For some reason I often thought of you during the summer, and this evening when I was getting ready to go to the theater it occurred to me that I might see you.'

"And she laughed.

" 'But you look listless tonight,' she repeated; 'it makes you seem older.'

"The next day I lunched at the Luganoviches'. After lunch they drove out to their summer villa to make arrangements to close it up for the winter, and I went along. I went back to the town with them, and at midnight we had tea together in quiet domesticity, while the fire glowed, and the young mother kept going to see if her little girl were asleep. And after that, every time I went to the town I never failed to visit the Luganoviches. They grew used to me and I grew used to them. As a rule I went in unannounced, as though I were one of the family.

" 'Who is there?' would be heard from a faraway room, in the drawling voice that seemed to me so lovely.

" 'It is Pavel Konstantinovich,' the maid or the nurse would answer.

"Anna Alexeyevna would come out to me with an anxious air and would invariably ask, "Why haven't we seen you for so long? Is anything wrong?'

"Her gaze, the elegant, exquisite hand she gave me, her simple dress, the way she did her hair, her voice, her gait, always produced the same impression on me of something new and extraordinary, and very significant. We would talk together for hours, there would be long silences, while we were each thinking our own thoughts, or she would play to me for hours on the piano. If I found no one in, I stayed and waited, chatted with the nurse, played with the child, or lay on the couch in the study and read a newspaper; and when Anna Alexeyevna came back I met her in the hall, took all her parcels from her, and for some reason I carried those parcels every time with as much love, as much solemnity, as if I were a boy.

" 'The old woman had it easy,' the proverb runs, 'so she bought a pig.' The Luganoviches had it easy, so they made friends with me. If I was long in coming to the town, I must be ill, or something must have happened to me, and both of them would be very anxious. They were distressed that I, an educated man with a knowledge of languages, instead of devoting myself to scholarship or literary work, should live in the country, rush around like a squirrel in a cage, work hard and yet always be penniless. They imagined that I was unhappy, and that I only talked, laughed, and ate to conceal my sufferings, and even at cheerful moments when I was quite at ease I was aware of their searching eyes fixed upon me. They were particularly touching when I was really in trouble, when I was being hard pressed by some creditor and was unable to meet a payment on time. The two of them, husband and wife, would whisper together at the window; then he would come over to me and say with a grave face:

" 'If you are in need of money at the moment, Pavel Konstantinovich, my wife and I beg you not to stand on ceremony, but borrow from us.'

"And in his agitation his ears would turn red. Or again, after whispering in the same way at the window, he would come up to me, his ears red, and say, 'My wife and I earnestly beg you to accept this present from us.'

"And he would hand me studs, a cigarette case, or a lamp, and I would send them fowls, butter, and flowers from the farm. Both of them, by the way, were very well off. In the early days I often borrowed money, and was not very choosy about it—borrowed wherever I could—but nothing in the world would have induced me to borrow from the Luganoviches. But why mention the matter?

"I was unhappy. At home, in the fields, in the shed, I kept thinking of her. I tried to understand the mystery of a beautiful, intelligent young woman marrying someone so uninteresting, almost an old man (her husband was over forty), and having children by him; I tried to fathom the mystery of this dull, kindly, simple-hearted man, who reasoned with such tiresome good sense, who at evening parties and balls kept near the more substantial people, looking listless and superfluous, with a submissive, apathetic expression, as though he had been brought there for sale, who yet believed in his right to be happy, to have children by her; and I kept trying to understand why she had met just him first and not me, and why such a terrible mistake need have happened in our lives.

"And every time I came to the town I saw from her eyes that she had been expecting me, and she would tell me herself that she had had a peculiar feeling all that day and had guessed that I would come. We would talk a long time, and then we would be silent, yet we did not confess our love to each other, but timidly and jealously concealed it. We were afraid of everything that would reveal our secret to ourselves. I loved her tenderly, deeply, but I reflected and kept asking myself what our love could lead to if we did not have the strength to fight against it. It seemed incredible to me that my gentle, sad love could all at once rudely break up the even course of the life of her husband, her children, and the whole household in which I was so loved and trusted. Would it be honorable? She would follow me, but where? Where could I take her? It would have been different if I had led a beautiful, interesting life—if I had been fighting for the liberation of my country, for instance, or had been a celebrated scholar, an actor, or a painter; but as things were it would mean taking her from one humdrum life to another as humdrum or perhaps more so. And how long would our happiness last? What would happen to her if I fell ill, if I died, or if we simply stopped loving each other?

"And she apparently reasoned the same way. She thought of her husband, her children, and of her mother, who loved her son-in-law like a son. If she yielded to her feeling she would have to lie, or else to tell the truth, and in her position either would have been equally inconvenient and terrible. And she was tormented by the question whether her love would bring me happiness—whether she would not complicate my life, which as it was she believed to be hard enough and full of all sorts of trouble. It seemed to her that she was not young enough for me, that she was not industrious or energetic enough to begin a new life, and she often said to her husband that I ought to marry a girl of intelligence and worth who would be a good housewife and a helpmate—and she would add at once that such a girl was not likely to be found in the whole town.

* * *

"Meanwhile the years were passing. Anna Alexeyevna already had two children. Whenever I arrived at the Luganoviches' the servants smiled cordially, the children shouted that Uncle Pavel Konstantinovich had come, and hung on my neck; everyone was happy. They did not understand what was going on within me, and thought that I, too, was happy. Everyone regarded me as a noble fellow. Both grown-ups and children felt that a noble fellow was walking about the room, and that gave a peculiar charm to their relations with me, as though in my presence their life, too, was purer and more beautiful. Anna Alexeyevna and I used to go to the theater together, always on foot. We used to sit side by side, our shoulders touching; I would take the opera glass from her hands without a word, and feel at that moment that she was close to me, that she was mine, that we could not live without each other. But by some strange misunderstanding, when we came out of the theater we always said good-bye and parted like strangers. Goodness knows what people were saying about us in the town already, but there was not a word of truth in it all.

"Latterly Anna Alexeyevna took to going away frequently to stay with her mother or her sister; she began to be moody, she was coming to recognize that her life was without satisfaction, was ruined, and at such times she did not care to see her husband or her children. She was already being treated for nervous prostration.

"We continued to say nothing, and in the presence of strangers she displayed an odd irritation with me; no matter what I said she disagreed with me, and if I had an argument she sided with my opponent. If I dropped something, she would say coldly:

" 'I congratulate you.'

"If I forgot to take the opera glass when we were going to the theater she would say afterwards:

" 'I knew you would forget.'

"Luckily or not, there is nothing in our lives that does not come to an end sooner or later. The time came when we had to part, as Luganovich received an appointment in one of the western provinces. They had to sell their furniture, their horses, their summer villa. When we drove out to the villa and afterwards, as we were going away, looked back to see the garden and the green roof for the last time, everyone was sad, and I realized that the time had come to say good-bye not only to the villa. It was arranged that at the end of August we should see

Anna Alexeyevna off to the Crimea, where the doctors were sending her, and that a little later Luganovich and the children would set off for the western province.

"A great crowd had collected to see Anna Alexeyevna off. When she had said good-bye to her husband and children and there was only a minute left before the third bell, I ran into her compartment to place on the rack a basket that she had almost forgotten, and then I had to say good-bye. When our eyes met right there in the compartment our spiritual strength deserted us both, I took her in my arms, she pressed her face to my breast, and tears flowed from her eyes. Kissing her face, her shoulders, her hands wet with tears—oh, how miserable we were!—I confessed my love to her, and with a burning pain in my heart I realized how needless and petty and deceptive was all that had hindered us from loving each other. I realized that when you love you must either, in your reasoning about that love, start from what is higher, more important than happiness or unhappiness, sin or virtue in their usual meaning, or you must not reason at all.

"I kissed her for the last time, pressed her hand, and we parted forever. The train was already moving. I walked into the next compartment—it was empty—and until I reached the next station I sat there crying. Then I walked home to Sofyino. . . ."

While Alyohin was telling his story, the rain stopped and the sun came out. Burkin and Ivan Ivanych went out on the balcony, from which there was a fine view of the garden and the river, which was shining now in the sunshine like a mirror. They admired it, and at the same time they were sorry that this man with the kind, intelligent eyes who had told them his story with such candor should be rushing round and round on this huge estate like a squirrel in a cage instead of devoting himself to some scholarly pursuit or something else which would have made his life pleasanter; and they thought what a sorrowful face Anna Alexeyevna must have had when he said good-bye to her in the compartment and kissed her face and shoulders. Both of them had come across her in the town, and Burkin was acquainted with her and thought she was beautiful.

IN THE RAVINE

The village of Ukleyevo lay in a ravine, so that only the belfry and the chimneys of the cotton mills could be seen from the highroad and the railway station. When visitors asked what village this was, they were told:

"That's the village where the sexton ate all the caviar at the funeral."

It had happened at a funeral feast in the house of the manufacturer Kostukov that the old sexton saw among the savories some large-grained caviar and began eating it greedily; people nudged him, tugged at his sleeve, but he seemed petrified with enjoyment: felt nothing, and only went on eating. He ate up all the caviar, and there were some four pounds in the jar. And years had passed since then, the sexton had long been dead, but the caviar was still remembered. Whether life was so poor here or people had not been clever enough to notice anything but that unimportant incident that had occurred ten years before, anyway the people had nothing else to tell about the village of Ukleyevo.

The village was never free from fever, and the mud was thick there even in the summer, especially near the fences over which hung old willow trees that gave deep shade. Here there was always a smell from the factory refuse and the acetic acid which was used in the manufacture of the calico.

The three cotton mills and the tanyard were not in the village itself, but a little way off. They were small plants, and not more than four hundred workmen were employed in all of them. The tanyard often made the water in the little river stink; the refuse contaminated the meadows, the peasants' cattle suffered from anthrax, and the tanyard was ordered closed. It was considered to be closed but went on working in secret with the connivance of the local police officer and the district doctor, each of whom was paid ten rubles a month by the owner. In the whole village there were only two decent houses built of brick with iron roofs; one of them was occupied by the district government office, in the other, a two-storied house just opposite the church, lived Grigory Petrovich Tzybukin, a townsman who hailed from Yepifan.

Grigory kept a grocery, but that was only for the sake of appearances: in reality he sold vodka, cattle, hides, grain, and pigs; he traded in anything that came to hand, and when, for instance, magpies were wanted abroad for ladies' hats, he made thirty kopecks on every pair of birds; he bought timber for felling, lent money at interest, and altogether was a resourceful old man.

He had two sons. The elder, Anisim, served in the police as a detective and was rarely at home. The younger, Stepan, had gone in for trade and helped his father, but no great help was expected from him as he was weak in health and deaf; his wife, Aksinya, a handsome woman with a good figure, who wore a hat and carried a parasol on holidays, got up early and went to bed late, and ran about all day long, picking up her skirts and jingling her keys, going from the warehouse to the cellar and from there to the shop, and old Tzybukin looked at her good-humoredly while his eyes glowed, and at such moments he regretted she had not been married to his elder son instead of to the younger one, who was deaf, and obviously no judge of female beauty.

The old man had always had an inclination for family life, and he loved his family more than anything on earth, especially his elder son, the detective, and his daughter-in-law. Aksinya had no sooner married the deaf son than she began to display an extraordinary gift for business, and knew who could be allowed to run up a bill and who could not; she kept the keys and would not trust them even to her husband; she rattled away at the abacus, looked at the horses' teeth like a peasant, and was always laughing or shouting; and whatever she did or said, the old man was simply delighted and muttered:

"Well done, daughter-in-law! Well done, my beauty!"

He had been a widower, but a year after his son's marriage he could not resist getting married himself. A girl was found for him, in a village twenty miles from Ukleyevo, Varvara Nikolaevna by name, no longer young, but good-looking, comely, and coming from a decent family. No sooner had she moved into a little room in the upper story than everything in the house seemed to brighten up as though new glass had been put into all the windows. The lamps gleamed before the icons, the tables were covered with snow-white cloths, plants with red buds made their appearance in the windows and in the front garden, and at dinner, instead of eating from a single bowl, each person had a separate plate set for him. Varvara Nikolaevna had a pleasant, friendly smile, and it seemed as though the whole house were smiling too. Beggars and pilgrims, male and female, began to come into the yard, a thing which had never happened in the past; the plaintive singsong voices of the Ukleyevo peasant women and the apologetic coughs of weak, seedy-looking men who had been dismissed from the factory for drunkenness were heard under the windows. Varvara helped them with money, with bread, with old clothes, and afterwards, when she felt more at home, began taking things out of the shop. One day the deaf man saw her take four ounces of tea and that disturbed him.

"Here, Mother's taken four ounces of tea," he informed his father afterwards; "where is that to be entered?"

The old man made no reply but stood still and thought a moment, moving his eyebrows, and then went upstairs to his wife.

"Varvarushka, if you want anything out of the shop," he said affectionately, "take it, my dear. Take it and welcome; don't hesitate."

And the next day the deaf man, running across the yard, called to her:

"If there is anything you want, Mother dear, help yourself."

There was something new, something gay and light-hearted in her almsgiving, just as there was in the lamps before the icons and in the red flowers. When on the eve of a fast or during the local church festival, which lasted three days, they palmed off on the peasants tainted salt meat, smelling so strong it was hard to stand near the tub of it, and took scythes, caps, and their wives' kerchiefs in pledge from the drunken men; when the factory hands, stupefied with bad vodka, lay rolling in the mud, and sin seemed to hover thick like a fog in the air, then it was a relief to think that up there in the house there was a gentle, neatly dressed woman who had nothing to do with salt meat or vodka; her charity had in those oppressive, murky days the effect of a safety valve in a machine.

The days in Tzybukin's house were busy ones. Before the sun was up Aksinya was snorting as she washed in the outer room, and the samovar was boiling in the kitchen with a hum that boded no good. Old Grigory Petrovich, dressed in a long black jacket, cotton breeches, and shiny top boots, looking a dapper little figure, walked about the rooms, tapping with his little heels like the father-in-law in the well-known song. The shop was opened. When it was daylight a racing droshky was brought up to the front door and the old man got jauntily into it, pulling his big cap down to his ears; and, looking at him, no one would have said he was fifty-six. His wife and daughter-in-law saw him off, and at such times when he had on a good, clean coat, and a huge black stallion that had cost three hundred rubles was harnessed to the droshky, the old man did not like the peasants to come up to him with their complaints and petitions; he hated the peasants and disdained them, and if he saw some peasants waiting at the gate, he would shout angrily:

"Why are you standing there? Move on."

Or if it were a beggar, he would cry:

"God will provide!"

He would drive off on business; his wife, in a dark dress and a black apron, tidied the rooms or helped in the kitchen. Aksinya attended to the shop, and from the yard could be heard the clink of bottles and of money, her laughter and loud talk, and the angry voices of customers whom she had offended; and at the same time it could be seen that the illicit sale of vodka was already going on in the shop. The deaf man sat in the shop, too, or walked about the street bareheaded, with his hands in his pockets, looking absent-mindedly now at the houses, now at the sky overhead. Six times a day they had tea; four times a day they sat down to meals. And in the evening they counted their takings, put them down, went to bed, and slept soundly.

All the three cotton mills at Ukleyevo were connected by telephone with the houses of their owners—Hrymin Seniors, Hrymin Juniors, and Kostukov. A telephone was installed in the government office, too, but it soon went out of order when it started to swarm with bugs and cockroaches. The district elder was semiliterate and wrote every word in the official documents with a capital. But when the telephone went out of order he said:

"Yes, now we shall be badly off without a telephone."

The Hrymin Seniors were continually at law with the Juniors, and sometimes the Juniors quarreled among themselves and went to law, and their mill did not work for a month or two till they were reconciled again, and this was an entertainment for the people of Ukleyevo, as there was a great deal of talk and gossip on the occasion of each quarrel. On holidays Kostukov and the Juniors would go driving and they would dash about Ukleyevo and run down calves. Aksinya, dressed to kill and rustling her starched petticoats, used to promenade up and down the street near her shop; the Juniors would snatch her up and carry her off as though by force. Then old Tzybukin, too, would drive out to show his new horse and he would take Varvara with him.

In the evening, after these drives, when people were going to bed, an expensive concertina was played in the Juniors' yard and, if the moon was shining, those strains thrilled the heart, and Ukleyevo no longer seemed a wretched hole.

II

The elder son, Anisim, came home very rarely, only on great holidays, but he often sent by a returning villager presents and letters written by someone else in a very beautiful hand, always on a sheet of foolscap that looked like a formal petition. The letters were full of expressions that Anisim never made use of in conversation: "Dear Papa and Mamma, I send you a pound of orange pekoe tea for the satisfaction of your physical needs."

At the bottom of every letter was scratched, as though with a broken pen: "Anisim Tzybukin," and again in the same excellent hand: "Agent."

The letters were read aloud several times, and the old father, touched, red with emotion, would say:

"Here he did not care to stay at home, he has gone in for a learned profession. Well, let him go his way! Every man to his own trade!"

It happened that just before carnival there was a heavy rain mixed with sleet; the old man and Varvara went to the window to look at it, and, lo and behold! Anisim drove up in a sledge from the station. He was quite unexpected. He came indoors looking anxious and troubled about something, and he remained the same for the rest of his stay; there was something jaunty in his manner. He was in no haste to go away, and it looked as though he had been dismissed from the service. Varvara was pleased to see him; she kept looking at him with a sly expression, sighing, and shaking her head.

"How is this, my friends?" she said. "The lad's in his twenty-eighth year, and he is still leading a gay bachelor life; tut, tut, tut. . . ."

From the adjacent room her soft, even speech continued to sound like tut, tut, tut. She began whispering with her husband and Aksinya, and their faces, too, assumed a sly and mysterious expression as though they were conspirators.

It was decided to marry Anisim.

"The younger brother has long been married," said Varvara, "and you are still without a helpmate like a cock at a fair. What is the meaning of it? Tut, tut, you will be married, please God, then as you choose—you can go into the service and your wife will remain here at home to help us. There is no order in your life, young man, and I see you have forgotten how to live properly. Tut, tut, all of you townspeople are sinners."

Since the Tzybukins were rich, the prettiest girls were chosen as brides for them. For Anisim, too, they found a handsome one. He was himself of an uninteresting and inconspicuous appearance; of a weak and sickly constitution and short stature; he had full, puffy cheeks which looked as though he were blowing them out; there was a sharp look in his unblinking eyes; his beard was red and scanty, and when he was thinking he always put it into his mouth and bit it; moreover he drank and that was noticeable from his face and his walk. But when he was informed that they had found a very beautiful bride for him, he said:

"Oh, well, I am not a fright myself. All of us Tzybukins are handsome, I must say."

The village of Torguyevo was near the town. Half of it had lately been incorporated into the town, the other half remained a village. In the first half there was a widow living in her own little house; she had a sister living with her who was quite poor and went out to work by the day, and this sister had a daughter called Lipa, a girl who went out to work too. People in Torguyevo were already talking about Lipa's good looks, but her terrible poverty put everyone off; people opined that only some widower or elderly man would marry her in spite of her poverty, or would perhaps take her to himself without marriage, and that her mother would get enough to eat living with her. Varvara heard about Lipa from the matchmakers, and she drove over to Torguyevo.

Then a proper visit of inspection was arranged at the house of the girl's aunt, with refreshments and wine, and Lipa wore a new pink dress made on purpose for this occasion, and a crimson ribbon like a flame gleamed in her hair. She was pale, thin, and frail, with soft, delicate features sunburnt from working in the open air; a shy, mournful smile always hovered about her face, and there was a childlike look in her eyes, trustful and curious.

She was young, still a child, her bosom still scarcely perceptible, but she could be married because she had reached the legal age. She really was beautiful, and the only thing that might be thought unattractive was her big masculine hands which hung idle now like two big claws.

"There is no dowry—but we don't mind that," said Tzybukin to the aunt. "We took a wife from a poor family for our son Stepan, too, and now we can't say too much for her. In the house and in the shop alike she has hands of gold."

Lipa stood in the doorway and looked as though she would say: "Do with me as you will, I trust you," while her mother Praskovya the charwoman hid in the kitchen, numb with shyness. At one time in her youth a merchant whose floors she was scrubbing stamped at her in a rage; she went chill with terror and there always was a feeling of fear at the bottom of her heart. And that fear made her arms and legs tremble and her cheeks twitch. Sitting in the kitchen she tried to hear what the visitors were saying, and she kept crossing herself, pressing her fingers to her forehead, and gazing at the icons. Anisim, slightly drunk, would open the door into the kitchen and say in a free and easy way:

"Why are you sitting in here, precious Mamma? We are dull without you."

And Praskovya, overcome with timidity, pressing her hands to her lean, wasted bosom, would say:

"Oh, not at all. . . . It's very kind of you, sir."

After the visit of inspection the wedding day was fixed. Then Anisim walked about the rooms at home whistling, or suddenly thinking of something, would fall to brooding and would look at the floor fixedly, silently, as though he would probe to the depths of the earth. He expressed neither pleasure that he was to be married, married so soon, the week after Easter, nor a desire to see his bride, but simply went on whistling. And it was evident that he was only getting married because his father and stepmother wished him to, and because it was the village custom to marry off the son in order to have a woman to help in the house. When he went away he seemed in no haste, and behaved altogether not as he had done on previous visits; he was unusually jaunty and talked inappropriately.

III

In the village of Shikalova lived two dressmakers, sisters, belonging to the Flagellant sect. The new clothes for the wedding were ordered from them, and they often came to try them on, and stayed a long while drinking tea. They were making for Varvara a brown dress with black lace and bugles on it, and for Aksinya a light green dress with a yellow front and a train. When the dressmakers had finished their work Tzybukin paid them not in money but in goods from the shop, and they went away depressed, carrying parcels of tallow candles and tins of sardines which they did not in the least need, and when they got out of the village into the open country they sat down on a hillock and cried.

Anisim arrived three days before the wedding, rigged out in new clothes from top to toe. He had dazzling india-rubber galoshes, and instead of a cravat wore a red cord with little balls on it, and over his shoulder he had hung an overcoat, also new, without putting his arms into the sleeves.

After crossing himself sedately before the icon, he greeted his father and gave him ten silver rubles and ten half-rubles; to Varvara he gave as much, and to Aksinya twenty quarter-rubles. The chief charm of the present lay in the fact that all the coins, as though carefully matched, were new and glittered in the sun. Trying to seem grave and sedate he screwed up his face and puffed out his cheeks, and he smelled of spirits: he must have visited the refreshment bar at every station. And again there was something free and easy about the man—something superfluous and out of place. Then Anisim had a bite and drank tea with the old man, and Varvara kept turning the new coins over in her hands and inquired about villagers who had gone to live in the town.

"They are all right, thank God, they get on quite well," said Anisim. "Only something has happened to Ivan Yegorov: his old woman, Sofya Nikiforovna, is dead. Of consumption. They ordered the memorial dinner for the peace of her soul from the confectioner's at two and a half rubles a head. And there was wine. There were peasants from our village, and Yegorov paid two and a half rubles for them too. They didn't eat a thing, though. What does a peasant understand about sauces!"

"Two and a half rubles!" said his father, shaking his head.

"Well, it's not like the country there. You go into a restaurant to have a snack, you order one thing and another, a crowd collects, you have a drink—and before you know it it is daylight and you've three or four rubles each to pay. And when you are with Samorodov he likes to have coffee with cognac in it after everything, and cognac is sixty kopecks a little glass."

"And he is making it all up," said the old man delightedly; "he is making it all up!"

"I am always with Samorodov now. It's Samorodov who writes my letters to you. He writes splendidly. And if I were to tell you, Mamma," Anisim went on gaily, addressing Varvara, "the sort of fellow that Samorodov is, you would not believe me. We call him Muhtar, because he is black like an Armenian. I can see through him, I know all his affairs as well as I know the five fingers of my hand, and he feels that, and he always follows me about, we're as thick as thieves. He seems not to like it in a way, but he can't get on without me. Where I go he goes. I have a true sharp eye, Mamma. I see a peasant selling a shirt at the rag fair, 'Stay, that shirt was stolen.' And really it turns out it is so: the shirt was stolen."

"How can you tell?" asked Varvara.

"I just know it, I have just an eye for it. I know nothing about the shirt, only for some reason I seem drawn to it: it's stolen, and that's all I can say. The boys in the department have got a saying: 'Oh, Anisim has gone to shoot snipe!' That means looking for stolen goods. Yes. . . . Anybody can steal, but it is another thing to keep what you've stolen! The earth is wide, but there is no place on it to hide stolen goods."

"A ram and two ewes were carried off from the Guntorevs's last week," said Varvara, and she heaved a sigh, "and there is no one to try and find them. . . . Oh, oh, oh . . ."

"Well, I might have a try. I could do that."

The day of the wedding arrived. It was a cool but bright,

cheerful April day. Since early morning people were driving about Ukleyevo in carriages drawn by teams of two or three horses, the bells jingling and gay ribbons decorating the yokes and manes. The rooks, disturbed by this activity, were cawing noisily in the willows, and the starlings sang their loudest unceasingly as though rejoicing that there was a wedding at the Tzybukins'.

Indoors the tables were already loaded with long fish, smoked hams, stuffed fowls, boxes of sprats, pickled savories of various sorts, and many bottles of vodka and wine; there was a smell of smoked sausage and of sour lobster. Old Tzybukin walked about near the tables, tapping with his heels and sharpening the knives against each other. They kept calling Varvara and asking for things, and she, breathless and distraught, was constantly running in and out of the kitchen, where the man cook from Kostukov's and a woman cook employed by Hrymin Juniors had been at work since early morning. Aksinya, with her hair curled, in her stays without her dress on, in new creaky boots, flew about the yard like a whirlwind, showing glimpses of her bare knees and bosom. It was noisy, there was a sound of scolding and oaths; passersby stopped at the wide-open gates, and in everything there was a feeling that something extraordinary was happening.

"They have gone for the bride!"

The carriage bells jingled and died away far beyond the village. . . . Between two and three o'clock people ran up: again there was a jingling of bells: they were bringing the bride! The church was full, the candelabra were lighted, the choir were singing from music books as old Tzybukin had wished it. The glare of the lights and the bright-colored dresses dazzled Lipa; she felt as though the singers with their loud voices were hitting her on the head with hammers. The stays, which she had put on for the first time in her life, and her shoes pinched her, and her face looked as though she had only just come to herself after fainting; she gazed about without understanding. Anisim, in his black coat with a red cord instead of a tie, stared at the same spot, lost in thought, and at every loud burst of singing hurriedly crossed himself. He felt touched and disposed to weep. This church was familiar to him from earliest childhood; at one time his dead mother used to bring him here to take the sacrament; at one time he used to sing in the choir; every icon he remembered so well, every corner. Here he was being married, he had to take a wife for the sake of doing the proper thing, but he was not thinking of that now, he had somehow forgotten his wedding completely. Tears dimmed his eyes so that he could not see the icons, he felt heavy at heart; he prayed and besought God that the misfortunes that threatened him, that were ready to burst upon him tomorrow, if not today, might somehow pass him by as storm clouds in time of drought pass over a village without yielding one drop of rain. And so many sins were heaped up in the past, so many sins and getting away from them or wiping them out was so beyond hope that it seemed incongruous even to ask forgiveness. But he did ask forgiveness, and even gave a loud sob, but no one took any notice of that, since they supposed he had had a drop too much.

There was the sound of a fretful childish wail:

"Take me away from here, Mamma darling!"

"Quiet there!" cried the priest.

When the young couple returned from the church people ran after them; there were crowds, too, round the shop, round the gates, and in the yard under the windows. Peasant women came to sing songs in their honor. The young couple had scarcely crossed the threshold when the choristers, who were already standing in the outer room with their music books, broke into a chant at the top of their voices; a band brought expressly from the town struck up. Sparkling Don wine was brought in tall glasses, and Yelizarov, a carpenter who was also a contractor, a tall, gaunt old man with eyebrows so bushy that his eyes could scarcely be seen, said, addressing the pair:

"Anisim and you, my child, love one another, lead a godly life, little children, and the Heavenly Mother will not abandon you."

He fell upon the old father's shoulder and gave a sob.

"Grigory Petrovich, let us weep, let us weep with joy!" he said in a thin voice, and then at once burst out laughing and continued in a loud bass. "Ho-ho-ho! This one, too, is a fine daughter-in-law for you! Everything is in its place in her; everything runs smoothly, no creaking, the whole mechanism works well, lots of screws in it."

He was a native of the Yegoryev district, but had worked in the mills at Ukleyevo and in the neighborhood since his youth, and had made it his home. For years he had been a familiar figure, as old and gaunt and lanky as now, and for years he had

had the nickname "Crutch." Perhaps because he had done nothing but repair work for forty years, he judged everybody and everything by its soundness, always asking himself if things were in need of repair. Before sitting down to table he tried several chairs to see whether they were solid, and he touched the smoked whitefish too.

After the Don wine, they all sat down to table. The visitors talked, moving their chairs. The choristers were singing in the outer room. The band was playing, and at the same time the peasant women in the yard were singing their songs in unison, and there was an awful, wild medley of sounds which made one giddy.

Crutch fidgeted about on his chair and prodded his neighbors with his elbows, prevented people from talking, and laughed and cried alternately.

"Children, children, children," he muttered rapidly. "Aksinya my dear, Varvara darling, let's all live in peace and harmony, my dear little hatchets . . ."

He drank little and was now drunk from only one glass of English bitters. The revolting bitters, made from nobody knows what, intoxicated everyone who drank it, stunning them, as it were. Tongues began to falter.

The local clergy were present, and the clerks from the mills with their wives, tradesmen and tavern keepers from the other villages. The clerk and the elder of the rural district who had served together for fourteen years, and who had during all that time never signed a single document for anybody or let a single person out of the office without deceiving or insulting him, were sitting now side by side, both fat and replete, and it seemed as though they were so steeped in injustice and falsehood that even the skin of their faces had a peculiar, thievish look. The clerk's wife, a thin woman with a squint, brought all her children with her, and like a bird of prey looked aslant at the plates, snatched everything she could get hold of and put it in her own or her children's pockets.

Lipa sat as though turned to stone, still with the same expression as in church. Anisim had not said a single word to her since he had made her acquaintance, so that he did not yet know the sound of her voice; and now, sitting beside her, he remained mute and went on drinking bitters, and when he got drunk he began talking to Lipa's aunt sitting opposite:

"I have a friend called Samorodov. A peculiar man. He is by rank an honorary citizen, and he can talk. But I know him through and through, Auntie, and he knows it. Pray join me in drinking to Samorodov's health, Auntie!"

Varvara, worn out and distracted, walked round the table, pressing the guests to eat, and was evidently pleased that there were so many dishes and that everything was so lavish—no one could disparage them now. The sun set, but the dinner went on: the guests were beyond knowing what they were eating or drinking, it was impossible to distinguish what was said, and only from time to time when the band subsided some peasant woman could be heard shouting outside:

"You've sucked the blood out of us, you plunderers; a plague on you!"

In the evening they danced to the band. The Hrymin Juniors came, bringing wine of their own, and one of them, when dancing a quadrille, held a bottle in each hand and a wineglass in his mouth, and that made everyone laugh. In the middle of the quadrille they suddenly crooked their knees and danced in a squatting position; Aksinya in green flew by like a flash, raising a wind with her train. Someone trod on her flounce and Crutch shouted:

"Hey, they have torn off the baseboard! Children!"

Aksinya had naive gray eyes which rarely blinked, and a naive smile played continually on her face. And in those unblinking eyes, and in that little head on the long neck, and in her slenderness there was something snakelike; all in green, with her yellow bosom and the smile on her lips, she looked like a viper that peers out of the young rye in the spring at the passersby, stretching itself and lifting its head. The Hrymins were free in their behavior to her, and it was very noticeable that she had long been on intimate terms with the eldest of them. But her deaf husband saw nothing, he did not look at her; he sat with his legs crossed and ate nuts, cracking them so loudly that it sounded like pistol shots.

But, behold, old Tzybukin himself walked into the middle of the room and waved his handkerchief as a sign that he, too, wanted to dance the Russian dance, and all over the house and from the crowd in the yard rose a hum of approbation:

"It's himself has stepped out! *Himself!"*

Varvara danced, but the old man only waved his handkerchief

and kicked up his heels; but the people in the yard, propped against one another, peeping in at the windows, were in raptures, and for the moment forgave him everything—his wealth and the wrongs he had done them.

"Well done, Grigory Petrovich!" was heard in the crowd. "Do it! You can still do it! Ha-ha!"

It was kept up till late, till two o'clock in the morning. Anisim, staggering, went to take leave of the singers and musicians, and gave each of them a new half-ruble. His father, who was not staggering but treading more heavily on one leg, saw his guests off, and said to each of them:

"The wedding has cost two thousand."

As the party was breaking up, someone took the Shikalova innkeeper's good coat instead of his own old one, and Anisim suddenly flew into a rage and began shouting:

"Stop, I'll find it at once; I know who stole it! Stop!"

He ran out into the street in pursuit of someone, but he was caught, brought back home, shoved, drunken, red with anger and wet, into the room where the aunt was undressing Lipa, and was locked in.

IV

Five days had passed. Anisim, who was ready to leave, went upstairs to say good-bye to Varvara. All the lamps were burning before the icons, there was a smell of incense, while she sat at the window knitting a stocking of red wool.

"You have not stayed with us long," she said. "You're bored, I suppose. Tut, tut, tut. . . . We live comfortably; we have plenty of everything. We celebrated your wedding properly, in good style; your father says it came to two thousand. In fact we live like merchants, only it's dreary here. We treat the people very badly. My heart aches, my dear; how we treat them, my goodness! Whether we barter a horse or buy something or hire a laborer—it's cheating in everything. Cheating and cheating. The hempseed oil in the shop is bitter, rancid, worse than pitch. But surely, tell me pray, couldn't we sell good oil?"

"Every man to his trade, Mamma."

"But you know we all have to die? Oh, oh, really you ought to talk to your father! . . ."

"Why, you should talk to him yourself."

"Well, well, I did put in a word, but he said just what you do: 'Every man to his own trade.' Do you suppose in the next world they'll consider what trade you have been put to? God's judgment is just."

"Of course, they won't consider," said Anisim, and he heaved a sigh. "There is no God, anyway, you know, Mamma, so what considering can there be?"

Varvara looked at him with surprise, burst out laughing, and struck her hands together. Perhaps because she was so genuinely surprised at his words and looked at him as though he were queer, he was embarrassed.

"Perhaps there is a God, only there is no faith. When I was being married I was not myself. Just as you may take an egg from under a hen and there is a chicken chirping in it, so my conscience suddenly piped up, and while I was being married I thought all the time: 'There is a God!' But when I left the church, it was nothing. And indeed, how can I tell whether there is a God or not? We are not taught right from childhood, and while the babe is still at his mother's breast he is only taught 'every man to his own trade.' Father does not believe in God, either. You were saying that Guntorev had some sheep stolen. . . . I have found them; it was a peasant at Shikalova stole them; he stole them, but Father's got the hides . . . so that's all his faith amounts to."

Anisim winked and wagged his head.

"The elder does not believe in God, either," he went on. "Nor the clerk, nor the sexton. And as for their going to church and keeping the fasts, that is simply to prevent people talking ill of them, and in case it really may be true that there will be a Day of Judgment. Nowadays people say that the end of the world has come because people have grown weak, do not honor their parents, and so on. All that is a trifle. My idea, Mamma, is that all our trouble is because there is so little conscience in people. I see through things, Mamma, and I understand. If a man has a stolen shirt I see it. A man sits in a tavern and you fancy he is drinking tea and no more, but to me the tea is neither here nor there; I see farther, he has no conscience. You can go about the whole day and not meet one man with a conscience. And the whole reason is that they don't know whether there is a God or not. . . . Well, good-bye, Mamma, keep alive and well, don't remember evil against me."

Anisim bowed down at Varvara's feet.

"I thank you for everything, Mamma," he said. "You are a great asset to our family. You are a very decent woman, and I am very pleased with you."

Much moved, Anisim went out, but returned again and said:

"Samorodov has got me mixed up in something: I shall either make my fortune or come to grief. If anything happens, then you must comfort my father, Mamma."

"Oh, nonsense, don't you worry, tut, tut, tut . . . God is merciful. And Anisim, you should pet your wife a little, instead you give each other sulky looks; you might smile at least."

"Yes, she is rather a queer one," said Anisim, and he gave a sigh. "She does not understand anything, she never speaks. She is very young, let her grow up."

A tall, sleek white stallion was already standing at the front door, harnessed to the chaise.

Old Tzybukin jumped in, sat down jauntily, and took the reins. Anisim kissed Varvara, Aksinya, and his brother. On the steps Lipa, too, was standing; she was standing motionless, looking away, and it seemed as though she had not come to see him off but just by chance for some unknown reason. Anisim went up to her and just touched her cheeks with his lips.

"Good-bye," he said.

And without looking at him she gave a strange smile; her face began to quiver, and everyone for some reason felt sorry for her. Anisim, too, leaped into the chaise with a bound and put his arms jauntily akimbo, for he considered himself a good-looking fellow.

When they drove up out of the ravine Anisim kept looking back toward the village. It was a warm, bright day. The cattle were being driven out for the first time, and the peasant girls and women were walking by the herd in their holiday dresses. The dun-colored bull bellowed, glad to be free, and pawed the ground with his forefeet. On all sides, above and below, the larks were singing. Anisim looked round at the elegant white church—it had only lately been whitewashed—and he thought how he had been praying in it five days before; he looked round at the school with its green roof, at the little river in which he used to bathe and catch fish, and there was a stir of joy in his heart, and he wished that a wall might rise up from the ground and prevent him from going farther, and that he might be left with nothing but the past.

At the station they went to the refreshment room and drank a glass of sherry each. His father felt in his pocket for his purse to pay.

"I will stand treat," said Anisim. The old man, touched and delighted, slapped him on the shoulder and winked to the waiter as much as to say, "See what a fine son I have got."

"You ought to stay at home in the business, Anisim," he said; "you would be worth any price to me! I would gild you from head to foot, my son."

"It can't be done, Papa."

The sherry was sour and smelled of sealing wax, but they had another glass.

When old Tzybukin returned home from the station, at first he did not recognize his younger daughter-in-law. As soon as her husband had driven out of the yard, Lipa was transformed and suddenly brightened up. Wearing a shabby skirt with her feet bare and her sleeves tucked up to the shoulders, she was scrubbing the stairs in the entry and singing in a silvery little voice, and when she brought out a big tub of slops and looked up at the sun with her childlike smile it seemed as though she, too, were a lark.

An old laborer who was passing by the door shook his head and cleared his throat.

"Yes, indeed, your daughters-in-law, Grigory Petrovich, are a blessing from God," he said. "Not women, but treasures!"

V

On Friday the eighth of July, Yelizarov, nicknamed Crutch, and Lipa were returning from the village of Kazanskoye, where they had been to a service on the occasion of a local church holiday in honor of the Holy Mother of Kazan. A good distance behind them walked Lipa's mother Praskovya, who always fell back, as she was ill and short of breath. It was drawing toward evening.

"A-a-a . . ." said Crutch, wondering as he listened to Lipa. "A-a! . . . We-ell!"

"I am very fond of jam, Ilya Makarych," said Lipa. "I sit down in my little corner and drink tea and eat jam. Or I drink it with Varvara Nikolaevna, and she tells some story full of feeling. She has a lot of jam—four jars. 'Have some, Lipa,' she says, 'eat as much as you like.' "

"A-a-a, four jars!"

"They live very well. We have white bread with our tea; and meat, too, as much as one wants. They live very well, only I am frightened in their presence, Ilya Makarych. Oh, oh, how frightened I am!"

"Why are you frightened, child?" asked Crutch, and he looked back to see how far behind Praskovya was.

"At first, after the wedding, I was afraid of Anisim Grigorich. Anisim Grigorich did nothing, he didn't ill-treat me, only when he comes near me a cold shiver runs all over me, through all my bones. And I did not sleep one night, I trembled all over and kept praying to God. And now I am afraid of Aksinya, Ilya Makarych. It's not that she does anything, she is always laughing, but sometimes she glances at the window, and her eyes are so angry and there is a greenish gleam in them—like the eyes of the sheep in the pen. The Hrymin Juniors are leading her astray: 'Your old man,' they tell her, 'has a bit of land at Butyokino, a hundred acres,' they say, 'and there is sand and water there, so you, Aksinya,' they say, 'build a brickyard there and we will go shares in it.' Bricks now are twenty rubles the thousand, it's a profitable business. Yesterday at dinner Aksinya said to the old man: 'I want to build a brickyard at Butyokino; I'm going into the business on my own account.' She laughed as she said it. And Grigory Petrovich's face darkened, one could see he did not like it. 'As long as I live,' he said, 'the family must not break up, we must keep together.' She gave a look and gritted her teeth. . . . Fritters were served, she would not eat them."

"A-a-a! . . ." Crutch was surprised.

"And tell me, if you please, when does she sleep?" said Lipa. "She sleeps for half an hour, then jumps up and keeps walking and walking about to see whether the peasants have not set fire to something, have not stolen something. . . . She frightens me, Ilya Makarych. And the Hrymin Juniors did not go to bed after the wedding, but drove to the town to go to law with each other; and folks do say it is all on account of Aksinya. Two of the brothers have promised to build her a brickyard, but the third is offended, and the factory has been at a standstill for a month, and my uncle Prohor is without work and goes about from house to house getting crusts. 'Hadn't you better go working on the land or sawing up wood, meanwhile, Uncle?' I tell him: 'why disgrace yourself?' 'I've got out of the way of it,' he says: 'I don't know how to do any sort of peasant's work now, Lip-inka.' . . ."

They stopped to rest and wait for Praskovya near a copse of young aspen trees. Yelizarov had long been a contractor in a small way, but he kept no horse, going on foot all over the district with nothing but a little bag in which there was bread and onions, and stalking along with big strides, swinging his arms. And it was difficult to walk with him.

At the entrance to the copse stood a milestone. Yelizarov touched it to see if it was firm. Praskovya reached them out of breath. Her wrinkled and always scared-looking face was beaming with happiness; she had been at church today like anyone else, then she had been to the fair and there had drunk pear cider. For her this was unusual, and it even seemed to her now that she had lived for her own pleasure that day for the first time in her life. After resting they all three walked on side by side. The sun had already set, and its beams filtered through the copse, gleaming on the trunks of the trees. There was a faint sound of voices ahead. The Ukleyevo girls had gone on long before but had lingered in the copse, probably gathering mushrooms.

"Hey, wenches!" cried Yelizarov. "Hey, my beauties!"

There was a sound of laughter in response.

"Crutch is coming! Crutch! The old horseradish."

And the echo laughed too. And then the copse was left behind. The tops of the factory chimneys came into view. The cross on the belfry glittered: this was the village, "the one at which the sexton ate all the caviar at the funeral." Now they were almost home; they only had to go down into the big ravine. Lipa and Praskovya, who had been walking barefoot, sat down on the grass to put on their shoes, Yelizarov sat down with them. If they looked down from above, Ukleyevo looked beautiful and peaceful with its willow trees, its white church, and its little river, and the only blot on the picture was the roof of the factories, painted for the sake of cheapness a dark sullen color. On the slope on the farther side they could see the rye—some in stacks and sheaves here and there as though strewn about by the storm, and some freshly cut lying in swathes; the oats, too, were ripe and glistened now in the sun like mother-of-pearl. It was harvesttime. Today was a holiday, tomorrow they would harvest the rye and cart the hay, and then Sunday a holiday again; every day there were mutterings of distant thunder. It was muggy and looked like rain, and, gazing now at the fields, everyone thought,

God grant we get the harvest in in time; and everyone felt at once gay and joyful and anxious at heart.

"Mowers ask a high price nowadays," said Praskovya. "One ruble and forty kopecks a day."

People kept coming from the fair at Kazanskoye: peasant women, mill hands in new caps, beggars, children. . . . A cart would drive by stirring up the dust, and behind it would run an unsold horse, and it seemed glad it had not been sold; then a cow was led along by the horns, resisting stubbornly; then a cart again, and in it drunken peasants swinging their legs. An old woman led a little boy in a big cap and big boots; the boy was tired out with the heat and the heavy boots which prevented him from bending his legs at the knees, but yet he blew a tin trumpet unceasingly with all his might. They had gone down the slope and turned into the street, but the trumpet could still be heard.

"Our mill owners don't seem quite themselves . . ." said Yelizarov. "It's bad. Kostukov got angry with me. 'Too many battens have been used for the cornices.' 'Too many? As many have been used as were needed, Vassily Danilych; I don't eat them with my porridge.' 'How can you speak to me like that?' said he, 'You good-for-nothing, you blockhead! Don't forget yourself! It was I made you a contractor.' 'That's nothing so wonderful,' said I. 'Even before I got to be a contractor I used to have tea every day.' 'You are all crooks . . .' he said. I held my peace. 'We are crooks in this world,' thought I, 'and you will be the crooks in the next. . . .' Ha-ha-ha! The next day he was softer. 'Don't you bear malice against me for my words, Makarych,' he said. 'If I said too much,' says he, 'what of it? I am a merchant of the first guild, your better—you ought to hold your tongue.' 'You,' said I, 'are a merchant of the first guild and I am a carpenter, that's correct. And Saint Joseph was a carpenter too. Ours is a righteous and godly calling, and if you are pleased to be my better you are very welcome to it, Vassily Danilych.' And later on, after that conversation, I mean, I thought: 'Which was the better man? A merchant of the first guild or a carpenter?' The carpenter must be, children!"

Crutch thought a minute and added:

"Yes, that's how it is, children. He who works, he who is patient, is the better man."

By now the sun had set and a thick mist as white as milk was rising over the river, in the church enclosure, and in the open spaces round the mills. Now when darkness was coming on rapidly, when lights were twinkling below, and when it seemed as though the mists were hiding a fathomless abyss, Lipa and her mother who were born in poverty and prepared to live so till the end, giving up to others everything except their frightened, gentle souls, may perhaps have fancied for a minute that in this vast, mysterious world, among the endless series of lives, they, too, counted for something, and they, too, were better than some-one; they liked sitting up there, they smiled happily and forgot that they must go down below again all the same.

At last they reached home. The mowers were sitting on the ground at the gates near the shop. As a rule the Ukleyevo peasants refused to work for Tzybukin, and he had to hire strangers, and now in the darkness it seemed as though there were men with long black beards sitting there. The shop was open, and through the doorway they could see the deaf man playing checkers with a boy. The mowers were singing softly, almost inaudibly, or were loudly demanding their wages for the previous day, but they were not paid for fear they should go away before tomorrow. Old Tzybukin, with his coat off, was sitting in his waistcoat with Aksinya under the birch tree, drink-ing tea; a lighted lamp was on the table.

"I say, grandfather," a mower called from outside the gates, as though taunting him, "pay us half anyway! Hey, grandfather."

And at once there was the sound of laughter, and then again they sang almost inaudibly. . . . Crutch, too, sat down to have some tea.

"We have been to the fair, you know," he began telling them. "We had a fine time, a very fine time, my children, praise the Lord. But an unfortunate thing happened: Sashka the black-smith bought some tobacco and gave the shopman half a ruble, you know. And the half-ruble was a false one"—Crutch went on, and he meant to speak in a whisper, but he spoke in a smothered husky voice which was audible to everyone. "The half-ruble turned out to be a bad one. He was asked where he got it. 'Anisim Tzybukin gave it me,' he said, 'when I was at his wedding,' he said. They called the police, took the man away. . . . Look out, Grigory Petrovich, that nothing comes of it, no talk. . . ."

"Gra-ndfather!" the same voice called tauntingly outside the gates. "Gra-andfather!"

A silence followed.

"Ah, little children, little children, little children . . ." Crutch muttered rapidly, and he got up. He was overcome with drowsiness. "Well, thank you for the tea, for the sugar, little children. It is time to sleep. I'm broken down, my beams have rotted away. Ho-ho-ho!"

As he walked away he said: "I suppose it's time I was dead," and he gave a sob. Old Tzybukin did not finish his tea but sat on a little, pondering; and his face looked as though he were listening to the footsteps of Crutch, who was far down the street.

"Sashka the blacksmith told a lie, I expect," said Aksinya, guessing his thoughts.

He went into the house and came back a little later with a parcel; he opened it, and there was the gleam of rubles—perfectly new coins. He took one, tried it with his teeth, flung it on the tray; then flung down another.

"The rubles really are false . . ." he said, looking at Aksinya and seeming perplexed. "These are those Anisim brought, his present. Take them, daughter," he whispered, and thrust the parcel into her hands. "Take them and throw them into the well . . . confound them! And mind there is no talk about it. Harm might come of it. . . . Take away the samovar, put out the light."

Lipa and her mother sitting in the barn saw the lights go out one after another; only up in Varvara's room there were blue and red icon lamps gleaming, and a feeling of peace, contentment, and happy ignorance seemed to float down from there. Praskovya could never get used to her daughter's being married to a rich man, and when she came to the house she huddled timidly in the entry with a beseeching smile on her face, and tea and sugar were sent out to her. And Lipa could not get used to it either, and after her husband had gone away she did not sleep in her bed, but lay down anywhere to sleep, in the kitchen or the shed, and every day she scrubbed the floor or washed the clothes, and felt as though she were hired by the day. And now, on coming back from the service at Kazanskoye, they had tea in the kitchen with the cook; then they went into the shed and lay down on the ground between the sledge and the wall. It was dark here and smelled of harness. The lights went out about the house, then they could hear the deaf man shutting up the shop, the mowers settling themselves about the yard to sleep. In the distance at the Hrymin Juniors' they were playing the expensive accordion . . . Praskovya and Lipa began to drop off.

When they were awakened by somebody's steps, the moon was shining brightly; at the entrance to the shed stood Aksinya with her bedding in her arms.

"Maybe it's a bit cooler here," she said; then she came in and lay down almost in the doorway so that the moonlight fell full upon her.

She did not sleep, but breathed heavily, tossing from side to side with the heat, throwing off almost all the bedclothes. And in the magic moonlight what a beautiful, what a proud animal she was! A little time passed, and then steps were heard again: the old father, white all over, appeared in the doorway.

"Aksinya," he called, "are you here?"

"Well?" she responded angrily.

"I told you just now to throw the money into the well, did you do it?"

"What next! Throwing property into the water! I gave it to the mowers . . ."

"Oh my God!" cried the old man, dumbfounded and alarmed. "Oh my God! you wicked woman. . . ."

He struck his hands together and went out, and kept talking to himself as he went away. And a little later Aksinya sat up and sighed heavily with annoyance, then rose, and, gathering up her bedclothes in her arms, went out.

"Why did you marry me into this family, Mother?" said Lipa.

"One has to be married, daughter. It was not us that ordered things so."

And a feeling of inconsolable woe was ready to take possession of them. But it seemed to them that someone was looking down from the height of the heavens, out of the blue, where the stars were, that someone saw everything that was going on in Ukleyevo, and was watching over them. And however powerful evil was, yet the night was calm and beautiful, and yet in God's world there is and will be righteousness as calm and beautiful, and everything on earth is only waiting to be made one with righteousness, even as the moonlight is blended with the night.

And both, huddling close to one another, fell asleep comforted.

VI

News had come long before that Anisim had been put in prison for counterfeiting money and circulating it. Months went by, more than half a year went by, the long winter was over, spring had begun, and everyone in the house and in the village had grown used to the fact that Anisim was in prison. And when anyone passed by the house or the shop at night he would remember that Anisim was in prison; and when they rang at the churchyard for some reason, that, too, reminded people that he was in prison awaiting trial.

It seemed as though a shadow had fallen upon the house. It looked more somber, the roof had become rusty, the green paint on the heavy, iron-bound door into the shop had faded; and old Tzybukin himself seemed to have grown darker. He had given up cutting his hair and beard, and looked shaggy. He no longer sprang jauntily into his chaise, nor shouted to beggars: "God will provide!" His strength was on the wane, and that was evident in everything. People were less afraid of him now, and the police officer drew up a formal charge against him in the shop, though he received his regular bribe as before; and three times the old man was called up to the town to be tried for the illicit sale of spirits, and the case was continually adjourned owing to the nonappearance of witnesses, and old Tzybukin was worn out with worry.

He often went to see his son, hired lawyers, handed in petitions, presented a banner to some church. He presented the warden of the prison in which Anisim was confined with a long spoon and a silver holder for a teaglass with the inscription: "The soul knows its right measure."

"There is no one to look after things for us," said Varvara. "Tut, tut. . . . You ought to ask someone of the gentry to write to the head officials. . . . At least they might let him out on bail! Why wear the poor fellow out?"

She, too, was grieved, but she nevertheless grew stouter and whiter; she lighted the lamps before the icons as before, and saw that everything in the house was clean, and regaled the guests with jam and apple tarts. The deaf man and Aksinya looked after the shop. A new project was in progress—a brickyard in Butyokino—and Aksinya went there almost every day in the chaise. She drove herself, and when she met acquaintances she stretched out her neck like a snake in the young rye, and smiled naively and enigmatically. Lipa spent her time playing with the baby which had been born to her just before Lent. It was a tiny, thin, pitiful little baby, and it was strange that it should cry and gaze about and be considered a human being, and even be called Nikifor. He lay in his cradle, and Lipa would walk away toward the door and say, bowing to him:

"How do you do, Nikifor Anisimych!"

And she would rush at him and kiss him. Then she would walk away to the door, bow again, and say:

"How do you do, Nikifor Anisimych!"

And he kicked up his little red legs, and his crying was mixed with laughter like the carpenter Yelizarov's.

At last the day of the trial was fixed. Tzybukin went away some five days before. Then the Tzybukins heard that the peasants called as witnesses had been fetched; their old workman who was one of those to receive a notice to appear went too.

The trial was on a Thursday. But Sunday had passed, and Tzybukin was still not back, and there was no news. Toward evening on Tuesday Varvara was sitting at the open window, waiting for her husband to come. In the next room Lipa was playing with her baby. She was tossing him up in her arms and saying ecstatically:

"You will grow ever so big, ever so big. You will be a peasant, we shall go out to work by the day together! We shall go out to work by the day together!"

"Come, come," said Varvara, offended. "Go out to work by the day, what an idea, you silly thing! He will be a merchant! . . ."

Lipa sang softly, but a minute later she forgot and began again:

"You will grow ever so big, ever so big. You will be a peasant, we'll go out to work by the day together."

"There she is at it again!"

Lipa, with Nikifor in her arms, stood still in the doorway and asked:

"Why do I love him so much, Maminka? Why do I feel so sorry for him?" she went on in a quivering voice, and her eyes glistened with tears.

"Who is he? What is he like? As light as a little feather, as a little crumb, but I love him, I love him as if he were a real person. Here he can do nothing, he can't talk, and yet I know from his little eyes what he wants."

Varvara pricked up her ears: the sound of the evening train coming into the station reached her. Had her husband come? She did not hear and she did not heed what Lipa was saying, she had no idea how the time passed, but only trembled all over—not with dread, but with intense curiosity. She saw a cart full of peasants roll quickly by with a rattle. It was the witnesses coming back from the station. When the cart passed the shop the old workman jumped out and walked into the yard. She could hear him being greeted in the yard and being asked some questions. . . .

"Loss of rights and all property," he said loudly, "and six years penal servitude in Siberia."

She could see Aksinya come out of the shop by the back way; she had just been selling kerosene, and in one hand held a bottle and in the other a can, and she had some silver coins in her mouth.

"Where is Father?" she asked, lisping.

"At the station," answered the laborer.

" 'When it gets a little darker,' he said, 'then I'll come.' "

And when it became known all through the household that Anisim was sentenced to penal servitude, the cook in the kitchen suddenly broke into a wail as though at a funeral, imagining that this was demanded by the proprieties:

"Who will care for us now you have gone, Anisim Grigorich, our bright falcon. . . ."

The dogs began barking in alarm. Varvara ran to the window, and rushing about in distress, shouted to the cook with all her might, straining her voice:

"Sto-op, Stepanida, sto-op! Don't harrow us, for Christ's sake!"

They forgot to set the samovar, they could think of nothing. Only Lipa could not make out what it was all about and went on playing with her baby.

When the old father arrived from the station they asked him no questions. He greeted them and walked through all the rooms in silence; he had no supper.

"There was no one to see about things . . ." Varvara began when they were alone. "I said you should have asked some of the gentry, you would not listen to me at the time. . . . A petition would . . ."

"I saw to things," said her husband with a wave of his hand. "When Anisim was condemned I went to the gentleman who was defending him. 'It's no use now,' he said, 'it's too late'; and Anisim said the same; it's too late. But all the same as I came out of court I engaged a lawyer and gave him an advance. I'll wait a week and then I'll go again. It is as God wills."

Again the old man walked through all the rooms, and when he went back to Varvara he said:

"I must be ill. My head's in a sort of . . . fog. My thoughts are mixed up."

He closed the door that Lipa might not hear, and went on softly:

"I am worried about the money. Do you remember before his wedding Anisim's bringing me some new rubles and half-rubles? One parcel I put away at the time, but the others I mixed with my own money. When my uncle Dmitri Filatych—the kingdom of heaven be his—was alive, he used to go to Moscow and to the Crimea to buy goods. He had a wife, and this same wife, when he was away buying goods, used to take up with other men. They had half a dozen children. And when Uncle was in his cups he would laugh and say: 'I never can make out,' he used to say, 'which are my children and which are other people's.' An easy-going disposition, to be sure; and so now I can't tell which are genuine rubles and which are false ones. And they all seem false to me."

"Nonsense, God bless you."

"I buy a ticket at the station, I give the man three rubles, and I keep fancying they are counterfeit. And I am frightened. I must be ill."

"There's no denying it, we are all in God's hands. . . . Oh dear, dear . . ." said Varvara, and she shook her head. "You ought to think about this, Grigory Petrovich: you never know, anything may happen, you are not a young man. See they don't wrong your grandchild when you are dead and gone. Oh, I am afraid they will be unfair to Nikifor! He is as good as fatherless, his mother's young and foolish . . . You ought to settle something on the poor little boy, at least the land, Butyokino, Grigory Petrovich, really! Think it over!" Varvara went on persuading him. "He's such a pretty boy, it's a pity! You go tomorrow and make out a deed; why put it off?"

"I'd forgotten my grandson," said Tzybukin. "I must go and have a look at him. So you say the boy is all right? Well, let him grow up, please God."

He opened the door and, crooking his finger, beckoned to Lipa. She went up to him with the baby in her arms.

"If there is anything you want, Lipynka, you ask for it," he said. "And eat anything you like, we don't grudge it, so long as it does you good. . . ." He made the sign of the cross over the baby. "And take care of my grandchild. My son is gone, but my grandson is left."

Tears rolled down his cheeks; he gave a sob and went away. Soon afterwards he went to bed and slept soundly after seven sleepless nights.

VII

Old Tzybukin went to the town for a short visit. Someone told Aksinya that he had gone to the notary to make his will and that he was leaving Butyokino, the very place where she had set up a brickyard, to Nikifor, his grandson. She was informed of this in the morning when old Tzybukin and Varvara were sitting near the steps under the birch tree, having their tea. She closed the shop in the front and at the back, gathered together all the keys she had, and flung them at her father-in-law's feet.

"I am not going on working for you," she began in a loud voice, and suddenly broke into sobs. "It seems I am not your daughter-in-law, but a servant! Everybody's jeering and saying, 'See what a servant the Tzybukins have got hold of!' I did not hire myself out to you! I am not a beggar, I am not a homeless wench, I have a father and mother."

She did not wipe away her tears; she fixed upon her father-in-law eyes full of tears, vindictive, squinting with anger; her face and neck were red and tense, and she was shouting at the top of her voice.

"I don't mean to go on slaving for you!" she continued. "I am worn out. When it is work, when it is sitting in the shop day in and day out, sneaking out at night for vodka—then it is my share, but when it is giving away the land then it is for that convict's wife and her imp. She is mistress here, and I am her servant. Give her everything, the convict's wife, and may it choke her! I am going home! Find yourselves some other fool, you damned bloodsuckers!"

The old man had never in his life scolded or punished his children, and had never dreamed that one of his family could speak to him rudely or behave disrespectfully; and now he was very much frightened; he ran into the house and hid behind the cupboard. And Varvara was so much flustered that she could not get up from her seat, and only waved her hands before her as though she were warding off a bee.

"Oh, Holy Saints! What's the meaning of it?" she muttered in horror. "What is she shouting? Oh, dear, dear! . . . People will hear! Hush. Oh, hush!"

"You have given Butyokino to the convict's wife," Aksinya went on bawling. "Give her everything now, I don't want anything from you! Go to hell! You are all a gang of thieves here! I have seen enough, I have had my fill of it! You have robbed people coming and going; you have robbed old and young alike, you brigands! And who has been selling vodka without a license? And false money? You've stuffed your coffers full of false coins, and now I am no more use!"

By now a crowd had collected at the open gate and was staring into the yard.

"Let the people look," bawled Aksinya. "I'll put you all to shame! You shall burn up with shame! You'll grovel at my feet. Hey! Stepan," she called to the deaf man, "let us go home this minute! Let us go to my father and mother; I don't want to live with convicts. Get ready!"

Clothes were hanging on lines stretched across the yard; she snatched off her petticoats and blouses still wet and flung them into the deaf man's arms. Then in her fury she dashed about the yard where the linen hung, tore down all of it, and what was not hers she threw on the ground and trampled upon.

"Holy Saints, stop her," moaned Varvara.

"What a woman! Give her Butyokino! Give it to her, for Christ's sake!"

"Well! Wha-at a woman!" people were saying at the gate. "She's a wo-oman! She's going it—something like!"

Aksinya ran into the kitchen where laundering was being done. Lipa was washing alone, the cook had gone to the river to rinse the clothes. Steam was rising from the trough and from the caldron near the stove, and the air in the kitchen was close and thick with vapor. On the floor was a heap of unwashed clothes, and Nikifor, kicking up his little red legs, lay on a bench near them, so that if he fell he should not hurt himself. Just as Aksinya went in Lipa took the former's chemise out of the heap and put it in the trough, and was just stretching out her hand to a big pitcher of boiling water which was standing on the table.

"Give it here," said Aksinya, looking at her with hatred, and snatching the chemise out of the trough; "it is not your business to touch my linen! You are a convict's wife, and ought to know your place and who you are!"

Lipa gazed at her, taken aback, and did not understand, but suddenly she caught the look Aksinya turned upon the child, and at once she understood and went numb all over.

"You've taken my land, so here you are!" Saying this Aksinya snatched up the pitcher with the boiling water and flung it over Nikifor.

After this there was heard a scream such as had never been heard before in Ukleyevo, and no one would have believed that a little weak creature like Lipa could scream like that. And it was suddenly quiet in the yard. Aksinya walked into the house in silence with the old naive smile on her lips. . . . The deaf man kept moving about the yard with his arms full of linen, then he began hanging it up again, silently, without haste. And until the cook came back from the river no one ventured to go into the kitchen to see what had happened there.

VIII

Nikifor was taken to the district hospital, and toward evening he died there. Lipa did not wait to be fetched, but wrapped the dead baby in its little quilt and carried it home.

The hospital, a new one recently built, with big windows, stood high up on a hill; it was glittering in the setting sun and looked as though it were on fire from inside. There was a little village below. Lipa went down the road, and before reaching the village, sat down by a pond. A woman brought a horse to water but the horse would not drink.

"What more do you want?" the woman said to it softly, in perplexity. "What more do you want?"

A boy in a red shirt, sitting at the water's edge, was washing his father's boots. And not another soul was in sight either in the village or on the hill.

"It's not drinking," said Lipa, looking at the horse.

Then the woman with the horse and the boy with the boots walked away, and there was no one left at all. The sun went to sleep, covering itself with cloth of gold and purple, and long clouds, red and lilac, stretched across the sky, guarded its rest. Somewhere far away a bittern cried, a hollow, melancholy sound as of a cow shut up in a barn. The cry of that mysterious bird was heard every spring, but no one knew what it was like or where it lived. At the top of the hill by the hospital, in the bushes close to the pond, and in the fields, the nightingales were trilling. The cuckoo kept reckoning someone's years and losing count and beginning again. In the pond the frogs called angrily to one another, straining themselves to bursting, and one could even make out the words: "That's what you are! That's what you are!" What a noise there was! It seemed as though all these creatures were singing and shouting so that no one might sleep on that spring night, so that all, even the angry frogs, might appreciate and enjoy every minute: life is given only once.

A silver half-moon was shining in the sky; there were many stars. Lipa had no idea how long she sat by the pond, but when she got up and walked on everybody was asleep in the little village, and there was not a single light. It was probably about eight miles' walk home, but neither body nor mind seemed equal to it. The moon gleamed now in front, now on the right, and the same cuckoo kept calling in a voice grown husky, with a chuckle as though gibing at her: "Hey, look out, you'll lose your way!" Lipa walked rapidly; she lost her kerchief . . . she looked at the sky and wondered where her baby's soul was now: was it following her, or floating aloft yonder among the stars and not thinking of her, the mother, any more? Oh, how lonely it is in the open country at night, in the midst of that singing when you yourself cannot sing; in the midst of the incessant cries of joy when you yourself cannot be joyful, when the moon, which cares not whether it is spring or winter, whether men are alive or dead, looks down, lonely too. . . . When there is grief in the heart it is hard to be without people. If only her mother, Praskovya, had been with her, or Crutch, or the cook, or some peasant!

"Boo-oo!" cried the bittern. "Boo-oo!"

And suddenly the sound of human speech became clearly audible:

"Hitch up the horses, Vavila!"

Ahead of her, by the wayside a camp fire was burning: the flames had died down, there were only red embers. She could hear the horses munching. In the darkness she could see the outlines of two carts, one with a barrel, the other, a lower one, with sacks in it, and the figures of two men; one was leading a horse to put it into the shafts, the other was standing motionless by the fire with his hands behind his back. A dog growled near the carts. The one who was leading the horse stopped and said:

"Someone seems to be coming along the road."

"Sharik, be quiet!" the other man called to the dog.

And from the voice one could tell that he was an old man. Lipa stopped and said:

"God aid you."

The old man went up to her and said after a pause:

"Good evening!"

"Your dog does not bite, grandfather?"

"No, come along, he won't touch you."

"I have been at the hospital," said Lipa after a pause. "My little son died there. Here I am carrying him home."

It must have been unpleasant for the old man to hear this, for he moved away and said hurriedly:

"No matter, my dear. It's God's will. You are dawdling, lad," he added, addressing his companion; "look alive!"

"Your yoke isn't there," said the young man; "I don't see it."

"That's just like Vavila!"

The old man picked up an ember, blew on it—only his eyes and nose were lighted up—then, when they had found the yoke, he went over to Lipa with the light and looked at her, and his look expressed compassion and tenderness.

"You are a mother," he said; "every mother grieves for her child."

And he sighed and shook his head as he said it. Vavila threw something on the fire, stamped it out—and at once it was very dark; the immediate scene vanished, and as before there were only the fields, the sky with the stars, and the noise of the birds keeping each other from sleep. And the landrail called, it seemed, in the very place where the fire had been.

But a minute passed, and the two carts and the old man and lanky Vavila became visible again. The carts creaked as they rolled out on the road.

"Are you holy men?" Lipa asked the old man.

"No. We are from Firsanovo."

"You looked at me just now and my heart was softened. And the lad is so gentle. I thought you must be holy men."

"Have you far to go?"

"To Ukleyevo."

"Get in, we will give you a lift as far as Kuzmenki, then you go straight on and we turn off to the left."

Vavila got into the cart with the barrel and the old man and Lipa got into the other. They moved at a walking pace, Vavila in front.

"My baby was in torment all day," said Lipa. "He looked at me with his little eyes and said nothing; he wanted to speak and could not. Lord God! Queen of heaven! In my grief I kept falling down on the floor. I would be standing there and then I would fall down by the bedside. And tell me, grandfather, why should a little one be tormented before his death? When a grown-up person, a man or woman, is in torment, his sins are forgiven, but why a little one, when he has no sins? Why?"

"Who can tell?" answered the old man.

They drove on for half an hour in silence.

"We can't know everything, how and why," said the old man. "A bird is given not four wings but two because it is able to fly with two; and so man is not permitted to know everything but only a half or a quarter. As much as he needs to know in order to live, so much he knows."

"It is better for me to go on foot, grandfather. Now my heart is all of a tremble."

"Never mind, sit still."

The old man yawned and made the sign of the cross over his mouth.

"Never mind," he repeated. "Yours is not the worst of sorrows. Life is long, there is good and bad yet to come, there is everything yet to come. Great is mother Russia," he said, and looked round on either side of him. "I have been all over Russia, and I have seen everything in her, and you may believe my words, my dear. There will be good and there will be bad. I went as a delegate from my village to Siberia, and I have been to the Amur River and the Altai Mountains and I lived in Siberia; I worked the land there, then I got homesick for mother Russia and I came back to my native village. We went back to Russia on foot; and I remember we went on a ferry, and I was thin as thin, all in rags, barefoot, freezing with cold, and gnawing a crust, and a gentleman who was on the ferry—the kingdom of heaven be his if he is dead—looked at me pitifully, and tears came into his eyes. 'Ah,' he said, 'your bread is black, your days are black. . . .' And when I got home, as the saying is, there was neither stick nor stone; I had a wife, but I left her behind in Siberia, she was buried there. So I am a hired man now. And I tell you: since then I have had it good as well as bad. Here I do not want to die, my dear, I would be glad to live another twenty years; so there has been more of the good. And great is our mother Russia!'' and again he gazed on either side and looked round.

''Grandfather,'' Lipa asked, ''when anyone dies, how many days does his soul walk the earth?''

''Who can tell! Ask Vavila here, he has been to school. Now they teach them everything. Vavila!'' the old man called to him.

''Yes!''

''Vavila, when anyone dies how long does his soul walk the earth?''

Vavila stopped the horse and only then answered:

''Nine days. After my uncle Kirilla died, his soul lived in our cottage thirteen days.''

''How do you know?''

''For thirteen days there was a knocking in the stove.''

''Well, all right. Go on,'' said the old man, and it could be seen that he did not believe a word of all that.

Near Kuzmenki the cart turned into the highroad while Lipa walked straight on. By now it was getting light. As she went down into the ravine the Ukleyevo houses and the church were hidden in fog. It was cold, and it seemed to her that the same cuckoo was calling still.

When Lipa reached home the cattle had not yet been driven out; everyone was asleep. She sat down on the steps and waited. The old man was the first to come out; he understood what had happened from the first glance at her, and for a long time he could not utter a word, but only smacked his lips.

''Oh, Lipa,'' he said, ''you did not take care of my grandchild. . . .''

Varvara was awakened. She struck her hands together and broke into sobs, and immediately began laying out the baby.

''And he was a pretty child . . .'' she said. ''Oh, dear, dear. . . . You had the one child, and you did not take enough care of him, you silly thing. . . .''

There was a requiem service in the morning and again in the evening. The funeral took place the next day, and after it the guests and the priests ate a great deal, and with such greed that one might have thought that they had not tasted food for a long time. Lipa waited at table, and the priest, lifting his fork on which there was a salted mushroom, said to her:

''Don't grieve for the babe. For of such is the kingdom of heaven.''

And only when they had all left Lipa realized fully that there was no Nikifor and never would be, she realized it and broke into sobs. And she did not know what room to go into to sob, for she felt that now that her child was dead there was no place for her in the house, that she had no reason to be there, that she was in the way; and the others felt it too.

"Now what are you bellowing for?" Aksinya shouted, suddenly appearing in the doorway; because of the funeral she was dressed all in new clothes and had powdered her face. "Shut up!"

Lipa tried to stop but could not, and sobbed louder than ever.

"Do you hear?" shouted Aksinya, and stamped her foot in violent anger. "Who is it I am speaking to? Get out of the house and don't set foot here again, you convict's wife. Get out."

"There, there, there," the old man put in fussily. "Aksinya, don't make such an outcry, my dear. . . . She is crying, it is only natural . . . her child is dead. . . ."

" 'It's only natural,' " Aksinya mimicked him. "Let her stay the night here, and don't let me see a trace of her here tomorrow! 'It's only natural!' . . ." she mimicked him again, and, laughing, went into the shop.

Early the next morning Lipa went off to her mother at Torguyevo.

IX

The roof and the front door of the shop have now been repainted and are as bright as though they were new, there are gay geraniums in the windows as of old, and what happened in Tzybukin's house and yard three years ago is almost forgotten.

Grigory Petrovich is still looked upon as the master, but in reality everything has passed into Aksinya's hands; she buys and sells, and nothing can be done without her consent. The brickyard is working well; and as bricks are wanted for the railway the price has gone up to twenty-four rubles a thousand; peasant women and girls cart the bricks to the station and load them up in cars and earn a quarter-ruble a day for the work.

Aksinya has gone into partnership with the Hrymin Juniors, and their mill is now called Hrymin Juniors and Co. They have opened a tavern near the station, and now the expensive accordion is played not at the mill but at the tavern, and the postmaster, who is engaged in some sort of business, too, often goes there, and so does the stationmaster. Hrymin Juniors have presented the deaf man with a gold watch, and he is constantly taking it out of his pocket and putting it to his ear.

People say of Aksinya that she has become a person of power; and it is true that when she drives to her brickyard in the morning, handsome and happy, with the naive smile on her face, and afterwards when she gives orders there, one is aware of her great power. Everyone is afraid of her in the house and in the village and in the brickyard. When she goes to the post the postmaster jumps up and says to her:

"I humbly beg you to be seated, Aksinya Abramovna!"

A certain landowner, middle-aged but foppish, in a tunic of fine cloth and high patent leather boots, sold her a horse, and was so carried away by talking to her that he knocked down the price to meet her wishes. He held her hand a long time and, looking into her merry, sly, naive eyes, said:

"For a woman like you, Aksinya Abramovna, I should be ready to do anything you please. Only say when we can meet where no one will interfere with us."

"Why, whenever you like."

And since then the elderly fop has been driving up to the shop almost every day to drink beer. And the beer is horrid, bitter as wormwood. The landowner wags his head, but drinks it.

Old Tzybukin does not have anything at all to do with the business now. He does not keep any money because he cannot tell good from counterfeit coins, but he is silent, he says nothing of this weakness. He has become forgetful, and if they don't give him food he does not ask for it. They have grown used to having dinner without him, and Varvara often says:

"He went to bed again yesterday without eating anything."

And she says it unconcernedly because she is used to it. For some reason, summer and winter alike, he wears a fur coat, and only in very hot weather he does not go out but sits at home. As a rule he puts on his fur coat, wraps it round him, turns up his collar, and walks about the village, along the road to the station, or sits from morning till night on the seat near the church gates. He sits there without stirring. Passersby bow to him, but he does not respond, for as of old he dislikes the peasants. If he is asked a question he answers quite rationally and politely, but briefly.

There is a rumor going about in the village that his daughter-in-

.w has turned him out of the house and gives him nothing to ıt, and that he is fed by charitable folk; some are glad, others ·e sorry for him.

Varvara has grown even fatter and her skin whiter, and as efore she is active in good works, and Aksinya does not inter-·re with her.

There is so much jam now that they have not time to eat it efore the fresh fruit comes in; it goes sugary, and Varvara lmost sheds tears, not knowing what to do with it.

They have begun to forget about Anisim. Some time ago there ame a letter from him written in verse on a big sheet of paper as ough it were a petition, all in the same splendid handwriting. vidently his friend Samorodov was doing time with him. Under e verses in an ugly, scarcely legible handwriting there was a ingle line: "I am ill here all the time; I am wretched, for 'hrist's sake help me!"

One fine autumn day toward evening old Tzybukin was itting near the church gates, with the collar of his fur coat ırned up, and nothing of him could be seen but his nose and the eak of his cap. At the other end of the long bench sat Yelizarov e contractor, and beside him Yakov the school watchman, a othless old man of seventy. Crutch and the watchman were ılking.

"Children ought to give food and drink to the old. . . . Honor y father and mother . . ." Yakov was saying with irritation, while she, this woman, has turned her father-in-law out of his wn house; the old man has neither food nor drink, where is he go? He has not had a morsel these three days."

"Three days!" said Crutch, amazed.

"Here he sits and does not say a word. He has grown feeble. nd why be silent? He ought to prosecute her, they wouldn't pat er on the back in court."

"Wouldn't pat whom on the back?" asked Crutch, not hearing.

"What?"

"The woman's all right, she does her best. In their line of usiness they can't get on without that . . . without sin, I ıean. . . ."

"From his own house," Yakov went on with irritation. "Save p and buy your own house, then turn people out of it! She is a ice one, to be sure! A pla-ague!"

Tzybukin listened and did not stir.

"Whether it is your own house or others' it makes no difference so long as it is warm and the women don't scold . . ." sai Crutch, and he laughed. "When I was young I was very fond o my Nastasya. She was a quiet woman. And she used to b always at it: 'Buy a house, Makarych! Buy a house, Makarych Buy a horse, Makarych!' She was dying and yet she kept o saying, 'Buy yourself a racing droshky, Makarych, so that yo don't have to walk.' And I bought her nothing but gingerbread.'

"Her husband's deaf and stupid," Yakov went on, not listening to Crutch; "a regular fool, just like a goose. He can understand anything. Hit a goose on the head with a stick an even then it does not understand."

Crutch got up to go home. Yakov also got up, and both c them went off together, still talking. When they had gone fift paces old Tzybukin got up, too, and walked after them, steppin uncertainly as though on slippery ice.

The village was already plunged in the dusk of evening an the sun only gleamed on the upper part of the road which ra wriggling like a snake up the slope. Old women were comin back from the woods and children with them; they were bringin baskets of mushrooms. Peasant women and girls came in crowd from the station where they had been loading the cars wit bricks, and their noses and the skin under their eyes wer covered with red brick-dust. They were singing. Ahead of the all was Lipa, with her eyes turned toward the sky, she wa singing in a high voice, breaking into trills as though exulting i the fact that at last the day was over and the time for rest ha come. In the crowd walking with a bundle in her arms, breathless as usual, was her mother, Praskovya, who still went out t work by the day.

"Good evening, Makarych!" cried Lipa, seeing Crutch. "Goo evening, dear!"

"Good evening, Lipinka," cried Crutch delighted. "Girls women, love the rich carpenter! Ho-ho! My little children, m little children. (Crutch gave a sob). My dear little hatchets!"

Crutch and Yakov went on farther and could still be hear talking. Then after them came old Tzybukin and there was sudden hush in the crowd. Lipa and Praskovya had dropped little behind, and when the old man was abreast of them Lip bowed down low and said:

"Good evening, Grigory Petrovich."

Her mother, too, bowed. The old man stopped and, saying nothing, looked at the two; his lips were quivering and his eyes full of tears. Lipa took out of her mother's bundle a piece of pie stuffed with buckwheat and gave it to him. He took it and began eating.

The sun had set by now: its glow died away on the upper part of the road too. It was getting dark and cool. Lipa and Praskovya walked on and for some time kept crossing themselves.

THE STUDENT

The weather was fine and calm at first. Thrushes were singing, and in the nearby swamps some creature droned piteously as if blowing into an empty bottle. A woodcock flew over and a shot reverberated merrily in the spring air. But when darkness fell on the wood an unwelcome, piercing cold wind blew up from the east and everything grew silent. Ice needles formed on the puddles and the wood seemed inhospitable, abandoned, empty. It smelt of winter.

Ivan Velikopolsky, a student at a theological college and a sexton's son, was returning home along the path through the water meadow after a day's shooting. His fingers were numb, his face burned in the wind. This sudden onset of cold seemed to have destroyed the order and harmony of things, striking dread into Nature herself and causing the shades of night to thicken faster than was needful. Everything was so abandoned, so very gloomy, somehow. Only in the widows' allotments near the river did a light gleam. But far around, where the village stood about three miles away, everything drowned in the dense evening mist. The student remembered that, when he had left the house, his mother had been sitting barefoot on the lobby floor cleaning the samovar, while his father lay coughing on the stove. There was no cooking at home because today was Good Friday, and he felt famished. Cringing in the cold, he reflected that just such a wind had blown in the days of Ryurik, Ivan the Terrible, and Peter the Great. Their times had known just such ferocious poverty and hunger. There had been the same thatched roofs with the holes in them, the same ignorance and misery, the same desolation on all sides, the same gloom and sense of oppression. All these horrors had been, still were, and would continue to be, and the passing of another thousand years would make things no better. He did not feel like going home.

The allotments were called widows' because they were kept by two widows, a mother and daughter. A bonfire was burning briskly—crackling, lighting up the plow-land far around. Widow Vasilisa, a tall, plump old woman in a man's fur jacket, stood gazing pensively at the fire. Her short, pock-marked, stupid-looking daughter Lukerya sat on the ground washing a cooking pot and some spoons. They had just had supper, obviously. Men's voices were heard, some local laborers watering their horses by the river.

"So winter's come back," said the student, approaching the fire. "Good evening."

Vasilisa shuddered, but then saw who it was and smiled a welcome.

"Goodness me, I didn't recognize you," she said. "That means you'll be rich one day."

They talked. Vasilisa, a woman of some experience—having been wet nurse to gentlefolk and then a nanny—spoke delicately, always smiling a gentle, dignified smile. But her daughter Lukerya, a peasant whose husband had beaten her, only screwed up her eyes at the student, saying nothing and wearing an odd look as if she was deaf and dumb.

"On a cold night like this the Apostle Peter warmed himself by a fire." The student held out his hands toward the flames. "So it must have been cold then. What a frightening night that was, Granny, what a very sorrowful, what a very long night."

He looked at the darkness around and abruptly jerked his head. "Were you in church yesterday for the Twelve Gospel Readings?"

"Yes," Vasilisa answered.

"At the Last Supper, you'll remember, Peter said to Jesus, 'Lord, I am ready to go with Thee, both into prison, and to death.' And the Lord said, 'I say unto thee, Peter, before the cock crow twice, thou shalt deny me thrice.' After supper Jesus prayed in mortal agony in the garden, while poor Peter was weary in spirit, and enfeebled. His eyes were heavy, he couldn't fight off sleep, and he slept. Then, as you have heard, Judas that night kissed Jesus and betrayed Him to the torturers. They bound Him, they took Him to the high priest, they smote Him, while Peter—worn, tormented, anguished, perturbed, you understand, not having slept properly, foreseeing some fearful happening on this earth—went after them. He loved Jesus passionately, to distraction, and now, afar, he saw Him being buffeted."

Lukerya put down the spoons and stared at the student.

"They went to the high priest," he continued. "They put Jesus to the question, and meanwhile the workmen had kindled a fire in the midst of the hall, as it was cold, and were warming themselves. Peter stood with them near the fire—also warming himself, as I am now. A certain maid beheld him, and said, 'This man was also with Jesus.' In other words she was saying that he, too, should be taken for questioning. All the workmen round the fire must have looked at him suspiciously and sternly because he was confused and said, 'I know him not.' A little later someone recognized him as one of Jesus' disciples and said, 'Thou also wast with him.' But he denied it again. And for the third time someone addressed him. 'Did I not see thee in the garden with Him this day?' He denied Him for the third time. And after that the cock straightway crowed, and Peter, looking at Jesus from afar, remembered the words which He had said to him at supper. He remembered, his eyes were opened, and he went out of the hall and shed bitter tears. The Gospel says, 'And he went out, and wept bitterly.' I can imagine it was a very quiet, very dark garden and his hollow sobs could hardly be heard in the silence."

The student sighed, plunged deep in thought. Still smiling, Vasilisa suddenly sobbed and tears, large and profuse, flowed down her cheeks. She shielded her face from the fire with her sleeve as if ashamed of the tears, while Lukerya, staring at the student, blushed, and her expression became distressed and tense as if she was holding back a terrible pain.

The workmen returned from the river. One of them, on horseback, was already near, and the light from the fire quivered on him. The student said good night to the widows and moved on. Again darkness came upon him, and his hands began to freeze. A cruel wind blew, it was real winter weather again, and it did not seem as if Easter Sunday could be only the day after tomorrow.

The student thought of Vasilisa. Her weeping meant that all that had happened to Peter on that terrible night had a particular meaning for her.

He looked back. The lonely fire quietly flickered in the darkness, no one could be seen near it. Again the student reflected that, if Vasilisa had wept and her daughter had been moved, then obviously what he had just told them about happenings nineteen centuries ago—it had a meaning for the present, for both women, and also probably for this godforsaken village, for himself, for all people. It had not been his gift for poignant narrative that had made the old woman weep. It was because Peter was near to her, because she was bound up heart and soul with his innermost feelings.

Joy suddenly stirred within him. He even stopped for a moment to catch his breath.

"The past," thought he, "is linked to the present by an unbroken chain of happenings, each flowing from the other."

He felt as if he had just seen both ends of that chain. When he touched one end the other vibrated.

Crossing the river by ferry, and then climbing the hill, he looked at his home village and at the narrow strip of cold crimson sunset shining in the west. And he brooded on truth and beauty—how they had guided human life there in the garden and the high priest's palace, how they had continued without a break till the present day, always as the most important element in man's life and in earthly life in general. A sensation of youth, health, strength—he was only twenty-two years old—together with an anticipation, ineffably sweet, of happiness, strange, mysterious happiness, gradually came over him. And life seemed enchanting, miraculous, imbued with exalted significance.